P9-CDT-026

# THE PALADIN

## Also by David Ignatius

The Quantum Spy

The Director

Bloodmoney

The Increment

Body of Lies

The Sun King

A Firing Offense

The Bank of Fear

Siro

Agents of Innocence

# THE
# PALADIN

## A SPY NOVEL

## DAVID IGNATIUS

W. W. NORTON & COMPANY
*Independent Publishers Since 1923*

*The Paladin* is a work of fiction. Names, characters, places, organizations, and events are the products of the author's imagination or are used fictitiously. Any resemblance to actual persons, living or dead, is entirely coincidental.

Copyright © 2020 by David Ignatius

All rights reserved
Printed in the United States of America
First Edition

For information about permission to reproduce selections from this book, write to Permissions, W. W. Norton & Company, Inc., 500 Fifth Avenue, New York, NY 10110

For information about special discounts for bulk purchases, please contact W. W. Norton Special Sales at specialsales@wwnorton.com or 800-233-4830

Manufacturing by Lake Book Manufacturing
Book design by Patrice Sheridan
Production manager: Julia Druskin

Library of Congress Cataloging-in-Publication Data

Names: Ignatius, David, 1950– author.
Title: The paladin : a spy novel / David Ignatius.
Description: First Edition. | New York, NY : W. W. Norton & Company, [2020]
Identifiers: LCCN 2019050473 | ISBN 9780393254174 (hardcover) |
ISBN 9780393254181 (epub)
Subjects: GSAFD: Suspense fiction.
Classification: LCC PS3559.G54 P35 2020 | DDC 813/.54—dc23
LC record available at https://lccn.loc.gov/2019050473

W. W. Norton & Company, Inc., 500 Fifth Avenue, New York, N.Y. 10110
www.wwnorton.com

W. W. Norton & Company Ltd., 15 Carlisle Street, London W1D 3BS

1 2 3 4 5 6 7 8 9 0

For Lincoln Caplan

and

Susan Carney

And ye shall know the truth and the truth shall make you free.

—John 8:32, *carved on the wall of the entrance to CIA headquarters*

There are two ways to be fooled. One is to believe what isn't true; the other is to refuse to believe what is true.

—Søren Kierkegaard, *Works of Love*

# THE PALADIN

# 1

Alexandria, Virginia—May 2017

At Michael Dunne's sentencing hearing at the federal courthouse in Alexandria, the judge asked if he was sorry for his crimes. She said that Dunne had flagrantly ignored the Central Intelligence Agency's legal rules, and lied about it, and worst of all, that he had violated the constitutional rights of others by running an intelligence operation against American journalists. Did he understand the seriousness of this offense? The First Amendment was first for a reason. Did he truly regret what he had done?

Dunne had been coached by his lawyer, Mark Walden, to respond with remorse and contrition. The hearing was "in-camera," and nobody cared what he said, other than the judge, so it should have been a no-brainer. A good man, a public servant, hardened by the world but still almost boyish with his thatch of red hair, a CIA officer who had made a mistake for which he was sorry. And he had planned to make the apology. He knew this was his best chance to recover what was left.

But Dunne couldn't do it. A ripple of anger had crossed his face as he listened to the judge's questions. He answered that he had done what he thought was right under the circumstances, on orders; he mumbled it at first, but then said it in a loud, unambiguous voice so there wasn't any mistaking his meaning.

He wasn't regretful in the least for his actions, only that he had failed in his mission. He had been assaulted by forces that he didn't understand. What did he feel? the judge had asked. He felt a throbbing, consuming anger and a determination to someday obtain justice. But no, he wasn't sorry for what he had done.

The judge applied the most extreme penalty that was available in the sentencing guidelines provided by the government in the plea agreement. She ordered Dunne to serve a one-year prison term on the single felony count of making false statements to the FBI about his violation of agency regulations. The judge glowered at Dunne as he was led out of the courtroom. *Arrogant man*, her face said. Dunne walked out with his head raised and shoulders back, refusing to slouch away like the beaten, destroyed man she wanted him to be.

Dunne wasn't any more repentant when his lawyer told him a few minutes later that he had been childish and could have gotten off with community service if he'd followed advice. "Fuck off," Dunne muttered, and then apologized. It wasn't Walden's fault. The fact was, Dunne truly didn't care. That's what happens to you when everything that matters has been shattered: You become so angry that you want to hurt people, starting with yourself.

But life changes. Or, as in Dunne's case, it gets ground up into little pieces that eventually begin to fit back into some kind of order, so that you begin to see things more clearly. Not at first, but after a while. You learn things about how the world works that you couldn't have imagined, even if you were in the business of stealing secrets, as Dunne had been. You see that the adversaries you have been chasing are allied with the friends you thought you were helping. The world slips and stutters, as you try to find your balance.

You learn a lot about revenge, too, when that becomes your consuming passion. You think at first that it's about driving toward a target as straight as you can, but you discover that it's more of an arc that bends back on itself, and you, the closer you get to the truth.

# 2

Pittsburgh, Pennsylvania—May 2018

On the morning that Michael Dunne was released from the Federal Correctional Institution at Petersburg, Virginia, the deputy warden offered him a $500 "release gratuity," which he refused. The deputy wished him well and, when Dunne didn't answer, he said, "I'm sorry."

Dunne was solid and contained as a toolbox. He had lost weight and added muscle since he'd gone to prison, so that his body fit like a suit that was a size too small. His striking red hair now enveloped his face, with a russet beard he had grown in prison. His eyes were bright and curious—still, after everything he had lived—but they were masked by the black frames of his sunglasses.

Dunne walked out of the gate feeling the lightness of freedom and the weight of anger. He was fitter than a year before. He had spurned the starchy food they pushed on inmates, and his chief pleasure all those months had been exercising his body. He could do more sit-ups than he ever imagined or wanted to. He had turned forty during that year in prison; he hadn't told anyone his birthday, but the warden saw it in Dunne's file and sent him a card.

Traveling home wasn't easy. Dunne took a bus from Petersburg to Richmond, and then a flight from Richmond to Pittsburgh, via Charlotte. The releasing officer had asked him to identify someone who would be meeting him when he arrived. Dunne had put down his mother's name, to be cooperative, but she had died four years before. He didn't want to see anyone yet. He had a new suit of clothes, but they smelled like prison.

*   *   *

The Pittsburgh horizon was a low, thin gray, the color of cigarette ash, as Dunne's taxi drove toward the Fort Pitt Tunnel from the airport. Dunne scanned the landscape, trying to remember what it had looked like when he was a boy. He closed his eyes; he hadn't eaten all day, and he felt light-headed.

And then, suddenly, he was home: When they exited the tunnel, he saw the dazzling flash of color and light at "the Point," where the Allegheny and Monongahela Rivers meet to form the Ohio, and between them the dense triangle of office towers of this beaten-down but resilient city.

Dunne whispered, "Wow," and the cabdriver answered, "Yes, sir."

Dunne didn't call anyone the first day, or the second. He thought of phoning his ex-mother-in-law, to ask about his ex-wife, but he knew that would be a mistake. He checked into a hotel downtown and slept for fourteen hours. It was the first time in a year he hadn't faced a bed count at midnight, three a.m., and five a.m.

When he awoke, he took a taxi to a car dealer south of the city and bought a used Ford Explorer. He paid cash, drawn from an account he had kept open through his incarceration. The salesman shrugged when Dunne listed his previous address as Federal Correctional Complex, Petersburg, Virginia.

"I'm from here, originally," Dunne said. "Mon Valley." The salesman nodded. He was from Youngstown, Ohio. He'd been selling cars ever since he lost his job in the mill, thirty years before.

Dunne drove the car off the lot and stopped at a supermarket a block away. He bought a Steelers hat for himself and some roses to leave at his mother's grave. He had missed her funeral back in 2014. He was on assignment and hadn't wanted to ask for compassionate leave. And he hadn't been ready to come home then.

Dunne studied his Steelers cap before he placed it atop his red curls. The colors of the three stars in the logo each used to mean something: yellow for coal; orange for iron ore; and blue for steel scrap. Now the pattern just reminded people of an NFL football team.

He steered his SUV down the twists of the Monongahela toward McKeesport. It was like an X-ray world, where everything that had once been bright had gone dark. The belching blast furnaces and coke ovens and the acres-long rolling mills that had lined the river were nearly all gone. The workers who had lost their jobs but stayed on stubbornly at first were mostly gone now, too; dead, like his mother, or run away to Florida with a new spouse, like his alcoholic father.

Dunne stopped the Explorer at the back entrance of the cemetery, halfway up Versailles Street. The grave sites down by the river were in neat, unbroken rows of bodies interred a century ago, but up here it was almost pasture, with a few scattered headstones and plenty of space around his mother's plot. Room for his father if he ever decided to come home, or for Dunne.

He began to pull the weeds around his mother's gravestone, and then let them be. It was late spring. The insects were thick by the stagnant water of a crumbling stone-ribbed fountain. He propped the roses up against the cold marble and then walked back to the gate.

Dunne dreaded seeing his old house. He hadn't been back in years, and for all he knew, it had been razed. He drove slowly up Versailles Street to his old high school, and then turned onto Grandview Avenue. The squat two-story house looked deserted, no curtains and empty, see-through rooms. At least it wasn't boarded up or demolished into an empty lot like so many neighbors' homes; half the houses in town seemed to have FOR SALE or FORECLOSURE signs. It looked like a city that had been defeated in war and then abandoned.

On an alley wall near his school was the faint trace of a mural his classmates had painted senior year, in 1996, when they were competing for the state football championship. GO TIGERS! You could barely see the faded letters now.

Dunne drove back to the river. The old National Tube Works gate at Third Avenue and Locust Street was a barren crossroads. The buildings that had housed the mills were mostly empty; many of them weren't even buildings, just roofs and some sideboard. Dunne looked for the Steelworkers Local 1408, where his grandfather had been a vice president. A little plaque marked the spot and gave an address, in a shopping center in North Versailles, where a remnant of the union could be found.

"I hate this," Dunne muttered to himself. The McKeesport plant had closed in 1987, when Dunne was ten years old. Several companies had tried to rehabilitate parts of the old tube works, but they were just tugging on bits and pieces of the corpse. The body had been dead a long time.

Dunne tuned the radio to Big 104.7, the local country music station. A DJ was telling sentimental stories about helping people in need. Dunne took off his Steelers cap and laid it on the seat next to him. He was back home, but it wasn't the same place and he wasn't the same person.

# 3

## Pittsburgh, Pennsylvania—May 2018

Michael Dunne's last stop that day was a modern office building down the Monongahela River, almost to Pittsburgh, in what was newly dubbed the Pittsburgh Technology Center. It stood in an empty field that had once housed the Jones & Laughlin North Side furnaces that fed molten steel across the "Hot Metal Bridge" to the rolling mills on the south side of the river.

Dunne was early for his appointment. He parked his SUV outside the anonymous, shiny building and sat silently in his car, thinking one last time whether he wanted to take this next step. It would be the beginning of his "R&R," he had been telling himself for months; his revenge and redemption. He had hungered for it through his year in Petersburg, but now he was like an overheated engine that was choked with too much fuel. He needed to cool off a little so the spark would take.

He had a tie and blazer on a hanger in the backseat. He knotted the tie and affixed it with a clip bearing a tiny American flag.

Dunne waited in the parking lot until four and then went into the building. There was no signage outside; a plaque behind the reception desk identified the office as the National Cyber-Forensics and Training Alliance. The only hint about who really occupied the building was the receptionist, who was wearing a badge with the symbol of the Federal Bureau of Investigation.

Rick Bogdanovich, the head of the FBI cyber center, was waiting upstairs in a big office overlooking the river. He had an FBI crew cut and a round, meaty face with thick pouches under his eyes. When he saw Dunne, he gave him a long hug.

"Hey, Red!" he said. "You're back, man."

"I guess," said Dunne, shaking his head.

"I feel like shit about what happened," said Bogdanovich. "We all do. You look solid, at least, whatever crap they pulled on you down there."

"Solid," repeated Dunne. "Thanks for seeing me, Rick. I'm glad the Bureau still remembers me. The agency wants me to go away."

"Don't get me started about the freaking agency. They hung you out to dry, my friend."

"Maybe," Dunne said. He looked at the floor and shook his head. He wasn't going to be polite and say it was all fine. It was past time for that. But he didn't want to talk about it, either.

The two men had become friends ten years before, when they were both assigned to a joint counterintelligence task force that was hunting for a penetration inside the CIA. It was a very small, highly compartmented program. They went six months without talking to colleagues outside their unit about what they were doing. Their agencies didn't get along very well, but they had developed a bond. And there was the Pittsburgh thing. Bogdanovich had grown up in Moon Township. He knew what failure looked like.

Bogdanovich offered his friend a chair and waited for him to speak. Dunne loosened his tie. There were beads of sweat on his forehead. His beard itched.

"I need help," Dunne said eventually. "You're my first stop."

"You got it, Mike. Whatever it is. So long as it won't send you back to the slammer."

"I want to start a company. A cyber consulting firm, sort of, just me at first. Kind of a boutique."

Bogdanovich gave him a thumbs-up. He looked relieved that this was what Dunne had come to ask about.

"Pittsburgh's a good spot for it. Carnegie Mellon, Pitt, Robert Morris, and our very own FBI forensics center. It's one-stop shopping. And it's a good time to be getting in the business. Every son of a bitch in the world wants to have his own cyber expert these days. The Bureau loses them as fast as we hire them. It's a hot market."

"I'm good at what I do, Rick. You know that."

"The best, in my book." Bogdanovich nodded respectfully.

"So, straight up, I've been worrying that because I have a criminal record, people won't hire me. That's why I need help."

Bogdanovich gave a dismissive wave.

"Easy to fix. Put up a nice storefront. Get a lawyer to create a shell company. Half the hackers in this business used to be criminals. It adds a little luster. Just make sure there's someone to cover for you."

Dunne folded his arms awkwardly, then unfolded them. He didn't like asking for favors.

"That's why I'm here. Will you vouch for me? Can I list you as a reference? Maybe get one of your ex-Bureau guys to be a silent partner. I hate to ask. But like I said, I need help."

Bogdanovich didn't respond right away. He wasn't a glad-hander, and he knew he would have to stand behind whatever he promised.

"What are you going to do in this little boutique, might I ask?" There was the slightest twinkle in his eye.

"The same thing I was doing before," said Dunne. "Except this time I won't get caught."

"The term in the trade these days is 'active defense,'" said the FBI man.

"Yeah. Very active. I don't want anyone, ever, to have to face what I did: information that takes them down, rips them apart, and they're defenseless. So, for sure, I want to offer my clients defenses that are, yeah, active."

"You have to be careful," said Bogdanovich. "This is a 'gray area' for the lawyers, including the Bureau's. Defending yourself against 'malicious intruders' is legal. Hacking them is illegal. A 'hack back' can get you busted. In theory, at least. If you violate the law, I can't do anything for you. Just so we're clear."

"Got it," said Dunne. "It's like anything else. Do it right, and don't get caught."

Bogdanovich shook his head and wagged a finger at Dunne.

"This is nasty shit, my friend. The toys aren't locked up anymore, at the agency or NSA or here. Everybody's playing. It's dangerous out there."

"That's why I want to start my company, to give the good guys a fair chance of stopping the bad guys, right? I'm a client's dream. I'm pissed off, and hungry, and I'll work cheap. So, will you help me?"

Bogdanovich looked at his old friend, lean, angry, needing a break. He nodded.

"Of course I will. Just so we understand the rules. I'm going to give you two names. One is the best start-up lawyer in town, who can do the paperwork. The other is a guy who used to do undercover cyber work for the Bureau. Vijay Prakash. He knows cyber better than anyone. He's got more clients than he can handle. He'll spin you some."

Dunne took a notebook from his pocket and began writing down the two names. Then he stopped.

"Why would this guy Vijay help me? He's a hotshot. I just got out of prison."

"Because I tell him to, that's why. And I'll do one more thing for you, Mike. I'll hire you myself, as an FBI consultant. Or, to be precise, I'll retain your firm. That's why you've got to create a front company. An LLC. The lawyer can do that."

"Thank you," said Dunne. It had been a long time since he had asked for anyone's help.

"Let's go get a beer," said Bogdanovich, rising from his chair. "They don't have plant whistles in this valley anymore, but I think it's quitting time."

"Can I still get an Iron City?"

"Definitely. And you'll be glad to know they have Iron City Light now."

"Iron City Light? What the fuck is happening to the world?"

Dunne pulled off his necktie as he walked out of Bogdanovich's office. He felt something like normal, really for the first time since had had gone into prison a year before. The FBI man was a step behind him, and they rambled down the stairs to the parking lot and the graveyard of what had once been the furnace of America.

# 4

Langley, Virginia—August 2016

How did it begin? The answer was simple, and complicated. Simple because Michael Dunne was asked, and he was a good soldier, and complicated because he knew even at the very start that there were a lot of reasons to say no. But one morning in August 2016, Sarah Gilroy, the head of the Directorate of Science and Technology, summoned Dunne to her office in the New Headquarters Building, and he breezed in the door.

Dunne was wearing jeans. He had just been on vacation, and he needed a haircut. He thought he was bulletproof, back then. He had a beautiful Brazilian wife, one young child and another on the way, friends who shared his taste for a drink after work. He didn't have to wear a tie to work, and he got paid more than a lot of the people who did. His life had been about taking risks and not making mistakes, and he was good at both. He understood cyber systems as well as any operations officer in the agency.

When he arrived, Gilroy suggested that they take a walk. She usually liked meeting with colleagues at her desk, flanked by protective pictures of government officials on the wall behind. If she wanted to leave the office, it meant she had something sensitive to say that was outside her comfort zone.

Gilroy was a slender woman, thin-boned, sandy blond hair, carefully dressed. She didn't look like a software engineer, but over the years she had become one of the most reliable computer specialists in the agency. When a woman got promoted, men sometimes told themselves it was an affirmative-action hire. But anyone who knew Gilroy's work recognized that she had risen through sheer, unassailable competence. Dunne trusted her, as far as he trusted anyone in management.

"We have a difficult target." That was all she said at first, leading him out the door and down the corridor to the elevator.

"Who is it?" asked Dunne.

"We aren't sure." She put a finger to her lips, warning Dunne to be quiet until they were outside. "That's why it's difficult."

"Russians?" asked Dunne as soon as they were out in the heavy August air.

"We don't think so. They're the flavor of the month, I know, but this is different. The techs say it's not like anything they've seen. Highly skilled cyber tools, zero attribution, zero motive. NSA says it's our problem. People are confused."

"Why me?" Dunne asked. But he knew.

Dunne had just finished a tour in Frankfurt. His cases there had mostly involved technical operations against the nations of the former Soviet Union, but Frankfurt also ran ops against the Iranians. Like nearly everyone from his generation at the agency, he had been sucked into Iraq and Afghanistan, but they'd let him operate out of Paris for those shit shows. He was the technical officer people trusted with complicated jobs, and he didn't have enemies. He was regarded as part of the CIA's Catholic mafia, even though he hadn't been to Mass since he was a kid. To the extent it could be said of anyone at the agency, he was "clean."

Dunne would think later of all these reasons why he was the obvious choice for what turned out to be his last CIA mission. He had more experience against hard targets than any of the other techs, and had run sensitive, compartmented operations. And he had a reputation from his early days as a hell-raiser, a quality that the agency still admired. It was only after it went bad that Dunne began to wonder about the provenance of the assignment.

Why had they chosen *him*?

* * *

Gilroy was wearing a lime-green cotton dress. She pulled down her sunglasses as they navigated the walkway toward the woods. It was one of those muggy days of Washington's late summer whose thick heat would eventually be relieved by a thunderstorm. The clouds were pillars of moistening gray as the two exited the building near the cafeteria and walked southwest toward the water tower and power plant and the fenced perimeter that bounded Route 123.

"What's this about, anyway?" asked Dunne. "You're not the nature-walk type."

Gilroy waited for two other strollers to pass.

"Have you ever heard of a leftie group called Fallen Empire?" she began. "They operate mostly in Europe. They work with some hacker punks who call themselves the Quark Team. That ring any bells?"

"Maybe," Dunne answered. "They're like WikiLeaks, right? They publish leaked shit on the Internet."

"Correct," she said. "But it's more complicated than that. They claim they're Robin Hood in cyberspace. They strike all the time, from different servers and websites. They have contacts everywhere. We're not supposed to penetrate them, because they're journalists, supposedly, but they keep blowing secrets. They use serious hacking tools, from Tailored Access at NSA and Information Ops here at the agency. People want to know where they get their stuff."

"Which people?"

"The seventh floor. The deputy director himself, George Strafe. He thinks there aren't enough so-called whistleblowers on the planet to keep these people afloat. He thinks someone is feeding them, and he wants you to prove it."

"What does Strafe have on them?"

"He hasn't told me, exactly. But something rang his bell."

"Liaison?"

"Correct. A foreign service has been watching them, and they pinged us. The boss wants us to have our own sources in Fallen Empire. He needs an org chart of this Quark Team, too. He wants to find their transmission belt. But he can't do that without getting inside."

"Sounds like a counterespionage case," said Dunne. "Why do you need me?"

"Because it's complicated, Michael, like I said. The person who runs Fallen Empire is an American. He claims he's a real journalist, though the seventh floor thinks that's nonsense. The main site where they post things says it's a news organization. Fallenempire.org, it's called. So, there's a problem, technically."

"You mean 'legally.' If he's an American, and he's a journalist, then running an operation on him is against the rules, isn't it? Like the First Amendment, specifically. I hate rules, myself, but I'm just checking."

Gilroy stopped to consider her answer. She removed her sunglasses. Her eyes were a luminous hazel-green.

"You're correct that there is a general administrative order banning operations with or against U.S. journalists. And you are also correct that there was a specific decision not to penetrate WikiLeaks or any of the other so-called free-speech groups after the Snowden affair. We aren't supposed to ask how WikiLeaks got the leaked emails from the Russians, that's a fresh order, as of last week. I know this history as well as you do. Better."

"Then why is this one okay? If the others weren't?"

"Because this is scarier. That's what Strafe says. He got the General Counsel's Office to approve it."

"What boxes did he check?"

"The target is outside the United States. The target is not a U.S. person, but a foreign organization with possible links to a hostile foreign intelligence service. The American in question is ancillary. Any collection about him would be incidental. The lawyers have reviewed the proposed operation carefully, at the request of the deputy director. I wouldn't be having this conversation with you otherwise. Obviously."

She looked pained. She didn't like this case any more than Dunne did, but she had been given an order.

"Sorry to be a jerk, Sarah, but I don't trust the General Counsel's Office. They were the ones who assured my friends in the interrogation program that everything would be fine. That passed muster with the lawyers, too, until it didn't."

Gilroy looked him in the eye for a moment, then glanced away.

"That hurt, Michael," she said. "I have friends who got burned, too. This isn't 'enhanced interrogation.' It isn't rendition. It isn't illegal. It's just unusual. Strafe is creating a special access program to look at it, and he wants you to run this program. You can say no. But you're the right person."

Dunne held up a hand. He would have put it lightly on her shoulder, to reassure her, but you weren't supposed to do that now.

"I never say no, Sarah. I just need to know a little more before I say yes."

She was walking again, more quickly. "What do you want to know?"

"Who's the target of this operation? Where does he work? How does this pass muster, in case there's a flap?"

"Strafe says it's in Europe. He doesn't know where yet, but he thinks maybe in Italy. The American who runs Fallen Empire is named Jason Howe. He's a big Snowden fan, by the way, if that turns up your animosity meter."

"I hate Snowden. But that doesn't get me to yes. What's this 'Quark Team' that helps the American kid out?"

"It's run by an Italian computer science wiz named Lorenzo Ricci. He used to publish a lot of flashy papers about cyber, then he went dark. That's suspicious, Strafe thinks."

Dunne nodded. The agency called it "the null set" when someone went off the grid like that. It was a "tell" that an operation had gone black.

"Would I have to penetrate a physical location?" asked Dunne. He was already thinking about operational details.

"Meaning, break in? Probably. Once you find it. Look, it's a legitimate target. We go after people like this every day."

"I'll be honest, Sarah, the seventh floor scares me. They play politics with everything. If these people are Snowden fans, there must be something wrong with them. But shit, even the Republicans are playing games with WikiLeaks. Why should I get near all that?"

"Because it matters. The seventh floor thinks this outfit behaves like an enemy intelligence service. They're strategic, deliberate, and covert. They operate on multiple fronts. I'll let Strafe tell you the details, because I don't know them. They're not the Russians or the Chinese, but something else. That scares people."

"Why me? Really. I just got home. Alicia's fixing up the new house. We're trying to be normal for a while."

"What I said: You're the best, and this is complicated. Sorry, this is the price you pay for being good."

"Maybe." Dunne cleared his throat. "Honestly, I don't do 'complicated' very well. I'm better at 'simple.' And the big shots scare me."

"Other people asked for you, too. Not just Strafe. People you trust."

"Right." He put his hands in his pockets. There was a saying in technical services, that an extrovert was someone who looked at the other person's shoes rather than his own.

"Would I have to transfer out of S&T? I like it here."

"No. This would be temporary."

"I don't know. I mean, I guess . . ." He couldn't quite say it.

"You won't have people looking over your shoulder, I promise you. The compartment will be tiny. I won't even be briefed, once you start. If you start."

Dunne took a deep breath.

"Come on, Dunne. It's like you said before, right? You always say yes, in the end. That's why we love you."

"Shit." He exhaled slowly. "Let's go back to your office and look at the paperwork." He said it wearily, with resignation.

"I don't have the clearances. They told me to send you to the seventh floor, if you agreed. You can do the paperwork there tomorrow."

They were walking back now. The sky had darkened. A breeze was rustling the trees, a sign that the thunderstorm was coming.

"Let's hurry," said Gilroy, "before we get drenched."

\* * *

The only person Dunne was authorized to discuss the new project with was George Strafe, the deputy director for operations. But people always talk to someone, and in Dunne's case it was Roger Magee, who had been his friend and mentor ever since he had joined the agency in 2002. Magee had run the Directorate of Science and Technology for more than a decade and was now the senior technical adviser to Gilroy. But, really, he was a sort of informal clan leader for the agency's blue-collar workforce.

Like every organization, the CIA had a class system. It was like a big suburban high school: The case officers were the cool kids who played sports and had good SAT scores. They ran operations and eventually they got to be the station chiefs. The smart, nerdy kids who didn't play sports were the analysts; they had fancy degrees and very good SAT scores, but they were fussy and didn't like to break things. When the case officers competed with the analysts, it was like *Mean Girls.*

And then there were the bad kids, the blue-collar rednecks who did the dirty work of planting bugs, hacking computers, stealing briefcases, and shooting people. This working-class CIA had various outposts, but S&T was the most celebrated. The S&T techs were whip-smart, and they reveled in the grunt work of espionage—breaking into places that were locked and stealing secrets. This work increasingly involved breaking into computers rather than safes, but it was the same idea. S&T had been Magee's domain since the 1970s, and he had embraced Dunne as a kindred spirit and fellow troublemaker.

*   *   *

Dunne met Magee in a bar in McLean that for decades had been an S&T hangout. Magee was in his sixties now, nearing retirement, and he had a long wispy beard that made him look like a guitarist for ZZ Top. He had been drinking for a while when Dunne got to the bar.

"What's up?" asked Magee. "Must be something bad, or you wouldn't have called me, you stuck-up son of a bitch."

"Hey, Roger. Nice to see you, too."

"So, what's got you so scared that you need to see big brother, 'urgently'? I hope you're keeping your pecker in your pants and taking care of your pretty wife, but if you aren't, I don't want to hear about it. What is your gal, anyway, African?"

"Brazilian. Her name is Alicia. She's fine, thanks. This isn't personal, it's work. Gilroy wants me to do something, on direct orders of the DDO. They want me to operate off-line, in a special compartment."

"Well, I don't know anything about it, and I'm supposed to be Gilroy's tech guru. So I guess it's too 'off-line' for me. What's it about, if you're 'allowed' to tell Grandpa?"

"They want me to penetrate a free-speech group that operates out of Europe. I don't know much other than that. Fallen Empire and the Quark Team are the target names. I'm supposed to see George Strafe tomorrow morning."

Magee shook his head. The long hairs of his beard grazed over his beer mug.

"Don't do it, Mike. Trust me. If there wasn't something wrong with this operation, then Strafe wouldn't be doing it sneaky-Pete, behind the woodshed. Strafe is a dirtbag. If he was only a double dealer you could adjust for that, but with him there are five or six layers. And don't mess with journalists. It's like having a pet rattlesnake."

"Come on, Roger, these Wiki bastards are bad news. They're like journalists, but worse. They print anything they want, and they don't give a shit. If Strafe wants to look up their butts, what's wrong with that?"

"A lot. This so-called information space is getting crowded, brother. The black arts have spread far and wide. Don't go making trouble. You'll step on your dick."

Dunne opened his palms. What was he supposed to do? Gilroy had asked him to take on a special mission, but she wouldn't say why, and his best friend had just told him to refuse, and he wouldn't say why, either.

"Cut the crap, Roger. Why should I refuse?"

"Because if it was straight-up, Strafe wouldn't need you." He wagged his finger. "Don't fucking do it."

"I thought you'd say that. The problem is, I already said yes, pretty much."

"Well, shit." Magee leaned back in his chair and swallowed the rest of his drink in one gulp. "You are one sorry-ass hillbilly, you know that? That being the case, I don't want to hear any more about it. Deaf and dumb. Shut the fuck up. That's my credo, brother, especially when I'm not invited to the party. Let's talk about something else."

So, they talked . . . about sports, and music, and girls. And mostly, they drank beer and remembered the good old days, which were so long before Dunne joined the agency that he could only pretend to recall.

*  *  *

Dunne kept at home a gift that Magee had given him when he first joined S&T. It was the unit's unofficial crest in the 1960s, before Dunne was born, back when it was called the Office of Technical Services. It showed a rotary telephone atop a castle and a drawing of a goofy guy with earphones and various other electronic paraphernalia, with the motto: "Stand By to Bug."

Dunne was always ready to plant a bug, or hack a computer, or otherwise break the laws of foreign countries, so long as he was given official permission. Many people who have a similar mischievous streak get into trouble, but they're reckless and stupid. Dunne was smart. He did well at McKeesport High School, and he got a scholarship to the University of Pittsburgh, which allowed him to take fancy computer science classes at Carnegie Mellon and to consider graduate school.

Then 9/11 happened, and like a lot of people from McKeesport and everywhere else, Dunne wanted to join the military. The Army recruiter was ready to offer him a bonus and a ticket to signals-intelligence school, but he flunked his physical because of a game leg from high school football.

Dunne was upset and asked the recruiter if he could suggest any alternative. He was thinking about the Coast Guard, maybe, or the Corps of Engineers. But the recruiter wrote out an address on Liberty Avenue and a room number that turned out to be a cover address for the local CIA base, and gave Dunne a letter of recommendation. Dunne filled out some paperwork, came back to take a bunch of tests, and a few months later he was taking a polygraph examination.

Dunne found that he liked having secrets. He gave his parents a lame explanation about a civil service job. His girlfriend went into a snit because he was leaving, so he dumped her and partied with a different girl every night. On St. Patrick's Day, just before he reported for CIA training, he dyed his red hair green.

*　*　*

Because Dunne was a geek, the CIA steered him toward a career as a technical operations officer. He bypassed the Clandestine Service Trainee Program, aka "the Farm," which was fine with him because CST trainees seemed to think they were better than other CIA recruits, whereas his tech colleagues liked to hang out with lock-pickers.

By 2010, Dunne was a rising star. S&T offered him a path to the management job that Sarah Gilroy had now, running the unit, which would have meant a fancy title and more money and a slot in the Senior Intelligence Service. Dunne said no. He had fallen in love with something other than his job.

\*   \*   \*

Dunne married a beautiful Afro-Brazilian woman named Alicia Silva. They were living in Paris then, where Alicia had a job with UNESCO. She was a tall, vivacious, honey-brown woman who charmed everyone she met. Dunne sensed from the first that this was it; he had met the girl of his dreams; it was time to stop playing around.

A secretary in the CIA station in Paris, who had served in Rio and spoke Portuguese, had introduced them. She brought Dunne to a hipster cocktail party at the Palais de Tokyo, near the Trocadéro. The art was weird, and the food was worse, and Dunne was about to leave when his friend tugged him over to meet the stunning Brazilian woman by the window overlooking the Seine. As Dunne approached, a Frenchman was harassing Alicia; she recoiled, and her heel slipped on the marble floor. Dunne caught her.

The Frenchman, intimidated by Dunne's bearing, slunk away. Dunne asked her out that night leaving the art gallery, but she said no. He asked her again.

*"Eu só me apaixono uma vez,"* she whispered the night they made love for the first time. Dunne asked what the Portuguese words meant. Her answer lingered in his ear. I only fall in love once.

Alicia's mother had been born in Mozambique, but she was a naturalized American citizen, which made it easier for the agency. Her Brazilian father was a doctor who had been studying in America when Alicia was born, but he had died when she was a toddler. He had never been there to catch her when she fell, never made her feel safe.

"I belong to you," she told Dunne when they got married, and then she laughed and gave him a little slap. But he knew: She was his, to cherish and protect.

Alicia loved to sing Portuguese songs to her new husband. She sang in the bathroom when she got up, in the car, walking down the street, whispering in his ear when they were falling asleep. She sang Afro-Brazilian capoeira songs, with call-and-response, in a deep voice that made Dunne laugh; she chanted maracatu songs she'd heard at Carnival; and she whistled the tunes of choro songs that were little laments of the heart.

But most of all, Alicia liked to sing samba music, and she had a favorite that she sang to him the summer after they were married, when they took a vacation on the beach in California, in Carmel. She eventually translated it into English, so Dunne would know: "We'll make such sweet music / Until the night is done / Just dance the samba with me . . . / This is the time for that song / And this is the time for that dance / I don't feel alone because / I know that you'll stay with me / To samba through life with me."

She would lean back her beautiful head as she sang, and shake her braids, and when she was done, she would give Dunne a kiss and take him to bed.

Alicia never asked Dunne about his work. But he had sensed, from the first encounter when he intimidated the Frenchman who was bothering her, that she knew what he did. He was strong, and he knew his way in the world, and he worked at the embassy. She said to him once, just before they married, "I'll never tell anyone your secrets."

They had a child when they moved to Frankfurt, a beautiful girl they named Luisa, who liked to sing with her mother as she was falling asleep. Alicia began teaching Portuguese at a German university, and she loved the work. She would save up stories about her little triumphs with difficult students and share them with Dunne when he returned home from long trips.

"I love my teaching," she would say. "But my family is my world."

Alicia and Dunne moved to D.C. in the summer of 2016, when the Frankfurt assignment ended. The crazy presidential election was in full swing, but they barely noticed. Alicia wanted to put down roots. Luisa was four, almost ready to start kindergarten. They bought a house in Arlington, near a golf course. Alicia got a part-time job teaching Portuguese at George Mason University. She was expecting their second child.

\* \* \*

Dunne came home after his meeting with Gilroy and his drinking session with Magee. It was late. Alicia had been waiting up for him. He told her that his boss wanted him to take a new assignment and unfortunately he would be traveling again, at least for a while. He hated having to be away, especially with a new baby coming, but people said they needed him, and Dunne didn't know how to refuse. He promised that he would get home when he could.

"*Nunca me esqueça, minha querida,*" she whispered in his ear when they were in bed that night. Don't ever forget me, my darling.

Alicia loved and believed in her husband so totally that when the crack came, it was shattering.

# 5

Pittsburgh, Pennsylvania—May 2018

After Dunne's release from prison he found an apartment in Shadyside, just off Fifth Avenue. When he was a college student, this had been the Pittsburgh neighborhood that seemed edgy and cool, but over the years it had gone upmarket, with the same stores you'd find in any prosperous suburb. Dunne bought some furniture from the IKEA out by the airport. He put up pictures of his daughter, now six, by the bed. The photos were out of date. His ex-wife refused to provide new ones, and she wouldn't post shots of her child anywhere he could find them on the Internet. He had a picture of Alicia, too, from early in their marriage, but he couldn't bear to look at it.

Dunne made himself dinner that first night in his new home, spaghetti with clam sauce. He opened a bottle of red wine, but after he drank a glass, he poured the rest down the sink. He watched the Pirates lose a game on his new television set. The Bucs' mediocrity had deepened in the years he had been away. The last time they had won a World Series Dunne had been less than a year old. Their theme song back then had been "We Are Family." That seemed like a joke now, in Pittsburgh and everywhere else. "Family" was what we weren't.

Before Dunne went to bed, he trimmed his red beard with a new electric razor he had bought at the appliance store along with the television. He thought

of shaving the beard off entirely to make a new start, but, staring at his face in
the mirror, seeing those hard, sunken cheeks through the whiskers, he decided
against it. He couldn't sleep, so he took one of the pills they had given him
in prison.

Dunne visited the lawyer that his FBI friend had recommended. He drew
up papers for the LLC, and helped Dunne rent an office on Forbes Avenue. The
lawyer asked Dunne what he wanted to call the dummy company. It had to
be "Something LLC"; Dunne said he didn't have a name yet but would think
about it.

*    *    *

The first call Dunne made from his new office was to Richard Ellison, his best
friend from college and the only person whose letters Dunne had answered
while he was in prison. Ellison was an African American from Oakland. His
father had been a friend of August Wilson, the playwright, or so he claimed. His
father might have been one of Wilson's characters; his life plan was to play by
the book and *win*—make it or die. Ellison Junior had made it. He had moved
back to Pittsburgh recently, too, to take a job as general counsel for one of the
local banks.

The two men had become friends at Pitt. One night during freshman year
when the dining hall was crowded, Dunne had taken a seat at one of the Afro
tables. All the other black students got up and moved. Ellison stayed. They
talked about computers. Dunne thought of him as his friend; not his black
friend, just his friend.

Ellison was the sensible, risk-averse person that Dunne would like to have
been. Ellison didn't want to break into anything; he liked to fix stuff. He had
gone to law school after they graduated from Pitt, and then, after clerking for a
federal judge, he had become an assistant U.S. attorney in the Eastern District
of Virginia.

Ellison had been finishing his assignment in Alexandria when Dunne's
case was prosecuted. He had asked not to be involved because of their friend-
ship, but he had been troubled by the case. Ellison had said, in several of his
letters, that his colleagues thought the one-year prison sentence the judge had

imposed had been outrageous. The prosecution had assumed Dunne would get work release, or a few months at most.

* * *

"I've been waiting for you to come home, brother," Ellison said on the phone. "We need to talk. There's something I've been waiting to give you."

They met at a bar on Grant Street, near Ellison's office. The lawyer was wearing a gray pin-striped suit and a regimental-stripe tie. His dark skin was glowing as if it had been buffed. The bartender called out his name.

"You look like a movie star," said Dunne, giving him a soft pat on the cheek.

Ellison laughed and put his arm around Dunne's shoulder.

"You look like a guy who just got out of the joint. Didn't they feed you in there? Shit! And that red beard! Did you join Aryan Nation?" He laughed. "But you're home now, man. That bullshit is over."

"Yeah, maybe," answered Dunne.

Dunne asked about Ellison's wife and family. His wife was a lawyer, too. They had just bought a new house in Fox Chapel, where the rich people lived. The children were going to a private school. Ellison didn't ask about Dunne's family. He knew that was an open wound.

They ordered beers, even though it was the middle of the afternoon, and they talked about people they knew from college. Ellison understood that he was talking to a man who was trying to put his life back together, and he didn't push. It was Dunne who eventually asked the question.

"You said you wanted to give me something. What is it?"

"It's a letter for you. It came after you went into Club Fed."

Ellison reached into the inside jacket pocket of his pin-striped suit and removed a long, thin envelope. He handed it across the table to Dunne.

Dunne read the envelope cover once, turned it over, and read it again. Typed on it were the words:

*For Michael Dunne. To Be Delivered Upon His Release from Prison. From a Lemon Squeezer.*

The letter was sealed tightly with several layers of plastic tape and embossed with seals that would show if the letter had been opened. There was no return address. Dunne laid it down on the table.

"Who sent this?" asked Dunne.

"I don't know," answered Ellison. "It was sent to the U.S. Attorney's Office. It arrived in a FedEx package. I tried to track the sender's address in New York. Nothing there. It's a mail drop."

"Did you keep the shipping label?"

"Yes, indeed."

Ellison removed the red, white, and blue document from another pocket and handed it over.

Dunne read the address. It was a post office box number in Manhattan. The sender obviously had taken precautions not to be discovered.

"Did you dust for prints?"

"Did that, too. Nothing." Ellison looked at his friend. "Come on, man, aren't you going to open it?"

Dunne shook his head. "Not now. When I'm back home. If I opened it here, you'd want to know what it says, and I'm not sure that's a good idea yet."

"Aw, shit! I should have just opened it back in Alexandria. That's what the other assistant U.S. attorney wanted to do. But I said no. It's a private communication, to be opened by Michael Dunne, personally, when he's a free man."

"I appreciate that, Rich. You're the only person who cares what I want. I'll tell you what's in the letter after I read it. Probably."

"Okay. Just one question. What's a 'Lemon Squeezer'?"

Dunne laughed.

"It's CIA slang, from the part of the agency where I worked. In the old days, a 'Lemon Squeezer' was someone who specialized in secret writing. You'd write the message in lemon juice, and then when the agent got the letter and heated the paper, shazam, the words would appear."

"Meaning the letter was sent by one of your former colleagues?"

Dunne nodded and put the envelope in his own pocket, along with the FedEx label.

"So it seems," he said. "Unless someone is just squeezing my lemon."

*  *  *

On the way back to his office on Forbes Avenue, Dunne bought a pair of surgical gloves. He put them on before he opened the letter. It was one page, neatly printed, no letterhead or markings, and, Dunne was sure, no prints that would give away its author. He laid it out on his desk, went to the cooler and brought back a glass of water, and then began reading:

Dear Mr. Dunne:

Like many people, I am very sorry about what happened to you. If we could have prevented it, we would have done so. You chose to say nothing publicly about your case, and we respect that. But if you are reading this, it means that you have finished your prison term and are thinking, as others are, about how to right the wrong that has been done to you. The advice from your friends is to be persistent but be careful.

When you were arrested, you were pulling on a thread that touches many powerful people. We hope that you will keep pulling. Look for other victims like yourself and try to help them. That's the best way to get started. Eventually, you will find the network that tried to destroy you. It operates more widely now. It is as efficient as a machine, for a reason. It is a machine.

Here are some tools that will help you.

First, here is the most recent IP address for the computer used by Jason Howe: 52.222.232.38. The domain registry is 1837442_DOMAIN_COM-VRSN. The server name is NS-2038 .AWSDNS-00.ORG. Howe is very hard to find now, but it will be worth the effort.

Second, here is the serial number for the iPhone most recently used by Howe. DDJXFDML6JC4D. The Sim card ICCID used most recently for this phone is 89148000004050207996.

Third, here are the registry numbers in the National Vulnerability Database for the zero-day exploits that have been used recently by Howe's group: CVE-2015-1425, CVE-2015-3690, CVE-2015-1763, CVE-2015-2029, CVE-2015-5078, and CVE-2015-6372.

Fourth, this network has been using as its principal malware a rootkit that intercepts application programming interfaces in the kernel and erases its tracks as it extracts data. The most recent software that can detect this kernel-mode rootkit is: http://www.antirootkit .com/software/IceSword.htm.

We wish it were possible to send you more information, or to update what we are sending in this message. But our points of access have disappeared. Anyone who is monitoring these accounts now is subject to surveillance and possible prosecution. Any serious investigation will have to be done outside government agencies. You have the motivation and skills to penetrate and disable this network. If you're successful, others will find you.

You will wonder who we are. Perhaps you have heard of the warriors who banded together in the time of Charlemagne, the ninth century king of France. Songs and legends celebrate their mission of assisting victims of injustice. They were called The Paladin. The name has survived over many centuries. They were the people's bandits, fighting for justice.

If you want to understand where this message comes from, think of this ancient fraternity that seeks to assist decent people who have been threatened by powerful and lawless forces, just as you were, and who stand invisibly behind you now. You have our apologies and respect.

The Paladin

*   *   *

When Dunne had read the letter, he went to the office of the lawyer who had been recommended by his FBI friend Rick Bogdanovich. It was late in the afternoon, and the lawyer was almost ready to leave work, but Dunne asked him to stay a few more minutes.

Dunne told the lawyer that he had decided on the name for his little company, the LLC that would serve as the legal shell for his cyber consulting venture. Paladin LLC. The lawyer asked what the name meant, and Dunne said it was a French word for an avenger.

"Is that like the old television show?" the lawyer asked. "Richard Boone. *Have Gun—Will Travel*?"

"No." Dunne laughed. "I don't have a gun. I just like the name." It was more complicated than that, but he didn't want to talk about it.

# 6

Langley—September 2016

George Strafe, the deputy director for operations, was waiting for Dunne in the secure conference room on the seventh floor, across the hall from the director's suite and its bank of windows overlooking the Potomac. Sarah Gilroy had accompanied Dunne up the elevator and down the corridor but left him at the door. The general counsel was supposed to attend the meeting, but her office said she wasn't feeling well that day.

Dunne hadn't worn a tie, even to see the boss. He was dressed in gray flannel slacks, a light tweed jacket, loafers, and an open-neck shirt. He'd gotten a haircut that morning on the way to work, and his red curls were, for once, neatly trimmed. He didn't like being on the seventh floor; this was where trouble began.

Strafe was seated at the conference table, reading from a file of blue-stripe cables, when Dunne entered the room. He looked up curiously. Strafe had a mottled face, scarred by what people said was a letter bomb he had opened early in his career. His brown hair was in short spikes that might never have seen a comb. A bald spot had emerged at the crown. He was wearing a skinny black knit tie and a rumpled black suit with an incongruous white silk handkerchief monogrammed with the initials *GS* in the pocket. The room was ringed with maps, digital clocks displaying the time in a dozen stations around the world, and television screens for secure video conferences.

"Hey, thanks for coming, Mike." Strafe's voice was affable and unconvincing. "Have a seat. Want some coffee? I hear you just moved back. Not an ideal time. We appreciate it."

"I'm fine, sir," said Dunne. He took a seat in a leather swivel chair across from his boss. He knew the deputy director from when Strafe had been an ambitious station chief making his way up the ladder and needed technical help on operations. Dunne had supplied some ingenious surveillance devices and Strafe had recommended him for promotion to GS-11. He was transactional that way.

"Relax," said Strafe. "This will work out fine. You know what Napoleon said? War is a matter of hiding fear as long as possible."

Dunne laughed uneasily. "I'm not afraid, sir. Just confused. I don't know what this is about."

"I can explain," said Strafe. "Give you a tour of the forest, before we drop you into the trees." He turned to his executive assistant, who was seated a few seats down, preparing to take notes.

"Jim, close the door on your way out, please." The aide exited the room, leaving the two men alone. Strafe removed his jacket and rolled up the sleeves of his shirt to the elbows, revealing a tattoo on his right arm that said, in small block letters, IPSO FACTO.

"We have a problem," Strafe began, his voice low at first. "What it is, exactly, I don't know, but it scares the shit out of me."

Strafe paused to let that sink in before continuing.

"Someone is turning off some of our cyber weapons in Europe. In Italy, Austria, and Serbia, for sure. They're supposed to beacon to us, securely, so we know they're in place and ready to go. But they've stopped beaconing. I don't like it, my friend. Not at all."

Dunne nodded. "Did the Russians do it?"

"Nope. Some of their malware has been taken down, too. They don't think we know that, but there's a lot they don't know."

"The Chinese?"

"Negative. They've also lost their beacons. They think we're doing it. But we're not."

"Well, it's a plus that the Russians and Chinese are unplugged, right?"

"Not so much. We had already turned off their nastiest malware ourselves. But we left the beacons in place, so they wouldn't know that their software wouldn't work. Someday they would push the red button and, surprise, nothing would happen. Now they know."

"I didn't realize that."

"Nobody does. But it's bad shit, like I said. Someone out there has a whole lot more technical expertise than we ever realized."

"So, who are these geniuses, sir?"

Strafe crossed his arms over his chest, so that the "Ipso Facto" tattoo was over his heart.

"That's what you're going to find out, my friend. But I'll get you started."

"Fallen Empire."

"Correct. We think that thread starts with these supposedly do-gooder hackers who want to purify cyberspace. The leader is named Jason Howe. He pretends to be a journalist, but that's horseshit. We think the top software engineer is an Italian named Ricci, who runs something he calls the Quark Team. But the rest is fuzzy."

"Sarah told me the names. She said she'd never heard of them before. What else can these people do, besides turn off malware?"

"Install it, for Christ's sakes. They think they have the secret sauce. Remember *Ghostbusters*? They want to be 'the Gatekeeper.'"

"Where are they?"

"We aren't sure. I know that sounds pathetic, but we just found out about this two weeks ago. My guess is Italy, because that's the last fix we had on both Howe and Ricci. But right now all we see is their exhaust."

"Are you sure they aren't fronting for the Russians?"

"I'm not sure of anything. The Russians may be their customers. The Chinese, too. Before Ricci hooked up with Howe, he was making the market in bad shit. Selling it to anyone. Password dumps. Keystroke logging. Rootkit control. The works."

"Do they write their own code?"

"God knows where they get it. From the Brits, or French, or Israelis, or us. Maybe all of the above. Or maybe they really are that smart. The point is, we want to take them down. Or, hell, maybe own them, I don't know. But first we need to know who they are. And that's your job, brother."

"I apologize, sir, but tell me again. How do we know it's not a Russian cutout?"

"We know the Russians aren't running it because we know from SIGINT that the GRU is trying to penetrate this outfit, too. Okay? I didn't tell you that, but that's the point, Mike. We want you to get there first."

"Got it." Dunne nodded. "Who has this Quark Team recruited? Any ideas?"

"Nope, but you read the same intel I do. There a lot of smart asshole kids out there. Throw a dart at the map. Russia. Ukraine. Germany. Iran. Saudi Arabia. Britain. America. There are hacker shitheads everywhere the dart lands."

Dunne cleared his throat. "And you want me to find this organization and get inside it?"

"Precisely. We haven't been tracking them because it's supposedly 'illegal' for us. But that's changing, starting now."

"Uh, these people have cover as journalists, from what you said," offered Dunne.

"They *claim* to be journalists, but that's bullshit. And you know why? Because they are too *good*. They pump stuff out faster than we can follow, and they crow about it. People who talk about openness that much must have something to hide."

"What do you want me to do that Tailored Access and Information Operations can't do better?"

"Penetrate them. Physically. Turn over the rock and shine a flashlight so we can see what's crawling around. We've been going in the front door with these Wiki-nuts and charging them when we catch them doing something illegal. Now we want to follow the little bastards out the back door to where they think nobody is looking. Out among the geeks and hackers and NSA haters. We want to hit the people they think we can't touch. How does that sound?"

"Fine, but I still don't know what you want me to do."

"Sarah said she told you a little about Fallen Empire."

"She told me about Howe."

"They claim to be the global fourth estate. Which is ridiculous. They shit on all the real journalists who refuse to publish the crap they steal. They've been off-limits for us."

"I gather."

"But not anymore. They started working recently with a Serbian illegal in Italy. We have that link solid, stone cold, or at least the Italians do."

"Who cares about Serbia?"

"Nobody. The point is that the guy is an undeclared intelligence officer. That changes the game. Anyone touched by an illegal is fair game. That's how the lawyers and I read the rules."

"Then why do you need me?"

"Because we want to get inside this so-called free speech underground. Recruit people. Mess with their shit. Take them down. After that, we'll see what's next."

Dunne lifted his brows. He was game, but he wasn't stupid.

"That sounds like covert action against a bunch of civilians."

"It's foreign intelligence collection. If it was covert action, we'd need a finding from the White House. But it isn't. So, we don't. You have it in writing, in the order creating your special access program. That's your get-out-of-jail-free card. Not that you'd ever need one."

"But you could never show the SAP authorization to anyone. It's code-word."

"We'll never need to. Because it's legal. I thought you were a stand-up guy, Mike. I didn't know you'd been to law school."

"Shit, sir. Give me a break!"

"Just teasing. I know you're solid, or you wouldn't be here."

"Thank you."

"So, listen up: These people are dangerous. They have all the tools. They could start pushing this stuff, and not to Human Rights Watch, either. Fallen Empire's target list doesn't make sense. They're omnivores."

"You sound almost jealous, sir," said Dunne.

"Maybe." Strafe allowed himself a smile. "I just want to find where they are, see what they've got, and own them, one way or another. But first you'll have to strip away all this free-speech, we're-just-journalists crap. You need to break their cover."

Dunne looked around the conference room at the array of command-and-control systems that connected the agency to everywhere that mattered on the planet. He took a breath, put his hands together, deliberating.

"There's one more thing you need to know," Strafe said quietly in the silence. "Some of this shit that Fallen Empire is putting out doesn't seem to be true."

"What do you mean?"

"Just what I said. There are voices, pictures, events that look real. But our analysts don't think they happened. So, it's like, what the fuck? These are smart bastards, and they're playing with, forgive the term, 'reality.' It's not fake news, like the Russians. It's fake events. That's why we need to get inside."

Dunne nodded again. "This is a pretty big deal, I take it."

"Yes, indeed, my friend. This is the star gateway. People in the USG have gotten so worried about authorities and technicalities that they don't realize the world has changed. That's why we need someone who hasn't lost his street smarts, who can break into this space and wire it up, get some ground truth so we know what the hell is going on."

"And I don't have to quit my directorate?"

"Nope. This is TDY."

"What if I get caught?"

"We'll deny it and pull you out."

"Right. But suppose they collect stuff on me. I'm a sitting duck. They're American 'journalists.' They could fry my ass."

"Hypothetical, but it won't happen. Once these people know we're coming after them, they'll scatter. These people are chickenshit, basically. Otherwise they wouldn't be sitting behind machines all day."

"Maybe they are machines," said Dunne.

Strafe laughed. "You're losing it, buddy."

"Suppose I get prosecuted. This is against the regs, technically."

Strafe laughed. "For god's sake, Mike. Chin up. We're the CIA. Nobody would bring a case. If they did, the judge would never convict. Don't be a baby."

Strafe checked his watch, unnecessarily, given that there were a dozen clocks on the wall. He stood and put his hand on Dunne's shoulder.

"Sorry, but I have another meeting. If you get cold feet, tell Sarah and we'll find someone else. Otherwise, good luck."

He was out the door before Dunne could answer that he was a pro, he would accept the assignment, and he wouldn't get caught.

# 7

Langley—September 2016

"European Special Collection" was the opaque name given to Michael Dunne's special access program. It was separate even from the normal review for compartmented work. Access was denied for European station chiefs and the Europe and Eurasia mission center. Because it wasn't defined as a covert action, it wasn't briefed to the White House or the congressional oversight committees. The operation was run directly by the deputy director for operations.

European Special Collection was given a small office in the basement of the Original Headquarters Building, in a restricted area that handled liaison with officers outside the building under non-official cover. Dunne was assigned a codirector named Morris Hoffman, a veteran Europe Division officer who was temporarily reassigned from his post as deputy chief in the Counterintelligence Center. Four support officers were assigned to the group, too, all experienced and read into some of the agency's most sensitive activities.

The group held a meeting the day it got office space, sitting on desktops because the chairs hadn't been unpacked yet. The Office of Security had delivered boxes of computer gear, but they were sitting on the floor, unopened.

"Welcome to the office that does not exist," said Dunne when they gathered in the cramped, windowless space. There was nervous laughter; their makeshift office looked like the storage room of a hotel.

"I've asked Mr. Hoffman to lead this first meeting," Dunne continued. "He's been around Headquarters for years, unlike me, and he knows how to make the bureaucracy work."

Morris Hoffman was bald, with a smooth oval face. He wore a suit with suspenders that accentuated the broad bulge of his stomach. His skin had the pink, slightly puffy tone of a man who preferred steam baths to exercise. He sat in his chair almost motionless, and conveyed an aura of benign, impervious calm.

Hoffman gave a broad, imprecise explanation of the operational objectives, authorities, classification procedures, and operational security requirements. He talked without modulation, like a flight attendant reviewing pre-takeoff safety procedures. He and Dunne would soon be preparing a detailed operations plan, he said, which they would share with the group when it was approved.

Hoffman asked for questions, and when there weren't any, he turned his round Humpty Dumpty frame toward Dunne.

"Shall we adjourn the larger group, Mr. Dunne? Go over some details?"

They retreated to the soundproof cubicle that was their shared office, for a private review of the program.

Dunne had a perverse admiration for his new partner. Hoffman was one of the exotic florae that still existed in the remoter parts of the agency, far from the hotshots and second-guessers. He was from a family of CIA spooks: His great-uncle Frank had been a legendary station chief in the Middle East, and various other relatives had navigated the secret world abroad, but Morris was the family introvert. He was an orchid that bloomed in the dark. He would be useless on an operation, but that was Dunne's realm; Hoffman understood the minefield of Headquarters.

"May I suggest that we take a month to organize our template?" proposed Hoffman.

"That's too long," answered Dunne. "Strafe is itchy. We should move out as soon as we know where our targets are based. Target location is your department."

"Indeed it is." He smiled like a maître d'hotel in a fine restaurant, whose only pleasure is to make the customer happy.

"We are looking for the obvious indicators," Hoffman continued. "Cyber operations require a large power supply, so we are looking for changes in local grids in Europe. They require advanced computing capability, so we are looking for shipments of graphical processing units and the most advanced NVIDIA cards. They require smart people, so we are looking for engineers who have been writing significant research papers who have suddenly stopped publishing. We'll find a location, I assure you. In the meantime, we are collecting all Fallen Empire communications, public and private."

"I want to be in Europe in two weeks," said Dunne.

"Very well. You are the 'operator.' I am your support staff. I gather, then, that as soon as you have a preliminary plan, you'll want to set up overseas. Am I right?"

"Yup," said Dunne.

"I promise you one thing, Mr. Dunne. I will stay out of your way. I am here to advise and consult."

"Have you worked overseas recently?" asked Dunne.

"Not for some years, I'm afraid." Hoffman smiled and clasped his hands across his tummy. "Many years."

"Operations is a different game these days. Everything leaves a digital trail. Unless we're very careful, people will see us coming. So, to do this right, I will need a base camp first to scout the people and terrain. I've been thinking that Switzerland is the best bet. It's a secure operational environment and the base chief can help with real estate."

"Whatever you say, Mr. Dunne. We are entirely at your disposal. Take as many of our support people as you need. Your budget, as I understand it, will be unlimited, essentially. You collect the information and we will analyze it, as needed. Does that make sense?"

"Sure, Morris. And by the way, it's Michael. Mr. Dunne is my father. I hope you'll at least come visit us overseas."

"Oh, I'd just get in the way, Michael," said Hoffman. "You'll do much better on your own."

# 8

## Geneva—September 2016

Michael Dunne established his base camp in a Geneva suburb called Carouge, south of where the Arve River joins the Rhône. The local CIA base had a never-used safe house there, a two-bedroom apartment in an old building. Dunne booked an overnight flight from Dulles to check the location and wander the neighborhood. It was a noisy district known as Little Italy, without the sheen of the chic, French-speaking Geneva by the lake. That suited Dunne; he liked the anonymity that came with crowds and commotion. Headquarters requisitioned the apartment and flew in a suite of computers and communications gear with its own satellite uplinks.

Dunne said an awkward goodbye to Alicia before he left. She was seven months pregnant. He told her he wasn't sure when he would be back. It was hard to look her in the eye.

"*Cuidado, meu querido,*" she said. Be careful, my darling. She never knew where he was going or what he did. Dunne's four-year-old daughter Luisa didn't want to let him go, and she cried at the door as the Red Top taxi arrived to take him to the airport.

Dunne brought his two best tech support people, Adrian White and Arthur Gogel, to assist him in Geneva. They arrived two days after Dunne, along with the computer gear. Like many of Dunne's S&T colleagues, they looked like hipsters on vacation, but they were meticulous at their jobs. They shared the front bedroom, which quickly took on the funky, chaotic look of a college dorm. Dunne claimed the bedroom in the back, overlooking a courtyard.

In the living room the team created a small computer lab, with secure servers, laptops, and a half dozen monitors, all shielded to prevent detection of signals. The team had two communications links to the outside: One was a high-speed broadband connection to the "dirty wire" of the public Internet; a second accessed a satellite array that carried CIA special-handling traffic. All the Internet connections were routed through two proxy servers, a first in Luxembourg that bounced to another in Thailand, to hide their tracks.

Dunne's team spent the first few days scouting Fallen Empire's messaging. Adrian managed the initial online research. After three days, he had enough to present a briefing.

"This is some weird shit," began Adrian, when he gathered his two colleagues. He was a dark-skinned Jamaican-born man, with dreadlocks falling to his shoulders. His ethnic identity had given him cover over the years to do close-in S&T operations in places where a white man wouldn't survive. He was beloved among colleagues as an unflappable professional, the man you would most want to have with you in a foxhole.

"First, let's look at some of the propaganda these so-called journalists have been putting online. They post from fifty different IP addresses, but all the stuff I'm going to show you gets the 'Fallen Empire' brand."

Adrian displayed a visualization he had created to map the messaging. It showed dozens of topic clusters, but he focused on four big themes: freedom for Edward Snowden; police violence against African Americans; environmental action; and anti-Semitic hate crimes in Europe.

"We'll start with Snowden," said Adrian. "It's the basic crybaby line you would expect." Over a career in the CIA, Adrian had developed the same conservative political views as most of his colleagues.

"They have a site called WeLoveSnowden.org," he began. "No shit. It's really called that. They quote various predictables demanding that Snowden be pardoned. Hollywood actors, a Black Lives Matter dude, some bleeding-heart novelists, even a British comedian. It's nasty, but let's face it, half the people in Europe feel the same way."

"Sad but true," said Dunne. "You finding any fakes? Anything that doesn't smell right?"

"Yes, indeed. The WeLoveSnowden site is circulating an NSA document that's supposedly a memo authorizing surveillance on European citizens, everywhere. Not just their metadata, but everything. It's backed up by a recording of the NSA director's voice, supposedly talking to the head of the German BND."

"And that's fake?"

"NSA hasn't issued any public statement. But I got a message overnight from the Fort that it's a crock. The voiceprint is flawless. It's the director. But his XO says he never said it. And there's a fake video, too, in which President Obama supposedly asks an aide off-line about a drone strike he ordered in Russia to kill Snowden."

"You're shitting me. That's online at the Fallen Empire site."

"It's password-protected, for their inner circle only, but yeah. It's fake, but unbelievably good. The video looks exactly like brother Barack, down to the white hairs on top. But Hoffman got confirmation from the NSC that it never happened. Here, take a look."

Dunne watched a figure identical to Obama, speaking in the unmistakable high, thin, precise voice of the president, inquiring about a drone assassination attempt on Snowden.

"That would fool Michelle," muttered Dunne. "What else have you got besides the Snowden file?"

"They're playing the race card pretty hard, even for me," said Adrian, flipping his dreads back from his shoulders. "Look at this stuff from Ferguson."

Adrian clicked through a string of images that had been posted since the killing of Michael Brown in Ferguson, Missouri, two years before. The recurring theme was that nonviolence was a mistake and it was time for a reprise of Black Panther radicalism.

One had a picture of Bobby Seale and the words, "Hands up. But next time we'll shoot!" Another featured the iconic photo of Huey Newton in a wicker chair with a spear in one hand and a rifle in the other. A third had a line of young black men in berets and leather jackets and the words, "Black Panthers tried to protect black people from the KKK. The government destroyed the Panthers but the KKK survives."

"You go deep into the site and there are lots of videos of black people getting whipped and shot. Close up, gory, makes your skin crawl. That shit happens in real life, but I asked Hoffman to do some tests, and this particular shit ain't real. It's staged. We're trying to figure out how they did it."

"These folks are going to get someone killed," said Dunne.

"Uh-huh," said Adrian. "I think that's the plan."

Dunne pointed to the "Fracking" cluster on Adrian's map. "What's that about? Does shale oil kill black people, too?"

"It kills everybody, according to our friends," said Adrian. "Check it out."

The screen displayed a series of the environmental posts that Fallen Empire had disseminated through social media. They all centered on the idea that finding oil and gas through the technique called hydraulic fracturing would contaminate groundwater and harm public health forever.

"Fracktivists Unite!" said one, showing a group of militants brandishing rakes and shovels. The slogans repeated versions of the message that fracking was a rip-off scheme to hurt ordinary people and help rich corporations: "We Can't Drink Money," "No Jobs on a Dead Planet," "Keep the Frack Out of My Water," "The Poison Doesn't Stay in the Ground."

"Maybe they have a point," said Arthur, the other tech. He was wearing a black football jersey with the name ORWELL over the number 84.

"Nah! They just hate oil companies," said Dunne. "They want to kill the energy business the way people killed the steel business. Believe me, I've seen this movie."

Adrian motioned for Arthur to come closer. "Check this out, brother, before you decide these dudes are the good guys."

He displayed a link analysis that showed the countries where most of the anti-fracking posts had been disseminated. Nearly all were in Europe.

"So, the funny thing about these European anti-fracking activists is that they're using some material that shows up on a Gazprom website," explained Adrian. "The Russians hate fracking because it would take away gas sales. Some of the video embedded in these sites looks too good to be true."

"Which means it probably isn't. Send it home to Hoffman. Tell him to put it in the 'Fakes' file."

"What about anti-Semitism in Europe?" asked Arthur, pointing to the fourth cluster. "That's not fake. My mother's family is French-Jewish, and I'm telling you, it's no joke."

"Understood, amigo," said Adrian, clicking on another link. "But watch this."

The images in the anti-Semitism cluster were a jumble. A synagogue in Brussels attacked by Arabs. A crowd of North Africans outside a kosher market in Paris chanting, "Death to Jews." A public mural in a Pakistani section of London showing Jewish bankers playing Monopoly on the backs of naked brown men. An image of Afghan refugees in Germany covered head to toe in burkas with the caption: "George Soros brought them here. Is there a terrorist underneath?"

"Jew-hating bastards," growled Arthur.

"Racist crap," agreed Dunne. "How does it fit with the other stuff?"

"Because it's so slick. I mean, there are videos of Muslim women being assaulted by Jewish men. Men in yarmulkes, men with side curls. They're obviously fake, but they don't look fake. They hired actors, or something else. I don't know."

"Send them to Hoffman," said Dunne. "What's the bottom line?"

"The anti-Semitism images are just like the rest. They're all about getting people ripshit-angry at each other. They start with real stuff and then crank in fake stuff. Muslims are killing Jews. Corporations are destroying the environment. Blacks should kill racist white people. It's all stirring the pot."

"What's the pot?" asked Arthur.

"Wrong question," said Dunne, half to himself. "Who's holding the spoon?"

"There's one more thing I've got to show you," said Adrian. "It's the weirdest part, really. I just found it last night, when I was putting the briefing together."

"Let's have it," said Dunne.

"Well, all this left-wing crap I just showed you, with the inflammatory fake images about surveillance, race, the environment, and Jews, that's all Fallen Empire, okay?"

"Check. We just watched the highlight reel. What's weirder than that?"

"Well, last night I came across the same stuff in reverse. Sometimes the same video links, but with the fake stuff spun the other way. In this other version, Snowden was a traitor. Obama was chickenshit for not having killed him. The police were the victims in Ferguson and the other shootings. The oil companies are under attack and losing jobs. Jews are creating phony evidence of anti-Semitism. It was the same narrative, upside down."

"Who was posting the counter-narrative?" asked Dunne.

"It's a right-wing group called Save the West. But they're playing with the same cards as Fallen Empire. It's like a hockey face-off. Mirror image. Two sides manipulating the same fake information for different purposes."

"These people are scary good," muttered Dunne. "Like the Russians, but better. How did you detect the fake stuff, Adrian?"

"Slow the imagery down. Your eye doesn't catch it, but if you go pixel by pixel, with a high-res image, you can see it. The splice isn't quite right. The lighting is off. It's a coherence problem. But they're seriously good at it."

"Who *are* they?" murmured Arthur. He had watched the anti-Semitic videos in horror and was now struggling with the possibility that the same team of Internet manipulators had created evidence that the Jews were really the aggressors. He took it personally.

Dunne moved to the center of his small team, his eyes blazing.

"We have to find these people, now. Stop looking at their videos and start messing with their shit. Do we have anything that can locate them physically? Servers, proxies, anything?"

"Not yet," answered Adrian. "They're bouncing around a bunch of different servers."

"Let's feed all the video to Hoffman. Maybe there's a tell we're not seeing. We need to get inside this organization, now, and see how it works its magic tricks, and then it's lights-out. Agreed?"

"Roger that," said Arthur and Adrian, in unison.

*　*　*

Hoffman called on a secure line later that day. His usual laconic manner was gone. His voice was thinner, and up an octave.

"I believe we have found something of interest," he said. "Something locational."

"I'm holding my breath," said Dunne.

"We think that many of the videos were created in northeast Italy. In a region called the Marche, in the mountains west of the Adriatic coast."

"And why do you believe that, pray tell?"

"Because different power grids have different signatures, dear boy. Tiny fluctuations in the current. No generator is precisely the same as another. That's something we learned when we were looking for Osama bin Laden. Videos have much hidden information. The slightest oscillation in the lighting. A flicker you can't see. Islamabad looks different from Peshawar, if you know what to look for. And we do."

"So where in the Marche were the videos shot?"

"The grid can't tell us that precisely. It's uniform in the region served by the central Enel station in Ascona. But . . ."

Hoffman paused for effect. This was his moment, and he wanted to savor it.

"But what? Come on, Morris. We're on the clock."

"We did discover that a significant new power transmission line was installed for the city of Urbino, in the Marche, a month ago, to meet a substantial increase in demand for power there. It's the sort of increased power consumption that we find when a small server farm is installed."

"Bingo!" said Dunne. "They're in Urbino."

"Quite possibly, yes. I should think so. Entirely possible. Likely, perhaps."

Dunne turned to his two support techs. They both had big smiles, as he did.

"Boys, we have a target. We need to start prepping it, which means close-in surveillance, name identification, plans for how to get in and out."

"*Mi deh yah!*" said Adrian, dropping a phrase of Jamaican slang. "I'm here."

# 9

Geneva—September 2016

A few blocks down the street from Dunne's little war room was a nightclub called La Minette. The Pussycat. It featured hip-hop and reggae music, and it got loud. Around midnight, the street filled with young people clamoring to get in. Dunne and his group had been working hard all day and into the evening and had ordered Indian food from a local takeout. But as the clamor outside increased, Adrian took off his headphones, which weren't keeping out the din.

"Hey, boss," he said to Dunne. "Let's go check out that place down the street."

Dunne shrugged. "I could use a drink," he said.

"You'll get more than that down the street," said Adrian with a mischievous smile.

Dunne and Adrian showered and changed. Arthur said he would stay and guard the equipment. He wanted to watch a video. Adrian pointed to his dreadlocks and asked if they should wear disguises. Dunne thought a moment and said no. They were clean, so far as they knew, and people on the street had already seen them come and go. Arthur let them out the door and powered down most of the equipment.

The club was upstairs in a simple stucco building. A DJ was spinning

records when they arrived. The dance floor was filled, bodies close under pulsing lights, purple and red, and a spinning globe that flashed in every direction.
In the crush of people, you couldn't really tell who was dancing with whom.
Dunne and Adrian stood on the side of the floor, drinking and watching the
action. Dunne had ordered a vodka.

Adrian had his shades on, chilling. Dunne had his eye on a blond woman
in a black leather skirt. In the heat of the room, her blouse was tight against
her body and with each beat the fabric moved with the sway of her chest. The
woman was lost in the sound of the music, eyes closed, arms raised above her,
somewhere else. And then she was looking at Dunne, returning his gaze.

Dunne raised his glass. She smiled and arched her back. The song ended,
and a new one powered up. As the beat changed and the crowd of dancers
re-formed, she was gone.

That's lucky, Dunne thought. He ordered another vodka. The DJ thanked
the crowd and stepped away from his turntable, and the lights dimmed. When
they came back up, a reggae band was on the little stage and tuning its instruments. Adrian went to the men's room; when he came back, he smelled like
weed. Dunne asked if he wanted to stay for the reggae set, and the Jamaican
mouthed the words, *Fuck, yes.*

The house lights darkened, so that all you could see was the spotlight on
the singer onstage. Dunne turned to pick up his glass from the rail, and in the
dark he didn't see at first that the blond woman in the black leather skirt was
standing next to him. She looked up at him with radiant blue eyes, freshly lined
with mascara. She had an unlit cigarette in her hand.

Dunne knew he should ignore her. She extended the hand holding the
cigarette.

"I don't have a light, miss," he said. "Sorry."

"Then buy me a drink," said the woman, in German-accented English.

* * *

Dunne bought her a glass of wine, and one more vodka for himself. They
retreated to a balcony at the back of the club, where it wasn't so noisy and she
could smoke her cigarettes. Dunne took her for a high-priced call girl.

"Where do you work, pretty lady?" asked Dunne.

"A bank." She winked.

"Which one?" he countered dubiously.

"Maison Suisse. Private Wealth Management."

Dunne had heard of it. It was one of the oldest private banks in Switzerland. If she was a hooker, she had a fancy pimp.

"So, what's your name, Miss Private Wealth Manager?"

She moved closed. "Veronika." She put her finger to her lips. "What's your name, Mr. Red Hair?"

"Joe," answered Dunne, using his cover name. "Plain old Joe."

"Why don't you dance, Mr. Joe? You have a nice body."

"Shy," he answered. His eyes were hungry. He was intoxicated by the sight of her more than by the booze.

"I don't believe it."

"So, what are you doing here, Miss Veronika?"

"I like to dance. And I like it when people watch me. I get a kick, you know. Is that okay?"

Dunne shook his head as he said yes. "Hey, sweetheart, everybody likes to look at a pretty girl."

"I like to be sexy, that's all. Every woman does. Is that okay?"

"Yeah, that's okay."

Get a grip, Dunne told himself. He was falling through space. He was lucky that it was so late, and that he was tired, or he would have been out the door with her already. She was leaning against him as they talked, so that he could feel the swell of her breast against his arm.

Adrian came looking for Dunne eventually. He had a woman on his arm, a dark-haired girl from Belgium who called herself Marina. Seeing his colleague shook Dunne out of his trance.

"Hey, man, we're leaving," said Adrian. "Marina is going to take me to see the water jet on the lake. You cool with that?"

Dunne knew that the right answer was no. But he had never, through his career, been a stickler for rules, and he wasn't about to become head nanny for his group.

"Yeah, sure," he said. Marina tugged Adrian toward the door. Dunne turned to Veronika, who had nestled closer. His eyes sharpened.

"Take a walk?" she asked.

Dunne was unsteady for a moment. He felt a rush he hadn't experienced for a long while. It excited him and frightened him. He closed his eyes and took several deep breaths until the vertiginous feeling went away.

"Sorry, sweetie, time for me to go home. It's a school day tomorrow."

"You don't go to school."

"Just an expression." He held up his ring finger, as if she hadn't seen the gold band already. "And I'm married. Wrong night, wrong person. But it was fun watching you dance."

"Maybe you'll come back," she said, fluttering those heavy lashes.

"I don't think so. But you never know."

She wagged her finger at him. "You are a naughty boy, mister. You can't fool me." She smiled and walked away.

*   *   *

Dunne walked back to their apartment. Arthur was still awake, binge-watching episodes of the fourth season of *Game of Thrones*. Dunne went into his room. He felt sad and empty, in addition to a little drunk. He missed his wife. He was a fool to be looking at pretty women, when he was married to the prettiest of all. He had a phone with photographs of her that he had taken on their honeymoon. Not pornographic, just sexy. Her body naked, after making love. Her sleepy face, rising from bed in the morning.

He told Alicia he'd deleted the pictures, but he never did. He sometimes took the phone with him when he traveled, to remember how beautiful she was. The soft curve of her bosom; the brown marble of her skin; the fullness of her lips. He thought he'd been careful with the phone. He'd disabled the Wi-Fi antenna and removed the SIM card to prevent any link to the Internet.

Tonight he wanted to see her, as a way of erasing what he had done at La Minette. He illuminated the old phone in airplane mode; no connection, nothing to worry about. And there she was. Alicia.

# 10

Pittsburgh, Pennsylvania—May 2018

Before Michael Dunne's new company was even registered, he printed up cards with the Paladin LLC name and his new email address. He thought of adding a logo, but the images he found showed medieval superheroes in outlandish capes and armor, so he let the mysterious word stand, with a brief explanatory phrase below: "Active Cyber Defense." He ordered a thousand cards.

True to his word, Rick Bogdanovich gave Dunne a quick $100,000 contract from his FBI center, so that his new consulting company had some working capital to get started. Dunne used some of the money to hire a young tech assistant named Jenny who had just graduated with a computer science degree from Pitt. He bought himself more office furniture, and a new couch for his apartment so that it didn't look quite so bare.

Dunne created a website, too, and a LinkedIn post that, in a matter of a few days, was visited by a dozen of his former colleagues, many of whom wished him good luck. His assistant logged a score of cold calls or emails from potential clients in the twenty-four hours after his Paladin website went live. As Bogdanovich had said, it was a hot market.

From his office on Forbes Avenue, Dunne could see the slope of Mount Washington, south across the river. When he had been a student at Pitt, he liked to take his dates up the tramway known as the Duquesne Incline to see the view of the three rivers. He rarely had enough money to buy them dinner at one of the fancy restaurants along Grandview Avenue, but it didn't matter; it was romantic, and he could usually convince his dates to come back home with him to his apartment. What an ass he'd been, Dunne thought.

The darkness that had enveloped Dunne's life while he was in prison had started to lift: A trickle of clients began making serious inquiries, thanks to referrals from Bogdanovich's former FBI colleague Vijay Prakash.

\* \* \*

Prakash invited Dunne to lunch at a local club, an almost comically old-fashioned establishment in a Gothic stone fortress downtown. The former FBI-man-turned-cyber-mogul was one of the few people of color in the dining room, a situation that he seemed to enjoy. Dunne hadn't thought to bring a tie, but the doorman insistently loaned him one as he walked into the club.

Prakash had a shaved head and a sprinkle of beard below. He was dressed in a pin-striped suit and a Ferragamo tie. He was a compact man, with an incongruously muscular upper body from too many workouts; he looked somewhere between a rich Indian oligarch and the oligarch's bodyguard.

Dunne looked around the room at the gnarled old gentlemen sitting at their luncheon tables. They ate slowly and talked loudly. They were hearty white men, nearly all; people you might see at a country club or an eleven-fifteen church service where children were discouraged. Prakash could see that his guest was curious about the membership. He thought Dunne was impressed, but it wasn't that.

"My father and grandfather worked for men like these," said Dunne. "They ran the steel industry into the ground."

Prakash shrugged. His family were engineers who had gone to work for technology companies the moment the airplanes landed from Delhi.

Prakash was something of a celebrity in the cyber consulting world. He was said to have operated for several years as an undercover personality in the "dark web," entrapping some of the nastiest people who did business there. Now he worked for one of the big cyber consulting firms and made so much money that he needed a portfolio manager to invest it all for him.

"How can I help you?" said Prakash. "Bogdanovich said you got seriously fucked over by the agency. What do you need?"

Dunne thought a moment. He wasn't used to people being generous. "Basically, I want to do the same thing as you. Cyber defense. To me, that means helping people who got chewed up the way I did."

"Hacked, you mean?"

"Yes, hacked, taken down, turned inside out."

"Do you know who hit you?"

"Other than the Justice Department? Honestly, I'm still trying to find out. I know who I was chasing when all this stuff came down, but they've vanished. To an apartment in Hong Kong, or a villa on the Black Sea, or the Faculty Club at Stanford, I don't know. If I'm lucky I'll find the thread again. I've got some tips. But right now I need to make some money."

"Okay, friend, here's the deal: People hire consultants who look safe, and they don't ask a lot of questions. They're scared. Bad guys have come at them from cyberspace and then vanished. They need help. That's my job now, but I do it for big banks and law firms. They're not going to hire you. But other folks might. The ones who want protection, maybe vengeance, no questions asked. That's business we turn away, but maybe I can steer some your way."

"Is it legal, the stuff you could send me?"

"Sort of. It's a gray area. You've got to be smart. Don't do stupid shit."

Dunne nodded. "I know about you. The Bogo case, where you broke the ring in Thailand for the FBI. How did you survive all that time underground? Those people are the worst of the worst."

"You know the Bureau. They train you for everything, even this crap. You get 'certified' for undercover. You go silent, no talking to anyone, sleep deprivation, nasty stuff. It makes sense, the Bureau is sending undercover people into Mafia families, terrorist cells."

"Must wear you down, though. Never talking to anyone. Like being in prison."

"Hey, the cyber stuff I did was easy: You make your bones with these deep web freaks by being an anarchist prick. You look at lots of sick pornography, and you sell a ton of illegal shit. But you get the hang of it, if you're a good liar. The FBI used to test us every six months to make sure we weren't getting too weird."

"I understand machines, but I'm not so sure about people," said Dunne. "I've made so many mistakes. If a client hires me, I want to do it right. The only client I ever had until now was the United States of America."

"You want some advice?" asked Prakash. "The clients who will hire you are the ones that can't afford me or are too embarrassed to tell me what happened. They need someone less visible. Which is you."

"Got it. That's where I want to operate." Dunne took a sip of his water from a heavy glass embossed with the seal of the club. "People with nowhere else to go, whose privacy has been ripped away. Naked people, emotionally. Can you help me find people like that?"

Prakash sat back in his chair a moment. He looked up at the frescoes and ornate moldings of the club dining room, and then back at Dunne.

"You're pretty passionate about this, man. What happened to you, anyway?"

"The worst," Dunne said. "Hacked, filleted, gutted. Whatever you can imagine, it was worse than that."

"I have one person to get you started, as a matter of fact. She runs a movie studio in California. Hackers took down all her company files, all her personal emails, every text. There's nobody in Hollywood who doesn't hate her now. She's gone to ground, up near Santa Barbara. She tried to hire my firm, but we can't touch her. She's desperate. Why don't you go see her, offer to help? Rick and I can vouch for you. I'll tell her that you're coming."

"What if she doesn't want to see me?"

"Be creative, my friend," said Prakash. "Get your foot in the door. Honestly, what have you got to lose?"

Dunne took the late plane to Los Angeles and was in Santa Barbara by the next morning.

# 11

## Montecito, California—May 2018

Michael Dunne approached the big house on San Ysidro Road warily from the back. The Santa Barbara County Sheriff's Office had thrown up a loose perimeter around the front, with orange tape that said CAUTION. It wasn't a crime scene so much as crowd control. A few cops stood outside the house, arms folded across their tan shirts and legs apart, telling people to go home. But that didn't stop the nosy neighbors and would-be paparazzi from snapping cell phone pictures through the windows of Hollywood mogul Pia Zimmerman and her actor boyfriend, Shawn Harris. They had the irresistible attraction of famous people who had been hit by a calamity.

The morning fog had burned off, and the air smelled of the pine trees above and the sea below. A television truck was parked outside the house, and a correspondent was doing a stand-up, in which she spoke with feigned horror about "the Hollywood hack of the century." She held up naked photos of the couple inside the house, with black squares covering their private parts.

"And sources tell KERT News Channel Four that some of the hacked material is much more personal and private than this!" said the reporter, puckering her cherry lips as she finished the stand-up. "Back to you, Stacey."

Zimmerman had retreated to the kitchen, in the back of the house, where her teenage son, Paul, kept telling his mother not to worry. She was a woman in her late fifties, a former actress and now studio chief, her face and figure sculpted by the finest cosmetic surgeons. Harris, the boyfriend, was a decade younger, but toned and dyed and waxed as expertly as she was. He was the sort of Hollywood personality that was featured in *In Touch* magazine, who was famous for being famous.

Outside, there was a rustle of noise. Harris had closed the curtains, but an agile busybody had climbed a tree behind the house and was shooting pictures through a skylight. As a camera flash went off, illuminating the darkened kitchen, Zimmerman screamed as if the house had been struck by lightning. Her son bounded from his chair.

"You fuckers!" screamed Paul Zimmerman.

He leapt toward the door and scrambled down the side-porch stairs. He grabbed several of the rocks that lined the driveway and began hurling them toward the snooping photographer in the tree. One of them hit the climber, who wailed as he clamored down, dodging more missiles and drawing more gawkers and police. It was pandemonium until one of the cops took the boy firmly by the arm, told him to calm down, and led him back to the porch.

*   *   *

In the disturbance, a figure moved to a door on the other side of the house. He was wearing a white shirt and gray flannel trousers; his red hair was combed neat, and his beard trimmed. The lenses of his dark glasses were glinting in the morning sun.

When a neighbor shouted to him as he neared the rear door, the man said, "Stand back, please," as if he were a plainclothes cop, and the neighbor retreated. He quickly picked the lock and entered the living room. There were noises in the kitchen, as Zimmerman hugged her returning son. The intruder walked quietly through the dining room and entered the pantry next to the kitchen before anyone noticed him.

"Hi, folks," said the man with the russet beard. He was perfectly calm, the opposite of threatening. "I think I can help."

"Who the hell are you?" demanded Harris. "Are you a cop? We already said, no police inside. Get out of here. Please."

The visitor reached toward the woman to give her his card.

She turned away, but the man's hand was still gently outstretched, and there was something in his demeanor that was reassuring. She took the card and studied it.

"Are you the person Mr. Prakash called about yesterday?"

"Yes, ma'am. My name is Michael Dunne. Paladin LLC. I am in the cyber business. As it says on my card, 'Active Cyber Defense.'"

"What does that mean, Mr. Paladin or whatever it is?" asked Zimmerman.

"It means that I will find the people who invaded your lives and make it impossible for them to do it again."

The woman shook her head. "Nope." She folded her arms tightly.

"Why not? I can help you."

"We have nothing left to steal," she said bitterly. "That's what I told your friend Prakash. You're too late."

"I didn't get the message. But it's never too late to protect yourself, Mrs. Zimmerman."

"It's *much* too late. It's all online. Every email I ever wrote. All my business messages. Every nasty word I ever said about anyone who wanted to work for Padaro Pictures. Every image that was on my phone. And Shawn's, too, that I stupidly backed up for safekeeping. Photographs that I would never want anyone to see, especially my son. And more. Lies and lies. It's all too horrible."

"I can help you fight back," said Dunne, speaking each word slowly and precisely.

"How are you going to do that, for Christ's sake?" broke in Harris. "We don't even know who these people are."

"Shush, honey!" said Zimmerman. There was something in the visitor's manner, so steady and deliberate, that made her want to hear his pitch.

"In our business, we call it attribution. It's not easy, but it's not impossible, either. Everything leaves tracks, electronically. It's like following a trail of crumbs. Eventually you find the cookie. Then you find the person holding the cookie. And then you make sure that he won't bother you again."

Zimmerman studied this calm, deadly serious man who had broken into her house to offer his services. She was a Hollywood studio executive. She had read a hundred pilots like this, but never encountered one in real life.

"What do you do to these people when you find them? Kill them?"

Dunne laughed and shook his head.

"Of course not. There are easier ways to disable an adversary. They have the same electronic vulnerabilities that you do. You just have to find them, and then shut down the capabilities that hurt you."

"You mean, like, hack them back?"

"I won't explain all the details of our services. I just promise you that this attacker will not cause you more trouble. The damage that's been done to you, I can't undo. But I'm confident I can find the attacker, disable him, and tell you who he is. I'll give you all the information I get—and then you can take whatever action you want. But not through me. I'm just the digital guy."

"Mr. Prakash said you used to work for the CIA, but then you got in trouble. And he said you were reliable."

"He's right, on all three counts. The FBI can explain who I am, if you have questions."

"What would you need from us, if we were interested?"

Harris, the boyfriend, raised his hand.

"Honey, I'm not sure you should do this. This guy is a nobody."

Zimmerman ignored him. "What would you need?" she repeated.

"A retainer of fifty thousand dollars, and another hundred thousand if I'm successful. That's the easy part. I also need access to all your computers, at home and at work. And your passwords."

"But they'll make even more things up. They'll publish everything. People will believe them."

"That's already happened," Dunne said quietly. "The attackers have taken everything they want. You're already completely vulnerable. You just need to start pushing back."

"You're not listening to me. *They made things up.* Some of the sex pictures are real, but a lot are phony. My head giving a blow job to an actor I don't even know. They're disgusting, all mixed together. I kept saying at first that they were fake, but nobody believed me. They look like me. But they're not."

"Say that again, please," said Dunne.

"They're fake. They've put my face on someone else's body. But it's done so well, you can't tell. They'll make more pictures like that. This won't end."

"Yes, it will," said Dunne calmly. "I want you to show me the fakes, if you hire me, so I can understand them. They will help me expose the people who have done this to you. You won't be hurt anymore. I promise."

She nodded. Despite herself, she was beginning to trust him.

"Let me talk to Shawn about this. Why don't you come back this afternoon?"

Dunne stepped toward her. In his face was determination, need, commitment, and the hint of a shared sense of vulnerability. He lowered his voice almost to a whisper, so that he was speaking to her, not her boyfriend.

"How about if I wait in the living room?" Dunne said. "If you decide yes, then I can get started right away, while the trail is still fresh. If you decide no, then we won't waste any more time. How does that sound?"

She returned his gaze. In the intelligence business, the mysterious process of establishing trust is called "rapport." Zimmerman had lived by a similar code through her career in the entertainment business. In an unlikely way, they understood each other.

"Shawn, you go upstairs and check your email. Mr. Paladin and I are going to talk here for a few minutes. Paul, get Mr. Paladin a cup of coffee."

"There's one more thing I didn't tell you before," Zimmerman said when they were alone. "Whoever is doing this is a crackpot. A zealot, like. He scares me, and not just because of all the pictures and emails he hacked and posted, which everyone in Hollywood is enjoying so much."

"Why does the attacker scare you?" Dunne asked.

"Because he hates Israel. He leaves horrible anti-Semitic messages. 'The Jews Run America.' 'Hollywood Is Kike City.' Vile things. Sick things. I called the Anti-Defamation League, but they say they can't help. America is full of crazy people who are anti-Semites. This president has made it worse."

"Don't blame the president," said Dunne gently. "He didn't send the messages. Let me find the person who did and stop him. Does that make sense?"

Zimmerman nodded.

"I hope you will hire me," said Dunne. "I know how to stop this person."

# 12

Los Angeles, California—May 2018

When Pia Zimmerman retained Paladin LLC, she turned over her computers, peripherals, and passwords, as Dunne had requested. She gave him a key to her house and an access card to enter the offices of Padaro Pictures. Dunne rented a cheap hotel room in Carpenteria, a few miles south of Zimmerman's grand, besieged home, where he began doing his initial forensic work. A few days later, he moved to West Hollywood, near the Padaro lot, where he began working on the servers and access points for the studio's accounts.

The hardest part was asking Zimmerman to show him which were the real sex pictures and which were the fakes. Her boyfriend had been in the habit of shooting videos of them having sex, so there was a trove of personal pornography that displayed every inch of this prominent producer's anatomy. She sat stoically as they searched the hacked archive for the fakes.

"This one," she said, pointing a thin, rigid finger at an image that showed her astride one of Hollywood's most famous actors. "And that one," she said with a shudder, pointing toward an image of fellatio. "And that one, too."

As they surveyed the fake images, Dunne was astonished by the clarity and detail. Somehow, a computer had created an image in which Zimmerman's face had been grafted to the lips and mouth of another woman. The famous faces had been melded with the bodies so artfully and seamlessly that they appeared to be entirely real.

"I'm so sorry," Dunne said.

Zimmerman was quivering. She put her hand over her face to hide her embarrassment.

"I've seen something like this before," ventured Dunne. "Not this good. But this same idea."

"When and where?" she asked.

"I can't talk about it," he said. "But we'll get these people."

\*    \*    \*

The job took just over two weeks. Dunne got lucky. He also had some technical assistance from a computer security company in Laguna Beach. The founder was a former colleague from the agency who owed Dunne a favor from long ago. He helped Dunne set up a command post in his hotel suite near the Padaro headquarters.

Dunne reconstructed the cyber assault step by step. The attacker had stealthily gathered his hacked information and then chosen a grand cover name, "Partisans of Freedom," to shield himself. The fictitious organization sent messages to Zimmerman and other Padaro employees, demanding a billion dollars as the price for not releasing intimate personal and corporate files of the company and its executives. The absurd size of the ransom made clear this wasn't a commercial hack, but something else.

Padaro had immediately called the FBI and hired a fancy cybersecurity firm, but by then it was too late. The attacker had been exfiltrating data for weeks and began messaging it to entertainment industry websites, directing the curious to torrent files that were cached online. The files' names were too tantalizing to resist: "Sex Tapes," "Zimmerman Feuds," "Nude Movie Pix," "Hollywood Whore," "Hooker of the Rich and Famous." Someone with system access had combed through Zimmerman's personal and corporate files and vacuumed up the most damaging information.

From the day he arrived in Santa Barbara, Dunne had suspected this was an inside job, and now he assembled the evidence that confirmed it.

His team found the malware quickly, with a standard hashing algorithm.

The tool had the same signature as a file-extraction program that had been used in a half dozen other hacks. The raider had obtained system-administrator privileges by targeting a phishing scam on a careless member of the Padaro IT department. Then the hacker went to work, using his stolen root access to get into Zimmerman's personal files and pick and choose the most damaging material.

* * *

Dunne's luck was that the attacker had beaconed back to a command server that could itself be hacked. A scan of the server's ports revealed an unpatched vulnerability, which Dunne used to invade the server. He found that one of the emails sent to the entertainment industry media disclosing the hack could be linked to an alias account used by a former producer at Padaro named Anwar Malek, who had been fired two years before.

Malek, the disgruntled employee, was born in Saudi Arabia, the son of a wealthy businessman who had helped finance Padaro's films years before. The son had gotten his first job at Padaro as a favor to the father. He had money and connections, but not enough talent. He was convinced that Jewish executives at Padaro and other studios were conspiring against him because he was a Muslim Arab.

Malek had filed a nuisance lawsuit the previous year claiming that Zimmerman had retaliated against him because he refused to have sex with her. The lawsuit was quickly dismissed, and everyone forgot about the case, except Malek.

The angry anti-Semitic messages were like watermarks. On Malek's computer, Dunne found reams of propaganda attacking Israel and Jews. Malek was a special devotee of an Israeli-Arab poet whose verses were included in messages Malek sent to his Arab friends: "The Creator sentenced you to be loser monkeys, / Victory belongs to Muslims, from the Nile to the Euphrates."

Dunne had promised Zimmerman that he would destroy the attacker's ability ever to harm her again. And after dismissing his helpers from Laguna Beach, he set about doing so. Hiding his tracks through proxy servers, Dunne inserted his own malware into Malek's computer accounts and froze them so that they couldn't be used to send or receive messages. He didn't wipe the data; he wanted it preserved, in case Zimmerman decided later that she wanted to prosecute.

From behind an impenetrable wall, Dunne sent Malek a final message before he froze the system, written in hacker jargon:

*Hi Anwar. You have been pwned. If you ever touch PZ again, your system will be Eternal Blue.* It was signed, *Partisans of Internet Security and Safety Offensive Forensic Force*, with a glowing acronym.

*   *   *

The fake photographs were a harder problem. They were masterful. They were like the false images Dunne had come across during his ill-fated pursuit of the Quark Team and Fallen Empire. But this version was two years better. It wasn't a head spliced onto a body, but a new image that was seamless.

Dunne took extra time on the fakes, even after he had neutralized Malek. He analyzed the images digitally over and over, deconstructing the electronic signature and the technique. The imperfections were subtle, but they could be found with the right tools. Dunne recognized the technology too well. How had Anwar Malek obtained access to it?

Dunne and his helpers posted some questions on cybersecurity forums, and they tested pieces of code against tools that had been used in other hacks.

They got a break after several days of quiet exchanges with master computer sleuths, including Vijay Prakash and Rick Bogdanovich. It emerged that some of the code was part of a hacking suite called Bariq that was sold by a firm in the United Arab Emirates, through a partner firm in Saudi Arabia. Bariq meant "lightning" in Arabic.

Dunne dug a little further. A thread on a hacking forum said that Bariq's suite of tools had been adapted from an Italian hacking group that had mastered deepfakes and then disappeared. The Italian software engineers, whoever they were, were the common ancestor of a dozen hacking packages that were being sold around the world by different vendors. Cyber consultants were so busy monitoring the outcroppings that nobody had bothered to go back and look for the original seed.

The Italian software engineers had insisted on encrypted messages, so it was hard to follow their tracks. The only readable message Dunne could find was in the very beginning: *Anwar, contact me on Viber. Ciao. Lorenzo.*

Dunne had planned to leave Anwar Malek alone and let Pia Zimmerman decide what she wanted to do. But as he gathered the forensic details, he wanted to meet Malek. Ask him where he made his contacts. Look him in the eye. He had been taught in the agency, years before, that asking a person stressful questions and then gauging his reactions was nearly as reliable as hooking him up to a polygraph.

Malek lived in Studio City in a small detached house. Dunne pressed the buzzer, but there was no answer. A week's mail was stuffed inside the screen door. Malek had evidently been away for a while. Dunne rang the doorbell at the next house down the block; an old man answered the door; he was unshaven in the late afternoon. Dunne said he had a message for Anwar Malek next door.

"He's gone, nearly a week. He's sick. An ambulance came. They took him out on a stretcher."

"Shit," muttered Dunne.

"Say what?" asked the man, offended that someone would ring his bell and then utter a curse.

"Nothing," said Dunne. "Nothing at all. Sorry to bother you." He wrapped his coat tight around his shoulders and pulled a cap over his red hair, so that it would be harder to identify him if he was photographed as he walked away.

*   *   *

Dunne returned to Montecito with a folder and a disk drive for Pia Zimmerman that contained all the information her lawyers would need if they wanted to pursue the matter in court. He explained that he had done what he promised. He had identified her tormentor and destroyed his ability ever to hurt her again. She had closure.

When he gave her the packet, she looked bewildered at first, and then she began to cry. That's the strange thing about revenge. Once people have cornered their enemies and gained the opportunity to take an eye for the one that was lost, they aren't sure what to do. She didn't want to take the packet, at first, so Dunne left it resting on the table.

"The name of your attacker was Anwar Malek," Dunne said quietly. "He used to work for you. He was an angry, sick man. He had help from others. But he won't bother you anymore. It's over."

Zimmerman tearfully said she would wire the $150,000 that afternoon, and tried to offer a bonus, which Dunne refused. His only request was that he be able to keep his own copy of the forensic materials he had compiled, for use in future cases.

"There's one more thing I should tell you about Anwar Malek," said Dunne. "He's disappeared. I don't think he'll be back."

*   *   *

As Dunne left her beautiful mansion in Montecito and headed south on the 101, he thought once more, as he had over the last several days, about the anomalies he had discovered in the Partisans of Freedom operation.

Malek had used a particular piece of malware hidden in a graphics driver. Dunne had seen that code before. And the attacker's messages had been masked by proxy servers from three disparate sites: a Polish import-export company; a university in Thailand; and a virtual private network exit point in Italy. All three were familiar IP addresses. And then there were the masterful fakes, and the anti-Semitic screeds.

Anwar Malek had accessed a market, operated by far cleverer people than he, where he purchased his tools of character assassination. On Dunne's first case, he had encountered traces of a network whose provenance he thought he knew. These were devils for hire. Dunne could see their shadows, but not yet their faces. He thought he knew, but that wasn't the same as knowing.

In this flush of his first success as a private businessman, Dunne had a powerful urge to contact his ex-wife, Alicia. Maybe she would be proud of him for protecting this woman, he imagined for a moment, but the thought darkened.

# 13

## Paris—August 2017

The young man had begun calling himself "Eric" after he left his friends in Italy. He told them he needed a break, but it was more than that. Doubt had intruded where before there was certainty. He had imagined himself as a digital bandit in Italy, but perhaps he was simply part of a business that had investors and clients. His mission had been to deconstruct "truth," to dismember it for the bourgeois lie that it was. But now he wandered amid the rubble of deconstruction wanting something that he could call fact.

From the window of Eric's apartment on the Rue de Valmy, he could see the Canal Saint-Martin, the poor man's River Seine, and the dense green of the Parc des Buttes-Chaumont beyond. The apartment was in the far northeast of Paris, the Cité Rouge, where the streets were named after socialist heroes like Jean Jaurès and Henri Bergson, and there was a Métro stop called Stalingrad. Rebels and outcasts had fled here for two centuries: The local cemetery Père Lachaise was a roll call of the defiant: Oscar Wilde, Marcel Proust, Gertrude Stein, Jim Morrison. Eric had fantasized a spot for himself among the forest of gray tombstones.

He had started reading newspapers for the first time in years, real ones that were printed on paper. His favorite French manifestos of post-structuralist philosophy and critical theory were still stacked next to his bed for reassurance. But he wasn't sure he believed the arguments anymore.

The French philosophers insisted that "truth" was an ambiguous word. Descriptions of reality were culturally determined; they were logocentric. "Universal" values were delusions; worse, they were instruments of oppression. There were not "facts," but narratives. The author was dead; the reader was king. Eric knew all the arguments. He'd been making them himself since he was an adolescent prodigy. But now, he wondered.

Eric wanted to take a solitary walk along the canal, or row himself across the pond in Buttes-Chaumont, or make any other escape from the "colleague" who had followed him from Italy and taken a bunk in the concierge's apartment. The colleague was there to "protect" Eric, that was what he said. He warned Eric that their movement had many enemies. If someone struggled for freedom, as Eric had, it was hard to be free.

Eric was tall and thin, with a frizz of blond curls atop his head and the thinnest sprouts of hair on his body. His trousers hung low from his hips like pants on a store rack; from the back he looked almost like a runway model, thin and androgynous and barely there in the material world but moving his thin legs like chopsticks. He lived like a recluse, forgetting to eat much of the time, but he was a glutton in one respect: the books he read, and the old movies he watched in the dark of his garret apartment.

"Eric" wasn't his real name. He'd used so many aliases the last few years that he couldn't always remember what was printed on his papers. But "Eric" was the name he gave himself now in his mind: Wake up, Eric! Stop being a prisoner in your head, Eric! Live and breathe, Eric!

The importance of being Eric. There was Eric Blair, Eric Clapton, Eric Idle, Eric Ambler, Eric the Red. But his true namesake was a British historian named Eric Hobsbawm, who had written a book called *Primitive Rebels* that explained the world. It celebrated the "social bandits" who had been the scourge of the wealthy and powerful in premodern times. Highway robbers like Dick Turpin and Jesse James; the fearless brigands of places like Calabria and the Marche in Italy, who hid away in the mountains sustained by the peasants, to harass the corrupt mercenaries of church and state.

Eric lay in his bed, trying to remember the last time he had eaten. He was hungry, certainly, but that gave him a measure of control and autonomy. Nobody could make him eat. The afternoon was deepening. From the street below, he could hear people gathering at the café along the quay. The light of the setting sun, filtering through the window, was a pale pink, not quite the color of blood.

By Eric's bed was his tattered copy of *Primitive Rebels*. The man hadn't even been a professor when he wrote the book in 1958, just a "reader in history." A lesson in humility. He opened the book to one of his favorite passages:

> *A few remarks may complete our sketch of the mechanics of the bandit's life. Normally he will be young and single or unattached, if only because it is much harder for a man to revolt against the apparatus of power once he has family responsibilities.*

That was the easy part, to rebel in your heart, to be one man apart, but eventually you needed brothers and sisters. Who would take you into their band? And at what price?

> *How long a band lasted we do not know exactly. It would depend, one imagines, on how much of a nuisance it made of itself, on how tense the social situation, or how complex the international situation was . . .*

Yes, but the people who took us up into the hills, who made us swear secret oaths in blood, didn't they draw us into their own version of the corruption we had been trying to escape? Even as we rebelled against one power, weren't we being absorbed into another that controlled us just as surely, so that all we had for ourselves really was the anger? Eric turned a few more pages.

> *The bandit is helpless before the forces of the new society which he cannot understand. At most, he can fight it and seek to destroy it "to avenge injustice, to hammer the lords, to take from them the wealth they have robbed with fire and sword to destroy all that cannot serve the common good: for joy, for vengeance, as a warning for future ages—and perhaps for fear of them."*

*   *   *

Eric slept for a time, the book beside him, and when he awoke, it was night and he was dizzy from hunger. His pants were falling off, so he put on a belt and then a T-shirt, and a schoolboy blazer. He had a phone with a new SIM card; he stuck that in the pocket of his jacket and headed downstairs.

Maybe tonight? He was light-headed; his body had no weight, and the part of him that felt fear had been starved into emptiness. He exited by the back courtyard, where they kept the rubbish bins. The colleague in the lair downstairs didn't stir, but there was a camera trained on the front door, and they always found a way to locate him, even when he thought he had disappeared. But perhaps not this time.

People were leaning against the railing along the quay, drinking wine and smoking weed. Eric went into a bar on a side street and ordered a double whiskey, which on his empty stomach was like the snort of a drug. He needed to eat something, but most of the restaurants nearby were closed. He found an Indonesian place that was still open, and he ordered a red curry whose aroma of coconut and spices made him even dizzier, but whose taste made him retch. He paid the bill and left the rich meal uneaten on the table.

In a little Arab takeout he bought some flatbread and a piece of chicken and a tomato, and made himself a dry, doughy sandwich that he ate until the nausea went away. He bought a bottle of rosé wine, too, and with some food in him, the wine tasted fine.

It was a cloudless night, and even in the center of the city he could see a few stars above. A woman tried to pick him up, and then a man. Eric shook his head. He was lost in himself, trying to think about a way to escape.

*I loved freedom*, he told himself. *That's why I joined a bandit gang, I thought I would free myself and others, but I am a prisoner. I thought I would do good, but I harmed people without knowing who they were. The people who bought the machines controlled them. I deconstructed reality, but they had another version waiting. I was an ant in their hill, not even human. How did this happen? Whom can I tell? How can I make things right?*

He had brought along a book from his shelf, this one not a call to rebellion or a post-structuralist text, but a meditation about release. It was called *Democ-*

*racy's Dharma*, about the practice of Buddhism in Taiwan. His colleagues, who kept him under such a tight watch, had suggested that perhaps he would be happier if he could move to Taipei and apply his technical genius to creating logic chips for a semiconductor company there. He was intrigued by the idea of mixing mind and no-mind as a Buddhist computer scientist.

But first there was someone else who needed release. It preyed on his mind, the wrong that he had done.

* * *

Eric walked south toward the Gare de l'Est. He approached a small park just south of the railway terminal; he saw some hookers, maybe, deep in the glen, but there was an empty bench near the entrance, well lit.

Eric took out his phone and began composing a message. It was an apology. Not in so many words, and not sent directly to the person to whom he owed the explanation, but through a cutout who would know how best to deliver it. It provided useful information. Some details about himself, references, points of contact. That was all he could do. He worked hard to disguise himself in the message, inventing a personality that would seem congenial, hidden with a bit of slang and a memorable nom de guerre. He was a good bandit, but one with a guilty conscience.

# 14

Geneva—September 2016

Michael Dunne didn't think he would ever see the woman called Veronika again, after the night he chanced to meet her in the club. He was busy the next few days with his support team, rising each morning at five-thirty and making breakfast the way he did for his techs on an operation. The three were at their computer screens by seven-thirty, combing the digital world for information that would decode the organization that called itself Fallen Empire, whose presumed base of operations was in the hills of northeast Italy.

Dunne was eager to take the next step of his mission. But only the deputy director for operations could authorize it, and he was on a tour of stations and bases in Asia, the watch officer said. So, Dunne kept gathering information. It was like tracking the call of a mockingbird that can mimic disparate sounds, but whose identity is elusive.

Fallen Empire was an anger machine, and it was accelerating. Nearly every day the group posted new videos of police brutality against black and brown people. On some sites, you could see a loop that showed a white fist punching a black face over and over. But race was just one channel of rage. Others conveyed different images of America's malign power, focusing on the martyr to Internet freedom, Edward Snowden: The group organized flash protests in several European cities to demand a pardon for Snowden. They were hashtag freedom fighters; the organizers never showed up at the Snowden rallies, only followers.

"Nobody is my leader," was one of the Fallen Empire slogans. They wore masks with the image of this Nobody—crew cut, bland demeanor, Snowden-like but not Snowden. It was the face of Nobody. But where did the masks come from, and the carefully painted banners celebrating Snowden and demanding his freedom?

*   *   *

Arthur Gogel found the next links in the chain. He had been up through the night reviewing video and running coherence and consistency tests on various bits of imagery and code. He knocked on Dunne's door at five-thirty, when his alarm went off.

"I've got to show you some stuff," he said, in the breathy voice of someone who was excited and exhausted at the same time. Gogel was a CIA "millennial." For his generation, the old exotica of tradecraft had collapsed into zeros and ones. Dunne put on a robe over his T-shirt and shorts and went into the study that had become a computer lab.

"Fallen Empire is a robot," Gogel said. "I mean, it's machine learning. A generative adversarial network. Nobody is feeding the machine. The machine is feeding itself."

"How on earth do you know that?" demanded Dunne, still groggy with sleep.

"I compared the source code of Fallen Empire's sites with those of Save the West, the right-wing version. And guess what? The right-wing sites use the same shortcut for coding images as the black-power sites, and the anti-fracking ones, too."

Gogel brought up the image-sizing code from a Save the West pro-police site, and then put it side by side with comparable code for one of Fallen Empire's sites supporting Black Lives Matter. The two sets of code were identical.

"The match is too perfect," said Gogel.

"Meaning this wasn't done by a person, but a machine."

"Correct. And let me show you another weird thing I found. Maybe I'm nuts, but I think they're trolling companies now."

"Show me," said Dunne.

Gogel called up several of the anti-fracking sites, on different screens. They were all linking to news footage of an oil spill from a huge tanker in the Sea of Japan.

Gogel clicked on the link. The imagery showed oil leaking from a hull-side storage tank directly into the water. The footage appeared to have been taken by a camera onboard the tanker. The banner across the bottom of the screen said: "Secret Video Shows Environmental Disaster."

"Holy crap!" said Dunne. "Where did this come from?"

"Supposedly it was posted by a whistleblower inside the oil company. But I did a very high-res check of the footage. The continuity is off. It looks real, but it isn't."

"What does the company say?"

"They deny there's any spill. But nobody believes them. Their stock price is tanking in Asia. The Japanese government has already said it's launching an investigation."

"My god!" said Dunne. "They're taking down companies they don't like, just for sport."

"Maybe they're shorting the stock," said Gogel, wide-eyed.

"Sure they are," said Dunne. "They're creating the news. Why not profit from it, too?"

Dunne drafted a message for Hoffman, copied to Strafe, asking them to look for recent product safety issues driven by insider documents or leaked videos. He gave some possible examples: lettuce producers quarantined for supposed food-poisoning scares; automobile recalls triggered by supposed internal documentation of safety flaws; fast-food chains accused of unsanitary conditions.

Slow down, Dunne told himself. One step at a time. If you start looking for a panic, you'll create one. He left the message unsent and went off to prepare breakfast for the boys.

\* \* \*

Dunne received an urgent message that afternoon from European Special Collection. It was from Hoffman, asking him to contact George Strafe immediately. Dunne used the secure-handling channel and routed the call through the operations center. He asked the watch officer to organize a time for a call with the deputy director. To Dunne's surprise, Strafe came on the line immediately.

"We need to hurry up," he said.

"What's happened?" queried Dunne. "Has the target gone to ground?"

"Worse. The Russians are sniffing up the same tree we are."

"How do we know that?"

"Special Intelligence. Don't ask. We just know they're getting close to the same target. I've taken care of it, for now."

"How, if I might ask?"

"The GRU case officer had an accident. He got caught by the Italian service. We managed to feed him some chickenfeed that makes him think he was looking at the wrong target. The Italians are running him as a double, but he'll play it all back to Moscow. They'll figure it out eventually."

"Meaning that we need to get there before the Russians wise up."

"Correct. There's one good thing in that respect, Mike."

"What's that?" Strafe rarely called Dunne by his first name.

"The Russians were using an illegal. He supposedly was a member of an underground hacking group in Germany. This gentleman was planning to visit a certain hill town in the Marche called Urbino, until the Italians convinced him it was a dry hole. That's what I needed, in terms of authorities."

"Sweet," said Dunne. "I'll head for Urbino and install some surveillance."

There was a long pause, and then Strafe came back.

"Send Adrian White to do the recon. Keep your powder dry. I need you for later."

"Are you sure?" Dunne was itching to move.

"Yup. Adrian is perfect. He's good at getting in and out of places. Prejudiced Europeans would never imagine that a black man could be installing a sophisticated surveillance device. It doesn't compute. The operational utility of racism."

"I'd rather do it myself."

"Soon enough, hotshot. The fun is just beginning. You'll get your chance."

*  *  *

Dunne accepted Strafe's decision, but he wasn't happy about it. He wasn't built for watching and waiting. He was always ready to plant the bug right now, up through the floor of the target's apartment or down from the ceiling above. Sometimes people get into a bar fight just because they want to feel the sting; there was something of that in Dunne when he got restless.

Hoffman supplied the target; it was called Digito Urbino, a computer company that had ordered the extra power lines. This was the front for Quark Team and its "news" operation, Fallen Empire.

Dunne told Adrian White to pack his bag. He proposed two surveillance cameras: One would watch the front door, the other the back. In the kit they had brought from Langley they had concealable cameras, signal processors, relays, and transmitters that would send the signals via satellite to Headquarters and then to their base in Geneva.

Dunne made the train reservation for Adrian. He tried not to act upset that he wasn't going himself. He was meticulous in designing and testing the gear that Adrian would install. But he was frustrated.

# 15

## Geneva—September 2016

Dunne exercised at a twenty-four-hour gym in Carouge. He worked the weights too hard, too long. His muscles were getting bulky and his shirts were tugging at the buttons. What was it that kept him on the bench doing set after set? Sometimes people get a loop inside their heads that keeps replaying: a song you've heard, or the image of a woman on a dance floor, maybe. The blink of her eyes, the feel of her skin; the mocking tone of her voice. What began as a mild buzz of desire becomes a throb in the gut. You could have forgotten about it another time, but now it's inside you, wanting to be fed.

Dunne walked past La Minette on his way to the gym one night and again on the way back. He returned the next night and stood in the shadows near the door. He was on the verge of going inside to look for her, but he stopped himself. Walking away, appalled by what he had nearly done, he muttered aloud. But the compulsion was still there.

Veronika had said she worked at a bank called Maison Suisse. That was the only thing Dunne knew about her, or thought he knew. Did she really work there? He wanted to be sure, though he couldn't have explained why.

One morning, after several hours of work, he told the boys he was going to take a walk. He put one of the burner phones in his pocket, and when he had walked half a mile from the office, he called the switchboard at Maison Suisse and asked to speak to Veronika. The operator asked, "Which one?"

"Private Wealth," said Dunne, and there was a click, and then a woman's voice answered.

Dunne felt a quickening in his stomach. He closed the connection and put the phone in his pocket, feeling an emotion somewhere between panic and exhilaration. He began walking northeast toward the business district, a block south of the Rhône, below the lake and the Jet d'Eau.

The bank's headquarters were on a tidy avenue a half mile from the river. Dunne had checked the address a dozen times already. He walked in that direction, swaying slightly on legs that didn't quite match because of his old football injury, slowly at first and then quickly.

Maison Suisse occupied an austere old building with a gray stone façade, no sign out front to advertise its business. Dunne approached from the south and walked past the building, not stopping, and continued all the way to the Rhône. He was going to go home then, after he had scratched the itch. But on an impulse, he turned and walked back up the street, pausing in the courtyard below the bank building and looking up at the windows, wondering if she was inside.

She was unsafe. That was what made her so tempting. Standing at the edge of a cliff, who doesn't think for a moment about jumping off?

*   *   *

Dunne was back again the next day at noon. Adrian had left that morning for Italy; Dunne told Gogel that he had to go out. Arthur shrugged; Dunne was the base chief; he could do a backflip out the window if he wanted.

Dunne sat across from the bank's entrance in a tearoom, where he could watch the front door. He waited through lunchtime, until two, but he saw no sign of her walking in or out of the building. Did he even remember what she looked like? He left the tearoom, but as he turned toward home, he felt a tightness in his chest and his breath came in quick, shallow gulps of air.

This time he walked right up to the front door, and stared at the porter who guarded the entrance. He caught his reflection in the window; saw the flush in his face. He took from his pocket a blank index card. He wrote the word

"Veronika" on one side and on the other side, "La Minette." He gave it to the porter, who took it silently.

Dunne asked him to deliver it to Miss Veronika in Private Wealth. The porter nodded; perhaps he thought Dunne was a reclusive investor considering opening an account.

*   *   *

Dunne came back that evening at five-thirty and waited for the office workers to leave at six. He was wearing a baseball cap and pretending to read a newspaper. His heart was racing as he watched the employees walk out the door one after the other.

And there she was: At six-fifteen, he saw the blond hair, the tight black skirt, the sheer white blouse, and the face. He folded his newspaper, wondering even then if he would walk toward her. We don't know until the coin falls whether it's heads or tails, and Dunne had never told himself what he would do if he saw her.

But he didn't have to decide. She strolled directly toward him, crossing the street to the far sidewalk where he was standing. She looked him in the eye just the way she had in the club and wagged her finger at him.

"You've been watching me," she said, smiling. She tilted her head and let those long lashes fall over her eyes. She was wearing fresh rouge and lipstick, and a dab of perfume. "Take off that silly hat so I can see your nice red hair."

Dunne smiled and removed the cap. "Walk with me," he said. He took a step before she could answer, but she was alongside him.

"I thought you had forgotten about the woman in the bar, Mr. Joe. I came back for two nights, and then I gave up."

"I didn't forget. I should have, probably, but I didn't."

She leaned toward his ear. "There's a park at the end of the street. We can talk."

They walked together in silence, crossing the tram tracks and into an open space, more pavement than trees and grass. She took his arm when they were inside the enclosure and pulled him toward an outdoor café about fifty yards away. They sat down at a wrought-iron table in the corner, hidden from view by the overhang of a shade tree.

She extended a cigarette toward him. This time Dunne had a lighter.

# 16

Geneva—September 2016

They sat in metal garden chairs and drank Chablis from a bottle that was chilling in a bucket of ice. Dunne wrapped his big arm around the back of her chair. An early evening breeze was blowing strands of hair across her face. The café was surrounded by plane trees, their bark mottled like sycamore and their branches pruned to nubs. Dunne stared at her, not knowing where to begin, but she laughed and gave him a playful poke in the chest.

"Hey, Mr. Joe? Is that really your name, anyway? You don't look like a Joe."

"Let's talk about you first, madame," he said. "I'm shy."

She shrugged. It was like a date: They had to go through the ritual of explaining who they were.

"Okay, Joe. My name is Veronika Kruse. I was born near Bern, in the mountains. Too much snow. I was a skier when I was a girl, but I crashed when I was little and after that the coach was not so interested. Then I became an ice skater, and then a dancer. A good one, ha, like you saw. I studied business and, after that, because I am a good Swiss girl, of course I went to work in a bank, like you already know. It was easy to be hired. I have relatives there. See? Not very complicated."

"Have you ever been married?" asked Dunne. She wasn't wearing a ring.

"Once. He was from Zurich. Too conservative for me. I was bored. He came home and caught me with someone else. Three years ago, we divorce. Mama was unhappy, but so what?"

"And your dad?"

"He's dead. But he would have been glad that I was alone, single again, you know. He was a mountain man. My mother left him. He wasn't rich or interesting enough for her, and she didn't like Bern. She was not, what is the word, *sympathique*."

"Is she rich now, your mother? Did she get what she wanted?"

"Too much. Her papa owned a bank. After she left my father, she married another man who owned a bigger bank, and when he died, she kept his money, and made her bank very big. She is too good at this money thing and when you start, there is never enough."

As Veronika talked, her face darkened.

"My mother is beautiful," she said. "Perfect. That's why I like to be a bad girl sometimes, you know. Take risks. Because it makes me forget I am not perfect like her."

Dunne touched her hand.

"She couldn't possibly be as pretty as you."

She smiled as if she were accepting a bouquet of flowers. Part of being a beautiful woman was knowing that you were beautiful.

Veronika looked at his hand.

"You took off your wedding ring."

Dunne nodded. "What about you? Do you have a boyfriend?"

"I see people. Men. And women too." She looked down at the table, and then back at him. "Is that okay?"

"Of course it's okay. Whatever floats your boat."

"What does that mean, about the boat? I love boats."

"Nothing. It's a stupid American expression. It means people should do what they want."

"Okay! That's me, then." Her face brightened again.

Dunne didn't say much about himself. He told her he was a contractor in Geneva on business, and she tilted her head and gave him a dubious look, as if she knew he was lying.

"I know why the caged bird sings," Dunne said. That had been one of his mother's favorite books.

"Silly boy." She laughed. "There is no bird. Just you and me, okay?"

*   *   *

This is a setup, Dunne kept cautioning himself: This is a play that has been constructed for you. But he knew women, too, and there were some things that could not simply be artifice. Even the most gifted deceiver can't fake everything: She can't be taught to arch her neck just so, to brush the hair back from her face because she feels self-conscious; or to tremble, for an instant, when she knows that she is an object of a man's desire.

Dunne was too intoxicated with her to walk away. But he made himself a promise, as he listened to her singsong, German-accented English, and her improbable way of ending her statements with, "Is that okay?" The pledge was that he wouldn't do anything that he could not explain, however lamely, to his wife. He was restless at work, that was all; he wanted to give himself a little treat. He told himself that he would stop in time. Just not yet.

Dunne asked if she could have dinner that night. She lowered her face. No, she had a date. That reassured Dunne for a moment. But it made him jealous, too. If he couldn't have her, he didn't want another man to take her, either.

"It's a woman," she said, as if reading his mind. "We're going to a club later. You can meet us there, maybe. It's private. People like to dance."

"I don't dance. I told you, I'm shy."

"You're not allowed to dance, silly," she said with a slight smile. There was a glow on her skin, not just the rosy light of the setting sun, but a blush.

"Why not? I thought it was a club."

"It's a club for women, mister! They don't allow any guests, especially men, but I am one of the organizers, so maybe they will let you in. Is that okay?"

"I don't know. I need to be careful."

"Don't worry, Joe. They have a private room. You'll be alone."

Dunne closed his eyes for a long moment. The right answer was no. "Sounds interesting," he said.

She reached in her purse and wrote an address in the district just north of the lake, near the fancy hotels. She wrapped it around one of her business cards and handed the slips of paper toward him.

"The club is called Stylet. Stiletto. It moves around in different clubs and houses. Members only. Come at midnight. Use the back entrance on Rue du Levant. Tell the concierge you're my special guest. She will expect you. I will, too, but I won't see you. Until later, maybe."

Dunne took the card.

"I'm dangerous, you know," she said, smiling and pushing a strand of hair off her brow.

Dunne nodded. That shouldn't have been a seductive line, but it was.

*  *  *

Dunne arrived at the address at 12:10. As he headed toward the back alley, he saw a half dozen stylish women at the front door, presenting their invitations for inspection. The women were all dressed in long coats, so it was impossible to tell what they were wearing underneath. They were bantering in a mix of German, French, English, and Arabic.

Dunne rang the buzzer at the back door. It took nearly thirty seconds before a woman in a blue maid's uniform answered the door. Dunne gave her Veronika Kruse's card; she examined it carefully and then opened the door and said, in French, that he should follow her. They mounted a narrow stairway at the back of the building and walked down a dark hallway to a door. The blue-uniformed woman took a key from her pocket and turned it in the lock. The door swung open.

It was a small sitting room with a velvet curtain at the far end, faced by two leather chairs. The light in the room was low and the maid turned down the rheostat until it was nearly black. She motioned for Dunne to take a seat in one of the chairs. Then she walked to the right edge of the curtain, reached behind it to a cord, and pulled the velvet shears open.

"C'est un miroir transparent," she said. And, indeed, the room below was visible. She turned and exited the room. After she closed the door, Dunne heard the turn of the key in the lock.

Through the mirror, he could see a dozen women clustered in small groups in a well-furnished salon, talking as if at a cocktail party. The coats were gone, but there was every variety of silk: slit skirts, gowns with plunging necklines, harem pants that rode low on the hips; and more exotic garb, too: bustiers, corsets, straps, and belts. Each woman was wearing black stiletto heels. The club motif.

Propped on an easel against the far wall was a placard with the words En Soie Ce Soir. In silk tonight. The women were all young and attractive; that appeared to be a condition of membership.

Another notice was displayed by the entrance door. Étiquette du club. Les membres doivent être approuvés à l'avance. Les hommes sont interdits. Pas de jouets. Les appareils photo ou la photographie sont absolument interdits. No men, no toys, no photos. Just Dunne.

A woman with short black hair moved to the center of the room. Her face was angular and severe, but her body was shapely. She was wearing a black silk corset, tightly bound with stays, and black stockings that descended to her black heels. She spoke to the group, but Dunne couldn't hear what she said. In the circle gathered around her was a blond woman, prettier than the rest, in a tight silk sheath. She looked up toward the mirror and smiled. Veronika.

A waitress arrived carrying a tray of champagne flutes. There was a toast, a clink of glasses. Some of the women downed the champagne quickly; the waitress circulated with another tray of champagne.

The dark-haired woman at the center of the group concluded her introductory talk by extending to her guests a silver bowl, from which each withdrew a slip of paper. These seemed to be the equivalent of dance cards, for the women began to pair off. Music had started, and some of the women began to sway rhythmically; Dunne could hear the thump of the bass notes through the thick wall.

The lights dimmed, as the women found their partners and moved to corners of the room and alcoves beyond. Dunne could scarcely see what was happening, but in the half-light at the left he saw the blonde nestled against a woman with jet-black hair, wearing bright red lipstick; Veronika gave her partner a kiss, first on the cheek and then on the lips, and then turned her head ever so slightly toward the mirror behind which Dunne was standing. She slipped the sheath dress from her shoulders and it fell to the floor.

\* \* \*

An hour later came a knock at Dunne's door, and then a turn of the key in the lock. The door swung open, and in the beam of light from the hallway, Dunne saw Veronika. She was wearing a silk robe, but as she entered the room, she let it slip. There was nothing underneath. She closed the door but didn't lock it.

Veronika approached him. Dunne's heart raced, with excitement but also with anxiety.

"Maybe you want some company, Joe," she whispered in his ear. "It's lonely up here, you know." She moved her hand to his thigh. He began to pull away but stopped.

"Are we safe?" asked Dunne.

"I think so." She moved her hand a bit farther. She was so close he could feel the soft weight of her against his chest.

"How do you know we're safe?" he asked.

"Nobody knows you're here. Except the woman who let you in. She is an old maid. Who would she tell? I am one of the bosses."

He looked at her, trying to decide. In that moment of silence, she undid his trousers and let them drop and tugged at his shorts. She moved her hand toward him.

"This is dangerous for me," he said. It wasn't a protest.

"It's okay, I think." She drew closer. "We can go somewhere else, maybe? But you are ready now." She held his rigid form gently in her hand.

Dunne was about to say yes, they should go somewhere else, when the door burst open. He couldn't see the face, but he saw the flash of the camera, one, two, three times, and then heard the slam of the door.

*   *   *

Dunne stayed that night in a hotel on the south side of the lake. He had left Veronika sobbing, protesting that she hadn't known that anything would happen. It didn't matter then whether she was lying or telling the truth. Someone had set him up, and he had had to escape. He had slipped out the back door and into the shadows of the alleyway behind the building. As he lay awake later, trying to think about what had happened, he had two certainties: She was very beautiful. He was very stupid.

*   *   *

Dunne managed to sleep a few hours before dawn. He awoke knowing what to do. He messaged the watch officer in the operations room and said that he needed to speak urgently, personally, with George Strafe, the deputy director for operations, as soon as he awoke that morning. That made it easier, knowing that he was going to confess his mistake, rather than hide it. He thought briefly about what he might do after he was fired from the agency.

Calm restored his appetite: He ordered a big American breakfast, eggs and bacon and a potful of coffee, in the hotel restaurant. He went back to his room and watched television, then tried to read, to pass the time, but he couldn't concentrate.

He left the hotel and found a sporting-goods store nearby, where he bought a T-shirt and some shorts and a cheap pair of running shoes. He ran along the southern rim of the lake to Anières, six miles east, and then ran back.

It was noon when Dunne returned to the hotel. An hour later, when it was seven a.m. in Washington, Strafe called him using an encrypted phone app.

"This better be important," said Strafe. His voice had the rough, unshaven edge of early morning.

"I fucked up," said Dunne. "I needed to tell you right away, so I don't make it worse."

"Uh, okay. Anybody dead? Anybody arrested? Anybody shoot the pooch?"

"No, it was a honey trap. Someone took a picture of me with my pants down and a naked woman with her hand on my dick."

Strafe laughed. It was a low, growly chuckle. "My, my," he said. Then he laughed again.

"What should I do? I can try to get the picture back."

"Fuck, no, forget that. Too risky. Who set you up?"

"I met a cute Swiss girl at a bar. She brought me to this, I don't know, lesbo club. I don't know if she did me, or the people who run the club. I can tell you the details if you want, but they're not pretty. I ran when someone opened the door on us and started snapping pictures."

"You are an idiot, Dunne. Let's stipulate that. You had trouble keeping your dick in your pants when you joined the outfit, as I recall. You're not the only person in Operations with that problem, but even so, grow up! Does this Swiss Miss know who you are or where you're staying?"

"No. I'm not that dumb."

"Yes, you are, probably. But we'll leave that for later."

"So how do I neutralize this? Should I tell my wife?"

"How would she react?"

Dunne paused a moment, thinking about Alicia. "She'd go batshit," he said.

"Then don't tell her. Don't do anything."

"Nothing? Really? I mean, I have to assume that I'm compromised, don't I? Someone worked overtime to frame me. This chick, or someone else. I'm a sitting duck."

The line went dead for twenty seconds, while Strafe considered various options. Then he came back. His voice was lighter.

"I'm underwhelmed. It's a tolerable risk. It's too late to organize another run at this target if I pull you, so I won't. My instinct is that you should keep your head down but continue moving. Get in place to do the op in Italy. Find out everything you can. Get it done. Then come home and we'll figure out what you do next. If someone tries to spin up your wife, we'll deal with that down the road. They can't blackmail you with the agency because I already know, so WTF, right?"

"You're the boss. If you say so. That's a relief. I thought you were going to fire me."

"Maybe later, asshole. But not now. For the moment, I want you to do your goddamn job. And if you see this woman, I want you to run the other way. Otherwise I am going to come after you with a meat cleaver and chop you off at the curly red roots. Understood?"

"Yes, sir. Thank you, sir. I'm sorry to be an idiot. It won't happen again."

Dunne waited for a response, but Strafe had already hung up.

# 17

Cheat Lake, West Virginia—May 2018

A six-figure wire transfer arrived in Pittsburgh soon after Michael Dunne had "pwned" the tormentor of Pia Zimmerman, the Hollywood producer who had retained him as a consultant. She was Dunne's new champion: She wanted to recommend him to her friends and urged him to build an L.A. cyber defense practice. Everyone in the entertainment and technology business had online persecutors, she said, of one sort or another. But Dunne demurred. He wanted to stay in the East and think about what to do next, now that he'd had a first blush of success after the year-long shaming solitude of prison.

Dunne was happy to return to his office on Forbes Avenue, with its glimpse of the Monongahela River, while he ruminated on his past and future. The first day back he contacted Vijay Prakash, the ex-FBI agent who had referred the California client, and offered to share the fee with him. But Prakash just laughed. Dunne's $150,000 was a rounding error in the world where Prakash and his big cyber firm operated.

Instead of taking a split of Dunne's money, Prakash offered him another referral, a lawyer in Evanston, Illinois, named Joseph Lee, whose business had been shattered three months before and was seeking "active defense" of a kind that Prakash's firm wouldn't provide.

"He asked for you specifically," Prakash said. "He said he likes your work."

"How the hell does he know about my work? I've only done one case."

"Beats me, bro. But word travels fast in our business."

"Is this guy legit?"

"I don't know. But he's rich. His law firm has offices around the world. This could put Paladin on the map."

Dunne deliberated. He'd just gotten his life back. He didn't want to give it away again, or even sell it. "Tell the Evanston lawyer I'm interested," he said. "But I'm still getting settled. I have a few things to work out. I'll get back to him in two weeks."

"You're nuts," said Prakash. "This guy will have found someone else in two weeks."

"Maybe," said Dunne. "Or maybe he'll want me more if he thinks I'm picky."

Prakash gave Dunne the man's contacts, and Dunne told his secretary to arrange a call in two weeks. Running a business can't be this easy, he thought. But in the flush of having money and clients, he didn't worry about it.

*   *   *

While Dunne had been away in California, his assistant Jenny had been developing other business prospects, fielding contacts from the website and LinkedIn. She had received retainers from three new clients and started providing them with basic security and forensic services.

Dunne had never been very tidy with money. He had showered presents on his wife and child when he was married. Now he had a fat bank balance, even after he paid his alimony and child support. He bought flowers for Jenny, and a fancy espresso machine for the office, so they could make good coffee at work, and he sent a check for $10,000 to his father in Tampa, who didn't deserve the money, given everything he'd done to Dunne's mother, but got it anyway. On a whim, he bought a fish tank for the office and filled it with a half dozen tropical fish.

In his newfound prosperity, Dunne tried not to think about revenge. But our pasts never really stay in the past.

Soon after he returned from California, Dunne retrieved the "Lemon

Squeezer" letter that his attorney friend Richard Ellison had given him after his release. At first Dunne hadn't wanted to do anything about it. It would suck him back into a time that he was beginning to escape. But he read it again carefully now. He paid special attention to the details about Jason Howe, the young American he had been chasing, on agency orders, when his world collapsed.

The anonymous correspondent had dangled some very specific leads. He'd provided the IP address, domain registry, and server name for one of Howe's computers, and the serial number and SIM card of his iPhone. These traces could perhaps help Dunne find Howe, the architect of his destruction, but he would need some help.

Sometimes, perhaps, we should just let go of what is troubling us. But Dunne wasn't built that way. He wanted to know.

*　　*　　*

Dunne invited Rick Bogdanovich for lunch a few days after he returned home from California. He said he wanted to thank his FBI buddy for getting him back on his feet, but he had more than that in mind. They went to a fancy Italian place along the Allegheny River in Highland Park and feasted on fried zucchini and veal marsala, two of the house specialties.

Bogdanovich had two glasses of wine and was reveling in his new friend's good fortune—until Dunne pulled out the letter that had arrived at the U.S. Attorney's Office so many months ago in a FedEx mailer.

"Maybe you can help me with something, Rick," Dunne began. He had the letter in a plastic sleeve and pointed through the sheen to the items about Jason Howe: the computer addresses and the iPhone identifiers.

Bogdanovich stopped him in midsentence.

"Hold on, brother," said the FBI man. "I can't do this."

"But I haven't asked you for anything yet, Rick."

"That's why I'm stopping you now, before you do something I might have to report to the SAC in Pittsburgh."

"But the Bureau helps people track leads like this all the time. You know that as well as I do."

"We help law enforcement agencies and other government officials, not private consultants. There's a difference."

"Does that mean I should get someone in government to make the ask?"

"No, Mike." Bogdanovich wagged a thick finger. "I am just telling you how the system works. You're getting stupid again. Be careful. Now put that fucking letter away so we can eat our veal."

*   *   *

One thing you learn gradually when the bottom falls out is that you need friends. Sitting in the dining hall at Petersburg night after night, it had seemed safer not to talk to anyone—not to owe any favors or grant any, either.

Now that he was out, Dunne wanted to see people he could trust, and there weren't many. The one man who knew the whole story, with whom Dunne wouldn't have to pretend, was Roger Magee, his old mentor at S&T. Like Dunne, he was divorced, and had free weekends and an appreciation for the great outdoors, especially when it included a cooler of beer.

Dunne called Magee at his town house in Reston and, after the preliminaries, asked if he wanted to go fishing that weekend. Dunne had been doing some research, and he proposed a spot between Pittsburgh and Washington, in the headwaters of the Monongahela, just across the West Virginia border. It was called Cheat Lake and Dunne told his friend that a local fishing website said anglers were catching smallmouth bass, largemouth bass, walleye, and catfish.

"Nobody just calls about fishing," said Magee suspiciously. Dunne had phoned him just once since he'd gotten out of prison, and that was to give him his new mobile number and email. "What do you want to talk to me about when we're at this Cheat Lake?"

"Fishing," answered Dunne.

"Yeah, right. Okay. Fine."

They met at a boathouse by the lake. Dunne had rented a small fiberglass bass boat with a little outboard in the stern. Both men had brought along spinning rods and other fishing tackle. Dunne's was new. Alicia had thrown his old gear away in her rage during their breakup.

It was a bright spring day. The sky was Carolina blue. Surrounding Cheat Lake on all sides were low hills, thickly forested, dropping to the water's edge.

"This ain't no lake," said Magee, when they were puttering toward a cove that Dunne said was a good fishing hole. "The hills are too steep."

"It's the backup from a dam built over near Morgantown back in the 1920s. That's older than you, old man."

Magee surveyed the calm water, dense green foliage, and clear blue sky. "It's pretty," he conceded.

"It used to be a dump. My dad brought me here once when I was a boy and it looked so nasty, he turned around and drove home to McKeesport. The only fish here then were bullheads and white suckers. Coal mines were all around these hills, and the waste drained into the Cheat, and acid rain did a number, too, back then."

"And the do-gooders saved it?" asked Magee, as he made his first cast toward the shadows of the cove. "The EPA?"

"Fuck the EPA. It was local folks. Back when I was in college, they had a group to clean all this shit up. And they did. By the time I graduated from Pitt, you could fish in it and swim in it. One of my girlfriends at Pitt, I brought her here and we went skinny-dipping. Memorable."

"Spare me," said Magee. A few moments later, his rod bent sharply. Magee let the fish play for a moment and then jerked the pole to set the hook. The spinner ran for a few seconds as the fish dove for deeper water, then Magee tugged hard again and slowly began to reel it in.

It was a nice bass, nearly eighteen inches long. Dunne took out the net and scooped the flopping fish out of the water.

"Are we catching these big boys or releasing them?" asked Magee.

"I just got out of prison. Let's give him probation."

Magee took out his pliers. He carefully removed the hook from the fish's mouth and dropped it gently back into the water, where it spurted away.

"Cheat Lake," said Magee, newly appreciative. "Back from the dead. My kind of place."

The fish were biting into the early evening, and they caught and released more than a dozen bass and walleye between them. They broke out the beer, too, so by the time the sun began to set, they were both feeling mellow. They returned the boat to the marina and walked to a seafood restaurant nearby. At the table, they ordered more beer, and whiskey, too.

"What did you want to talk to me about?" asked Magee. "Other than fishing."

"I need some help."

"I had a feeling. So, what's pulling your chain? I hope you don't want your old job back."

"I'm thinking maybe I should try to rewind the tape on what happened to me. Just to satisfy my own curiosity. People did me dirt. Maybe I should look for them. Starting with the people I was chasing back then, who posted all my private stuff online."

"Don't do it. I said that to you once before and you didn't listen to me, and you fell into a big pile of shit. Now that you finally got yourself cleaned off, you want to jump back into the pile again. What is wrong with you, Mike?"

"I want to understand. People messed me up. I want to find out who they are. I think I have some leads on the chief bad guy, and I want your help. So please don't tell me to piss off, because that's not what a friend would say, and you're my friend."

"Oh, shit. Is this going to be a test of character and loyalty? Because I don't have any. I'm a burnt-out intelligence officer. I'm tapped out in the good-guy department."

Dunne ignored the gruff words. He knew that Magee was listening, and deliberating.

"Here's what I need from you," said Dunne. "Someone sent me the coordinates of the kid that Strafe had me tracking. His name is Jason Howe. I have a computer address and SIM card numbers. He probably has ditched those, but if I can find out where he was, then maybe I can locate him. I have all the numbers here. What I need is for someone from the intelligence community to ask the FBI to do a search. Can you do that for me?"

"Maybe. Rather not. Who sent you those coordinates in the first place, anyway?"

"They came in an anonymous letter from someone who called himself 'Lemon Squeezer.' That had to be someone who knows tech ops, because who else would understand what that phrase means? That wasn't you, was it?"

Magee cocked his head. "Hell, no! Why would I help your sorry ass?"

Dunne smiled and shook his head. He had no idea whether Magee was lying or telling the truth. That gift for ambiguity and concealment was one reason he liked the man so much.

"Okay, I'm just going to give you the coordinates, and hope to God you do the right thing with them."

Dunne took a sheet of paper out of his pocket and handed it across the table. Magee let it sit there while he finished his whiskey and then ordered another. Eventually he folded it and put it in his pocket.

"Okay, dipshit. What else?" he said.

"The network I was chasing in 2016, with all the smart hackers, was called the Quark Team. Remember them?"

"Vaguely. Strafe was spun up about them. I guess they went away."

"The network is still out there, and I think it's getting nastier. They're not saving the world anymore, they're selling shit. I ran into traces of it when I was working a cyber case this month for a woman who got hacked by a former employee. I just started a consulting company. Just had my first big case."

"So I heard. What was your fancy case, Mr. Big-Shot Consultant?"

"I hacked a hacker. I know this will sound weird, but the malware tools the hacker was using were branded by this old network I was after. I saw some of the same malware from before. These people are serious assholes. They hate America. I want to take them down."

Magee didn't say anything for so long that it made Dunne nervous.

"What the fuck, Roger? Talk to me."

"My friend, you do not realize what you are up against here."

"What's that supposed to mean?"

"Just what I said. You are running into a free-fire zone and you are clueless about who your enemies are. There is some serious juju on this case. Why do you think you got your ass fried and had to spend a year in prison, for Christ's sakes?"

"Because I went after a journalist and pissed off the free-speech crowd."

Magee laughed, slapped the table.

"That's rich. Little brother, you truly do not have a clue, do you? No, and I'm not going to tell you, either. Because I like fishing and drinking beer, and I don't intend to spend a year protecting my butthole from your boyfriends in Petersburg."

"Howe and his friends ruined my life. I'm asking you to help me find him and make him pay."

"I feel sorry for you, man. Truly. The problem with you is, you have a big, gooey wad of idealism down there with all the badass cynicism. You're smart, but you're just stupid enough to think you can make a difference on this stuff. You can't."

"Help me, Roger. People shouldn't be allowed to destroy a man's career, marriage, reputation, everything he cares about. There has to be an accounting."

Magee sighed wearily. He wasn't going to talk his protégé out of his revenge mission, but he wasn't volunteering to help, either.

"If you have a problem, son, leak it to the newspapers. Let them do the dirty work. I keep a yellow old clipping from the *Washington Post* of an exposé that blew up a commie dictator we'd been trying to bust for a year. People didn't believe the U.S. government, but they believed the newspaper. Weird, but true."

"I hate reporters. The people who took me down claimed they were journalists, too."

"Suit yourself. And on this payback thing, *Ahlan wa sahlan*, as our Arab friends say. Be my guest. But when the shit hits the fan again, don't say you weren't warned."

"Fuck you, too," said Dunne. He clinked the other man's glass.

They drank a while longer, until they were both way too drunk to drive. Dunne had reserved two motel rooms at the marina complex, and they staggered off to their beds. When Magee left the table, he still had the information about Jason Howe in his pocket.

*   *   *

Dunne and Magee both awoke the next morning at six. Dunne knocked on Magee's door a few minutes later and suggested they have breakfast together at Hardee's, a few miles down I-68, but Magee said no, he had a long drive ahead and wanted to get on the road. The older man had dark circles under his eyes, as if he hadn't slept much the night before.

Dunne hadn't slept very well, either. He had been thinking about Magee. He trusted him, by force of habit as much as anything else. But there was a part of Magee's character that was remote and, ultimately, impenetrable. Maybe he was Dunne's secret deliverer, with the "Lemon Squeezer" letter sent when he was in prison, but maybe he wasn't.

"I've got a weird question," said Dunne. "Humor me."

"Sure, buddy. Ask whatever you like. If I don't want to answer, I'll just lie."

"Okay, here goes. Do you speak French?"

"Hell, no! I speak American. Period. What a dumbass question."

"Then how did you know about Paladin? I mean, they're French."

"What's a Paladin?" snarled Magee.

Dunne looked his friend in the eye, and then gave him an even smile. Magee was genuinely, unmistakably mystified by the question.

"What the hell has gone wrong with you, boy? You're scaring me."

"Oh, forget it," said Dunne genially. "Just some goofy stuff. I got confused about something, that's all. Don't pay me any attention."

Magee wagged a fat finger at Dunne.

"Be careful, Hoss. This shit is bigger and weirder than you know. You keep turning over rocks and you're eventually going to find a rattlesnake."

"Maybe I already have. But if you get bit once, you start to develop resistance. It can't be any worse than it's already been, right?"

Magee shrugged. "If it were me, I wouldn't try my luck in the snakebite department."

Dunne heard the warnings. But he had set his compass, and he wasn't a man to change that, especially now.

"I need your help, brother. Plain and simple. Will you send the coordinates I gave you to the Bureau? Rick Bogdanovich, the guy who runs Cyber-Forensics in Pittsburgh, is a friend. He'll track the information down if someone official makes the request. Will you do that for me?"

"Of course I will," said Magee. "You don't have to ask twice."

They began to shake hands, but Magee wrapped the younger man in a bear hug and clasped him tight for a long moment and then pulled back.

"Just don't assume you can put this one back together the way it was, Mike. Things don't work that way."

# 18

Pittsburgh, Pennsylvania—June 2018

Michael Dunne's mother Gloria worked at the Carnegie Library in McKeesport for more than two decades. She began as a clerk, and by the time she retired she had become the head librarian. The library was the emotional center of her life when Dunne was a boy, along with the church. Her husband had slipped away into drinking and time-wasting with his jobless friends after the mill closed. McKeesport and the neighboring steel towns were being leached of prosperity and self-confidence, but the library was still indomitable in its stone castle atop Union Avenue. Mrs. Dunne would take her son there every Saturday to sit under the dome in the big reading room while she wrote her plan for the next week. When Dunne got his first library card, she told him never, ever to lose it.

Maybe it was the guilty feeling we all carry from childhood, or perhaps the loneliness of middle age, with no family around. But Dunne decided that he wanted to spend some of his new money to help the library where his mother had worked, maybe buy some books in her name, or donate a bench where people could sit outside and look at what was left of McKeesport. He made an appointment to see the new librarian, Edith King, and drove down there one morning in the week after his return from the fishing trip.

The building was as forbidding as Dunne had remembered it. It was a small

Gothic fortress set on a grassy hill, built back in 1902 by Andrew Carnegie himself in the first trickle of what would be an ever-widening stream of philanthropy. Mrs. King was waiting for him in the same head librarian's office that his mother had occupied. It looked tidier, without his mother's notes stuck to bulletin boards and her stacks of newly acquired books waiting to be filed. Where his mother had kept her clunky IBM Selectric typewriter, Mrs. King had installed a sleek computer monitor and keyboard.

The library was nearly empty; that was the first thing Dunne noticed. Two old men were sitting at the big table in the reading room, with their heads slumped down on the wooden desktop. They looked like the homeless people who haunt most public libraries. Dunne saw one other person, a middle-aged woman sitting at a computer, earbuds dangling from her head, lost in an electronic world.

Dunne took a seat in the librarian's office, across from Mrs. King's tidy desk. She was a black woman, hair shaved close, wearing a dress of colorful African cloth, wanting to be helpful but not sure how. She had the strong, empathetic, but unyielding face of a school principal or guidance counselor.

"Did you ever meet my mother, Gloria Dunne?" he asked. "This used to be her office, twenty years ago. She's the reason I'm here."

"Goodness, yes," answered Mrs. King. "Your mother was retiring when I transferred here from Duquesne, after their library closed. And we went to the same parish, until she passed."

"She loved the library," said Dunne. "She told me once that it was the only place in this town that hadn't gone broke."

Mrs. King laughed. "People in McKeesport still read, a few of them, at least. And we have a Friends of the Library group that helps pay the bills. They're mostly from Pittsburgh. God bless them."

"They have guilty consciences," said Dunne. "They're prospering, and McKeesport is dead."

"I'm a librarian, not a politician," Mrs. King answered firmly, wanting to close off the subject.

"Right. Well, I wanted to do something to remember my mother. Give some books or make a donation."

"You can join Friends of the Library. It's a 501(c)(3) organization, tax deductible. I'm sure they would be pleased to accept your donation."

Dunne reddened, not quite the shade of his hair, but close. Somehow, the tax-exempt status of the prosperous do-gooders got on his nerves. He suspected that the "Friends" were all Democrats who thought the world ended when Barack Obama left the White House.

"I want to do this myself. These 'Friends' wouldn't have been friends of my mother's. They would have looked down on her. Just like the trustees did when people wanted to make her librarian."

Mrs. King studied her visitor. She was used to escorting out drunken hobos and disciplining unruly children. Pissed-off white men were not a problem for her. She was calm and direct.

"You seem quite angry, Mr. Dunne. I'm not sure the library can help you with that. But do go see the president of the Friends. His name is William Hundley. I can give you his phone number."

"I *am* angry," said Dunne, ignoring her advice. "I just moved back home, and it upsets me. I'm sorry, but it's true. This valley is like a country that got defeated in a war. Maybe I'm crazy, but it doesn't seem right for this place to be destroyed and people pretend that everything is fine just because Carnegie Mellon University is designing a bunch of fancy software."

"I understand," she said gently. "Many people are angry, just like you. But if you had grown up in my neighborhood in the Hill District, where the only white faces we saw were policemen and steelworkers who were making five times what my daddy made, you would understand that some of us think the world has gotten better, not worse."

Dunne's eyes flared for a moment. How predictable, that this black woman was telling him his anger was just a white man's rage against loss of status. But then he softened. She was sitting in the same place his mother had. She'd made it to head librarian, probably against protests from people who thought she wasn't "smart enough," just as his mother had.

"You said you went to the same church as my mom. Was that Pius the Fifth? She loved Father Steve."

"Father Steve is gone. So is Pius the Fifth. It was closed in 2010. Now it's Corpus Christi Parish."

"I'm not following."

"The Catholic church is like the rest of this valley, Mr. Dunne. The jobs left, the people left, the churches closed. Once this town had Holy Trinity for the Slovaks, St. Stephen's for the Hungarians, St. Mary of Czestochowa for the Polish, Sacred Heart for the Croatians, Pius the Fifth for Scotch-Irish white folks like your mother and a few black folks, too, like me. But it's all gone now."

Dunne shook his head. It was the call of the dead. He gazed about the tidy librarian's office, and through the glass partition to the shelves of books in their assigned Dewey decimal positions, impervious to time and politics.

"He felt guilty, didn't he, Mr. Carnegie, when he built this library? He was trying to make amends."

"I suppose so, maybe. I don't know."

Dunne pulled out his checkbook and scribbled in the blank spaces.

"Here's a check for five thousand dollars," he said. "Do something good with it."

"I can't accept it," she said. "I told you."

"Yes, you can. It's made out to Friends of the Library. Give it to Mr. Hundley, with my blessing."

Mrs. King took the check gratefully, and escorted Dunne out of her office. But he didn't want to leave the building yet. He wandered over to the stacks and began looking for some of the books he had read as a boy. A few were still there. In one, a dusty history of the D-Day invasion, he even found his name atop an old dog-eared card.

*   *   *

Roger Magee did as he had promised, and a week after the fishing trip, he sent Dunne an encrypted note on Signal. It was brief and to the point:

> Here's what you asked for, courtesy of your Feeb friend Bogdanovich. The last known location of the cell phone and computer IDs was in London. The address is 84 Dover Street in London. Fancy digs. I checked. Most of the floors in the building belong to a law firm called Clissold Partners. They're registered in the Channel Islands. Very hush-hush about their clients. Their email drop address is enquiries@clissold.com.uk. Don't ask me for anything else.

Dunne pondered his next step. A fancy Mayfair law firm hadn't been the address he had expected for the free-speech agitator Jason Howe. But there was so much about this case that he didn't understand.

The Clissold office could perhaps be monitored through electronic or physical surveillance, but it would be expensive and as likely to draw false leads as good ones. Dunne decided to knock on the front door, present a calling card, and see who answered.

Dunne sent his message via email, unencrypted, to enquiries@clissold .com.uk. The message read:

> To the Managing Partner, Clissold Law Firm. I am seeking information in a complex legal matter involving an American named Jason Howe. I am advised that your firm can be helpful in this matter. Please contact me at this email address. Yours sincerely, Michael Dunne, Paladin LLC.

Dunne received an answer forty-eight hours later. It was from a man named Tom Goldman, who identified himself as a partner at the law firm. He invited Dunne to meet him in four days on a yacht that was moored in Sardinia. The name of the yacht was *Cosmos*. The message said Dunne would have no trouble finding it, for it was the largest boat in the harbor.

# 19

When people want to forget a mistake, they busy their minds with images drawn from work, sports, television—anything that will dull the visceral scene they're trying to suppress but can't. It comes back when they're taking a shower, or driving a car, or some other moment when the mind is blank. The scene intrudes with such sharp, sudden intensity that it brings a wince, or a few desperate words of regret. Or just a shudder and a curse. People can try to repress the memories with alcohol, or drugs, or physical exhaustion, but they're simply pushing them into the unconscious where they haunt dreams or bleed out in moments of panic. The bad memory doesn't go away; it just hides.

Michael Dunne couldn't undo his mistake with the woman he'd met in a reggae club and then stalked all the way to the click of a camera shutter. He had confessed the security breach to his boss and received a professional reprieve. He had offered to make a similar confession to his wife and been told no, let the matter rest for now. Do your work; finish the job; save penance for later. Let's get on with it; that was the tribal code. And so he did.

Adrian White returned from Urbino. He had installed cameras to monitor everyone who entered and left Digito Urbino, the front company they were targeting. The computer firm occupied the upper two floors of an ocher-washed building near the Centro; it was centuries old but modernized with new windows and lifts. The heavy power cables had been fed in underground from a new switching station. The office was above a local bookstore and near the university, so hundreds of young people streamed past every day.

At the front entrance was a thick metal door with a buzzer and videophone; a back door opened onto a narrow alleyway lined with trash bins, scooters, and bicycles. Adrian had covered each door with a camera, to monitor the faces of everyone who entered or left. Arthur Gogel had hacked the computer firm's own CCTV surveillance cameras, so they had that record, too.

The surveillance feeds were sent to Dunne in Geneva and Hoffman at Langley. By tapping public and private databases, the team began identifying faces and building a registry of names. The regular traffic in and out included a dozen European and American hackers and left-wing activists, a half dozen young computer scientists. But the monitoring didn't identify any known intelligence connections.

The team found records that four months before, the Urbino municipal government had approved a request for new electrical transmission lines that could carry four hundred kilowatts per day to the building. That was enough to power a farm with twenty servers, the techs back at Langley estimated. Extra systems for coolant had been added, too.

*   *   *

One morning just after ten, Arthur Gogel summoned Dunne to the monitors. "You better check this out," he said. "I think it's your guy."

A tall young man with a tuft of blond hair had entered the bookstore beneath Digito Urbino. He was so thin and small-hipped that he kept tugging at his trousers to hold them up. The young man spent five minutes browsing in the bookstore, and then exited to the adjacent metal door, rang the buzzer, and went upstairs to the computer work area. A surveillance microphone and the company's own video camera both picked up the same words.

"This is Jason Howe," said the thin figure on the screen. He had an ethereal look, an almost angelic sweetness in his face. "Buzz me in now."

Ten minutes later, a white Range Rover deposited a man in his early forties, dressed in a finely woven beige suit, near the door. He had long, lustrous hair, a thin beard, and wore a white shirt that was open at the neck. His eyes were masked by thick black glasses. He might have been a tycoon visiting from Milan, or a professor from Bologna or Rome, with the stylish grace that Italians sometimes call *la bella figura*.

The only anomaly was that he was carrying a leather computer bag. Before he reached the metal door, an assistant emerged to greet him.

"That's Lorenzo Ricci," said Dunne. "The hacker-in-chief."

"He looks like a movie star," said Arthur Gogel.

"To these people, he is," said Dunne. "He's the engineer prince. According to the traces he took a doctorate in computer science at Georgia Tech, before he went wiggy."

\* \* \*

Dunne requested an urgent talk with George Strafe. It was five p.m. Geneva time before Strafe responded on the special-handling encrypted phone. Dunne wanted to move quickly, himself, and he needed Strafe's blessing.

"The eagle has landed in Urbino," said Dunne.

"Our American friend?"

"Yes, sir. Along with Ricci and some computer-science guys we've been tracking. It looks like a convention."

"Time to move in, then. If you're asking for my permission, you have it. What's your operations plan?"

"I'm Edward Spitz, a whistleblower software engineer. I'm going to meet one of Howe's colleagues. Tell him I can help them. Then I could send in one of my team, if you like."

"No way. You're my guy. I trust you, assuming you keep your pants zipped."

"Just what I wanted to hear," said Dunne. "I'll leave tomorrow morning. Any last advice?"

"The usual, squared, cubed. Do. Not. Get. Caught. Make sure your identity is backstopped. If anything bad happens, keep your mouth shut until we figure out how to get you out. Remember, these people are very smart, in addition to being immature little creeps. Don't take anything for granted."

"My identity is solid. Social media tells the whole legend. Microsoft's databank has fifteen years of history on me. I hate the government. I'm Snowden's big brother. They'll like me."

"Do you want an abort signal, if something's going down wrong?"

"Why would we abort this? It's a makeable putt, totally. I know I fucked up with the woman, but I can do this."

"It's your ass. No abort signal, then. Just remember: When you shake the tree, you never know what's going to come down. If it feels hot, get out."

"What's your collection priority? So I don't waste time."

"Order of battle. I want to know what they've got, hardware and software. How did they pull all their fancy tricks, turning off malware and creating perfect fakes? What capabilities do they have? What game are they playing? Who are they playing it for? How do we neutralize them?"

"What buttons do I push when I get inside?" ventured Dunne. "Are we collecting intel, or sabotaging them, or something else?"

"I haven't figured that out yet. We'll buy them, maybe. Control them. Or just run this shit ourselves. I don't know yet. First you've got to get inside and see what they've got."

"Should I look for the code that took out our malware beacons in Europe?"

"No. Don't look for anything now. They've stopped unwiring the beacons anyway. Just get inside and chill."

"One more question: Will I have backup?"

"Nope. Just you. Your guys will monitor everything, but I don't want any other footprints. After this case is finished, you're going to have to carry your balls around in a wheelbarrow."

*　*　*

Dunne spent that evening reviewing his operation plan. He and Hoffman had decided that the most pliable access point was a hacker and would-be new age philosopher named Jacob Rosenberg. He had gone to college with Howe at Stanford, joined the Chaos Computing Club during a summer trip to Germany, and was deeply embedded in the Wiki underground. He hung out at a bar in Urbino called the Morgana. He liked to drink alone.

Dunne sent Rosenberg an encrypted message on Signal, in his Edward

Spitz cover identity, promising Microsoft exploits, zero-days that the company hadn't patched. He offered to come to Urbino. Rosenberg didn't say no.

Adrian White knocked on Dunne's door that night as he was packing. The train left the Geneva station the next morning at 5:39. Dunne was trying on some of his cover wardrobe. He had added an earring, and some fake tattoos, and packed some computer science magazines in his backpack. His body looked less muscular in a baggy black T-shirt. The red curls looked just punk enough when they were disheveled.

"There's some new stuff you ought to look at," said Adrian. "We just processed it."

He led Dunne back into the main workspace. Gogel had mounted a spacey, futuristic poster for Radiohead, his favorite band. It was time to leave Geneva. Everyone had gotten too comfortable.

"Look at this," said Adrian, sliding into a chair next to Dunne before a bank of monitors. One screen displayed a headline promising a leaked document about an Iranian plan to assassinate the U.S. secretary of state.

Dunne clicked on the link and studied a Farsi document and its English translation, which talked about the purported assassination at the United Nations General Assembly later that month. Next to the document was a photograph of a senior officer of the MOIS, the Iranian intelligence ministry. It linked to an audio recording. Dunne clicked and heard a voice in Farsi, sounding like a hundred SIGINT intercepts he had listened to over the years. It was followed by an English translation.

"If this is for real, someone has intercepted a hit man talking to his boss. Who posted this?"

"It's a new site, called DeadlyIran. It just popped up today, but it has the Fallen Empire tags. People are going nuts about this online, as you might expect. The site claims this shows its sources are everywhere. They have whistleblowers even in Iran."

"Cocky little bastards," muttered Dunne. "How did they manufacture this one?"

"Who knows? I checked the Ops Center a few minutes ago. They confirm that the recording is a fake. A very, very good one, simulating the voice of a real MOIS officer. But they don't think there's any such plan."

"How can they be so sure it's bogus?"

"Because they have HUMINT coverage in Tehran, and their source tells them it's bullshit. The DDO cleared the Ops Center to tell us. He thought we should know."

Dunne smiled. Fallen Empire and its digital wizards had gotten too confident. They were overreaching.

# 20

Urbino, Italy—October 2016

Dunne's trip to the hill town in the Marche took nine hours. A train from Geneva to Milan, another to Bologna, and then south to the coastal town of Pesaro, and finally by bus inland for an hour to Urbino, which sat atop Italy's mountainous eastern spine. History is capricious: A city-state that had once dominated a whole region of Italy was now so insignificant it didn't even have a railway station.

The brick walls and turrets of the Ducal Palace were pale pink in the late afternoon light when Dunne arrived. It was nearly a mile walk uphill from the bus station to the city center. Dunne tramped up as the day-tourists flowed downhill, back to the parking lots and buses, in a polyglot stream.

Dunne found his hotel; it was a simple three-story brick building, centuries old, on a street barely wide enough for a single car. Dunne checked in with his alias name, unpacked and showered, and slept for a few hours. He awoke at nine p.m., put on a black T-shirt and a suede leather jacket, and headed off to the pub where he planned to meet Jacob Rosenberg.

The Morgana was noisy with students carousing over beer and pizza. Dunne searched for a man with a shaved head and thick goatee, which was how Rosenberg looked in recent pictures gathered by European Special Collection.

On a quick tour of the bar he didn't see anyone who resembled the photos, so he took a seat alone and waited. The waitress flirted with him. Dunne smiled and shook his head. Not now; not anymore.

After thirty minutes, Rosenberg appeared; he scanned the crowd, looking for the person who had introduced himself electronically as Edward Spitz. He looked eager and wary at the same time. Dunne approached him and extended his hand.

"Hey, man, I'm Edward."

"Jake," answered the bald, goateed man. He was shorter than Dunne had expected. There were deep circles under his eyes. Dunne waited for him to say more, but he was silent.

"Pretty town. I've never been here before."

"Nobody has. That's one of its attractions. How'd you find us?"

"Everybody on 4chan knows Fallen Empire, dude. I've been communicating with your guys on message boards for a long time. You just didn't know it was me."

"What's your 4chan handle?"

"Coredump76," answered Dunne. His anonymous message-board life had been carefully backstopped, too.

"We'll check you out."

"Game on," said Dunne.

\* \* \*

They talked until midnight that first night. Dunne was good at building rapport. He didn't push, he teased. He let out a little about his purported work at Microsoft, and then a little more, and soon Rosenberg had dropped his reserve and was pulling for information. When Rosenberg asked him about the zero-day exploits, Dunne took a flash drive from his pocket, gave it a kiss, and then put it back in his trousers.

"I'm too drunk to talk serious coding shit," said Dunne. "Tomorrow."

"Is this for real?" asked Rosenberg.

"Most definitely," answered Dunne. "Hack the planet."

\* \* \*

They met the next morning at the office of Digito Urbino, near the university. Upstairs a small welcoming committee had gathered in a conference room. There were whiteboards on two walls, but no other decorations. Dunne had imagined a messy office decked with left-wing posters, but this space was clean and almost antiseptic.

Dunne recognized many faces from the surveillance cameras that Adrian had installed. A young man with a bushy beard, whose name traced as Manuel Sepulveda, guarded the door; Rosenberg sat in the center of the room; next to him was a black man with a tight Afro, who was identified in the traces as Marcus Cliff. Leaning against the back wall was Jean-Marc Silwan, pencil-thin, dressed in a gray cashmere sweater. At the table beside Dunne was Antonia Lucca; with Silwan, she was one of the three founders of the Fallen Empire news site. The chair on the other side of Dunne was empty.

"Tell the group about yourself, Edward," said Rosenberg. "They're curious."

Dunne extended his hands toward those gathered around the table. His body language said that he was a man who had nothing to hide. With his clear, taut face and carrot-top hair, he looked younger than he was.

"I'm a software engineer," he said. "I work for Microsoft in Redmond. Or did. I quit two weeks ago."

The room was silent. People stared at Dunne.

"Why did you leave?" asked Silwan from the back of the room. He spoke with the roll of a French accent.

"And why are you here?" added Lucca. She had bright eyes and prominent cheekbones. Her black hair was long and lustrous on one side and shaved close on the other.

Dunne didn't answer for a good ten seconds. His face was motionless; his eyes were closed. His was utterly still, while he considered their questions.

"There's an operating system that runs the world," he said. "I was part of it. I don't just mean Microsoft, it's all the companies and governments. I couldn't continue. I wanted to break the machine. It's like when you're sick. You don't decide to vomit. It just happens."

"But why us?" said Lucca. "We didn't invite you. You found us. Why?"

"Because you're serious. It's not an ego trip for you, the way it is with WikiLeaks or Anonymous and the other groups. I've been watching you for more than a year. You know what you're doing. You can break the machine. I can help, if you'll let me."

"How can you help us?" asked Silwan from the back. "You told Jacob you brought something to show your good faith. What is it?"

Dunne took the flash drive from his pocket and laid it on the conference room table.

"I have a zero-day exploit for Microsoft Office. Microsoft sent out a patch, but there's still a hole in the code."

"Why would we want a zero-day?" asked Lucca. "We are journalists, not hackers. We spread truth, not malware. I think you came to the wrong place."

Dunne nodded. He understood. They didn't trust him yet.

"I brought other exploits," he said. "They're not public. But they'll help you."

"Like what?" asked Rosenberg.

"Microsoft has a personal security product. It's called MS Security Essentials. I brought something that can get around it."

"Interesting," said Silwan.

"I also brought a beaconing tool. It works with all Microsoft Office documents. It's like a watermark. When the document is opened, it generates an HTTP request that you can see on your server."

"Nice, if you're a hacker. Or an intelligence service," said Lucca. "But like I said, we're journalists."

"I can help you," Dunne repeated.

There was a sound of footsteps in the hall, behind where Dunne was sitting. The door opened, and into the conference room walked a tall young man, baby-blond hair, even thinner than Silwan, dressed in skinny jeans that bagged around his legs and a charcoal-gray hoodie. He wore glasses with thick black frames and lenses that were tinted pastel-blue. He took the empty seat next to Dunne.

"I'm Jason," he said, extending his hand toward Dunne. "I was listening. I like what you had to say. Thanks for coming."

Heads around the room nodded. The leader of Fallen Empire had spoken.

"Hey," said Dunne, shaking Jason Howe's hand. "Glad to be here."

*   *   *

They talked for forty-five minutes. Howe asked Dunne more questions about himself and his work at Microsoft. He probed Dunne's technical background: where he had studied; what he had built; which programming environments and frameworks he preferred. Dunne was fluent, relaxed, believable. His legend tracked his own studies in college and his technical work over the last dozen years.

"You've got the chops," said Howe eventually. "But explain to me why you want to help us so much. We're anarchists, basically. You seem too sane to do something this crazy."

Dunne paused and thought for a long moment. He answered not with a rote script, but a version of what he really thought.

"I don't like the way the world is going. We've been fighting wars in the Middle East that don't accomplish anything except make people hate us. The political system in Washington is completely fucked up. When we get a new administration, it just means a new set of Goldman Sachs partners running the economy. I'm sick of it. It's like you say, America is a fallen empire. Time for something different."

Howe shrugged. "Makes sense to me," he said. "Just one last question. Are you a bandit, Edward?"

"I don't know," answered Dunne. "Never tried."

"Because real journalists like us, we're bandits. We're not like the ass-kissers who sit in Washington and write columns to make powerful people happy. We steal shit that matters, and then we publish it. Powerful people are our enemies, you understand? Sometimes the only way to serve the people is by being a bandit. Does that make sense to you?"

"I guess so. I need to think about it."

"I'll give you a book by a British professor. It will explain all about bandits. How's that sound?"

"Sounds good, dude," said Dunne.

Howe chuckled at the bro-talk. He took from the conference table the flash drive that Dunne had laid there more than an hour before.

"Okay, *dude*. Let's go upstairs to the lab. Show you around."

\* \* \*

The computer lab was on the top floor of the building, up a metal staircase. The windows were shuttered and bolted, and all you could hear in the room was the low hum of the air-conditioning system and the tapping of fingers on computer keyboards. There were more people here, and many of them looked more like Microsoft software engineers than apprentice anarchists. They whispered to each other in Italian and darkened their computer monitors as Dunne entered the room.

Howe escorted Dunne through the lab. The front of the room had a series of workstations, manned mostly by people Dunne recalled from the surveillance videos. Howe handed the flash drive to the chief of the tech team, an elegant Italian man in a beige suit, whom Dunne recognized as Lorenzo Ricci.

"*Illustrissimo*," said Howe to the Italian, with a flourish.

"Cut the crap," answered Ricci. He spoke perfect English, with a slow cadence that was somewhere between Milan and Atlanta. "What do you want?"

"We have a volunteer. The one I told you about. He offers us tribute. This flash drive, to be exact, which he claims has exploits that he purloined from Microsoft, his former employer. Could we, do you think, perhaps run a scan on a machine that isn't connected to anything else? Make sure there aren't any viruses, and then see what's on it."

"I'm very busy," said Ricci. "Is this worth the time?"

"I wouldn't have asked otherwise."

"*Bene*." Ricci took the drive, tossed it in his hand so that it spun a half dozen revolutions, and then gave it to his assistant. "Take this to the back office. Check it out," ordered the Italian.

"Slick operation, for a bunch of bandits," said Dunne.

"Just wait," said Howe when they got to the last of the workstations. He pointed to the back of the room. "There's the sweet spot."

Behind a glass partition was a cluster of servers, stacked five high on four black metal racks. Howe opened the glass door so Dunne could see better. The room had high-voltage power lines to feed the computer stack, and its own air-conditioning system to keep it cool.

"The best," said Howe. "Twenty blades, each with the latest NVIDIA graphical-processing cards. We can do almost anything. Correct that: Anything."

Dunne studied the array and tried to memorize each of the items on display. As he studied the clusters, he saw Ricci walking toward a door at the far end of the server room, which was protected with a cyber lock.

The Italian punched a code into the lock and the door swung open, and for the briefest moment Dunne saw into the room. He could see two dark-haired men with beards, who appeared to be Arabs, and, oddly, a man standing next to them with what looked like a yarmulke on the back of his head. The door closed as quickly as it had opened.

Howe tapped him on the shoulder. "Cool, huh?"

"What are you running here, a server farm?" Dunne laughed. "Are you guys trying to put Amazon Web Services out of business?"

"We're running a neural network. The architecture is optimized for reinforcement learning," said Howe proudly. "Lorenzo put it together, with his Italian friends and some other studs. Sweet, no?"

"Sweet. But what the hell do you need a neural network for?" asked Dunne. "Back at Microsoft, they'd only use an array like this for big machine learning or graphics projects. What gives?"

"Imagine playing politics with machines, the way you can teach a computer to play chess."

"What's that supposed to mean?" asked Dunne.

"Well, suppose I created one network that was assigned the job 'Subvert the system,' and then another one whose task was 'Detect subversion.' What do you suppose that would produce?"

Dunne thought a moment, then answered.

"You'd have a system that was awesomely good at subversion, because it could beat sophisticated attempts at detection."

Howe clapped his hands silently.

"Clever man," he said. "Murder and create, as the poet said. Destroy and build."

"I don't get it," said Dunne, fishing for a little more. "Explain it to me. And what's in the back office, where your man Lorenzo hangs out?"

Howe shook his head. Nice try.

"All in good time, my friend," he answered. "All in good time."

# 21

Jason Howe invited "Edward," the Microsoft defector, for dinner that night at a small trattoria near the city center, in the basement of an old town house. The brick of the walls and arched ceiling absorbed the noise, and in the crowded roomful of people they heard only each other. Howe ate ravenously; he ordered an antipasto of salt-cured ham and a soft pork salami, pasta with meat sauce and truffles, and then stuffed pigeons. They drank a bottle of Sangiovese, and then another.

Dunne imprinted every detail of the encounter. Howe was a finely embroidered self-creation. He was so blond and fair-skinned that he looked like a choirboy, but he could be as pugnacious about his mission as a football lineman. His clothes hung on his thin body as if he were a stick man, but he ate voraciously. He kept talking about himself as a bandit, but before he began eating he said a Buddhist prayer, in Chinese.

After Howe had eaten the antipasto, pasta, and one of his two stuffed pigeons, he pushed his plate away. In the low light of the cavernous dining room, he took off his blue-tinted glasses and put on another pair, round with simple metal rims. He leaned toward Dunne.

"I call myself a journalist, but that's not quite right. I'm a meta-journalist."

"What's that?" asked Dunne. "I've never heard that word."

"It means I don't care so much about facts, because they're momentary and malleable. I care about the narrative. It's like Bob Dylan said in *Don't Look Back*: Every word has its big letter and little letter, like 'truth.' The little letter is printed in the *Washington Post* and the *New York Times* every day and it's crap, right? It's not 'True,' with the capital letter. It doesn't mean anything. It's just what some people said happened yesterday. But the big letter, that's what we're working on. You follow me?"

"Mainstream journalism is bullshit," affirmed Dunne. "I don't trust reporters. What you're doing is different."

"Precisely. And sometimes the little-letter facts get in the way, so we have to, like, blow them up and create some new ones, right?"

"I guess so. I'm a software engineer. I write code."

"Well, it's right. Or at least I think it's right. Like I said today: Murder and create; destroy and build. That's what we do. Or at least I think that's what we do."

"You sound like you have doubts."

Howe laughed. "Me? Never."

Howe drained the last of his wine, and Dunne did the same. As they were drinking, Howe's phone buzzed. He saw that he had a WhatsApp message and read it quickly.

"Ho-ho!" he said. He called to the waiter.

"*Senta*. Bring us some cheese. Casciotta d'Urbino. Local specialty. And a sweet wine with the cheese. The local Vin Santo. And three plates, please, and three glasses."

"Another guest?" asked Dunne.

Before Howe could answer, there was a commotion at the door and in swept Lorenzo Ricci. He was wearing a jacket of black leather, soft as baby's skin, and a black cashmere turtleneck.

Howe gave the big boss a salute, and the Italian pulled up a chair.

*   *   *

"I wanted to see our visitor," Ricci said, sitting down. "People keep telling me about you."

Dunne's face didn't move a muscle. "Good things, I hope," he answered.

"Of course, of course. And you've taken so much trouble to come see us. I hope it will be, what, a 'killer app.'"

Ricci laughed. Howe was looking at the screen of his phone, checking messages.

Dunne stayed silent. A thought darted through his mind that maybe he had made a mistake when he told Strafe several days before that he didn't need an abort signal. But it was too late, and he had to play the cards in his hand.

Ricci ate a forkful of the Casciotta cheese, then took a long sip of the local Vin Santo, and exhaled happily.

"*Perfetto! Giusto!*" He smiled and turned to Dunne. "Do you know why we decided to make our headquarters here in Urbino?"

"The food," ventured Dunne.

"Of course. But there is something more special here. Just for us." He lowered his voice. "The history of this city is encrypted. You don't believe me, but it's true."

Ricci leaned closer, as if he were confiding the big secret at the center of all the little secrets.

"Urbino, this little nothing of a city on top of a hill, had the most powerful army in Italy at the end of the fifteenth century. Nobody knows that today, but it's a fact."

"*Sic transit gloria mundi,*" said Dunne. His high school Latin teacher had closed every class with that phrase.

"*Precisamente*. And do you know why Urbino was so strong, in its moment of glory? Because it had mastered the technology of war. Kings and dukes and even popes hired the mercenaries of Urbino to fight their battles, and they never lost. And you wonder: How was that possible?"

Ricci's eyes brightened as he talked. Howe had left the table and was talking to a skinny girl at the bar. Dunne beckoned Ricci on. He wanted this river to run its course.

"Urbino had a genius for a duke during its one golden hour. Federico da Montefeltro. The man with the big nose and the red hat in the Piero della Francesca painting. Remember him?"

"I'm a computer guy. Not an art guy."

"It doesn't matter, because I'll tell you. Federico dominated everyone because he had the best weapons. He had cannons and siege engines to knock down city walls; he even experimented with chemical weapons. His machines threw stones that weighed four hundred pounds. Boom, boom, boom, until the walls began to crumble. Are you following me?"

"That's what you're doing with Fallen Empire and the Quark Team. You're taking down the walls of the city."

Ricci took another drink of the Vin Santo.

"Maybe," he said. "But you missed the point: We're mercenaries, like Federico, and we need to avoid his mistake. He got too ambitious. In the beginning he was careful. But he got so famous that he was lured into conspiracies. You understand?"

"Explain it to me. If I'm going to be part of your team, I want to understand the origin story."

Ricci smiled.

"They were right about you. You're smart. So, listen to my story: The Pope and his allies, the Pazzi family, wanted to kill Lorenzo de' Medici in Florence. To do the dirty work, they hired Federico here in little Urbino. Lorenzo was supposedly his pal, but Federico agreed to knife him in the back."

"I didn't know that," said Dunne.

"It was a secret. They devised their plot in encrypted letters. Federico had a code that was strings of numbers and letters. It looked like Arabic or Armenian. Unbreakable, he thought. And it was, back then."

"But not now, I take it. Because otherwise, how would you know about it?"

"*Certo!* Anything can be decrypted today, my friend. Federico's problem was that the plot backfired. His operatives only wounded Lorenzo. He went on to be 'Lorenzo the Magnificent' and the Pazzi family was expelled from Italy."

"What about your hero, Federico? What happened to him?"

"He was unlucky in his heirs. When he died in 1482, Urbino was a jewel. It had the best architects, the best painters, the most money. But two generations later, it was all gone. Weak leaders, corrupt courtiers, bad luck. Poof. Now who's ever heard of this place?"

"Sad story. What's the moral?"

"Money is power. Rich people who don't have weapons can rent them. But for us mercenaries, the lesson is that if we don't have the best weapons anymore, our customers disappear. Tell that to your friends."

"What friends?" asked Dunne.

Ricci gave a thin smile and shook his head. He stood from the table. "*Ciao. Buona notte. Ciao.*" He gave the waiter a hug and a hundred-euro note.

Howe scurried back from the bar and walked his chief to the door, and then returned.

Dunne told himself to calm down. Howe took his old seat at the table.

"So?" asked Howe.

"Interesting man."

"Uh, yeah. The smartest software engineer I ever met."

"What's his game?" asked Dunne. "He doesn't seem like you. He seems more like, I don't know. A businessman. Someone you'd meet in Redmond."

Howe turned away. Dunne had touched a nerve.

"He's the head of the Quark Team. They help us, but they aren't part of us. Lorenzo has his own vision. His own people. What can I say?" He downed his glass of Vin Santo and ordered another.

Dunne took a guess. "He's selling hacks to clients."

Howe shrugged. "Not my department. But let's imagine that's so. Let's assume that Lorenzo has mastered every trick that a computer can do, every exploit imaginable, and he wants to sell those tools. Who do you suppose his customers would be?"

"I don't know. The Americans and the Brits."

"Fuck, no. Saudi Arabia, China, the United Arab Emirates, Singapore. Governments that repress people. Israelis who work with Arabs. Russians who work with Germans. Strange world, huh? But I don't care, because I want to bring it all down. The Americans and Chinese are all the same to me. P-I-G-S."

Dunne thought of the brief scene he had witnessed in Lorenzo's back office upstairs, when the door briefly opened. "I don't know, man. Some of those countries scare me."

Howe looked away, and turned back, sad-eyed. "I mean, maybe it's good to raise money by selling bad ops, to pay for the good ops. I don't know. Tricky business. I'm surprised the USG hasn't tried to stop them."

"Maybe the USG doesn't know."

"Maybe they just want a piece of the action. I say, fuck all these people. Fallen Empire is about destroying the power of governments, not helping them. I told Lorenzo I'm moving to Paris next year. *Finita la commedia.*"

"Right on," said Dunne. He brought his hand down on the table in assent.

Howe drained the last glass of Vin Santo and burped. He looked glassy-eyed suddenly. He rose from his chair and took a wobbly step. "I'm knackered, my friend. I need to get some sleep."

"I'll pay the bill," said Dunne.

"Forget about it. It's already taken care of." He started uneasily toward the door and then stopped and turned back toward Dunne.

"Just don't fuck me. That's the one thing you need to understand. I have tools you can't imagine, Mr. Microsoft. Those neural networks are operating twenty-four seven. If I find out that you have been jacking me off, I can put you in the hurt locker. Take you apart. Everything that matters to you, wiped out. Okay? Capisce?"

"Sure, man." Dunne put his big hand on Howe's slouching shoulder. "I'm solid. You'll see."

"Just don't forget: These people are all bastards. I'm a bastard. This is a dirty business and there aren't any clean people in it."

Dunne thought he understood what Howe was saying. People in the intelligence business talked like that, too. But usually it was just to make themselves sound meaner and tougher than they really were. Dunne understood one thing about Howe: He recognized how powerful Ricci and the Quark Team had become, and it worried him.

# 22

Urbino, Italy—October 2016

Michael Dunne walked slowly back to his hotel a half mile away. When he returned to his room, he looked for signs that it had been entered surreptitiously while he was away, but he didn't find any. Still, he wanted to be careful. He took his covert-communications device from a hidden, locked compartment in his suitcase. It was very late, but he wanted to send an encrypted message to George Strafe back at headquarters. He turned off the lights and sat down on the bed and typed out his message.

Dunne used careful language, but he wanted his boss to know that he had encountered something very puzzling in his visit to this crypto-anarchist den in the remote hills near the Adriatic coast. He described the racks of servers, the powerful graphics processing units that were engines of artificial intelligence. He summarized Jason Howe's statement of how he was running a neural network using custom algorithms that played against themselves to improve their results. He described Quark Team's tools and its unusual array of helpers in the back office.

At the end of his message, Dunne tried to explain the most salient piece of intelligence. Ricci and his team seemed to dominate Howe and his meta-journalists. Ricci spoke of himself as a cyber mercenary who knew that he had the best tools and wanted to sell them to people who could pay. Dunne explained that Howe was wary and suspicious of his boss, and his worry about Saudis, Israelis, Emiratis, and Chinese all working together under Ricci's umbrella. He proposed that Howe could be recruited as an asset, if he was developed carefully.

Dunne sent the message. As he lay awake that night, tired as he was, he thought that he had succeeded: He was inside his target, just as Strafe had ordered. And he had delivered to Strafe precisely the intelligence that he had requested. And it appeared to be as timely and potentially valuable as Strafe had thought. If there were laws forbidding what he had just done, well, he had violated them. But as he fell asleep, that didn't seem to matter.

*    *    *

Dunne received a brief reply cable overnight from Strafe, congratulating him and telling him to remain in place and continue working the case. The deputy director cautioned Dunne not to make any further contact with Ricci, but to await instructions.

Dunne spent the next two days trying to fit in with a group of thirty-something misfits. Howe left Urbino the next afternoon, without explanation. Rosenberg didn't meet Dunne for dinner again. Antonia Lucca invited Dunne, but he declined. Dunne worked all day in the lab, writing starter code for Fallen Empire websites. Nobody asked him to adapt the zero-day exploits he had brought, or the other potentially useful tools. The glass door to the server room remained locked.

Everyone was friendly; nobody had much to say. Dunne knew that something was wrong.

*    *    *

When Dunne returned to his hotel room the third night he had been in Urbino, he retrieved his covert-communications device from its hiding place and checked for messages. An urgent cable had arrived from Strafe's office, requesting that Dunne call headquarters immediately on an encrypted line and speak with the deputy director. Dunne sensed that it was unwise to make the call from his hotel room, so he stuffed the communications device in his jacket pocket and left the hotel.

It was dark, and the October night air was cool in the hills. Dunne buttoned his jacket tight. He looked up and down the narrow, steeply pitched street, but it was empty. The tourists had all gone home.

Dunne made a brief surveillance-detection run. He walked uphill, stopping occasionally to look for shadows and listen for sounds. He turned up several tight switchback alleys until he came to an open space atop the hill. He found a bench far from any buildings and cradled the small communications device in his lap.

Dunne punched the keys for the Operations Center. When the watch officer answered, Dunne gave his pseudonym and a password, and then asked to speak to the deputy director. Strafe came on the line ten seconds later.

"You've got to get out of there—now," said Strafe.

"Why? I'm in tight with these people. We have access. This is what we've been building toward. Why give it up?"

"They're on to you. There's going to be a flap."

"What do you mean, 'a flap'? My identity is solid."

"A serious flap. These little fuckers are about to expose you. There will be newspaper headlines. You've got to get out now."

"Holy shit," said Dunne. Instinctively, he checked the time, the landscape, the paths off this hilltop. "What should I do? Go back to Geneva?"

"No. Geneva is too hot. I've already shut it down. The equipment has been pulled and your assistants have gone to ground."

"Where should I go, then?"

"Come home," said Strafe. "Face the music. This will pass."

"I don't understand. What music? What the hell has happened?"

"Come home. In true name. As soon as you can. I have to go now."

Dunne asked another question, but Strafe had gone. When Dunne tried the Ops Center again, the watch officer said he didn't recognize Dunne's password and hung up.

# 23

Langley, Virginia—October 2016

Dunne was the iceman. That's what his colleagues always said. When an IED went off nearby, or a surveillance team tagged him while he was planting a bug, or any of the other things happened that would cause a normal person to panic, Dunne's body went cold; his heartbeat declined; his sweat glands went dry. He was strange that way, reverse-wired from most people. But this felt different. He didn't know what the threat was or where it originated.

He cleared out his room as soon as he got back to his hotel. There was a 10:55 bus that night to Pesaro, which he almost missed, and then a train a few minutes after midnight from Pesaro to Rome, which he barely caught. He was on the flight from Fiumicino to Dulles the next morning at 10:10.

Dunne went straight to Headquarters when he arrived. His badge didn't work at the front entrance. When he asked the security guard to call George Strafe's office, the DDO's secretary said she would come down immediately to escort Dunne.

"Where are you escorting me?" Dunne asked her on the phone.

"To the Inspector General's Office," she answered.

"I want to see Mr. Strafe. Now." Dunne was so tired from travel that there was a tremor in his voice.

"The deputy director is away," she said, her voice as opaque as a blacked-out window.

"When will he be back?"

"He didn't say."

When the secretary arrived downstairs, she was accompanied by a guard from the Office of Security. Dunne asked her once more when Strafe would be back, and when she didn't answer this time, he didn't press again. Whatever was happening, it wasn't her fault.

The deputy inspector general was waiting in a tight, boxy room in the New Headquarters Building. The agency lawyer introduced herself and said this was not a criminal investigation, which could only be conducted by the FBI, but an internal fact-finding effort.

"What does that mean?" Dunne asked. Her only answer was to repeat that this wasn't a criminal investigation, which could only be conducted by the FBI, but an internal fact-finding effort.

Dunne was exhausted and disoriented. He knew what Strafe would advise: Keep your mouth shut. He focused his eyes on the lawyer.

"This matter is compartmented," said Dunne, saying the last word slowly, breaking its syllables apart. "I cannot answer any questions until I have talked to the deputy director for operations. I operate under his personal orders."

"Mr. Dunne, I have already checked," she answered gently. "There is no record of any such orders or authorities in this matter. You are mistaken."

Dunne felt a lurch in his stomach, and a sudden weightlessness. It was like a free-fall parachute drop.

"What am I being investigated for?" he asked.

The deputy inspector general pulled from her drawer a copy of Executive Order 12333, the administrative regulation that governed the CIA and other parts of the intelligence community. She read two paragraphs:

*Section 1.1(b)(b) The United States Government has a solemn obligation and shall continue in the conduct of intelligence activities under this order, to protect fully the legal rights of all United States persons, including freedoms, civil liberties, and privacy rights guaranteed by Federal law.*

*Section 2.13 Limitation on Covert Action. No covert action may be conducted which is intended to influence United States political processes, public opinion, policies, or media.*

As the lawyer read this flat but incandescent language, there was a knock on her door. An aide stepped into the room and handed her a sealed envelope. On it was written the name "Michael Dunne." She handed it to him.

Dunne opened the long, thin envelope. Printed in the upper left-hand corner was the standard cover address: Central Intelligence Agency; Washington, D.C. 20505. Inside was an unmarked piece of paper.

The message had only one sentence: *You should get your own lawyer.* It was signed *GS.*

The next morning, the *Washington Post* carried a story on the bottom of the front page. The headline read: "CIA Officer Accused of Spying on Liberal Media Group." The story said that the FBI was launching a criminal investigation.

# 24

Costa Smeralda, Sardinia—June 2018

Michael Dunne's journey from Pittsburgh to Sardinia was long and uncomfortable. Despite his new prosperity, he flew economy via Detroit and Rome to Olbia Airport on the northern tip of the island. His body was too big to lie easily in the seat and he spent the night in uncomfortable contortions. When he finally arrived in midafternoon, he was so exhausted that he checked into the most lavish accommodation in town, a five-star hotel overlooking the Marina di Porto Cervo, where his meeting was scheduled the next morning.

He had brought along a small suitcase and a backpack with an unusual feature: It had a lock to protect the contents, and a locking metal chain to secure it. Dunne placed the pack in a corner of the closet, locked it to the leg of the minibar, and then flopped into bed for a few hours' sleep.

When Dunne awoke, the sun had set, and the harbor glowed with the lights of the giant luxury yachts and racing sailboats stacked at the piers of the marina. He stood at the window in his T-shirt and boxer shorts, staring at the armada bought with wealth looted from around the world and moored here for safekeeping. He closed the blinds and examined his too-expensive room, which was decorated with photographs and memorabilia of the Aga

Khan, who had made the Emerald Coast his summer playground and turned it into a hub for the unseemly rich.

From the moment Dunne had been invited here a few days earlier by a partner from the Clissold law firm in London, he had been struggling to understand the chain of communication that had led to his trip.

Dunne wanted to be the hunter, but someone, unknown, had pursued him. He had received an anonymous letter that revealed the coordinates of Jason Howe, the self-described cyber bandit who with his colleagues had turned Dunne's life upside down. The letter promised to help Dunne right the wrong that had been done to him. But when Dunne had tried to locate the "meta-journalist," using the anonymously provided information, he had been summoned to the biggest yacht in the fanciest harbor in the Mediterranean.

Dunne took a tiny bottle of vodka from the minibar, and then a second, and poured them over ice in a crystal glass. He took a long, burning swig, and another, and quickly drained the glass. He didn't understand the story any better with the vodka infusing his brain than he had sober.

What was the chain of provenance? The vodka in the minibar was gone, but there was a half bottle of Chablis. Dunne drank it down and, just before midnight, fell asleep with a cool evening breeze on his flushed face.

*   *   *

Dunne awoke early; through a crack in the shades, the Sardinian sun was shining bright in his eyes. He went to the hotel gym and lifted weights for an hour; a woman in her twenties, dressed in a one-piece pastel workout suit, asked if Dunne could help her adjust the treadmill. Dunne shook his head and said he didn't know how the machine worked.

The appointment was at ten aboard the *Cosmos*. An hour before, Dunne made his way downhill to the gleaming turquoise waters of the bay. The only things he took with him, apart from the clothes he was wearing, were electronics: a burner phone he was prepared to lose, and a few pieces of surveillance equipment, powerful but miniaturized so well that they were undetectable even to a practiced eye.

The marina had eight long docks, each accommodating a half dozen yachts. As Dunne walked seaward past the whitewashed splendor of the Yacht Club Costa Smeralda the boats became bigger and gaudier until he reached the last pier, where the mega-yachts were berthed. Under the yacht club's blue-and-red pennant, he glimpsed a discreet price list. For boats over 180 feet, the cost of a slip was fifteen hundred euros a night.

Dunne surveyed the yachts moored at this last pier, facing the mouth of the bay and the rising morning sun. They were all giants, well over two hundred feet; each was painted in the too-bright colors that you see on race cars. A metallic silver yacht with a knife-edge prow stood alongside a grand blue floating palace with five decks stacked like a wedding cake. Next was a sleek black hull, clad with blackened windows, that looked like a twenty-first century pirate ship.

Dunne stopped a marina dockhand and asked him where the *Cosmos* was berthed. The young man pointed toward the far end of the dock, where the very largest yacht of all rode in its slip. "Eighty-eight meters," he said, as if that told you everything that mattered. That was nearly the length of a football field.

Dunne walked down the wooden planks of the dock. He was dressed in a blue blazer, white trousers, and a pair of white sneakers. He had shaved off his red beard. He looked almost like he belonged.

As Dunne approached the yacht, it seemed to get even bigger. The hull was a metallic gray, like smoke. The superstructure was a creamy ivory. There were four separate decks above water; two of them had small swimming pools. The bow of the ship was perpendicular to the water, almost a submarine nose; it looked like it could plow through a gale. Just aft from the bow was a helipad marked with a giant *X*.

At the stern, in pristine white letters against the gray hull, was the yacht's name, *Cosmos*, and its home port, GEORGE TOWN, CAYMAN ISLANDS.

Dunne stood looking up at this skyscraper of a yacht and didn't notice, at first, an electric golf cart that was noiselessly approaching from the other end of the dock. The cart stopped next to Dunne and a tall, slender man stepped from the passenger seat. He was wearing matching powder-blue jacket and trousers with *Cosmos* written in script on the breast pocket.

"Please, Mr. Dunne," said the man. He spoke with a slight German accent. "Where's your luggage? I'll help you get it aboard."

"I didn't bring any luggage," said Dunne. "Are you Tom Goldman?"

"I'm Rudy, the steward. Mr. Goldman is on board waiting for you. We'll get you clothes. What size are you?"

"Large," said Dunne. The steward was still looking at him expectantly. "I'm a thirty-two waist, thirty-four inseam, forty-two regular jacket. You want my hat size?"

"The hats are adjustable, sir."

Rudy escorted Dunne down a red-carpeted gangway to the floating sun-deck attached to the rear of the boat; they passed through a hatchway, broad as the door of a two-car garage, that opened to the interior. An elevator took them up a floor to a lower salon that looked aft to a teak-lined pool; small wooden plaques pointed toward a beauty salon, a screening room, a gym, and a spa.

The steward motioned Dunne toward a circular stairway that rose to the main lounge. It looked like the lobby of a futuristic boutique hotel. There were twin white-marble cocktail tables, each with a bouquet of fresh irises; three white silk couches framed the seating area; and behind them along the walls were modern abstract-expressionist paintings with bold vertical strokes of color that matched the tint of the flowers. Beyond was a dining room with a white stone table, set amid walls of honey-colored marble.

Dunne stopped to admire the flowers. As one hand stroked the purple petal of the iris, the other attached a translucent sticky microphone to the inside of the ceramic vase.

Crew members, dressed in the same blue livery as Rudy, were standing midway through the gallery. Dunne looked for his host, but the room was empty except for the staff. He turned quizzically to the steward.

"Mr. Goldman is upstairs one more flight, in the master salon," said Rudy. "He thought you would enjoy it there."

The stairway was between the living and dining rooms. It was made of plexiglass and conveyed the sense of ascending through space.

At the top of the stairs stood a man in faded khaki shorts, a slim white T-shirt, and sandals. He looked like a beach boy more than a mogul. He waited for Dunne to climb to the top of the stairs, and then extended his hand.

"I'm Tom," he said warmly. "Thanks for coming so far to see me."

Goldman was a slim, sculpted man of medium height. He had an easy smile and his skin glowed with hydration and good health. His face was smooth and unlined, his hair sandy blond in a brush cut, his teeth perfect and immaculately white. He looked to be in his late thirties, but it was hard to be sure; he could have been a decade older than that, but he was so well maintained that the aging process seemed to have been suspended. He spoke with a cosmopolitan American accent that connoted good education, but not a geographical place.

Dunne looked at this sunny lawyer, thought about all the dark things that had happened to him in the last two years, and made himself a silent promise not to forget his desire to avenge the past.

"Nice boat," offered Dunne. "You're Jason Howe's lawyer, I take it."

"His legal representative, let's say. But we'll get to all that, I promise you. Relax, chill out. You've come a long way and you're on the nicest yacht in the prettiest port in the Med. Enjoy. What the hell, eh?"

"What the hell," repeated Dunne.

Goldman motioned for him to sit in one of four white leather chairs that surrounded a table set with another lavish bouquet of flowers. On all four sides of the room were windows looking out on the azure harbor. It was a cloudless day; the electric blue of the sky met the sparkling sapphire of the sea at the far horizon.

As Dunne was taking his seat, a woman dressed in a form-fitting, low-cut version of the blue *Cosmos* uniform entered the room with a tray of fresh-squeezed fruit drinks.

Dunne asked for water and a double espresso.

"You're making a mistake, my friend," said Goldman. "After a long flight, you need some Vitamin C. I'll have them make you a mixed-berry cocktail." He nodded to the woman with the tray. A few moments later, the cocktail appeared.

"I'm a prisoner in paradise," said Dunne, taking a sip. The casual bonhomie was getting on his nerves.

Goldman laughed. He turned to the steward and whispered a command. In the next moment, the hull of the great vessel began to move. The crew down below had cast off the lines, and small thrusters nudged the ship gently out of the slip; then the great, churning propellers under the hull began to drive her toward the open sea.

"I didn't know we were going for a cruise," said Dunne. "Lucky me."

"*Cosmos* at sea is an experience not to be missed," said Goldman. "Do you know what the root of 'cosmos' means? Probably not, nobody studies Greek anymore, not even the Greeks. The word means both 'world' and 'order.' I like to think of the two of them together. World order. Isn't that reassuring?"

"Not necessarily. Who owns the boat? Would that be you?"

"Certainly not. Don't be ridiculous. It belongs to one of our clients. The client lends it to me when it's not in use."

"Who's the client, if I may ask?"

"Of course you can ask, but I can't tell you. Won't tell you. If you checked the boat's registry, you'd find that it's owned by a trust in the Cayman Islands. The trust has a number of beneficial owners."

"How congenial." Dunne squinted at his host. He took another sip of the berry drink, at once sweet and tart. His eyes panned slowly across the sunny, floating lounge to his genial, smooth-faced host.

It was too perfect. Dunne wanted disruption.

He took the crystal glass holding the dark red juice and let it fall to the polished teakwood floor of the salon, where it splintered into a dozen jagged pieces. Sprays of juice stained the white fabric of the couch and the bright paper on the walls.

"Oops," said Dunne. "I dropped it."

Goldman shook his head, but his composure didn't break.

Two stewards emerged quickly from the pantry, as if summoned by the sound of the breaking glass. One began sweeping the shards into a stainless steel dustpan; the other doused the spots on the furniture and walls with cleaning solvent.

In the commotion of the cleanup, Dunne removed from his blazer pocket one of the tiny electronic devices he had brought with him and, as deftly as a magician, placed it invisibly into the fabric of the couch.

"That was rude, and unnecessary," said Goldman evenly, as the cleaners retreated. "I can see why you got in so much trouble at the CIA. You're an impulsive, angry man. But I will admit, that's why you interest people like us. You're a man with flair."

"Bullshit," said Dunne. "Who the hell are you? I go looking for Jason Howe and you come out of the bubble-gum machine. You keep talking about 'us' and 'we.' Do you represent Howe or not? He's an anarchist punk. What would he have to do with the billionaires who own this boat?"

Goldman kicked off his sandals and crossed his bare legs on the white leather chair.

"You need to calm down, Michael, or this will end as unhappily as your other adventures. Mr. Howe is not available. Our law firm was retained to represent the interests of him and his associates, which were larger than the little collective you visited in Italy. That chapter is over. It's time to turn the page, don't you think?"

"I'm 'interested' in him because he destroyed my life. Or tried to. He found every secret I had and exposed them all on his websites. He hurt the people I loved the most. I have business to settle with him. And with his associates, and their lawyer. That's why I'm here."

Goldman shook his head. "You're like a dog chasing a car. What on earth will you do if you find him?"

Dunne was silent. He didn't know the answer.

"I have another proposition for you," said Goldman. "It's revenge of a different sort."

"What's that?"

"Come work for us. Help tend the machine. It's not what you think. I promise. We can make all your other problems go away."

"You're kidding, right?" Dunne shook his head. "Have you Botoxed your brain? You work with the people who tried to ruin my life. Why would I have anything to do with you? I hate you."

"So sad. You don't even know who we are."

Dunne stared at him with a combination of indignation and curiosity.

"What's this about? I don't get it. Why are you pitching me, of all people?"

"Because you're the best. That's what your former colleagues such as George Strafe think, or so I'm told. They say you're the best person to keep this precious technology out of the hands of the Russians and Chinese. You're still a patriot, surely."

Dunne cut him off.

"What do you know about Strafe?"

"Nothing." Goldman backed off, after dropping the card. "I'm just a London lawyer. A name-dropper, with a big boat. Don't mind me."

Dunne kept silent. There was too much he didn't understand. He gazed out the broad windows of the salon. *Cosmos* was moving rapidly through the twin points that formed the harbor and toward open water. The yacht, under full power now, steered north toward the lighthouse at Capo Ferro at the northern tip of the island.

Goldman leaned toward his guest solicitously.

"Let's relax. Too much business is a mistake at the beginning of a meeting. Your stateroom is on the deck below, just forward of the dining room. Freshen up. Get changed. We'll go for a swim, and have some lunch, and then we'll talk."

Rudy showed Dunne to his room. It was a small suite, with a sitting room opening onto a bedroom done in blue and white: blue-veined marble on the walls, white linens topped by a blue twill spread. Laid out on the bed was a small wardrobe. Trousers, shirts, sweater, all made of the finest Italian fabrics. At the foot of the bed was a royal-blue swimsuit.

Dunne stripped and walked to the bathroom. Like everything else in this fantasy vessel, it was perfectly crafted, with a double sink, toilet and bidet, and a massive tub and shower. When he returned to the bedroom, Dunne put on his swimming trunks and sandals and a cotton piqué polo shirt. He lay down on the bed and closed his eyes so that he could think.

When Dunne felt the boat begin to slow, he roused himself from bed and went back on deck. The crew had maneuvered the giant craft into the bay of an offshore island. The water was a shade of iridescent green; truly, an emerald coast. The crew dropped the anchor and opened the back hatch to launch the motorboat, Jet Skis, and other paraphernalia of wealthy leisure.

Goldman beckoned from the lower deck. He was dressed in a bathing suit, a baggy shirt, and a Boston Red Sox baseball cap. The launch pulled aside the stern, and Dunne and his host sped off with a rooster plume of wake behind them toward the beach. Goldman turned toward him and spoke above the roar of the outboard motor.

"Isn't this better than being angry?" said the smiling lawyer.

"Who said I'm not angry?" answered Dunne.

# 25

Costa Smeralda, Sardinia—June 2018

Tom Goldman tossed a bag of snorkeling gear to Dunne and grabbed a set for himself as the motor launch idled just offshore. They waded a few dozen yards through the low surf to a crescent beach ringed by rocks and low brush. The cove was deserted, other than the giant gray yacht anchored a half mile offshore. Goldman put on his fins, mask, and snorkel, and Dunne did the same. The water was so clear that the black damselfish darting past might have been in an aquarium. Before Goldman fastened his mask, he called out to Dunne. "The octopuses are harmless. But stay away from the jellyfish. The medusa. They're nasty."

Goldman paddled off, and Dunne followed. His host was a strong swimmer. Dunne watched him drive through the green bay toward a cluster of undersea rocks a hundred yards away. As they neared the formation, schools of fish skittered past in regimental colors: the pink horizontal stripes of the porgies, black zebra stripes of the combers, and speckled gold of the royal dorade. Goldman dove toward an octopus hidden among the rocks and came so close it flared a tentacle. Dunne followed him down toward the creature, which retreated deeper into the rocks.

When they surfaced from the underwater grotto, Goldman spotted the fins of two bottlenose dolphins breaking the water in the seaward channel and drove toward them with his flippers; Dunne raced alongside him. Through the clear water, they could see the big creatures plunge toward the bottom and then power up to the surface to leap in tandem before descending again. The two snorkelers followed them for as long as they could, but the dolphins were stronger and sportier than the humans.

They swam for more than an hour, evading several red-tentacled jellyfish drifting toward them as they neared shore. When Dunne emerged from the water, he peeled off the mask and fins and collapsed, spread-eagled, on the sand. He closed his eyes and let the sun bake his pleasantly exhausted body. It had been a miserable, enervating season for Dunne. The sun, seawater, and intense exercise felt like an escape from a dark place into the light.

*   *   *

Back at the *Cosmos*, a magnificent lunch awaited them. It was served under a white awning on the top deck, behind the captain's wheelhouse. Dunne was ravenous. He attacked the oysters first, then the crab and shrimp, and finally a grilled branzino flavored with lemon and garlic. The steward poured a first-growth Chablis and kept refilling the two glasses until they were halfway through a second bottle. As they ate, Goldman talked about his adventures snorkeling and scuba diving around the world.

When the stewards had cleared the meal and served the espresso, Goldman put his feet up on the table. Dunne did the same. He was well fed and relaxed, and ready to stop sparring with his host and communicate.

"What's all this about?" asked Dunne. "I came here wanting to settle scores, and you're treating me like royalty. What's the hustle?"

"We're getting to know each other," said Goldman. "You knocked on my door. I answered. I offered you an opportunity, you said no, so we went swimming and had lunch."

"Come on, man. Cut the crap. I'm serious."

Goldman studied his guest. Dunne looked like a big red cat, now that he'd had some exercise and been in the sun. Goldman was warier, moving in diagonal steps toward what he wanted to say.

"Do you read much history, Michael? That was my undergraduate major, before I went to law school. My senior dissertation at Princeton was about Roman forts in the third century. It's still sort of a hobby, ancient history, and I keep seeing ways in which it's relevant to us right now."

"I can't help you much there," said Dunne. "My senior project was partying and hacking computers."

"Your education was more practical. But indulge me about the Romans. Why did they build all those forts? And so far from Rome. I mean, they constructed them in Jordan and Egypt. They had a string of forts along the Danube and the Rhône. They built Hadrian's Wall in Britain. What was that about?"

"Beats me," said Dunne. "I didn't go to Princeton. I'm a Pitt guy. The only British wall I remember from college is a song by Pink Floyd."

Goldman laughed and shook his head. He was used to smart people trying to pretend that they were dumb.

"As I said, indulge me. The Romans had an empire, and they wanted to protect it, and they thought the only way they could do that was by getting their forces out to where the threats came from."

"They were threatened by the barbarians. People like your friend Jason Howe."

"Jason isn't a barbarian, and it doesn't matter, because he's harmless now."

"Okay, then habeas corpus. Produce the body; I want him."

"We'll come back to Howe, but let me finish: The Romans had enemies in the provinces, yes, but the real problem was that they were rotting at the core. Rome had lost its confidence and conviction. The empire began to crumble, with commanders grabbing for the spoils. The walls were breached, but not far away, close to home. 'Rome' survived only because the culture had taken root somewhere else, in Byzantium, where it could be protected. Are you following me?"

"Frankly, no. Forget about Pitt and Princeton. I really don't get your point."

"Let's take a break," Goldman said. He stood up and arched his back to stretch his tired muscles. He called for another espresso and a bottle of mineral water. He rubbed some lotion on his tanned face, so that it glowed a silky gold. He looked like he owned the yacht, despite what he'd said. He sat down again, refocused, and turned back to Dunne.

As Goldman was speaking to a member of the staff, Dunne had reached into his pocket and removed a toothpick to clean his teeth. And something else, a tiny object that imperceptibly found its way into the upholstery in this upper lounge.

"Okay, sorry about the Rome lecture," said Goldman. "Here's the simple, straight-up version of what I'm trying to say. Unless you're an idiot, you can see that America is rotting from the inside out, too. It's breaking apart. When America tries to project power, it fails. Iraq, Afghanistan, zilch. When it builds walls, they crumble."

"I've been living that story. America first, baby. What else is new?"

"Well, come on, think about it. That same thing is happening with most other countries. Russia, China, Saudi Arabia, the United Arab Emirates, Britain, Germany, France. They're all stressed. Their wars are as messed up as ours. Ukraine, Yemen, the Uighurs. The big powers are paper tigers, all of them. Power doesn't live in nation-states anymore. It's gone somewhere else."

Dunne arched his eyebrows. "To the *Cosmos*, maybe."

"Clever man. 'World order,' as I told you earlier, for when the normal order isn't working. That's the idea. I represent a group of prominent people from all over the world. We don't want to be on the receiving end of history, we want to shape it. Think of a private group, almost a club, that exists for the preservation of culture. We're 'Byzantine.' And I mean that in the very best way."

"Big ideas make my head hurt, man," said Dunne. "You said we'd talk about Jason Howe later. What about now?"

"Okay, fine." Goldman took the espresso from the steward and took a sip that left a black froth on his lower lip. He dabbed at it with his linen napkin.

"Jason Howe was a test kitchen. He was a trial run. He imagined that he was the director of the show, when he was really just an actor. But that's okay. People make that mistake all the time."

"So, he wasn't the person who took me down."

"He pulled the trigger, but it wasn't his gun. I could explain what happened to you, but it's complicated. And it would only piss you off more, which is a waste of talent. That's why I thought it was easier to offer a new start."

"You motherfucker."

"Excuse me?" Goldman pretended he hadn't heard.

Dunne strode to the edge of the awning. He looked over the side of the railing of this upper deck, as if estimating whether there was space to dive and clear the hull of the boat into the water.

"Motherfucker," he repeated. "A guy who fucks his mother."

Goldman took a deep breath. He finished his espresso. Against Dunne's anger, he was a silk cushion.

"You're an idiot. Seriously. Your idea of vengeance against Howe is understandable, but misplaced. But attacking the larger forces in play here would be completely crazy. You really don't appreciate what's going on."

"This conversation is over," said Dunne. "Take me back to the dock. Or shoot me, or whatever you're planning to do on behalf of your bullshit league of pirates."

Goldman put up his hands in protest. He was a movie star, this one. Peter Pan with a snorkel.

"I'll take you back, of course I will. We're not gangsters. Quite the opposite. We're the good guys. We know how to do things that would make your head spin. Truly, all that crap you did for the CIA is kindergarten compared to the tools we have. We need smart people who can get around corners. Honestly, you're missing the opportunity of a lifetime."

"No. Fucking. Way. I'm going back to my cabin. Knock on my door when we get to Porto Cervo."

"What a pity," Goldman called out after him. "What a damned shame."

Dunne stopped as he reached the salon door, propping his arm against a teakwood shelf.

"I'm touched that you would pay so much attention to a guy with a prison record."

As Dunne made his wisecrack, gesturing dismissively with one hand, he moved the other to insert a sliver of wood, housing another microphone, into the inner corner of the shelf.

"Maybe you have a guilty conscience," said Dunne, heading toward his stateroom.

By the time Dunne was ready to leave the boat, he had placed microphones in its main seating areas, each with a minute radio-frequency transmitter that would feed a parabolic amplifier he intended to plant in the hills above the ghastly billion-dollar marina. The tiny bugs wouldn't last forever, but they would transmit long enough to provide Dunne with more information than he had.

"I could say it was dangerous for you, leaving us like this," said Goldman as he escorted Dunne toward the white leather balustrade of the gangplank. "But that wouldn't motivate you to reconsider, I gather."

"Nope. That's the only good thing about having your life destroyed. Threats don't work very well."

"I could say that you're being incredibly stupid, giving up a potential fortune."

Dunne laughed as he stepped onto the deck. "Why would I want to be rich, if I couldn't be pissed off anymore?"

It was late afternoon when Dunne got back to the hotel. He spent the evening in the bar, watching a series of pretty girls looking at him flirtatiously, and then went to bed.

# 26

Washington, D.C.—October 2016

On the day that Michael Dunne was summoned home to Washington, his wife Alicia Silva was teaching two classes, introductory and intermediate Portuguese, at George Mason University. She was eight months pregnant with their second child. Her belly was so big that she could barely fit behind the wheel of her car. Her face had the radiant glow of expectant motherhood, warming and softening the honey brown of her skin.

Alicia liked her teaching. George Mason was a sprawl of a suburban campus, just outside the Beltway but in the gravitational field of Washington. The university was big and anonymous, but the Portuguese program was tiny, with one permanent faculty member and Alicia as a part-time adjunct. Many of the students were military, foreign service, or intelligence officers preparing for a next assignment. They didn't want to read fancy writers like José Saramago or Antero de Quental, they just wanted to be certified as language-proficient and get on the job.

Which was fine with Alicia. Her Brazilian father had been a brooding doctor who according to family lore had dreamed of being a poet; her mother was a slim, Mozambican-born nurse who had aspired to be a dancer. Over time, Alicia had grown to like uncomplicated people, like her George Mason students and, she thought, like her husband.

Michael had dazzled her when they met in Paris. She was a translator at UNESCO, the tall, beautiful, vivacious Brazilian girl who danced until the sun came up but never went home with anyone. She was a virgin when she met Dunne. She had been waiting for someone like him, she said. "*Amor verdadeiro, não envelhece.*" True love is always the same age.

She liked to sing in bed, or in the car, almost anywhere. Samba, Carnival, Brazilian pop music, or Top 50 songs by Rihanna and Beyoncé. She had named their first daughter Luisa after the most famous pop star in Brazil.

Sometimes Alicia would whisper a Portuguese proverb in Dunne's ear as they were falling asleep. "*A noite é boa conselheira,*" she would say. The pillow is a good counselor. Sometimes, when he had just returned from a long trip, she would wake him in the middle of the night and want to make love again.

Alicia's class ended at seven, so she didn't return home from Fairfax until nearly eight. Michael had texted her that he was arriving that day but had to go to the office first. He had been away nearly two months. Her first thought when she got his text message was joy; now, maybe, he would be home when the baby was born.

Alicia found her husband collapsed on the sofa, his head in his hands. The babysitter had already put their daughter to bed and gone home. Alicia walked toward him. He touched his palm to the fullness of her womb. The crescent bump in her tummy when he left had become the rounded, heavy form of his unborn child. He was smiling, but there was a sadness in his face.

Dunne took his wife in his arms. As he rocked her, tears formed in his eyes. He excused himself and went to the bathroom and poured water on his face. When he looked at the image in the mirror, frightened and hollow-eyed, the face of a condemned man, he choked back tears again.

"*Está tudo bem, meu querido?*" called out Alicia. She knew that something was wrong. Michael asked her if she wanted a drink, but she patted her stomach. He poured himself a vodka over ice, to the rim of the glass. He sat down next to her again on the couch. He took her hand in his. She was trembling.

"I'm in a lot of trouble," he said.

"What is it, my darling? Is it a problem at work?"

"I'm not even sure I understand it. Something went bad. They're investigating me. I don't think I did anything wrong, but they're saying I broke the law and that I should get my own lawyer. The FBI wants to interview me."

"*Oh, meu Deus. Nos salve,*" she whispered. She wasn't religious, but reflexively she made the sign of the cross.

Tears came to Dunne's eyes again. He brushed them away with his sleeve. There was so much he needed to say but couldn't. He looked into her eyes, and then away.

"If people say bad things about me, don't believe them," he said.

"Never." She took his hand. "Never."

"You know I would never hurt you. My work is crazy sometimes, and I make mistakes. But I love you."

"Of course. Why do you say these things? You are scaring me, Michael. It will be okay. Your friends at work will take care of you."

"I don't know," said Dunne. He shook his head. "I don't think so." Now Alicia began to cry.

*　*　*

The next morning, the first newspaper story appeared in the *Washington Post*. Dunne picked the paper up off the lawn at six, standing in his bathrobe as he read the headline, front page, below the fold: "CIA Officer Accused of Spying on Liberal Media Group." Dunne read the story all the way through, standing outside in the October morning chill, the sunlight rising through trees that were nearly bare of their leaves.

The story was a hit job; the first paragraphs quoted congressional sources who had been briefed by the CIA inspector general on a violation of agency regulations that had been discovered overseas. The IG's office hadn't even waited twenty-four hours to brief Congress and leak the story. "Fuck, fuck, fuck," Dunne whispered to himself.

He turned to page A-23 and read the jump. The story was written in the breathless style that newspapers reserve for conduct that's presumed to be scandalous but whose details aren't yet clear enough to describe in simple declarative sentences.

The indignation factor was a presumed CIA attack on the free press. Despite a specific prohibition on agency operations against American journalists, an undercover officer had penetrated the overseas offices of an Internet publication called Fallen Empire, which was run by a crusading American journalist named Jason Howe; the CIA officer had sought to manipulate the news organization for intelligence purposes.

The story quoted an anonymous member of the Senate Intelligence Committee: "Russian intelligence may do things like this, but not the CIA." The head of a press-freedom group was quoted talking about the sanctity of the First Amendment. An unnamed "U.S. official" said that the officer under investigation had exceeded his authority, and that the matter was being referred to the FBI for possible criminal prosecution.

The *Post* story didn't identify Dunne by name, describing him only as an operations officer who had recently returned from assignment abroad. The committee had his name, obviously. The *Post* did, too, probably. It wouldn't stay secret for long. Dunne had watched this process a dozen times with his colleagues. Shit flowed downhill. When a flap surfaced, the officers who had been asked to do the dirty work were advised to get legal counsel.

Dunne finished the piece. His first sensation, other than the burning shame of being the target of a public investigation, was anger at himself for having been so foolish. He had known it was unwise to have trusted George Strafe's assurances, but he had done it anyway.

Dunne thought of hiding the paper from his wife, but when he turned back toward the house, he saw that she had been watching him through the window. He carried the paper inside and gave it to her.

"It's pretty bad," he said.

She read the story, and then walked to the kitchen, where Dunne was glumly eating his breakfast cereal, and put her arms around him. Dunne could feel the baby kick as she pressed against him.

"It doesn't mention your name," she said hopefully.

"The next story will, or the one after that. It will all come out." As Dunne said those last words, he shuddered.

\*    \*    \*

It didn't take long. The *Post* may have been cautious, but the Internet wasn't. Fallen Empire that afternoon published photographs of the supposed Microsoft employee named Edward Spitz who had wheedled his way into the "news organization's" offices in Italy. Microsoft denied that it had ever employed Spitz. His social media history was briefly available, and then deleted, which made it worse. By then Michael Dunne's true name was bouncing around the Internet, along with pictures of him from McKeesport High and the University of Pittsburgh.

The CIA public affairs director asked the *Post* and the *New York Times* not to publish Dunne's name, but when it surfaced on BuzzFeed, the mainstream papers went ahead. They named Dunne, interviewed former classmates, and patched together more comments from human rights groups about what a terrible thing he had done. Other than privately requesting caution in publishing details about sources and methods, the CIA had no comment.

Dunne spent the day at home, in his office on the third floor overlooking the fifth fairway of the nearby golf course. There was early frost on the greens, and the rough looked tangled and brown. Dunne had planned this room as his special place, where he would put his technical books and computer gear. The books were still in boxes, and the only technical equipment Dunne had was a three-year-old Dell laptop.

The FBI had requested an interview the next day. Dunne needed a lawyer, but even more, he needed advice from his former colleagues. Dunne made calls through the day, with mounting anxiety.

He rang George Strafe's office number, but the secretary repeated her line that he was away. He tried the DDO's personal cell number, but the call rolled immediately to voice mail. He phoned the Ops Center and gave them Strafe's personal alias and asked to be connected on an operational matter; but when Dunne supplied his password, the watch officer said it wasn't valid and hung up. When he tried the number again, his call was blocked.

Dunne reached Sarah Gilroy, the assistant deputy director for S&T. The call was put through only because Gilroy's secretary didn't know any better.

"I've been told not to talk to you," said Gilroy.

"By whom?"

"Legal. The Inspector General's Office came yesterday afternoon."

"What did you tell them?"

"I'm not allowed to say. They were very specific about that. They threw around stuff about obstruction of justice and conspiring to interfere in an investigation. Oh, my god! What have you done, Mike?"

"You know very well what I've done. You told me to do it. You asked me to accept a special mission, and then you sent me to see Strafe. Don't hang me out to dry here, Sarah. I know too much."

"Don't threaten me, Mike. And especially not on an open phone line. Any suggestion that I told you to bug an American news organization is false. I should tell you, although I'm not required to, that I am recording this call for my own protection. Get a lawyer. Don't call me back."

Finally, Dunne tried Morris Hoffman. No one answered at the office number; an email to Hoffman's address bounced. He and the group appeared to have vanished from the CIA's grid.

Dunne had Hoffman's home address in Alexandria, so he drove down Glebe Road to Old Town and rang the bell for thirty seconds, until someone inside said, "Stop."

It was Hoffman's voice, but he didn't open the door. Dunne could see the dark of an eyeball on the other end of the peephole. He pounded the door some more until Hoffman opened it a few inches, protected by the chain bolt.

Dunne could see his round, patrician forehead through the crack. He was wearing his bathrobe, in the middle of the day.

"What do you want?" asked Hoffman.

"We need to talk," said Dunne. "I'm being thrown under the bus."

"My lawyer says I am forbidden to talk with you. I'm paying him a lot of money. I need to listen to him."

"What are you telling them about our operation?"

"That it's classified and compartmented, and that I am not authorized to speak about it."

"And they're letting you get away with that."

"I am not getting away with anything. This conversation is over."

"Have you been diming me, Morris?"

"Go away!"

Hoffman slammed the door. Dunne tried ringing the bell and pounding some more. He heard Hoffman's voice through the wooden portal telling him to go away, and after another thirty seconds of useless buzzing and pounding, Dunne left.

Dunne had one last person he trusted, and that was his mentor, Roger Magee. Unlike the others, Magee took his call and proposed to meet at Legal Seafoods in Tysons Corner in thirty minutes.

Magee was wearing jeans and a red-checked woolen shirt. With his long beard, he looked like a lumberjack.

"I told you not to do this," said Magee.

"Spare me, Roger. I don't need another lecture. You're the only friend I've got. What should I do?"

"Get a lawyer. Here's the name of someone I trust. He's at Warren and Frankel. White-shoe firm, but don't let that put you off. He has all the clearances. The agency trusts him. He knows how to clean up a mess. He can help. If he tells you to plead, take his advice."

Magee handed Dunne a card with the lawyer's name, phone number, and email.

"But I didn't do anything wrong, Roger. I just did what Strafe told me."

"My friend, there is a big avalanche of shit that is going to fall on your head if you don't play along here. People haven't told me anything, and I haven't asked. But this is one where I humbly suggest that you take one for the team. Stay down for the count. Don't get up swinging. If you do, it's going to be ugly."

Dunne shook his head. His Scotch-Irish temper was rising. A whole team of friends and counselors couldn't have kept him from fighting back in that moment.

"No fucking way," he said. "I'm not taking a fall for Strafe. I'm going to tell the truth. If that causes problems for anyone, that's just the way it is. They can lawyer up, too. Fuck them."

"Cool down, brother. The world doesn't work that way. You're a little fish in this pond. The big fish eat the little fish."

"I'm not going to play, Roger. I'm sorry. I'll call your lawyer and try to follow his advice. But I won't cave."

"Suit yourself." Magee shrugged. "As I said once before, you have been warned. I don't like to see good people get hurt."

"No point in talking anymore, I guess," said Dunne.

"Nope." Magee turned and walked back toward the parking lot. Dunne sat for a moment on a bench in the restaurant lobby, and then called the lawyer and arranged an appointment for late that afternoon. For the first time in his life, he was truly frightened.

*   *   *

Mark Walden, a spry Warren and Frankel partner in his late sixties, welcomed Dunne to the firm's offices in a showy new building downtown. He had a top-secret security clearance and had represented many CIA officers in past litigation. He was temporarily cleared for Dunne's compartment, so that he could discuss the case with him.

"Maybe you should explain this matter from the beginning," said Walden.

So, Dunne did: He described the first approach from Sarah Gilroy; the meeting with Strafe and the discussion of targeting Fallen Empire and the Quark Team; the legal paperwork he had signed to create the compartment; the anodyne name "European Special Collection" for the office he had shared with Hoffman and the support techs; the forward post in Geneva; the move into Urbino to collect detailed intelligence about the targets.

Walden took careful notes, and stopped Dunne after the first run-through, to focus on details he didn't understand clearly.

"Tell me more about the Geneva and Urbino operations," Walden said. "Was that all authorized?"

"Yes. I was in regular contact with George Strafe. He knew about every move that I was making."

"Just so you know: That's not what he has told the inspector general and, I assume, the FBI. He says that you were on a technical-collection assignment in Geneva but were behaving erratically. He says that there was a personal matter that showed you had been using bad judgment. He considered replacing you then, but didn't, to his subsequent regret. He says it's all documented. You were unstable and off the reservation. That's his version of events."

Dunne groaned as he heard the reference to his personal life. It sounded like a warning. It should have made him scared, but instead it deepened his anger.

"I followed orders. My instructions came directly from the deputy director for operations. I may have made mistakes in my private life, but that's my problem."

"It's not just your problem, I'm afraid. Things like this sometimes become public."

"I pray they don't," said Dunne, his face reddening. "But I'm not backing down."

Walden nodded. He couldn't tell his client what to do. He knew that anger was the least useful emotion in dealing with a complex legal matter. But even if he had tried to explain that, Dunne wouldn't have listened.

"What should I tell the FBI?" asked Dunne. "They want to see me tomorrow morning."

"Don't talk to the FBI. My advice as your lawyer: Don't tell them anything."

"But I didn't do anything wrong. I don't want to look guilty, because I'm not. My best defense is to tell the truth."

"I repeat: My recommendation is don't talk to the FBI."

"But I've worked with the Bureau my whole career. I can't play games with them or take the Fifth. I'd look like a crook."

Walden sighed. A righteous client was a legal liability.

"Your call, in the end," he said. "If you see them tomorrow, tell the truth. It's always a mistake to lie to the FBI. Always."

"What if my version of the truth doesn't match what Strafe and Gilroy and the others are saying?"

Walden sat back in his chair and thought a moment. The lights from the luxury boutiques that surrounded his office were beginning to twinkle. Louis Vuitton. Gucci. Tiffany's. The rewards for playing the game, or having powerful friends protect you if you happened to cheat.

"If there is a conflict about the factual evidence, as I suspect there will be in this case, that ultimately will be up to a judge to resolve. But I don't think it will get that far. The government will offer you a plea agreement, and if it's reasonable, I will advise you to accept it."

"But I didn't do anything wrong," repeated Dunne.

"I believe you. I am your lawyer. But I must caution you that this is a matter where the facts are in dispute. There are a number of powerful people who apparently are prepared to say that you did do something wrong. My job is to get the best outcome for you."

"Too late for that," said Dunne. "My reputation has been destroyed."

Walden glanced at his watch and began tidying his notes. Another client was waiting.

"There's just one more thing," said Dunne. He hadn't been sure how much he would reveal about Strafe's complicity, but it was obvious now that there was no benefit in holding back.

"Please," said Walden gently.

"Strafe warned me that my actions in this operation might technically be illegal, but that if anything went wrong, I would never be prosecuted. And if I was prosecuted, I would never get convicted."

Walden smiled, and then pursed his lips.

"Did you get that in writing?"

"No. Of course not."

"Was anyone else present?"

"No. Just the two of us."

Walden nodded. He looked Dunne in the eye.

"Let me give you a piece of advice. Do not describe that conversation to the FBI. If you do, you will be accusing Mr. Strafe of a serious felony. Perhaps he committed it, but you have no proof. And your own testimony will be insufficient, given the questions about your own reliability. So the principal effect of such a statement will be to reduce the likelihood of the government offering you a favorable plea agreement."

"But what I just told you is true," said Dunne. There was a rasp of frustration and anger in his voice.

Walden sighed. A lawyer could counsel, but not decide.

"Please think about what I said. Would you like me to come with you to the FBI interview tomorrow?"

"I don't know. Would that be a good idea?"

"If you feel you have criminal jeopardy, certainly."

"I didn't do anything wrong," Dunne repeated. "I don't want you telling me to shut up."

"Then go alone. And tell the truth. And don't start a fight you can't finish."

# 27

Washington, D.C.—October 2016

The FBI Washington Field Office was a bland, eight-story limestone block in the hodgepodge of construction between the Capitol and Pennsylvania Avenue. It was framed by the red-brick hulk of a building constructed in the 1880s to process pension checks for Civil War veterans, which was now a museum, and a little Catholic church where penitent special agents could duck out for confession and Mass in the lunch hour.

Dunne entered the front door alone. He had breezed through the entrance before when he came to meetings with the Bureau on surveillance plans. But now he had surrendered his CIA badge, and the privileges of access. He was an ordinary person—worse than that, a suspect in a criminal case—and was alone and unprotected against the weight of a government that had identified him as a target.

A security officer escorted Dunne to an interrogation room, where two special agents greeted him solemnly. Candy Velazquez was a short Latina woman; Jeff Rudd was a tall, bull-necked man with a shaved head. They both wore the bulky black suits that were the FBI dress code. Dunne wore a blue blazer, white shirt, and a tie that was fraying along the edges.

Velazquez, who was the senior agent, read Dunne his Miranda rights. She was meticulous. "You must understand your rights before we ask you any questions." He nodded. "You do not have to make any statement or answer any questions." He said he understood. "Any statement you make or any answers you give may be used against you in a court of law or other proceedings." Right. "You have the right to talk to a lawyer for advice before you answer any questions and you have the right to have a lawyer present during the interview." Okay.

Even with that preamble, Velazquez still asked Dunne to sign a written waiver of his rights. As he did, he could see Rudd staring at him across the table, wondering, maybe, how Dunne had gotten himself in such a mess.

"Do you know my friend Rick Bogdanovich?" asked Dunne, as he was signing the waiver. It was an inappropriate, ingratiating remark and he regretted it immediately.

"We don't know anyone by that name," said Velazquez coldly. "Let's begin the interview. We appreciate your voluntary cooperation, which will be noted favorably in any report that's made to the U.S. Attorney."

Dunne took a drink of water from the bottle on the table. They hadn't even begun the interview, and they were already talking about a criminal referral.

"Just to be clear, we are recording this interview on audio and video."

"Fine. Go ahead."

"We have received a referral from the CIA inspector general." She was reading from a paper in front of her, to make sure she got the details right. "The inspector general found 'reasonable grounds' to believe that you violated Executive Order 12333, specifically the section that requires intelligence-community personnel to, and I am quoting, 'protect fully the legal rights of all United States persons, including freedoms, civil liberties, and privacy rights guaranteed by Federal law,' and the section that forbids any covert action, quote, 'intended to influence United States political processes, public opinion, policies, or media.'"

"I deny violating anything. I didn't do anything wrong."

"Hold on, Mr. Dunne. We'll get to all that. I need to read you what's on my sheet."

"Okay, sorry."

Velazquez looked down at her paper again.

"We are conducting this interview because Section 1.7(a) of Executive Order 12333 requires senior officials of the Intelligence Community to report to the attorney general possible violations of the federal criminal laws by employees, in a manner consistent with the protection of intelligence sources and methods."

"Is that it? For the boilerplate, I mean?"

"Yes, that's it," she said, putting the paper in her black briefcase. She didn't like reading the canned legalese any more than he liked hearing it, but it was required.

"Now, rather than me asking you questions, Mr. Dunne, perhaps you could just tell us what happened in your dealings with the journalistic organization called Fallen Empire, which is headed by a U.S. person named Jason Howe, who falls under the protection of Executive Order 12333. We call it a 'free narrative.' You can tell us what happened, from your recollection. How does that sound?"

Dunne cleared his throat and then faced them with a look that said: *Here goes.*

"I did what I was ordered to do, by my boss. Like I said, I didn't do anything wrong."

"Could you be more specific?"

"I was asked by George Strafe, the deputy director for operations, to conduct a special collection operation to gather information about a group operating overseas, with the same name you used, 'Fallen Empire,' same person, 'Jason Howe,' and some associates who called themselves the Quark Team. I asked Mr. Strafe if this was a covert action, because I knew we couldn't do that without a finding from the White House, and he said no, it was just collection. Because Howe was an American, I asked if that would violate the rules—all the gobbledygook you just read. And he said no. Howe's group had been in contact with a Serbian intelligence officer, and that made it a legitimate collection target."

Dunne reached into his blazer pocket for a sheet on which he had written some notes.

"There was also an undeclared Russian intelligence officer later, operating from Germany. We received a liaison report that he had met with the Fallen

Empire group in Urbino, Italy, and after that, with Mr. Strafe's approval, I went in."

Rudd spoke up. "You don't need to share classified information with us if it's not relevant." He was from the Counterintelligence Division, Dunne guessed.

"But it is relevant. It was the legal justification for the operation."

Velazquez and Rudd both made brief scribbles in their notebooks. They didn't ask any questions, so Dunne continued.

"I wasn't sure it was kosher in the beginning, so I asked Mr. Strafe what would happen if I got caught. Suppose Fallen Empire cracked my cover, and put out a press release saying there was a CIA witch hunt or something, what would happen then?"

"And what did Deputy Director Strafe say, allegedly?" asked Velazquez.

Dunne took a deep breath. He looked at the two special agents across the desk in this tight, low-ceilinged interrogation room. He hated being in this situation. He wasn't a rat. But if you were threatened, you had to fight back, or you would be destroyed. He felt dizzy for a moment. He closed his eyes, and then opened them and began to speak.

"Mr. Strafe said that if anything went wrong, he would take care of it. Fix it. He said that even if there was a flap, nobody would prosecute me, and if they went ahead, they wouldn't get a conviction."

"How could he promise you that?" asked Rudd. "The Justice Department makes decisions about prosecution."

"I know. I was stupid. I shouldn't have paid any attention. But I did."

"Do you have any record of this alleged exchange with Deputy Director Strafe?"

"No. It was in his office. We don't take notes about stuff like this. Sorry."

"Did you report it to anyone? I mean, if what you say is true, you were being asked to do something illegal. You had an obligation to tell the inspector general. Did you do that?"

"No. This is the CIA. Not the Boy Scouts. When we get an order from the boss, we follow it."

"What about any of your friends? Did you tell any of them?"

Dunne thought a long moment about his friend Roger Magee, who had in fact warned him against taking the assignment. Magee had spent his whole career avoiding mistakes like the one Dunne had made. If Dunne named him as a confidant, the FBI would be up his ass in twenty-four hours. Dunne didn't know whether Magee would back him up, but he didn't want to put him in that situation. Dunne would have to clean up his own mess.

"No," he said. "I didn't tell any friends."

"So there is no record of any kind, written or oral, to corroborate the allegations that you have made about Deputy Director Strafe."

"Just my word. And I'm telling you the truth. I did what I was told. I didn't do anything wrong."

*　*　*

They spent another ninety minutes taking Dunne through the details of his account. After the free narrative, they switched to rote questions. The agents were trying to fill in pieces of the chronology they'd received from the CIA, rather than add new facts. It was only near the end of the session that they asked a question that made Dunne's stomach tighten.

"Who is Veronika Kruse?" asked Rudd.

Dunne didn't say anything at first. He took a drink from the water bottle. Rudd and Velazquez waited. "Take as much time as you need," she said.

"Veronika Kruse is a woman I met in Geneva. I met her at a club."

"Did you have any reason to believe that she was a security risk? That she could compromise your operation?"

"No. Not in the beginning. Then, later, I don't know. I can tell you what happened. Probably you already know."

"We don't need to ask you any more questions about her now. All we want to know now is whether she tried to obtain any classified information from you."

"No," said Dunne. "That wasn't the problem."

"I see. What was the problem?"

"Personal."

They let it lie. They didn't pursue the matter of Veronika Kruse, and the interview ended a few minutes later.

Dunne left the FBI Washington Field Office with a sense of dread. He thought he should go home and warn his wife what might be coming. But by the time he got there, it was too late.

# 28

Washington, D.C.—October 2016

Alicia Silva was sitting at the breakfast table in the kitchen, staring at her laptop computer, when Dunne returned home. There was a box of tissues next to her. When Dunne entered the room, she looked away. "*Desgraçado,*" she said, barely audible. She closed the lid of her laptop and went into the bathroom. Their four-year-old daughter Luisa was taking a nap on the couch in the living room; Alicia checked her and closed the living room door. When she returned to the kitchen, she stared at Dunne. The corners of her lips were trembling.

"How could you?" she said. "I've always loved you. You were my only love."

"We need to talk," said Dunne. He pointed to the computer. "What have you been looking at?"

"What is Stylet?" she asked coldly.

"It means stiletto, in French," answered Dunne.

"I know that," she said. "What were you doing at the Stylet Club in Geneva?"

"How do you know about that?"

"Someone sent me an email. It said you were at this club with a woman. They sent me pictures. You pig."

"What pictures?" said Dunne.

This last bland, equivocating question from Dunne drove Alicia into a fury. She picked up a coffee cup from the counter and threw it at him. It missed his head and hit the wall with a splintering crash that woke the four-year-old sleeping in the next room.

"Pictures of you and this naked woman," she screamed. "This one. Right here! You see? She has her hand on your cock. Big tits. Brazilian wax. Did she blow you or fuck you? I cannot look at you. You're a liar and a cheater and a shit. I'm leaving!"

The child was wailing now at the sound of her mother's screams. Alicia waddled into the next room. She took Luisa in her arms, wrapped her in a coat, and whispered to her in Portuguese as she walked to the door.

"*Nós estamos indo embora. Eu vou cuidar de você minha querida. Nós vamos encontrar uma nova casa.*" We're leaving him, my darling. We'll find a new home.

Alicia took her purse and a warm coat, and a bag by the door that Dunne had overlooked when he arrived. She slammed the door behind her and carried the child to the car.

*   *   *

Dunne sat down at the kitchen table and looked at the computer screen. The image had the grainy look of a tabloid photo: the flash of the camera illuminating her white skin; the sheen of the blond hair against the dark, empty room; the slight bend in her knee as the hand reached toward him. And the absurd, humiliating portrait of a man with his trousers and shorts around his ankles, staring wide-eyed at the camera in the horror of being exposed.

Dunne shut the lid of the laptop. "I'm a fool," he muttered, and then a whimpering groan. He ran to the door to chase after his wife, but Alicia was gone.

He returned to his seat at the counter. He was shivering, though it wasn't cold. The screen of the laptop wasn't quite closed. It gave off a glow around the edges. He took out his cell phone to call his lawyer, Mark Walden, and then put it away. What would he say?

Dunne raised the screen again. The photograph had been sent as an attachment to an email. It came from a throwaway address, "stilettogirl674@yahoo .com." If Dunne had still been a member of the intelligence community, he might have been able to track the sender, but not now.

*Thought you should know . . .* was the subject line of the email. The body of the message read: *The Spy Michael Dunne at Stylet Club in Geneva, September 27, 2016, with Veronika Kruse, before he attacked the Citizen Journalists.*

"Motherfuckers," Dunne muttered. He wondered for a moment how they had gotten Alicia's email address, but that was so easy. They had everything.

Dunne went upstairs and put on a sweater to stop his shivering. He returned to the open laptop. His fingers paused above the keyboard. If they would do this, what else would they do? He typed his name into the Google search box.

At the top of the list was the *Post* story from two days before, but below that was a new web posting from Fallen Empire, with the headline "CIA Snoop Caught in Sex Club." It showed the top half of the lurid picture, with Veronika's face blurred. Other sites weren't so chaste. A web search quickly turned up a dozen copies of the full photo, on Reddit and 4chan. Dunne's humiliation had gone viral.

Dunne's hand was shaking. His bowels felt loose. He coughed as if something were caught in his throat, but he was gagging on his own shame and revulsion.

He needed to call Walden. He took some deep breaths as he punched the lawyer's number into the phone. When Walden's secretary asked why he was calling, he wouldn't answer. "Private matter," he said. She wouldn't put him through without an explanation, but Walden called back five minutes later, upbeat and solicitous.

"Hey, Michael, how did the FBI interview go?" he asked. "I need a debrief."

"I'll get to that," Dunne said. "Something bad has happened. I am all fucked up here. My wife has left me."

"Slow down. Tell me what happened."

"It's pathetic, I'm sorry. Someone sent Alicia a photograph of a naked woman holding my penis in her hand. She went nuts. She took our daughter and left. She's eight months pregnant. What am I supposed to do? The picture is all over the Internet."

"One step at a time. First, is the picture real?"

"Yes. I'm such an asshole. The woman's name is Veronika Kruse. Can you get it taken down?"

"Probably. Not everywhere, but most sites will delete it. Do you know who sent it?"

"They're punishing me," said Dunne. There was a tremor in his voice.

"What are you talking about? Who's punishing you?"

"Everybody. The people I was spying on. Maybe someone at the agency. George Strafe knew about the photograph, because I told him. I don't know, but this is payback from somebody."

"Calm down. Don't blame your colleagues. Things don't work like that."

"The FBI asked me about the woman in the photograph. They asked if Veronika Kruse had requested any classified information. How did they know about her, if someone didn't tell them?"

"Don't jump to conclusions, Michael. You're stressed. It will only make things worse. I'll contact the General Counsel's Office when we hang up. All right?"

"It won't make any difference, but okay." Dunne took a breath. He didn't want to look weak and disoriented. Not with his lawyer, or anyone.

"What else did you tell the FBI?" asked Walden. "I hope you were careful."

"I was truthful. I told them that George Strafe authorized everything I did and that he promised that if anything went wrong, he would fix it. The Feebs asked if I had any proof, or if I'd told anyone about what Strafe told me. I said no. Then the email with the dirty picture arrived."

"I wish you hadn't made the accusation against Strafe. It won't help. But we'll settle this case. Believe me. I've been in many negotiations with the agency that were more complicated than this."

"I don't want to settle. I didn't do anything wrong."

"Let me be the lawyer for a while, and you be the client. Okay? Tell me what else the FBI asked about."

Dunne was going to argue again, but he caught himself. Walden was right. He was just digging a deeper hole. He summarized his interview with the two special agents: what he had said in his own narrative, and then the interrogatory, back and forth. Walden took notes and stopped Dunne every few sentences to clarify. It was reassuring, to have someone else worrying about him.

"Send me the picture of you and the woman, please," Walden said when they had finished the reprise of the FBI interview.

"Give me a break. Is that necessary?"

"Sorry, I know it's embarrassing, but I can't get websites to take down a photograph unless I have a copy of it. I'll have a couple of my associates start calling social media companies as soon as we get the picture."

"I want to die," said Dunne.

"Stop it!" said Walden sharply. "Pull yourself together. If you'd like me to talk with your wife, I'd be happy to."

"I think she'll want a divorce lawyer," Dunne said. He meant it as a wisecrack, but as he said the words, he knew they were true.

\* \* \*

Alicia returned just after seven that night. A cold October wind blew some leaves over the threshold. She was holding their daughter. Her face was wan; her lips were dry; her eyes were puffy from tears.

"Mommy has been crying," said Luisa. "She's upset."

Dunne tried to embrace his wife, but she pulled back. She spoke coldly, flatly, the life crushed from her voice.

"I didn't come back for you, Michael. I need to be in the house. It's bad for my new baby if I leave now. And for Luisa. She doesn't know what's wrong, seeing her mother like this."

Dunne reached to comfort his daughter, but she cringed and grabbed for her mother's blouse. She was a striking child, with her father's red hair and her mother's radiant skin. Alicia put her down, but she continued to cling to her mother.

"I want you to leave this house tomorrow," Alicia said. "I've talked to a lawyer. I want us to meet with him as soon as possible."

"You want a divorce?" asked Dunne.

"Yes." She put her head in her hands. The tears came again. "Oh, Michael, my heart is broken."

"I'm so ashamed. I don't know how to make it better."

"I loved you so much." She said the words despondently. In the past tense. Dunne struggled for some way to connect with the woman who had slipped away from him.

"Let me get you something to eat. Have you eaten dinner? Or a cup of tea, or something."

"I can't keep anything down," she answered. "I keep throwing up. But get Luisa something simple."

Dunne knelt toward his daughter. He wanted desperately to be useful to someone.

"Do you want some cereal, Lou?" he asked. "Or some scrambled eggs?"

"Lucky Charms," she said, staring up at him. He reached out his arms, and she deliberated and then let him pick her up.

Dunne went to the kitchen and filled a bowl with cereal. Luisa sat at the table while he poured the milk. "Apple juice?" he asked.

"Yes, please." He gave her the glass, and then kissed her forehead.

"I'm going to talk to Mommy," he said. "I think she's thirsty."

Dunne poured a glass of Gatorade and brought it to his wife in the living room. Alicia waved him off.

"You need to drink something. You'll get dehydrated otherwise. Take a sip." She tipped the glass toward her lips but gagged at the taste.

"I can't," she said. "Not now."

"You need fluids. You'll get sick."

"I am sick. I'm going upstairs to bed. You can sleep on the couch in your study on the third floor."

"What about Luisa?"

"I called Heidi's mom next door, Annie. She's coming in a few minutes. Luisa is going to have a sleepover with Heidi tonight."

"Okay," said Dunne. He wasn't fit even to be in the same house with his daughter.

When the doorbell rang, Alicia walked Luisa out to meet the next-door neighbor. Dunne watched his daughter walk away, trying not to cry.

"Goodbye, Daddy," she said.

"I need a hug," Dunne called out, as his daughter was almost to the door.

He took Luisa in his arms and held her tightly, as if there might never be another time. She looked at him quizzically when he finally let her go.

"It's okay, Daddy. Mommy will feel better."

Alicia tried to smile, but it didn't hold. She took her daughter's hand, whispered something in her friend Annie's ear, gave her daughter a kiss, and closed the door. She walked past Dunne in the living room, but he called to her.

"Hey. Can we talk?"

"Not now. I'm going to bed."

"Drink some water, darling."

"I tried. It didn't stay down. I'll try again in a little while. Don't call me darling." She took slow, square-footed steps up the stairway to her bedroom.

\*   \*   \*

Dunne lay on the couch, eyes open, his mind a black knot of disgust. From the bedroom he heard muffled sobs from his wife, interrupted every half hour by her unsteady steps toward the bathroom and the sound of her dry retch over the toilet. He went upstairs when he couldn't bear to hear her suffer any longer.

"I'm frightened for you, baby," he said. "I'll take you to the doctor."

"Go away!" she wailed.

"Take a pill so you can sleep, at least."

"I can't," she said, sobbing again. "It will hurt my baby."

"What about aspirin?"

"I've already taken some. I'm cramping and I'm hot. I can take care of myself."

"Please, please," he said.

"Go upstairs. Leave the house tomorrow. That's all I want."

The phone rang just before midnight. Dunne picked up the extension and listened into the call.

"Are you Mrs. Alicia Dunne?"

"Silva is my last name, but yes. Who is this? What do you want?"

"I'm Jennifer Paige from the *New York Examiner*. I'm calling to check an item we're running on page three tomorrow."

"I don't want to talk," said Alicia. Her voice was as thin as a frayed piece of thread.

"Please don't hang up, Mrs. Dunne. I know what you're going through. We just want to get the facts right. Is it true that you're getting a divorce because your husband cheated on you? We have the picture. How terrible. I'm so sorry. Has he been fired from the CIA, your husband?"

"Please stop," she said. Her voice was barely audible now.

"Were there other women, Mrs. Dunne, besides the blond one in the picture? You've seen the picture, right? Just to confirm."

"Agh!" It was between a whimper and a sigh, as if she had been pierced by a knife but had too little strength to scream.

Dunne heard a click as the phone went dead. It rang again a few moments later, but Alicia let it continue until Dunne heard the beeping noise of a phone off the hook, and then silence. She was crying again, a low moan.

He went to her room again and knocked softly on her door.

"Go away," she said. "Just go away."

"I think we should we go to the hospital."

"Not now. Tomorrow. Leave me alone. Please, that's all I ask."

Dunne retreated to his study on the third floor and listened as she cried and gagged. He thought of calling an ambulance but decided that would be a last assault on her dignity and privacy.

Just after two a.m., she was quiet. Dunne tiptoed down to her second-floor bedroom and listened at the door for the sound of her breathing, to make sure that she was alive.

*    *    *

Dunne came downstairs the next morning. Alicia was already in the kitchen, hollow-eyed. She had a bowl of Raisin Bran in front of her getting soggy in the milk. She looked up at Dunne reproachfully, and tried a tiny spoonful. She nibbled at a few flakes and put the spoon back.

"I'm spotting," she said.

"What does that mean?"

"I'm bleeding."

"We should go to the hospital now."

"I'm waiting for the contractions to begin. Otherwise they'll just send me home."

Dunne reached out his hand to feel her distended belly and the baby inside.

"Don't touch me," she said. She lifted another soggy half spoonful toward her mouth.

Dunne hear the ping of a WhatsApp message on his mobile phone. Alicia's phone made the same noise an instant afterward. Someone was sending them a message. They both ignored the alert at first, and then Alicia pulled the screen toward her.

Alicia clicked the green WhatsApp icon. Dunne leaned toward her and saw that a new message was highlighted. *Pictures of someone you know*, read the first few words. Alicia held the phone tight in her hand; as sick as she was, she was still burning with jealous rage and hurt.

"What else?" she screamed. "*Você é o diabo!*"

Alicia clicked the icon. The screen displayed a sequence of a pictures taken with a cell phone camera. The first showed a naked woman in bed, flawless gold skin, a radiant glow of love on her face. The second caught her from behind, as she was about to get dressed and looked back toward the camera. The third showed the woman sunning herself on a private beach, her skin oiled and glistening in the sun.

With each click, Alicia struggled for breath. Then came an enraged cry from the core.

"This is me! My body! *Mãe de Deus*. How could you?" She moved to strike him, but she lacked the strength and instead collapsed on the table, sobbing.

Dunne tried to speak, but that roused her to greater fury, and now she was pounding his chest.

"You liar. You promised that you deleted these pictures. Did you sell them?"

Dunne tried again to speak, but he was so stunned himself, all he managed was to choke out the words, "I'm sorry."

"Dirty pig liar. You promised me! *Que Deus te destrua*."

From Alicia's phone there was the sound of two more pings, as the phone registered new messages. Dunne reached for hers, but she was quicker.

*Naughty Girl*, read the subject line.

"Bastard. Bastard. Bastard," she raged as she pounded the icon with her thumb.

Alicia gagged as she clicked on two more images. Dunne saw that these weren't erotic pictures. They were raw pornography. The first showed the same honey-colored woman, the same sweet face, but now her lips were formed around a man's penis. The second caught the woman atop the man, her hands clasped behind her head, her eyes closed in a moment of ecstasy.

Alicia fell to the floor in a swoon. Her belly hit first. She was silent for a moment, as if mortally stricken, and then began a piercing scream that lasted until her breath gave out.

Dunne fell to the floor beside her. Her forehead was burning hot.

"Oh, my God, my God," Dunne wailed.

"I want to die," she groaned, hiding her face. "How could you do this to me? I have nothing left. Who will take care of my babies?"

Dunne choked back the vomit in his mouth.

"I didn't take these. Baby, darling, please. These are fakes. Someone wants to ruin us." He tried to stroke the back of her head, but she recoiled.

Her voice was a dark whisper, near the edge of consciousness.

"I don't believe you. You only lie."

"Please, Alicia, breathe."

"Go away," she whimpered. She was tightening in a ball, but the pressure increased the flow from her womb.

"I'm taking you to the hospital," said Dunne, reaching for arm.

"No!" she moaned. "No. Don't touch me. I'll get myself and my baby there myself. You have destroyed me. At least my new child will never know you."

Dunne touched her belly. He felt kicks, but they were irregular. The V of her elastic pants, between her legs, was wet with blood.

Dunne took the phone.

"Let me call. Go away. Let me call," Alicia moaned. She was too weak to stand.

Dunne called 911.

"I need an ambulance now," he said. "I think my wife is going into labor. She's bleeding. Something's wrong. A miscarriage."

"How many weeks pregnant is she, sir?" asked the dispatcher.

"Eight months."

"It's not a miscarriage. She's having the baby. What's your address, sir? Tell me slowly, number and street."

Dunne gave the address. "Come quick," he said. "Please. Right now."

He put a cool washcloth on Alicia's forehead and a pillow under her head, and made her lie flat and bring her knees up so he could clean underneath. She was so weak and feverish now that she didn't resist. He ran upstairs and threw a fresh set of clothes and underwear into a canvas bag, along with her toothbrush, and then went back to his wife, who was half delirious on the floor.

"It's going to be okay," he said. "Stay with me."

He felt her belly again. The kicks were less frequent, and feebler. A new pool of blood had formed beneath her.

Dunne took Alicia's hand. "Please, God." He murmured a prayer, half aloud, the words set against her pants and moans.

A few minutes later, Dunne heard the siren of the ambulance, and then a ring at the doorbell. The emergency team moved Alicia tenderly onto a gurney and asked her questions, but her answers were only half coherent.

Dunne followed them out the door to ride with Alicia in the ambulance. She protested "No!" but Dunne and the technicians ignored her. As they loaded the gurney into the ambulance, Dunne took out his phone and stared at its toxic, radioactive face. He was about to hurl the device against the pavement, but the technician pulled him into the vehicle. The siren was already wailing, and the lights were blinking red.

*   *   *

Dunne's son died that morning at Virginia Hospital Center. Alicia was severely dehydrated and had a high fever, so the doctor recommended that the dead baby be removed by cesarean section. Dunne consented. He sat in the waiting room for many hours, until the operation was done and his wife was out of the recovery room.

A nurse brought him a manila envelope. "Would you like a picture?" she asked.

"Of what?" Dunne answered.

"Of your baby boy. He's with God now, but maybe you would like to see what he looked like."

Dunne was numb. "What did my wife say? Did she want the photograph?"

"We haven't asked her yet. She's still recovering from surgery."

Dunne took the envelope and pulled out a somber black-and-white image. The dead child was laid out in a plastic tray. He had a little cloth cap on his head. His mouth was open. The tiny eyelids were closed. Tears streamed down Dunne's cheek. He handed the photograph back to the nurse.

"I don't want to keep it. Maybe my wife will. When can I see her?"

"We'll let you know when she's ready," said the nurse.

Dunne waited until late that night, asking every hour or so whether his wife was ready for a visit. Eventually a nurse came out and asked Dunne to join him in a private room. At first he thought he would see Alicia there, but that wasn't it.

"Your wife doesn't want to see you. She's too upset. She asked me to tell you that. She has seen a priest, and a counselor, and her mother is on the way from Brazil. Your wife wants her mom to take care of your daughter when she arrives. She said that until she gets here, the child will stay with your neighbor."

"Alicia said that? She doesn't want me to be with Luisa?"

"She told me that you had already moved out of the house, Mr. Dunne."

Dunne turned away to hide his emotion, then turned back with a tearful plea.

"Please, nurse. I need to see my wife. I need to tell her something." Dunne was choking back sobs, trying not to give way yet to the black tide of grief.

"Not now," the nurse said gently. "She needs to heal. You both do. Get some sleep. Would you like to see a counselor or minister? We can help with that. You've had a terrible loss."

"No," said Dunne. There wasn't anyone he wanted to talk to, in truth, except Alicia.

"I'm sorry," said the nurse. "I'll keep the picture of your son for a few days, in case you change your mind."

"Give it back to me," Dunne said quietly. "I've changed my mind." He took the manila envelope with the picture inside and clutched it in his hands.

# 29

Arlington, Virginia—December 2016

Michael Dunne moved into a studio apartment on Lee Highway in Arlington. It was a dreary home, but it suited his mood. He joined a CrossFit gym nearby and punished himself physically. The most pleasurable parts of his day were when he became so exhausted and depleted from exercise that he couldn't think. He began drinking more heavily to get to sleep, but he was still waking up in the middle of the night, so he cut back on the booze and began taking pills, which didn't help him sleep, either.

Alicia's mother moved into the tidy house by the golf course in Arlington, and she guarded Alicia and Luisa ferociously. Dunne wasn't welcome there, and he didn't protest. He picked up Luisa every Saturday morning and played with her all day, but he returned her by dinnertime. He knew that his one-room apartment on a suburban street overlooking a tattoo parlor and a body-piercing studio wasn't the right place for a four year old.

Dunne didn't contest the divorce. Alicia asked for sole custody of their daughter, and Dunne didn't fight that, either. He knew that Alicia's lawyer could present evidence of his gross infidelity and whisper to the judge how the father had cruelly allowed dissemination of X-rated pictures of his wife; but it wasn't simply that. After what Dunne had been through, he wasn't sure that he merited custody rights. His actions had destroyed the happiness and stability of his family. They had led unintentionally to the death of his unborn child. He didn't deserve anything.

Dunne was technically on leave from the agency, suspended with pay pending resolution of the FBI criminal investigation. He sent most of the money to Alicia. He had lost his badge and his clearances, so he couldn't go to the agency, and none of his old colleagues would see him, except Roger Magee. The two would go drinking, and talk about sports and, occasionally, politics. Magee loved Donald Trump, and when Trump won in November, the two men stayed up until three a.m. election night drinking tequila shots. Dunne couldn't get drunk enough to stop thinking about what he had done to his wife—and what others had done to them both.

Dunne's remorse deepened after the first weeks into a gnawing hunger for revenge. He brooded over every step he had taken along the path to personal and professional ruin. His mind became a slow-motion, stop-frame video, starting from his first conversation with Sarah Gilroy all the way to the labyrinth of destruction constructed by Jason Howe and the Quark Team of hackers. Dunne had penetrated the bandit lair of Fallen Empire and become its victim. How had that happened?

Mark Walden gave Dunne a small windowless cubicle at the offices of Warren and Frankel downtown, where he could plug in his computer and do research about his case. He sat there in anguished retrospection day after day, trying to reconstruct the catastrophe that had surrounded the operation with the anodyne name, European Special Collection. He reviewed the Fallen Empire websites and message groups he had examined a few months before with his team, Adrian White and Arthur Gogel. He saw the same babble of competing message platforms, each trying to outdo the other in outrage. He remembered his talks with Jason Howe in Italy, and the glimpse Howe had offered of his technical suite. What were they building? Whose hand was on the switch? Dunne didn't understand now any better than he had two months before.

At the heart of this puzzle was the most grotesque mystery of all. Who would assault his wife with the most intimate and embarrassing photographs, first real and then doctored, in a way that had caused her to have a breakdown and lose a baby? It was an attack on Dunne, but to what end? And who would be capable of such cruelty?

As much as he disliked George Strafe, it was hard for Dunne to imagine a colleague stealing images from an old cell phone, unconnected to the Internet—and then sending them to Dunne and his wife at a moment of maximum vulnerability. Harder still to imagine a deliberate manipulation of the images of this flawless, blameless woman. That required a viciousness that Dunne associated with criminal syndicates in Latin America or Eastern Europe. He had never seen those qualities in his CIA colleagues, not even Strafe.

As for Veronika Kruse, someone had set Dunne up. But if it had been Strafe, why had he used the blackmail material when he did? What was the leverage people wanted on him? Had they been saving it for later? The questions knocked around Dunne's brain like pachinko balls, but they didn't come to rest.

Dunne looked for new electronic traces of the Quark Team networks, but after the election, the wires began to go cold. Fallen Empire's posts were mostly rote repurposing of items found on other left-wing websites. He read a story online, from Wired, that said the NSA had secretly replaced all its malware implanted abroad, after discovery that hackers had tampered with its beacons.

Jason Howe, Lorenzo Riccci, and the other Quark Team technicians Dunne had met during his foray in Urbino seemed to have vanished. Had they been caught, or disbanded, or recruited for something else? Or maybe they had never existed in the first place. Digito Urbino, too, had vanished from the web. Like an electronic Brigadoon, it had disappeared in the mist.

After the election, the newspapers couldn't stop talking about Russian hacking. Dunne wondered why reporters didn't ask about the "citizen journalists" who had helped the Russians turn the global information space into a free-fire zone. These Wiki-crusaders had fronted for the Russians, carried their messages, acted as their cutouts. Dunne made a cold call one day using an encrypted Signal line to a reporter at the New York Times who was famous for his scoops about cyber war.

Dunne used a fake name. He said he was a former CIA officer with damaging information about a group called Fallen Empire and a hacking operation in Italy called the Quark Team. The reporter chuckled. "You mean the Dunne case?" he said. "Yeah, we've looked into that. What an asshole. Otherwise, we don't think there's much there."

Dunne's dislike for journalists grew the more he dealt with them. They knew everything and nothing.

Dunne tried contacting former friends in the agency, despite Walden's admonitions not to do so. Most had changed their numbers. Adrian White and Arthur Gogel, the members of Dunne's team, had disappeared completely. The few who answered texts or Signal calls said they couldn't talk.

Dunne was too hot to touch. He had violated regulations. He had wandered into a sex trap. His wife had divorced him. The agency had cut him loose. His former colleagues knew what everyone knew. Talking to Dunne was like drinking an Ebola cocktail.

When Dunne listened to supporters of the new president-elect talk about the "deep state," the conspiracy of intelligence officers who really ran the country, he wondered if maybe they were right. His friend Roger Magee had started wearing a MAKE AMERICA GREAT AGAIN hat when they went drinking on Old Dominion Drive. But when Dunne pushed him about whether the new administration might review his case, Magee waved him off.

"This is all bullshit," he said. "Cop a plea. Do your time. Forget about it."

Alicia decided in November to move to Los Angeles. She applied for a job teaching Portuguese at the University of California at Irvine, starting in the fall term of 2017. Until then, she would do part-time tutoring and translation work for a Brazilian aircraft company that had offices in Los Angeles. California was on the other side of the country, which meant that Dunne wouldn't be able to see his child, but he didn't try to talk her out of the move. She planned to leave in January.

They put the house on the market in early December. It sold within a week for the asking price. The house had nearly $500,000 equity. Dunne said that his ex-wife and daughter could have nearly all of it. Money couldn't remove the pain he had caused, but it would help pay the bills. Dunne kept $50,000 in the bank for emergencies. He had a legal insurance policy that was paying his lawyer's bills at Warren and Frankel, for now.

A week before Christmas, Mark Walden summoned Dunne to his corner office downtown. He said he had just received a formal notification from the U.S. Attorney's Office in Alexandria that Dunne was the target of a grand jury investigation, and that he would be named in a sealed indictment early in the new year unless he accepted a negotiated plea. The initial offer from the prosecutors was that Dunne must plead guilty to three felony counts, with a sentencing recommendation of three to five years in prison.

"Are you kidding me?" responded Dunne. "How can they squeeze three counts out of a nothing case?"

"They're claiming that you lied to the FBI about Strafe and your instructions. That's two counts. The other one is for criminal violation of agency regulations."

Dunne shook his head. "No way. Strafe is the one who's lying. This is bullshit."

"I think I can bargain it down," said Walden. "I'm going to ask for one count, with a sentencing recommendation of community service."

"Can you get that?"

"Probably not. They'll want you to do some jail time. The media will crucify the Justice Department if it goes easy on someone who attacked the press, and so will the oversight committees."

"But it's all crap. Can we fight it?"

"You can try, but you'll probably lose. And your legal insurance probably won't cover a trial, if you decide to reject the settlement. It will be expensive. I strongly recommend that you take the plea agreement, if I can bargain it to one count."

"And if I want to take it to trial? Will you represent me?"

Walden looked at Dunne, and then glanced away, out the window to the Louis Vuitton store across the courtyard.

"I don't think so. I've given you my best recommendation. If you reject it, you would be wise to seek alternative counsel that sees the case the way you do."

"You're all I've got, Mark. I've been fucked by everyone. Come on."

"I'm giving you the best advice I can. Let me settle this case. That's in your best interest, and your family's."

Dunne thought about it overnight. When he made his decision, he slept well for the first time in several months.

The next morning, he called Walden and told him to begin settlement negotiations. If the prosecutors would agree to a single felony count, Dunne would plead guilty.

# 30

Costa Smeralda, Sardinia—June 2018

The spring sun was setting on Sardinia's western horizon, and a thin late afternoon mist was rising in ribbons of vapor. The shimmering sea began to dull into deep blue patches where the sun was gone and islands of reddish turquoise where the low rays still caught the water. The pink flowers of the cactus plants in the hills began to close, and the white blossoms strung along the roadside that had puffed up like tissue-paper snowflakes at midday fell into shadow. Down in the harbor, the giant yachts were preparing for nightfall as the crews did their last scrubbing and polishing and arrayed the cocktail lights for the owners and courtiers to begin their evening partying.

Michael Dunne returned to his too-fancy hotel room. From his window, he could see the gray vastness of the *Cosmos*, dominating the other boats at the dock. There were five billion dollars afloat in the harbor, maybe double or triple that if you counted all the vessels spread around Porto Cervo. Pirate ships. Dunne changed clothes, packed his bag, and paid his bill at the reception desk.

The clerk regretted that it was too late to cancel that night's reservation. Such a shame. Perhaps someone waiting for him in another port? Dunne played along: Yes, another warm bed awaited; he could not refuse. The clerk asked if he could order a cab, but Dunne said not yet, first he wanted to take a walk in the last bit of the afternoon sun. He left his suitcase with the porter and set off with the backpack he had locked in the closet while he was aboard the yacht.

Dunne had studied the terrain when he arrived the day before. He knew precisely where he wanted to go. He left the hotel's manicured grounds and traversed the ridge that overlooked the harbor until he came to a Catholic church atop a hill a few hundred yards above the marina where the *Cosmos* was berthed. The chapel was a little work of art, white adobe nestled among topiary hedges. The bells were muffled; the doors locked.

Dunne walked along the lower side of the hedgerow that bounded the churchyard. When he came to a spot that offered a direct line-of-sight view of the *Cosmos*, he stopped, set down his backpack, and opened the padlock that protected its contents. He removed from the pack a small beam antenna that could power the miniature microphones he had secreted in the salons of the yacht and receive their transmissions. Next to the antenna he placed a compact, high-resolution video camera that could monitor the vessel. He attached both devices to a small server, the size of a lunch box, that could process the images and relay them via its own encrypted wireless network and transmission antenna to Dunne, who would be several miles away. Finally, he connected the little network of monitors and processors to a small battery pack. He covered the array with a cloth that was the same flat green as the shrubbery.

Dunne had spent much of his career installing surveillance tools like these, small and powerful and easy to hide. He had a hobbyist's fastidiousness, as if he were building a model plane out of balsa wood, or a ship inside a bottle.

When the monitoring platform was complete, Dunne closed his nearly empty pack and slung it over his shoulder. All that remained inside the pack was his computer to monitor the information provided by the sensors.

He returned to the lavish hotel, retrieved his suitcase, and took a cab to a cheap *pensione* a few kilometers west, near a local ferry terminal. There, he closed the curtains of his room, opened his computer, and began to study the sounds and images from the vessel.

*   *   *

The *Cosmos* was still as night fell. Tom Goldman remained on board; the lights were glowing in the top salon, and Dunne's camera caught his slim form through the window. A steward brought Goldman dinner, and Dunne heard through the hidden microphone the low, sonorous bowing of the Bach cello suites, but no voices. Perhaps Goldman was reading or reviewing the portfolios of his mysterious clients as he listened to the music. Or perhaps he was waiting.

Just after nine that evening, midafternoon on the East Coast, Goldman's phone rang. The bug captured only Goldman's end of the conversation. It was like watching one player in a tennis game; you could infer what was happening at the other end even if it wasn't visible.

"Hey, yeah, I was waiting for your call," Goldman began. "He left a few hours ago. This guy won't play ball. He's arrogant. Monkey on his back, like you said. I don't understand people who walk away from money because they think they have a higher cause. They're snobs, in my book. Anyway, he's gone."

Goldman was talking about Dunne, evidently. There was a pause while Goldman listened to the response and queries from the other end, and then he was talking again, answering another question about what had gone wrong.

"The pitch about the Russians and Chinese didn't work. His enemies are personal."

Another break, while Goldman's contact deliberated about the failure to recruit Dunne, and its implications. And then Goldman's languid response.

"I don't think he knows all that much, really. He saw the operation in Italy, but he didn't understand it. Certainly not what we're planning to do with it. He thinks his problem is Howe. Not very curious. Strange for an intel officer. Is that because he's a tech? They're mules, right? Or maybe he's just stupid."

Dunne flushed, sitting in the darkened room with his earphones on, listening to Goldman badmouthing him. There was another silence, as the caller asked some more questions, and then Goldman's response.

"Sure, he's on the prowl, but so what? He came to see me because he was looking for Howe. He'll never find him. All the threads are cut, in and out. Howe is stashed in Taiwan, building chips for that semiconductor company and chanting in his spare time. He's living in an old hutong house by the river in Taipei, last I heard. The service there monitors all his communications. They won't let anyone near him."

Dunne closed his eyes and registered the information. The monitor was silent as Goldman listened to more questions, and then his voice again.

"No. We didn't follow him when he left. I don't have the resources here, and we have no need to do it, anyway. He's an ex-felon. He's radioactive. We can pick him up whenever we want. If we track him, we just call attention to ourselves. Don't complicate things. Never be in a hurry to make a mistake."

Goldman's dismissive comments seemed to draw a sharp response, because he interrupted several times to say, "Yes, but—" and "That's not what I meant" and "Calm down." Eventually the storm passed, and Goldman adopted his accommodating, lawyerly voice again.

"Sure, if you want. Makes sense to get the group together. We could organize a dry run, go over the logistics and assignments. I thought we could do all that in a month or two, but we can start earlier, if you like. How soon can you get here, assuming you want to meet on the boat?"

Silence again, as Goldman's caller pondered the timing of a meeting.

"Two days is too soon. People's schedules are busy. Let's say four days. Next Monday. That will give me time to do a sweep of the boat."

Goldman's comment caused another eruption, and he was defensive again.

"Stop worrying. Dunne was here only a few hours. I'll bring a crew in tomorrow. If he left anything, it will be gone. You're worried about nothing. If it really bothers you, I'll tell the Italians to watch the airports and pick him up. Okay? Are we cool?"

And then: "Yeah. Bye-bye."

The audio monitor went silent, and after several minutes the video feed captured the lights being extinguished on the top deck. From the lower salon came the sound of a Mozart violin concerto, which stopped a few minutes into the first movement, as Goldman made another phone call.

"*Buonasera. Questa è la stazione dei Caribinieri?*"

When the duty officer responded, Goldman asked to be transferred to his friend Major Tomassino. The desk patched through a call to Tomassino's mobile.

"*Caro maggiore,*" Goldman began, and then switched to English. "This is Mr. Goldman aboard the *Cosmos*. I am so sorry to bother you. But I want to report a thief, who has damaged my vessel, the *Cosmos*. The thief's name is Michael Dunne. He's an American, red hair, about six feet tall. Dangerous man, I fear. I'll send you his passport details later. If he tries to leave Italy, you should stop him. Issue, you know, a *mandato di arresto*. Tonight's probably impossible, but tomorrow, please."

The police official agreed, evidently, because Goldman ended that call and placed another one.

"Ciao, Bruno. I need a nonlinear junction detector. Here, tomorrow morning. If you've got a Scantron system, I need that, too. And Delta X. The works. Can you come at ten? . . . Okay, by noon."

Dunne knew the brand names: They were fancy surveillance-detection devices, and Bruno was evidently a security consultant who specialized in finding bugs, probably a lucrative trade in the richest harbor in the Mediterranean. The hardware Goldman had requested could find any of the bugs Dunne had installed that were still transmitting.

\*    \*    \*

Dunne's only protection was that Goldman thought he was slow and incurious. His Sardinian adventure was over. On his computer, Dunne found a late ferry that left that night for Corsica from a port at the northern tip of Sardinia. Corsica was in France. Once he arrived on French territory, Dunne would be invisible long enough to get back to America.

Dunne needed to move quickly. He reprogrammed the surveillance camera he had embedded in the hedgerow below the church so that it uploaded to a cloud server that he could access from anywhere. He powered off the beam antenna that had been receiving sound signals. Bruno might find the bugs Dunne had hidden aboard the yacht, but he would have to be lucky. They wouldn't be sending or receiving electronic signals. They were now dead pieces of metal and fiber.

\*    \*    \*

Dunne checked out of his lodging for the second time that night. He took a bus north to the port. He found a café there with a bathroom, altered his appearance and clothing, and left by a back entrance. Corsica was eight miles north, across the Mediterranean. The ferry left just before midnight. The trip to Bonifacio took just fifty minutes.

Dunne arrived on the French island before one a.m. Thanks to Schengen rules, nobody checked his passport.

The bars and clubs were still jumping. He found a hotel near the port that overcharged him for a noisy room on the second floor, but he didn't care. He had a map in his mind now. He knew where he was going, and perhaps began to understand better who was coming after him.

Dunne needed to get home quickly, without attracting attention. He rose early the next morning and took a three-hour bus ride up the eastern coast of Corsica to Bastia, where he caught a cheap flight to Marseilles. From Marseilles, he booked a late afternoon flight to JFK via Paris, and slept through the second leg over the Atlantic.

He was back in Pittsburgh on Sunday afternoon, in his office on Forbes Avenue. The tropical fish had died, but otherwise the place looked tidy. He slept on the office couch Sunday night for a few hours, but he awoke at one a.m., as dawn was breaking in Costa Smeralda.

# 31

Pittsburgh, Pennsylvania—June 2018

Michael Dunne read the *Post-Gazette* sports section early Monday with one eye, while the other watched the live feed from the surveillance camera trained on the sleek gray cruiser forty-five hundred miles away. Dunne didn't want to miss any movement in or out of the vessel, so he toted the screen along with him when he went to the toilet or made coffee. He propped the sports section against the monitor so he could see it while he thumbed the pages.

Dunne stared at the screen for seven empty hours, until the sun had come up over the Monongahela River and it was two p.m. in Sardinia. The crew of the *Cosmos* had been busy enough, scurrying in and out of the vessel to load provisions and prepare for a voyage. But all the faces visible through the cabin windows and at the dock were familiar. The guests that Tom Goldman had invited four days earlier hadn't arrived, and Dunne wondered if the gathering had been moved to another time and place.

Just after two-thirty, as the shadows were beginning to lengthen, there was a bustle of action dockside. Three stewards descended the gangway; two stood at attention by the boat, and a third, dressed more elegantly in a double-breasted blue blazer, jumped into a waiting golf cart and steered it up the dock and out of sight of the fixed frame of Dunne's video camera. Dunne recognized the driver as Rudy, the chief steward who had greeted him when he arrived at the marina the week before.

Dunne peered intently at the screen, wondering who Rudy was fetching. He hoped to identify the mystery guests through facial recognition software, if the images were clear enough to be processed digitally. Dunne waited anxiously for several long minutes as the greeting party awaited the new arrival.

The golf cart rolled back into the frame suddenly. Dunne hunched forward to see the image, but the vehicle and its passenger were obscured by a plastic screen that had been unfurled to cover the cabin. The cart halted, and a steward sprang toward the screen and drew it back so that the guest could exit. In that same moment, the steward popped open a large black umbrella and held it low over the emerging passenger, so that the face was obscured.

Dunne saw the flap of a pair of baggy black trousers and the skirt of a matching jacket under the umbrella, but no more. As the new arrival shambled toward the gangway, the steward protectively handed him the umbrella, so that the face remained covered all the way up into the cabin. This was a practiced maneuver; they were carefully hiding the identity of their visitor.

"Shit," muttered Dunne. He rubbed his eyes. After all his preparation, and the hours of waiting, all he had seen was a black apparition hidden under a canopy. Who had arrived in such secrecy? Who would work so hard to remain invisible?

Dunne was exhausted, and he needed sleep after so many hours of staring at the computer monitor. He scanned the boat for a hint of who was inside, but the curtains of the salons and staterooms had been drawn tight, blocking any observation. Dunne thought of giving up, but Rudy was still poised at the dock, sitting in his golf cart, as if awaiting more guests.

The cart whirled off again a half hour later. This time it returned with an elegant man with a thin beard, dressed in slacks and a tailored jacket. As he exited the cart, he slung a computer bag over his shoulder. The arrival ceremony wasn't elaborate or secret this time. The man walked himself to the boat and climbed the gangplank unaided.

As Dunne studied the image, he recognized the face. The man with the computer bag was Lorenzo Ricci, the Italian computer scientist who had secreted himself in the back room of the laboratory in Urbino when Dunne made his fateful visit there, and then spoken so mysteriously over cheese and dessert wine.

*   *   *

It was nearly five p.m. in Costa Smeralda when the golf cart suddenly sped out of the frame again. Before it returned, the whole troop of cabin stewards came down the gangway one by one and lined up on the dock to greet this special arrival. Goldman himself followed and stood at the head of the line. He had put on a coat and tie.

The golf cart glided back, and with a flourish, Rudy deposited the last arrival. The plastic cover had been re-furled, so the side of the cart was open. The stewards bowed; Goldman extended his hand. From the cart stepped an elegant woman in her fifties, immaculately coiffed, her short blond hair tight against a sculpted face.

Goldman gave the lady his arm and escorted her to the steps as if she were royalty. Scrambling behind was an assistant laden with two cases that appeared to carry computer gear and were stamped with big letters that said BLOOMBERG.

Dunne stared at the woman's face. She had a beauty that reminded him eerily, disturbingly, of Veronika, the Swiss girl who had unzipped his marriage, but this woman was older. What registered was the deference with which she was treated. Whatever enterprise this might be, she appeared to be the chief executive. Dunne prayed the camera had captured an image clear enough to be processed digitally.

The woman was installed in a cabin that faced toward Dunne's camera. The curtains remained open enough long enough for Dunne to see the woman's assistant set up a Bloomberg terminal, with two screens to display market data and chat room talk, just like in the trading room of a large bank or hedge fund. The woman, dressed more casually now in a sweater, sat down behind the screens, and the assistant closed the curtain.

Ten minutes later, the crew cast off the bow and stern lines, and then the spring line between; the water churned and eddied under the propellers of the great yacht, and the Cosmos began to slip away from its berth toward open water.

As the boat headed east toward Italy, the last of the evening sun caught the fantail and illuminated the yacht's grand name, evoking the power of the global dominion, and its inscrutable home port of George Town, in the Cayman Islands.

*    *    *

Dunne collapsed on the office couch and slept through the rest of that day and into the night. When he awoke before dawn Tuesday morning, he went to his computer and retrieved the best image of the mystery woman who had boarded the *Cosmos* so grandly. He cropped the frame as tightly on her face as he could. Then he uploaded the image to two facial recognition sites on the Internet. Neither returned a match; or, more precisely, they returned too many matches to be useful.

Dunne found a third facial recognition site, a German company that required registration and payment. The site claimed it could review 101 different facial attributes to make a match. It promised a 90 percent success rate; Dunne paid the fee online, 199 euros. He uploaded the blond woman's face in the most precise images he had captured.

The software churned for a few seconds and then spit out a name: Adele K. Hecht. She was the head of a network of private banks with offices in Switzerland, Luxembourg, and the Cayman Islands. She was in her mid-fifties, and the profiles said her former husband, Hecht, was dead and that she had a child, unidentified, from an earlier husband, also deceased.

The name of Adele Hecht's largest financial holding was a bank in Geneva called Maison Suisse.

Dunne closed his eyes. The images cascaded in his mind: the perfect, intolerant mother; the mesmerizing, rebellious child; the perfume of danger; the ruinous consequences.

Psychologists speak of "paramnesia," in which reality and fantasy are momentarily confused, and a person can feel as if a new discovery is duplicating an earlier one in every detail; he may be uncertain for an instant whether he is in the past or the present. Dunne felt some of that disorientation now, as he stared at the information on his computer screen. The arc he had been following was bending back toward him. The knot he thought he was untying had become more tangled.

Move, Dunne told himself. When the present collapses into the past, the only path of escape is to drive toward the future. When you don't understand a problem, that means you haven't yet gathered enough information.

*   *   *

Dunne went back to his computer and found a flight later that day to Taiwan via San Francisco. Goldman had let slip in the monitored conversation that Jason Howe was working in Taipei. Dunne didn't have an address or number; just the fleeting reference that Howe was designing chips for a semiconductor company, and living on a lane in the old part of town near the river. Goldman had also said that Howe was watched carefully by the local security service.

Dunne had never operated in Taiwan. He couldn't advance without help. But the S&T fraternity was large, and Dunne had done favors for most of his colleagues over the years, without asking for much in return.

As Dunne pondered the Taiwan challenge, he recalled an old friend from S&T named David Mazor, who had sometimes used Taipei as an operational base a decade ago and knew the local service there as well as anyone in the agency. Dunne had rescued Mazor from a jam once, when Mazor had planted a bug that didn't work in the hotel suite of an Iranian diplomat in Paris and Dunne had quickly improvised another.

Roger Magee would know how to find Mazor. But Dunne hesitated as he was about to dial Magee's number. He felt a shadow of doubt, not rooted in anything specific, but he had started to obey such warnings even if he didn't understand them.

Who else would know where to find David Mazor? Dunne consulted his mental list of contacts. He had another former chum from S&T, a colleague who'd been in his trainee class and had sent him a heartfelt letter of support when he was sentenced to prison. Dunne had never answered the note; he was too angry then to accept kind words from anyone. But now he called the man, who had retired in Camden, Maine, and asked if he had any way of contacting their former colleague Mazor.

And, of course, he did. These were fraternity brothers in the secret world. Mazor was now living in Santa Clara, California, reported his Camden friend, and getting rich working for a social media company there.

Dunne called the number his friend provided, waking his former colleague in the California predawn. He said he needed a favor, big time. He was heading for Taiwan that day and needed to find an American who was working for a semiconductor company there and living in the old part of Taipei.

"You're the one who got screwed," said Mazor, sleepy but wanting to be helpful.

"That's me," answered Dunne. "And, yes, I did."

"Will this help you get even?"

"Maybe," answered Dunne. "Right now it's the best shot I've got."

"Edward Chen is the man to call. He can find anyone in Taipei, if I ask him. Hold on while I look." The phone was dead for a moment, and then Mazor's voice returned. "Chen's WhatsApp number is 886-955-5273-88. I'll message him now and tell him to help you."

Dunne paused. He'd been burned so often, there was scar tissue.

"Why would this guy Chen help me, David? We've never met, and if he does any research, he'll know I'm trouble."

"He'll do it because I ask him to. I helped him a lot once. Really a lot. He's never forgotten it. And look, in our work, you've got to trust someone in the end. Isn't that right?"

Dunne closed his eyes. "That's right," he said.

Mazor offered to come meet Dunne's plane at SFO and to buy him dinner in the city if he could stay overnight in San Francisco. Dunne said his connection time was too short.

"Okay, my friend, you're getting the special former-colleague-who-got-fucked package, okay? I'm going to reserve you a room at the Regent Hotel in Taipei, hire a car and driver to meet you at the airport and drive you around Taiwan. When we hang up, I'll send you on Signal the private number of the director general of the National Security Bureau, in case you get in any trouble. You have any problem with that?"

"I'm grateful," said Dunne. "I need help. I wouldn't have called you otherwise. I'll explain when it's over."

"No need," said Mazor. "Explanations are bullshit. Good luck. I hope you get what you want."

"Okay," said Dunne. "So, like, just, thanks."

# 32

Taipei, Taiwan—June 2018

The big Boeing jet touched down a day later in a rainy Taipei, bathed in the sweet, moist perfume of late June. Dunne had slept for the first half of the flight and awakened to watch an adolescent Bill Murray comedy movie; he laughed so loudly at the jokes that his Chinese seatmate glared at him. He moved through passport control and customs easily; whatever mischief had been done to him in Italy hadn't followed him to the other side of the world. As he approached the baggage claim carousel, he saw a jaunty Chinese man carrying a sign displaying the name DAVID MAZOR.

Dunne gave him a thumbs-up. The man approached and took the handle of Dunne's bag; he offered to carry the padlocked backpack, too, but Dunne demurred.

"I'm Tony Tsai," the man said, with what sounded like a New York accent overlaying his Chinese accent. "I'm your driver, secretary, whatever you need, that's what Mr. Mazor told me. In America, people call me TT, or Taiwan Tony, or whatever you like, it's cool."

"Thanks. Tony." Dunne stuck out his hand. "You a Yankees fan or a Mets fan?"

"Are you kidding? Yankees. Okay, Mr. Dunne. Follow me. My car's in the next lot. Come on, we'll get you to your hotel, take care of business."

They walked out of the immaculate, pagoda-shaped terminal toward the adjoining parking lot. Tsai had a black Lexus sedan. He opened the back door, limousine-style, but Dunne slipped into the front passenger seat. Tsai steered the vehicle out of the airport compound and onto the elevated highway into the city.

The rain was pelting as fast as the wipers could push it away.

"Rainy season, Mr. Dunne. May and June, you need to be a duck to live in Taiwan."

"You sound like you lived awhile in New York, Tony."

"The Bronx, then Queens, then Long Island City. And you asked me about the Yankees. I was there when Chien-Ming Wang won nineteen games for the Bombers. Do you feel me, Mr. Dunne?"

"Definitely," said Dunne. He gave Tsai a sidelong glance. How long had this polyglot Taiwanese man been on Mazor's payroll, and in how many places had he operated?

As they entered the city, the rain slowed and banks of fog settled over the low-rise skyscrapers. Taipei had the shopworn look of a capital whose wealthy younger residents had decamped for the mainland to embrace the "China Dream." Left behind were Grandma and Grandpa, a whole lot of money, and some rambunctious kids who liked the idea of living in a democracy, even if it wasn't quite a country of its own.

They rolled up a driveway past an ostentatious fountain to the Regent Hotel entrance, flanked by French luxury boutiques. Dunne told Tony to wait while he checked in. The reception clerk treated him like a viceroy; he upgraded Dunne's room to a junior suite, overlooking a park that was like a box of green velvet in the concrete jumble.

*   *   *

Dunne unpacked and took a catnap for an hour. When he awoke, he called David Mazor's Taipei contact, Edward Chen.

"I have been expecting you," said Chen, soft-voiced, his speech plump and well turned. "I hope you had a good flight. How I can be helpful?"

"Maybe I should come in person," said Dunne. "I'll be able to explain better."

"Come now, if you're not too tired. I'll give you a glass of very good whiskey." He provided an address on Xinyi Road, near the financial center. Dunne put on a crisp white shirt and a suit and tie. In Asia, it was never a mistake to overdress.

Chen's assistant was waiting in the lobby of the office building. He escorted Dunne to the twenty-eighth floor, where Chen's holding company had its headquarters. Night had fallen, and the city was twinkling all the way to the Taiwan Strait. The offices were understated; the décor, like Chen's business, was between China and the West.

Chen was wearing a tweed sports coat in the air-conditioned chill of the skyscraper. He offered Dunne a selection from a cabinet of whiskeys. He was a collector, he explained. He liked to take a trip every summer with one of his sons to a distillery in some remote bog or island in Scotland and add to his cache.

Dunne asked for a suggestion, and his host proposed a twenty-one-year-old Glen Dronach, which he said was his own favorite. It had been aged in casks that had previously held sherry, so it had a hint of sweetness along with its peaty Highlands flavor.

Chen poured two glasses and handed one to Dunne. He waited while Dunne took a sip. It was unlike any whiskey Dunne had ever tasted, sharp and spicy, with caramel-sweet flavors that lingered in his mouth. Chen looked pleased. He liked doing favors for members of the fraternity that had helped him build and protect his business empire.

"Tell me how I can help you, Mr. Dunne. David told me that you are looking for someone here in Taiwan. An American who is a chip designer. That is a big category, but this is a small island, and the odd peg sticks out. I'd like to invite my assistant, who has a better brain for these things than I do. You can trust his discretion."

"I'm happy for your help, Mr. Chen. But can our conversation be private? You must have many friends at the American Institute in Taiwan, and probably back at Langley. But this is a personal matter, and I don't want it showing up in message traffic. If that's an impossible request, let me know, and I'll finish this delicious whiskey and go back to my hotel."

"I understand. Life has compartments, just as intelligence work does.

David told me that you had encountered difficulties with your former employer. I gather that you were treated in a way that was unworthy of your fine organization. I'm sorry for that. I give you my word that these conversations will be entirely private. No tracks, no traces, no traffic."

Dunne thanked his host, and Chen picked up his desk phone and summoned a young man named Alton Chen, whom he introduced as his youngest son. The young man was dressed in a blue blazer and a striped tie bearing the colors of his Cambridge college.

Dunne and Chen sat together on a couch, facing the lights of the city. Alton sat in a straight-backed chair a few feet to the side.

Dunne began to unspool his request. The assistant took notes on his iPad as Dunne spoke, while Old Man Chen smiled and poured himself another dram of Glen Dronach.

"The person I'm looking for is named Jason Howe," said Dunne. "He is a computer scientist who made a reputation as a free-speech activist. He ran a website called Fallen Empire and worked with a group of hackers called Quark Team that was based in Urbino, Italy. They had top-of-the-line servers, way beyond what they needed. I'm still not sure just what their business was, but part of it involved putting damaging, often false, information on the Internet. Sometimes they tried to destroy people using their information."

Chen reached out his hand toward Dunne, not quite touching his guest.

"I gather that this Mr. Howe was involved in the events that led to your own personal and professional difficulties. Is that so?"

"He harmed me and my family, in a way that can't be fixed. That's why I've come here to find him."

"I understand, of course I do. Forgive my interruption. Please provide any details that can help Alton find this unpleasant fellow."

"I don't know much. I'm told he's working in Taipei, helping design logic chips for one of the big semiconductor companies. He's a tall white guy, lab rat, wispy blond hair, so thin he can barely keep his trousers on. I don't have a photograph, but I could work up a sketch."

"Let's do that," said Chen, nodding to his son. "Then we can run the image against data from the police bureau's surveillance cameras. They have installed quite a few of those nearly everywhere, and my friends give me a back door. Nobody does anything in Taiwan that is not knowable these days."

Alton brought over his iPad, on which he had loaded a modern photo-based version of the old Identikit system that police used to sketch portraits of suspects. Dunne sorted through pictures of eyes, cheeks, noses, foreheads, hairlines, lips, and chins until Alton had assembled a pretty good likeness of Jason Howe, as Dunne had last glimpsed him in the dim light of an underground trattoria.

"Anything else we should know about this character?" asked Chen.

"I was told that Howe lives in a lane house in the old part of the city, in a hutong, if that's the right word, near the Tamsui River. The only other thing I heard was that your National Security Bureau keeps a close watch on him. I know that makes it complicated for you. I apologize for that."

"We have a Chinese saying, if you will forgive me, Mr. Dunne. 'Before telling secrets on the road, look in the bushes.' As I said earlier, a well-ordered life has compartments. People who have secrets know that other people have secrets, too. That's how we all get along."

Chen sat back in his chair and stared for a moment at the lights of the city he had helped to build, and then turned to his ruddy red-haired guest, who was an animal of a slightly different species.

"Here in China, we think red is a lucky color. But red-haired people, I don't know. Sometimes people say '*ang mo kui*,' which means red-haired devil. But that was a superstition from a long-time ago, when people were afraid of Dutch traders. Now I think red is a good omen."

"I hope so," said Dunne. "I could use some luck."

\*   \*   \*

Chen sent his guest back to the Regent to get some sleep and promised that he and his son Alton would get to work immediately on the missing-person request. For that's all it was. A "*gweilo*," a white ghost, had vanished into an enclosed island space that numbered just twenty-three million residents. He would be found. Dunne should await a call.

Chen dispatched his son to an office in the interior ministry, in the Zhongzheng District near the old monuments and museums of the Chiang Kai-shek era. Everyone owed favors in this country, but few people had larger networks of *guangxi* than Edward Chen. It was convenient for the deputy chief of the national police to assist in Mr. Chen's search. It would have been inconvenient to refuse.

When Dunne awoke, he went to the gym in the subbasement of the hotel. The air didn't circulate very well down there, and the exercise room had the smell of old sweat flavored with garlic and fish sauce. Dunne watched Chinese cartoons on television while he jogged on the treadmill. Dunne returned to his room and was finishing his breakfast when the phone rang, just before ten a.m. It was Chen.

"I think we have something," he said. "It's not so hard, when you know where to look. Alton will come by the hotel presently. I believe that he will be able to take you to see your Mr. Howe. There will be a policeman there, in plain clothes. If you have a score to settle, please don't do it there, with my son and the policeman present."

"Thank you, sir," said Dunne. He was astonished that his request had been answered so quickly and efficiently.

"It is *my* pleasure," said Chen.

# 33

Taipei, Taiwan—June 2018

Alton Chen arrived at the Regent Hotel entrance in a small yellow Toyota taxi, the last car anyone would think to follow. He was dressed more casually than the night before, in jeans and black sneakers and a flowered shirt he had left untucked.

Dunne entered the cab; he had worn a tie but removed it. They drove east from the hotel toward the old city and the river; the streets got narrower and the shops were no longer selling Western goods but more exotic Chinese wares: teas and herbs and traditional medicines.

When the cab reached a derelict temple, with the round, battered face of a smiling Buddha peering down at them, Alton told the driver to stop and paid the fare. He beckoned for Dunne to follow him on foot. They walked from the bustle of the shops down a narrow lane toward a park by the river. The river smells of early June were in the air: diesel oil from the ships passing down the Tamsui to the mouth of the strait, and fish rotting where they had washed up against the riverbank.

As they neared the corner, Alton stopped at an old brick building bearing intricately carved stone and wood panels on the façade. A square-legged man in a bulky suit stood outside. Evidently he was the plainclothes cop Chen had mentioned. Alton whispered in his ear, and the policeman nodded. He stood at ease, hands together behind his back, to guard the site while they entered.

The first interior room was a commercial shop selling porcelain. Alton approached the shopkeeper and spoke in her ear. She nodded and escorted Alton and Dunne into an inner courtyard, hidden from the street; it was a small garden amid the city, with orchids in bloom, and lush ferns and several potted bonsai trees.

A sound of chanting came from the inner courtyard. The words were Chinese, but the voice had the flat throatiness of American English, even as it intoned the words: *Na mo ho la da nu do la ye ye . . .*

The shopkeeper motioned for Alton and Dunne to follow her upstairs, following the voice, to a wooden balcony with a couch and chairs that overlooked the courtyard. The chanting continued from an interior room. *An, sa bo la fa yi, su da nu da sia . . .*

As Dunne listened to the pious tones, spoken by a voice he recognized, he exploded with an anger that had been building for months.

"Shut the fuck up," shouted Dunne.

The voice stopped.

The shopkeeper knocked on the door of the apartment from which the sound of the chanting had come, and then opened it. A tall, gaunt man peered through the opening and walked out slowly, gazing curiously at his visitors.

Dunne wasn't sure at first that it was Jason Howe. He was as thin as before, but he had shaved his head. He was dressed in a long linen shirt, matching linen trousers, and a pair of sandals, the sort of simple garb a mendicant monk might wear, or a college kid traveling in Asia for his summer vacation. There were deep circles under his eyes, and stress lines on the face that Dunne didn't remember.

Howe stared at the muscular, red-haired American. It took him a moment to recognize Dunne. He put his palms together meekly and addressed Dunne.

"I'm sorry," said Howe. "I was meditating. It's the great compassion mantra."

"You prick," said Dunne. His body instinctively tensed to swing a punch at the man who had put him in prison for a year.

Howe bowed again submissively. There was an odd smile on his face, the opposite of fear. More like relief.

"I knew you would come," said Howe. "I prayed for it. I am happy to see you."

Dunne took a step back.

"Why are you happy, you shit? You tried to destroy me. Why would you care if I'm alive or dead?"

"We need to talk. Too much bad karma. You've got this upside down."

"Don't fuck with me," snarled Dunne. "There's a big part of me that wants to kill you."

Howe bowed again, and then put up his hand gently in caution and protest. "I understand. But you are chasing the wrong person. I have been trying to help you."

"Bullshit. What are you talking about?"

"Sit down. You've come a long way. I can help you. This is satori. It's why you came."

Dunne took a seat on the wicker couch, and Howe dropped his thin, gangly form into a chair alongside.

Alton Chen kept his composure amid these loud voices, standing against the rear wall of the balcony.

Dunne glared at Howe, cheeks red, eyes still flashing. "Do you have any idea what you did to me?"

"I am very, very sorry for what happened. But it wasn't me. That's why I wanted you to find me. That's why I sent you the letter when you went into prison, because I felt so bad about what happened."

Dunne cocked his head. His back quivered. He shook his head.

"What are you talking about?" pressed Dunne. "What letter?"

"The one with my contact info. I said I was a Paladin, a righteous avenger. I said it was from a 'Lemon Squeezer,' to look like one of your pals. I thought that if I contacted you directly, you'd send the cops after me. Or they would . . ."

Howe's voice trailed off. He didn't explain what he meant by "they," and Dunne for the moment didn't ask.

"You're the 'Lemon Squeezer'?" asked Dunne, his voice rising. "Are you kidding me? Where did you learn to talk tradecraft?"

"I found it on the Internet. That's how I know everything. I wanted you to come and find me, when you got out of jail, so that I could tell you."

"You could tell me what?"

"That I didn't do it. I'm not the guy who wanted to publish the dirt on you and your wife. That wasn't me. They were cutting me out already by then."

\* \* \*

Dunne closed his eyes. Sometimes when you first consider that a story may be very different from what you had believed, you feel a sense of disorientation, as if waking up from a dream and sensing, but not being quite sure yet, that what had seemed so vivid wasn't in fact real.

Dunne muttered, under his breath, a groan that expressed his recognition.

"Who took my life apart, then, if it wasn't you?"

"The boss. The owner. The board of directors. I don't know. I was exiled from the inner circle of the Quark Team after you came to see us in Italy. But I was always fronting for other people, I knew that much. I didn't buy all those GPU clusters you saw in Urbino, that's for sure."

"It wasn't you," said Dunne, affirming to himself what he had just heard.

"No."

Dunne stood up. Alton Chen was standing quietly by the wall. Dunne walked to the edge of the balcony and peered over the rail. The shopkeeper was in the front part of the store, evidently minding her business, but Dunne didn't feel secure. He was in a location where he had no operational control, talking about the most sensitive issues in someone else's space.

"Let's take a walk," he said to Howe. "You and me. We need to talk where I'm sure people aren't listening."

"Okay. No problem. Let me put on some shoes." He went back into his room and returned wearing a pair of Chuck Taylor All-Stars with the laces undone.

Dunne turned to Alton, his unofficial minder.

"We need to get out of here, somewhere outside where we can talk. Is that cool?"

Alton gave half a nod, respectful but not quite giving permission.

"Let me check with my dad. To make sure you will be safe."

Alton took out his cell phone, turned toward the wall, and dialed his father's private number. He began speaking quickly in Mandarin Chinese, relaying the situation and waiting for instructions.

"My dad says it's permissible. The policeman will stay here, but I must accompany you while you walk. Not close, I'll leave you alone, but my dad says that to make sure you are both safe, I should come along. Is that acceptable?"

"That's fine," said Dunne. "Keep ten yards back. If you see something you don't like, come grab us."

*   *   *

Dunne and Howe departed the hutong and crossed a busy street toward the park that ran along the bank of the Tamsui. Alton stood back respectfully, just as he had promised, protective but not intrusive.

They walked beneath a six-lane expressway, traffic humming on the concrete above, and through a grove of trees to the grass-lined sidewalk by the quay. Dunne waited until they were in the park before he began quizzing Howe in earnest.

"You owe me," Dunne began. "I need information in a hurry. Even the stuff that doesn't seem important. So, take me back to the beginning. How was the Quark Team put together? Who was the founder?"

"Before we start, Mr. Dunne, I need to ask you something. Can you get me out of here? Because I'm in danger."

"I'll try. But right now, I found you, and I own you. Just talk."

Howe nodded. In a sense, this debriefing was what he had wanted when he had reached out to Dunne, guilt-laden, back in Paris. But we never know just what it will feel like, when we get what we want. Howe didn't look like a Buddhist novitiate, but a scared guy on the run.

"You want the whole story of how we got to Urbino?"

"Everything that matters."

"We were just some nerd-balls at the start," Howe began quietly. "Geeky kids at Brookline High School. My dad taught at MIT and he was always at the lab; he and my mom had just gotten divorced, so I had lots of time and nothing to do. And I was pissed off. So, I started programming, and then a few months later I started hacking into university computers and met other people like me, and by junior year in high school I was seriously good at it. I started making money for a hacking group that operated out of Europe, or at least that's what they said."

"What was the group? How did they pay you?"

Howe scratched his shaved head and shrugged his stooped shoulders.

"They were just, you know, hackers. They were anarchists. They liked to rip shit off and make trouble. Like me. They wanted to send me money through PayPal but I said forget it. It was a kick. We didn't really have an ideology, except the Internet should be free and governments were bad. We liked pulling people's chains. That was the beginning of the Quark Team. Smart kids who wanted to raise hell using computers."

"Where did Fallen Empire come from?"

"That was Dmitri's idea. He was my best friend at Brookline High. His parents had emigrated from Russia. He thought America was getting like the Soviet Union, invading Afghanistan and Iraq, pushing people around, and letting rich crooks steal everything from other people. I decided he was right. We both got into Stanford and began doing serious computer science stuff, but we started doing Fallen Empire posts, too. And then politics began to get crazy in 2015. I was pissed off about Snowden. You know all that crap."

"What happened to you and Dmitri?"

"Dmitri got hired by Google. He said it wasn't about the money, but I didn't believe him. He had all the chicks he wanted, and coke, and pills. I thought that was bullshit. Everybody I knew at Stanford was on a money-and-death trip. So, fuck it, I dropped out and went to Europe. I had met Jake Rosenberg at Stanford. He thought I was cool, so he dropped out, too."

"You sound like me when I was twenty."

"Probably everybody is like that when they're twenty."

"What did you do, when you dropped out?"

"I had these hacker friends, like I told you. I went to live with them. First in Berlin, which is, like, hacker paradise, and then in Italy, we began to form this Quark Team thing, in addition to all the trolling we were doing with Fallen Empire."

"Did you move to Urbino then?"

"Not right away. We started in Milan. There were some super-smart hackers there. The number-one guy was Ricci. He was like the alpha hacker. He'd been at Georgia Tech, published a lot of articles. Very, very smart dude."

"I remember him from Urbino," said Dunne. "And guess what? I just saw him less than a week ago."

"Say what?"

"I'll tell you later, maybe. Keep going with your story."

"Ricci had a cybersecurity business, on the offensive side. He'd been running it for a couple of years when I met him, and he wanted me to help. Do you really want to hear all this, man?"

"Absolutely. Every word. What was the business?"

"Ricci understood cell phones. I think he had worked for Apple for a while. He realized that people were just stupid with their phones. They said anything they liked, they took pictures of their dicks, and fucked around with each other. It offended him. He was a very bourgeois guy, really, despite all the hacking lingo. He figured out ways to get inside people's phones. Tap their cameras; use the microphones to listen in on them. And he began selling his little phone-cracker malware back in 2014."

"Who were his customers?"

"He didn't care at first. Private security. Women who wanted to find out if their husbands were cheating. Whoever paid him. But eventually people found out what he could do with iPhones and, boom, everybody wanted to be his customers."

"Like who?"

"Governments. They wanted to use this stuff to spy on people they didn't like. Ricci didn't care. He had contempt for people, really. I mean, he had rules, but they were crap: People had to sign agreements saying they were using his software for 'lawful purposes,' to 'catch criminals' and 'prevent terrorism,' but who was he kidding?"

"Who was on the Quark Team, besides you?"

"He began hiring people who had worked for government agencies in Russia and Israel. But not America. He thought the CIA and NSA would try to control everything. He said that I was the only American he trusted, because I was such a flake. He let me play with Fallen Empire, as long as I helped him with the Quark Team stuff."

"That sounds like a devil's bargain."

"I guess. Kids are stupid. I had this badass idea of myself as a bandit, robbing people to help humanity."

"Kids are stupid," Dunne assented.

"It doesn't matter now. I was delusional. But back then I thought we were serious about doing good. Even when they began to put all those new GPUs into Urbino, I still thought it was okay. And then, blam! Everything blew up."

"I'm listening," said Dunne. "And keep your voice down."

# 34

Taipei, Taiwan—June 2018

The clouds over Taipei were thickening with the moisture that would become the afternoon rain. Taiwanese kids were skimming along the path on bicycles, and occasional knots of people were gathered at benches. Michael Dunne and Jason Howe walked slowly down the riverside path, followed by the discreet shadow of Alton Chen. A bridge over the Tamsui loomed a quarter mile ahead, where the quay ended.

Dunne looked at his watch. Time was running out. At some point, Chen's magic with the authorities would disappear. But there was too much Dunne didn't understand yet. He grabbed Howe's arm and steered him in the opposite direction, back upriver. Chen, still ten paces behind, made the same maneuver.

"I still don't get it," said Dunne. "Help me out. What were you doing with all the fancy computers, anyway? That didn't make any sense when you showed them off in Urbino, and it still doesn't."

"Man, you are a lamer. How did they ever let you in the CIA? This whole thing was a phreak. We were building a world made of Astroturf."

"That's not responsive. Be specific. And, honestly, you're not the person to call me lame. You would piss in your pants if you tried some of the stuff I've done. So, cut the crap and explain what you were doing."

Howe laughed for the first time. He liked pulling Dunne's chain. He leaned closer and continued his narrative.

"Ricci and I agreed on one thing, which was that politics was bullshit, no matter where. It was all lies. And we realized that with the Internet we had this theater where we could create whatever effects we wanted, so we just let it rip. That was our thing, back in 2016, before you showed up."

"Were you working with the Russians?"

"Hell, no. We watched the Russians, for sure, with their troll farms and websites and agitprop. They were obvious, if you had friends in St. Petersburg, which we did. And at WikiLeaks, which we did. We saw the Russian hacks going down, and it was lulz, for sure, but it was so basic, and then the Democrats went nuts. It was a goof, basically."

"What did you do that was fancier than the Internet Research Agency and the GRU?"

"We took it to the next level. Instead of posting fake-news sites, we started creating fake events and putting them online. And guess what? Nobody could tell the difference. That's how fucked up politics is. People traded on our information on the stock market. They referred to it in news stories. We started trolling companies just for fun. And Ricci had this pet project to defang all the malware the Russians and Americans had installed. He was pumped about that."

"Why? What did he get out of it?"

"Advertising. And just to show he could."

"Why did you help? He's the kind of person you should have hated."

"I thought it was cool bandit stuff, for a long time. I finally realized that, for Ricci, it was just business."

Dunne thought about some of the fake events he'd watched online back in Geneva, when he was preparing for his trip to Urbino. He thought of poor Pia Zimmerman, and the created image of her lips around the penis of a man she'd never met. Zimmerman's Saudi tormentor had purchased the deceptive imagery from someone, and now it was evident from whom.

He saw the image in his mind, too, of his wife Alicia. His arm twitched and he felt a gag in his throat. He made himself think about something else.

"You started selling this technology to other people," said Dunne, barely audible.

"Ricci did. He and his partners were ready to sell one-offs to anyone, so long as they kept the technology in-house. They were doing some very creative things. People call this stuff deepfakes, but that doesn't do it justice. Technically speaking, it's sweet."

"It's sick. How do you make it look so real?"

"The technical term is 'generative adversarial networks.' GANs, we call them. That's how you create a believable fake. You have one cluster of graphical processors that's programmed to create images from all the video and photos you can upload. And then you have another GPU cluster that's programmed to detect fake images, by seeing anomalies and blips. And then you feed the glitches back to the first cluster, so it can fix the flaws and make a better image, and then you test that one, and it's back and forth like that until you have an image that is so good your mother couldn't detect the real one from the fake."

"And Ricci sold this stuff?"

"He was just starting to, when you visited. He was playing with the technology, to see what it could do. He created fake events about the weather, drug trials, earnings reports. Anything that would move markets. And then he began selling 'trading opportunities' to hedge funds. Little market-timing moments, where he knew something would happen but never told his customers why he was so smart. He loved that. He's been tinkering these last two years, getting ready."

"Ready for what?" asked Dunne. "What's he planning now?"

"Something big. Ricci and his friends don't tell me much anymore. They have new partners who don't want a leftie Buddhist wannabe like me around. They put me on ice. First I was in this big old apartment in Paris with nothing to do. Then they stashed me here in Taiwan. Out of sight, out of mind. Until you showed up, that is. Satori."

"You said that word before. What does it mean?"

"Sudden awakening. Comprehension. Understanding."

Dunne nodded. He studied the landscape as Howe talked, thinking about how he might extract him from Taiwan without putting others in danger. Even a small island had hiding places. Across the river was New Taipei City, a commercial district, unfashionable and anonymous. To the south were miles of rugged hills, dotted with parks that most Taiwanese were too busy to enjoy. But before he thought about escape, Dunne had to know more.

"We need some leverage. Otherwise I'll never be able to get you out of here. What do you know about Ricci's plans?"

"Honestly, man, I don't know any details. Before they transferred me here, they talked about a major score. Ricci called it 'La Festa.' The Party. But I have no idea what that means. Ricci said it was going to make him so rich he could buy his own country. He's got investors now, too. 'Associates,' is what Ricci called them."

"Like who? People, countries, what?"

"I don't know, for Christ's sake. That's why I'm here and not in some fancy spa in Europe. Because they don't trust me. Maybe it's because Ricci didn't want me to know that some Americans had gotten involved."

"What Americans? How do you know that? This is important, my friend."

"Because right after you got busted and it went into the newspapers, we had some visitors in Urbino that I didn't recognize. They spent all their time in the back office with Ricci and his Italian computer-science geniuses, and they came and went by a different entrance. When I was in the server room, working on the GPUs, the door opened, and I heard them speaking English, with American accents."

"What did they look like?"

"There was one old guy, black suit, with spiky brown hair, bald spot. He looked like shit. A black guy came with him, with long dreadlocks."

"Fuck me," said Dunne. He exhaled and shook his head.

In that moment, Dunne felt a taste of what his wife Alicia had known, the mute, helpless sense of having once trusted someone who destroyed your happiness. Now it was his turn.

Howe saw Dunne's ashen face.

"What's wrong, man? Do you know those guys?"

Dunne took a deep breath and nodded.

"The two gentlemen you described are George Strafe and Adrian White."

"Who the hell are they?"

"I worked with them at the CIA. They're the ones who fucked me up."

"Wow. I'm sorry, man. That is some very bad shit."

*   *   *

Dunne closed his eyes for a moment and made himself a vow. He would find, expose, and destroy George Strafe. He put his hand awkwardly around Howe's shoulder, then let it drop. They weren't enemies anymore. Dunne had gone down a long road and found what he was looking for, even if it wasn't what he expected. Now he needed to know the rest.

"Who else joined your group, Jason? Who was working with my CIA colleagues?"

"There was a smooth lawyer from London. Neat, compact, American, but not so much. I met him in Mayfair on my way here. He bought me my plane tickets and told me to shut up."

"The London lawyer is named Tom Goldman," Dunne said quietly.

"Whatever. And there was one other person. A woman. I never met her, but the lawyer and Ricci kept talking about her. They called her 'La Patronessa.' Like, the Boss. Does that make any sense to you?"

Dunne nodded. He felt a budding kinship with Howe, the man he had hated for so long.

"I saw that woman on a computer screen a few days ago. Her name is Adele Hecht. She was getting on a big yacht in Sardinia. The *Cosmos*, it was called. Ricci was on board. Probably Strafe, too. Goldman was the host."

"A yacht, huh? That figures. Ricci was always talking about buying himself a big-ass boat, but he never had enough money. And now he's got it. And you found it. Maybe you're not as lame as I thought."

"Maybe not. The question for now is how we get you out of here."

"Can Junior help?" asked Howe, nodding toward Alton Chen, who was keeping his usual distance.

"Possibly. His father can do anything on this island. But we need to make it worthwhile. Maybe we can tip him about Ricci's big party. Tell me something we can use as a tease."

"I assume it involves financial markets. Something that turns everything upside down, so that the Consortium can profit."

"What's the 'Consortium'?"

"That's the name that Ricci gave to his partnership, when he began to draw these other people in."

They were near the overhead expressway and the roar of the traffic. Dunne surveyed the landscape. Old Taipei, New Taipei, the factories and office blocks that embodied Taiwan's two defining traits: Money and survival.

Dunne turned back toward Alton Chen.

"Alton, could you come here?" he called out. "Can you arrange for us to go see your dad?"

Young Chen approached, nodded, not quite a bow, and then retreated to make the phone call.

*   *   *

Dunne's head was buzzing. He closed his eyes. He could almost touch the pieces of this puzzle. He thought of the ways he could eclipse the distance so that he could grasp it all, but he needed help. An access agent, he would once have called such a person, but that just meant someone who could get into a place that was otherwise closed.

"Hey, Jason," he said. "Do you have friends who are still working with Ricci? People who would help you out, if you asked them?"

"Just one, really. You met him in Urbino. Jacob Rosenberg. He worked with me on Fallen Empire in the beginning. They trust him. He's working on this 'Party' thing. Jake sends me encrypted texts sometimes. They're paying him a lot of money now."

"What does Jake do for the Consortium?"

"He writes code. And he does social engineering sometimes, to get information for an operation. He hangs out with people who know stuff and talk too much about it. Engineers, security people. They go to their favorite bar and they lose their minds. We call it a 'watering-hole attack.'"

"The CIA calls it that, too, just so you know. What else does Jake do?"

"Last message I got, he was in New York, working on a deepfake they're using for the show."

"Can you can get in touch with him?"

"Yeah, sure. He thinks Ricci is an asshole. He just likes the money."

"Would he help you, if you asked for it? Even if it was a little risky?"

"Yeah, man, I think so. He's bored. Just don't get him killed, but otherwise, sure. Everyone wants some lulz."

"You stay in touch with Jake, okay? Just like before. Keep him on a string. That's what you can do for me, in exchange for my getting you out of your permanent assignment to Taiwan."

*   *   *

Alton returned after making the call to his father. It was all arranged, he said.

# 35

Taipei, Taiwan—June 2018

The patriarch sent an absurdly luxurious Mercedes Maybach limousine to pick up his son, Dunne, and Howe. The sedan cruised down Xinyi Road, past the headquarters of the big banks and manufacturing companies, toward the ungainly 101-story financial center known as Taipei 101 that rose from the western end of the avenue like a symbolic finger stuck in the eye of mainland China across the strait.

Chen's building was a half mile away from the monumental tower. He was not a man to poke anyone in the eye. Alton scurried into his father's office for a private chat when they arrived, and a few minutes later the old man welcomed them. He cast a skeptical eye toward Howe, with his shaved head and hippie clothes, but he was polite as ever. As they took their seats, a servant arrived with a pot of tea, scones, strawberry jam, and whipped cream.

Dunne didn't waste time. His window of maneuver with Howe was closing. He opened his arms, palms out, in gentle supplication.

"I need to ask you another favor, Mr. Chen. You have already been so generous that I'm sorry to be knocking on your door again so soon. But I must ask, because it's important."

"You are welcome, esteemed Dunne. As we say, if you always give, you will always have. Alton tells me that you had a very busy morning with Mr. Howe. He says that you had a great deal to talk about. And privately, too, which means it was a serious conversation. Perhaps you will share it someday. But, please, tell me how I can help now."

"Jason needs to go home to the United States, urgently. An important business matter has come up. I'd like to help him get home as soon as possible."

Chen put his finger to his lips. He closed his eyes for a moment.

"Perhaps his employer can make the arrangements," said Chen. "Taipei Silicon Technology is a large and successful company. I'm sure they would want to assist one of their trusted employees."

"Well, that's the problem. The reason Jason needs to get home so quickly is that he has discovered a technical problem that could be very damaging if it isn't fixed. He can't tell his company yet, because it's so sensitive, but he wants to protect all companies in Taiwan, and probably elsewhere, sir, because it's one of these cyber issues. Malware."

"Dangerous for all Taiwan?" That fixed Chen's attention.

"Yes, sir. As I'm sure you know, Mr. Howe is an expert in these matters. And if you ask our mutual friend David Mazor, he will tell you that I am quite knowledgeable, as well. Not bragging, Mr. Chen, being honest."

"Just so. David's confidence in you was renewed to me overnight, by the way, in a private message. So, whatever you say, I am inclined to believe you. I don't know your friend, Mr. Howe." He nodded toward the mendicant hacker. "But if you say it's urgent, well, you must have a reason."

"Jason frequents a world where you and I don't travel, Mr. Chen. In this hacker underground, he's hearing about danger ahead. A malware problem that's worse than anything we've seen. His friends are calling it 'La Festa.' The Party."

"My goodness. What will it do?"

"I can't say. I shouldn't say. I'm asking you to trust me. And I give my promise that if we can't stop this malware attack, I will give you advance notice so that you can take special precautions to protect your business from any harm. Would that be useful?"

"Oh, yes, quite useful. My friends have lost hundreds of millions because of these attacks in cyberspace. Making chips is the most profitable business in

Taiwan, and if this industry were compromised, it would be catastrophic for us. Advance word of such an attack would be, well, sir, a lifesaver."

"Here is what I need: Two tickets on the next flight from Taipei to San Francisco. And your help in getting Jason through security and onto the plane. I know that's a lot to ask. But I promise you that your assistance will be repaid."

Chen summoned his son and went through a list of things that he wanted Alton to check. The young man began making inquiries using his iPad. Dunne leaned toward Howe and spoke in his ear.

"Do you have your passport?" whispered Dunne.

"Sort of. It's locked in a safe at my office, near the technology center out by the airport."

Dunne nodded. "I'll get into the safe, if you can get us in the door."

Alton Chen stepped forward, displaying the tablet screen so the two Americans could see.

"You missed the eleven-thirty flight to San Francisco. The next one is at seven-fifty tonight. You need to be at the airport two hours early. My father says that I should accompany you all the way to the door of the airplane. We should leave for the airport in two hours, at most."

"My stuff is ready to go at the Regent. Jason, how fast can you pack?"

"The packing is ten minutes. All I have is simple clothes like these. But I need my computer. And like I told Mr. Dunne, I need to stop at the office to get my passport. There's security there."

Edward Chen nodded. He folded his hands and closed his eyes. It was a good fifteen seconds before he opened them again, long enough for Dunne to worry that he was having second thoughts, but he was just letting the decision settle.

"I think you must leave now to get your things and go to the airport. Alton will accompany you, as he said, to make sure you don't encounter any difficulties. If any problem arises, he will call me. And I will fix it."

"Thank you, sir," said Dunne.

Howe put his palms together in a Buddhist gesture of thanks and submission. The patriarch, puzzled, stared at him and then shook his hand.

*   *   *

Chen insisted they take the Maybach, for security. And there was also the intimidation factor. Nobody in Taiwan was going to trifle with someone traveling in a car that costs more than $200,000.

They stopped first at the Regent. The car waited downstairs while Dunne packed his suitcase. He felt sticky from the summer morning outside in the humid air, so he took a quick shower. The last item was his backpack, locked to the closet door. He hoisted it on his back and took the elevator down eighteen floors to the gaudy lobby. The clerk, who had seen the Maybach in the drive, was deferential.

They drove east toward Dadaocheng, in the old district of the city. The big car had trouble navigating the last few small streets before they reached Howe's hutong and the old red-brick house with the inner courtyard.

Alton accompanied Howe. The cop was still standing guard in the porcelain shop. Alton spoke to him, but he already seemed to understand. Alton pressed a crisp thousand-New-Taiwan-dollar bill in his hand as he shook it. Howe descended from the balcony with a well-stuffed backpack, pairs of sandals and sneakers dangling from the drawstring, and a computer bag strapped over his shoulder.

*   *   *

The Maybach rolled east from the old quarter, crossing the Tamsui River and heading along the expressway toward the airport perched along the Taiwan Strait. After about thirty minutes, Alton told the driver to take an exit off the highway toward an industrial park that housed the headquarters of Taipei Silicon Technology.

A guard station blocked the entrance to the complex. Howe showed his company badge. The guard checked his watch list, and then approached to ask some questions, but Alton Chen had already sprung from the front passenger seat of the car, handed the guard his card, and talked to him rapidly in Chinese. Chen walked to the guardhouse with the security officer and spoke over the phone to his boss. The metal gate pulled up, the stanchions were lowered, and the Maybach cruised to the front entrance drive.

Flapping in the breeze by the front door was the Republic of China flag, a white sun in the corner of a field of red.

The chief security officers were standing inside the door. Alton had a conversation, but they evidently had already received approval from someone. There were no more phone calls, and Alton beckoned for Howe and Dunne to come inside. Dunne unlocked his backpack, which was beside him on the rear seat of the limousine, and removed a small kit of tools, which he put in his jacket pocket. He and Howe were escorted to the elevator.

They rode to the seventh floor, accompanied by a security officer with a TST logo on his uniform. Howe's badge buzzed him through the door of his office; his workspace with the safe was in a rear office. He led Dunne toward this last redoubt. The security officer followed.

"We need a little privacy here," said Dunne.

Alton turned to the security man and spoke in rapid Chinese. This drew a sharp response; Alton tried again, more gently, but the man wouldn't budge. His instructions were to accompany the two Americans.

"A little problem," said Alton, then adding, "No problem."

He took out his mobile phone and called his father. Alton explained that they had run into difficulty at Taipei Silicon. Edward Chen's eruption was so loud that even Dunne and Howe could hear him through the speaker.

Alton passed the phone to the security chief, who got an earful from the patriarch. He trembled slightly as he handed the phone back to Alton, bowed, and left the room.

*　*　*

Howe led Dunne into the back room and opened the closet where the safe was anchored. It was a standard gray model with a big black dial lock.

"Shit," muttered Dunne. "They must want to keep you here."

Dunne took his kit from his jacket and removed an array of tools. He had a small drill and a tiny piece of plastic explosive, but he prayed he wouldn't need those extreme tools, which would cause problems for Edward Chen and his dutiful son.

Dunne put on the plastic gloves that were folded inside the kit. He attached a small electronic monitor and amplifier to the face of the dial, plugged in a pair of noise-canceling earbuds, and then began feeling his way around the dial, listening for the sound of the wheel pack and the contact points where each of the four wheels would line up.

Dunne had cracked dozens of safes in his career. He had liked to tell colleagues that he knew the feel of a safe the way he knew his wife's body. As that recollection flew through his mind, it sickened him, that he had ever thought or said something so crude.

This lock didn't give up its secrets easily: Dunne turned up the amplifier and attached a meter that registered changes he might not hear. He removed some graph paper from his kit, to record precisely the contact areas for each wheel. He got the click of the first wheel that way, and the next three were easier. There was the sweet moment in the end, where the contact points of all the wheels lined up and the pin fell through and with a turn of the bolt the locked clicked open.

Howe removed his passport. There was a wad of cash inside the safe, too, wrapped in rubber bands, but Dunne said to leave it. He put his tools back in the kit, closed the safe carefully, quickly wiped the room of fingerprints, and then pushed Howe toward the door. Alton was outside waiting. He looked enormously relieved that they were finished.

Dunne got back in the limousine, returned his lock-picking tools to his pack, and closed his eyes. The Maybach rolled toward the gate and powered back onto the expressway.

"Shit, man. You're good," said Howe.

Dunne didn't open his eyes.

They reached the airport a few minutes later. Alton took them to the VIP departure area, walked them through passport control and customs. The authorities had been alerted. They were elaborately polite and seemed barely to look at the documents that Dunne and Howe presented. Chen escorted them to the gate as he had promised.

An hour later, Dunne and Howe were in big seats on the EVA Air flight. Dunne ordered a glass of champagne. The flight attendant asked him if he wanted pajamas to sleep in on the flight to San Francisco. Dunne said yes, he would like pajamas, then fell asleep.

# 36

## Whippany, New Jersey—June 2018

Tom Goldman took a seat at the bar, next to two young men who had just finished their shifts at Data-Save, a data-recovery center that had opened a half
mile down the highway in one of the pitted exurbs west of Newark, New Jersey.
One had a sleeve of tattoos; the other had gold rings piercing the lobes of each
ear. They were watching the Yankees and talking about the dumbass mistakes
that other engineers had made in designing the server farm where they worked.

Goldman drank his beer and listened. With his bland, unlined face and
noncommittal smile, he was easy to overlook in the bar. He wore jeans and an
untucked blue shirt. He seemed to be listening to music through his earbuds,
but they were microphones that amplified the sound nearby.

"The heat sensors are kludgy on the third floor," said the first engineer. As
he drank his beer, the scales of the lizard tattooed on his left arm seemed to ripple at the joints. "I mean, really. They. Do. Not. Work. How fucked up is that?"

"We are working for morons. They could be one degree away from frying
every circuit in the place and they wouldn't even know it," said the young man
with the pierced ears. He pounded the bar with his fist and said, "Yes!" A Yan-
kee batter had just hit a double off the left-field wall at Fenway.

The engineer with the tats burped loudly.

"Yowzah!" He gulped down the rest of his beer.

"The NYSE techs came out today to test the system," he said, after he had wiped the foam from his mouth.

"Charlie and them?"

"Yup. They spent an hour in the data center, punching their tickets. They checked the bandwidth, sort of, checked the certificates, blah, blah. Then they drove back to Manhattan as if they had a clue whether we meet the specs."

The Yankees fan got a mock-serious look on his face.

"This is a test," he said in a radio voice. "For the next sixty seconds this data-recovery center will conduct a test of the emergency response system. This is only a test. If this had been an actual emergency, you would have been instructed to jump out the fucking window. This concludes this test of the emergency response system."

They both laughed. Data security was a joke to people who understood how porous most of the systems were.

Goldman sat atop his barstool, seemingly preoccupied with his music. He doodled with numbers on a piece of paper in front of him. Four thousand four hundred thirty-six. That was the number of companies that were publicly traded on U.S. financial exchanges. Thirty-one trillion dollars. That was the market's current capitalization, the three thousand biggest companies multiplied by the price of their stocks. One-point-eight billion. That was the number of trades per day.

He looked at his numbers, smiled, and then began to add little fillips: extra digits and half-written numbers, dividing lines and misplaced commas. And then, to cover the whole thing, a sprout of dragon's wings and sine curves and oscillating rays, so that it was a compendium of nonsense.

Life happens at the margins. That was what Goldman understood. The integrity of a system wasn't the big aggregates, but the smaller individual numbers that summed to the large ones. Reality was degraded a decimal point at a time. Once the individual numbers became suspect, so did the composites. Trust eroded in small fissures, and as they widened, people began to doubt the integrity of the entire system.

The Yankees game ended. The two engineers finished their beers. The one with the tattoos, who had been in the control room with the visitors from the

New York Stock Exchange, paid with a credit card. Goldman took a picture of it, the name and card number, with a camera hidden in his sleeve. Joseph Zelwig. Finding his address and other contact details would be comically, tragically easy.

The two friends walked noisily to the door. Goldman quietly followed twenty seconds behind, as if he were heading to the men's room, but then slipped out the side entrance. From the shadows of the parking lot, he registered the make, model, and license plate number of Zelwig's car.

Goldman went back to his seat at the bar and closed out his tab. Fifteen minutes later, he left the bar and walked back out into the sticky New Jersey summer night.

*　*　*

Goldman sat in his car, with the lights out, in the shopping center down the road from the Data-Save recovery center. He was surrounded by the charmless, anonymous landscape of far suburbia. Glowing beyond the Applebee's he had just left were a Taco Bell, a McDonald's, and a Chili's. So many choices; so little choice.

Goldman took his phone and called a number in Italy, using an encrypted Signal connection. It was early morning there, but he had promised a report, and Ricci probably hadn't gone to sleep yet.

"*Ciao, Lorenzo,*" he said. "*Questo è Tom.*"

" 'Sup?" answered the Italian.

"This is doable," said Goldman. "I'm at the backup site. We can, what shall I say—adjust—the trading records here in a way that will produce a panic."

"*Stai calmo, amico mio.* We don't need a panic. We just need a ripple. A demonstration. As my countryman Niccolò Machiavelli advised his prince: 'Never attempt to win by force what can be won by deception.' "

"I'm a lawyer. I want what my client wants."

"What about Michael Dunne? Did you hear the news from Taiwan? *Quest'uomo è noioso.* We squeeze him, box him, bribe him, and he doesn't go away. *Sono stufo di lui,* you hear?"

"I'll make him go away."

"I thought we did that before. But here we are again. *Basta.*"

"Heard. Understood. Acknowledged. It will be party time soon. The wires are ready. You just have to plug them in."

Heat radiated from the server farm as the summer night grew steamier. Goldman turned the ignition and the car rumbled off down the highway toward Paramus and then Hackensack and, beyond, the lights of New York City, which on this night seemed suspended from heaven as if by a billion invisible digital threads.

# 37

San Francisco, California, and Pittsburgh,

Pennsylvania—June 2018

Michael Dunne arrived in San Francisco with his mind in the traveler's in-between state, where pills couldn't quite put him to sleep and coffee wouldn't really wake him up. He'd been trying to think through all the activities he needed to set in motion now. Jason Howe clambered after him on the jetway; he was visibly delighted to be back in San Francisco. He put a fist in the air like a 1960s radical, and said to nobody in particular, "Right on!"

Dunne had warned Howe on the flight, before the sometime-Buddhist had had his fourth glass of wine, that he needed to be careful. After his escape from Taipei, his "colleagues" might be suspicious of him. But Howe insisted that he would be fine. He was a career bandit; he knew how to take care of himself. And the Bay Area was his safe place. He'd gone to Stanford. He'd get high for a week and stay in touch with Dunne on Signal.

"Slow down, Mr. Bandit," said Dunne, as they walked down the terminal toward the exit. "This is just starting to get serious. I want you to ping your friend Jake. You said he'd help you."

"Sure. I hired him, washed him, waxed him. He'll talk to me."

"Get in touch. Tell him you need a favor. Tell him you want to come East and see him. Reconnect. Find out what he's preparing for the Party. I need to know when and where it is. He may be the only way to find out."

"You got it!" said Howe, with a star-child buzz in his eyes.

Howe turned toward the TSA exit sign and freedom. He grabbed his backpack, with its flopping sneakers and sandals, and trotted off toward the door. Dunne thought of chasing after him, but he was tired, and it was pointless. He'd rescued the young man and downloaded what he knew. If Howe wanted to play outlaw again, that was his problem. Just so long as he made the connection with his former colleague.

*   *   *

Dunne spent the hours of his layover shopping in the airport. He bought himself two new Android phones that were unlocked, so he could install any chip he wanted. To connect them, he purchased four prepaid phone cards. He bought a fancy new backpack, too, to carry his expanding tool kit.

Flying over the Pacific was the easy part, but the two hops back to Pennsylvania were crushing. Flight delays, overcrowded planes, surly passengers. Dunne was in a foul mood as he rolled his bag to his apartment building in Shadyside and mounted the steps to the second floor.

*   *   *

The first sign that anything was wrong was that the door had been splintered and sloppily repaired around the lock.

Inside the apartment, they hadn't bothered to clean up. The closet and drawers were still open, and loose papers and articles of clothing were strewn across the floor. The mattress and pillows had been cut open to search for hidden material, as had the cushions for the sofa and chairs in the living room. Dunne had taken his laptop with him on the trip, but all the other computer equipment, the monitor, printer, even the mouse, had been looted. The burglars' goal had been information, obviously, but also raw intimidation.

Dunne called his office on Forbes Avenue. His assistant Jenny didn't answer the main number, and a call to her cell phone rolled to voice mail, too. That worried him.

Dunne found his Ford Explorer on a side street, untouched, and he was at the office in fifteen minutes.

The scene there was worse than at the apartment. Broken glass, a smashed copying machine, desk drawers ripped off their tracks and left in a heap, files either carted off or dumped on the floor. The burglars had even trashed the nice De'Longhi espresso machine that Dunne had bought when he had his first big payday. The office computers were gone, along with the peripheral equipment. Dunne didn't see any surveillance devices, but he assumed they had been installed.

Dunne's first thought was for Jenny, who must have discovered the upheaval when she came in for work and panicked.

Dunne called her cell again and left a gentle message advising her not to worry and to return his call as soon as she could. Then he called the police, who sent a squad car, and then a van with a forensics team.

While he waited, Dunne went to the place in his mind where he dealt with operations that had been disrupted. The process was more like spontaneous muscle memory than thinking, less conscious and more intuitive. He was getting close now, and he had to push on through.

*   *   *

The police did the standard crime-scene investigation. They took photographs, dusted for prints, and made an inventory of items that were stolen or damaged. They interviewed neighbors along the corridor and the guards in the lobby, and they examined the video archives of the surveillance cameras.

The detective took a statement from Dunne. He asked about motives and possible suspects. Dunne was politely unhelpful. He said he was in the private-security business and probably had a lot of enemies, but he couldn't think of anyone in particular. When the detective asked about his previous employment, he recited his State Department cover jobs. His résumé had a bland, not-quite-real quality, with so many seemingly unrelated overseas postings.

Dunne described the break-in at his apartment, too, and asked the police to go gather evidence there. The detective asked skeptically why Dunne hadn't immediately reported that other break-in and had come to his office instead. What was he worried about?

Dunne volunteered, since he knew the cops would find out anyway, that he had served a year in prison for making false statements to the FBI. After that, the detective quizzing Dunne subtly switched gears. Dunne was a certified bad guy; he'd been to prison; now some other bad guy had messed with his stuff. Maybe they'd find the perpetrator, and maybe they wouldn't.

The detective handed Dunne his card and advised him to contact his insurance company. The police department would do its best, he said, but since this wasn't an armed robbery and nobody had been hurt, they'd have to fit it in with other work. Meaning, don't hold your breath.

After the police had left, Jenny returned Dunne's phone call. Her voice was tight, and it sounded like she had been crying. She said she had discovered the break-in that morning. She knew her boss was traveling, so she had waited until he returned.

"Should I be scared?" she asked. "They have my cell phone number and email address. They know where I live." That information had been in her employment file, which was missing from the cabinet along with every other important record the little start-up company had gathered.

"Don't worry," said Dunne. "We'll keep you safe."

She was trying not to cry. Dunne told her to pack a bag and wait outside her apartment in Squirrel Hill. He would pick her up in fifteen minutes. Dunne retrieved his dusty SUV from the parking garage. He unlocked the glove compartment, removed a thick stack of bills, and peeled off a wad. He stopped at an AT&T store on Forbes Avenue on his way and bought a cheap cell phone and ten gigabytes of data, for cash. He opened the phone, noted its number, and put it in his pocket.

*  *  *

Jenny was sitting on the concrete steps in front of her building, with a suitcase and a shopping bag of clothes beside her. She was wearing a Pitt sweatshirt. She waved when Dunne rolled up.

"Hi, boss," she said. "I'm sorry about the phone call. I was a little nervous. Everything's okay, right? The office was such a mess. But it's just a burglary, yeah?"

Dunne laughed. "It's all good," he said. "We just need to chill for a little while."

She laughed, too, and then looked perplexed. "What do you mean? Chill how?"

"Where do your parents live? You told me, but remind me."

"Weston, Massachusetts. Boston Post Road." She rattled it off as if she were reciting a lesson.

"Well, maybe you should go there and spend a week with them. All expenses paid. I'll give you your salary, and a bonus, now, and money for the airfare. You can't come back to work, anyway, until we clean up the broken glass and fix the office."

Dunne took five banded packs of ten bills each and handed them to her. She counted the money carefully.

"There's five thousand dollars here," she said. "I can't take this. I don't make that much in a month, for gosh sake."

"Give me anything that's left over when you get back. Deal?"

"Yeah, I guess."

"Do you have your cell phone?"

"Of course! God, I can't get rid of it. I am so sick of social media."

"Me, too," said Dunne. "Listen, do something for me. Go to 'Settings,' and then 'Privacy,' and turn off 'Location Services.' Can you do that?"

Jenny clicked away at the device. When she had completed the change Dunne had requested, she looked up at him. Real concern showed on her face.

"What's wrong?" she asked. "Is someone after you?"

"I'm just being careful. There are a lot of screwballs out there. Until I know who trashed the office, I don't want anyone to know anything. It's none of their beeswax."

Dunne laughed again. She wasn't convinced.

"Have you called the police?" she asked.

"Yes. I just finished with the detective before coming to get you. They're doing all the right stuff. Fingerprints, photos, lists of what's stolen. I'm sure they'll catch the guy. And I'm going to call the FBI, too, my friend Bogdano-vich. You remember him? He helped me set up the business. Anything the police can't solve the FBI will figure out. It's all cool."

She looked at him skeptically. "What aren't you telling me, Mr. Dunne?"

"Nothing interesting." He smiled. In the afternoon summer sun, on the sidewalk of a neighborhood full of college kids, he might have been her older brother.

"I'll drive you to the airport. I think there's a flight to Boston on American at five."

"It's JetBlue. And it leaves at five twenty-four. My roommate can drive me. She'll want to say goodbye."

"Well, all right, then. One more thing."

Dunne took the burner phone out of his pocket and handed it to her.

"When we've put the office back together and everything is cool and it's time for you to come back to work, I'll call you on this phone. I have the number. Use your regular phone for everything else but keep this one clear for me."

"What if I need to get in touch with you, Mr. Dunne?"

Dunne offered one last, unconvincing laugh.

"I'll be kind of hard to reach for the next while. Send me an email on my Paladin account. I'll call you back."

Jenny shouted for her roommate, who had been waiting just inside the screen door. Dunne climbed into the cab of his big Ford.

"See you soon," Dunne called out. She nodded but couldn't form the words of an answer.

*   *   *

Dunne's last stop that day was Rick Bogdanovich's office at the FBI's cyber lab on the banks of the Monongahela.

In the fading light, there was a fragile, temporary look to the new office parks that occupied some of the empty space on either side of the river where the vast Jones & Laughlin steel complex once stood. In their day, the mills and furnaces here had looked so solid they would last a thousand years: the blast furnaces on the north side feeding molten steel to the rolling mills on the south side, to be welded and pounded into cars, trucks, trains, and buildings. How could that tower of steel ever crumble?

Now it was a technology park, feeding off bits and bytes from Carnegie Mellon and other local universities. The soot in the sky that had blackened men's shirts, and lungs, too, was gone. Fish swam in the river again, and so did people. So maybe it was better, but it was different. The strong, sturdy men and women had been replaced by coders, processors, and marketers.

Bogdanovich was waiting in his office. Dunne had called ahead and said he had a big problem and needed help urgently. It was past five-thirty when Dunne arrived, and most of the special agents and technicians had left for the day. Bogdanovich badged him past security and led him upstairs to his corner office, glinting with the light of the low, fierce sun above the grand span of the Liberty Bridge.

"I need help, Rick," said Dunne. "I've got a red-hot mess on my hands."

"I hear that someone tore up your office, and your home, too."

"Who told you?"

"The Allegheny County Police Department. They know we're friends. They seem to think it's your fault."

"That's ridiculous."

"Obviously. But what's going on? Otherwise I can't help you. No way. I'll get busted."

"Crazy story. If I tell you all of it, you won't believe me."

"Tell me part of it, then."

Dunne scratched his red beard. He hadn't shaved in nearly a week.

"You know how weird shit sometimes happens that goes off the books. The 'Executive Series' traffic from NSA suddenly isn't available on a particular subject, or the distribution list gets cut down to a few people? Does that ever happen in the Bureau?"

"Sure," answered the FBI man. "Lots of times. When something is hot, or it's bad news for the big shots, they put it in a separate compartment so that most people won't know about it. Or they just kill it off in cable traffic."

"But ask yourself: How does one of these weird busted operations get started? Somebody is sent on an assignment, and they find out something important, and the big shots say: Holy shit! This is important. We want a piece of this action. And then the games begin."

"Sorry, Mike, I'm not following you."

"You're not supposed to. Listen, do you believe in government conspiracies?"

"Not usually. Most government agencies can't do simple things right. How could they pull off something really complicated?"

"I used to think the same way. But not anymore. Because I'm caught in one."

Bogdanovich shrugged. "You're not telling me anything useful here, Mike. What's the problem? Who's chasing you? What's so important that people took apart your home and office trying to find out what it is? Level with me. Otherwise, this is bullshit."

Dunne looked at his friend, smart, solid, trustworthy. Would he understand? Dunne was about to speak, but then he shook his head.

"You wouldn't believe me. You'd think I was nuts, and then I'd lose the last friend I have. Let me work this alone a little while longer, until I have some pieces that fit together in a way that I can explain."

"But you're in danger, Mike. Someone is coming after you. You know something that can blow them up, and they're ready to take you down to stop you. You're not exercising good judgment here. You need to trust people."

Dunne shook his head. "I did that once before."

Dunne looked out the window toward Pittsburgh. A fallen empire. Jason Howe was right about that, at least. He turned back to Bogdanovich.

"I need someplace to hide for a few days. A safe house. Someplace where you stash your snitches and informants. Just a few days. And some documentation, like you'd give to one of your people if they were in trouble. Just a few days. Then I'll be cool."

"Why the hell should I do that, man?"

"Because I asked you. That's the main reason."

"I need another reason."

"We've known each other for, what, fifteen years. Have I ever told you a lie?"

"Nope. That's why we're friends."

"Okay. Something terrible is going to happen unless I can stop it. People have built some wicked cyber tools. They can take down financial markets, create panic, ruin the lives of ordinary folks. If we miss this, people will be asking for years why we didn't do anything."

"If it's that big a deal, let the government handle it."

"I'm trying to tell you, Rick: 'The government' is part of the problem. You need to give me a little space, to figure some things out. Then it's all yours, and I promise, it will be the biggest case of your career."

"I liked the first reason better."

In the silence, they both watched a coal barge move slowly down the Monongahela. There weren't many of those left. The old ways of doing things were nearly obsolete, but not quite. Bogdanovich leaned toward his friend.

"Let's just say you are a confidential source. You're in danger, obviously, given the attacks on your home and office. We're just doing what we'd do for any source who was at risk. No more, no less."

\*　　\*　　\*

Bogdanovich picked up the bulky phone that he used for talking about classified information. He called his colleague Janelle Martin, who was the special agent in charge of the FBI field office for Pittsburgh, located in a plain, flat, low-rise building across the river.

"I'm sending over an informant," he said. "I've got all the paperwork here. He's part of a dark-web undercover operation we're running. He needs papers. Fake ID, Social Security number, credit cards, new phone, all that stuff, billable to us. We need to do it quick, like today, so he doesn't get burned."

Bogdanovich paused, while SAC Martin asked several bureaucratic questions and otherwise covered her ass so that she wouldn't get in legal trouble if something went wrong with this operation, and then came back.

"He's a big guy, red hair. Scotch-Irish, I'm guessing. Use whatever cover name you like. He needs a safe house, too, an address that will match his ID. You got some apartments you aren't using?"

Martin scrolled through her inventory and reported back to Bogdanovich. He put his hand over the phone and spoke to Dunne.

"You can stay here in Pittsburgh, or in York, or in Erie. What do you like?"

"I like Erie," said Dunne. "By the lake. My dad took his boat up there sometimes."

"Erie," Bogdanovich told his colleague. "I'm sending this guy over right now. He needs new tags for his car, too, I guess. Don't ask questions. I've got the file here. Don't worry about it."

He paused a moment while Martin ran her name search, and then said, "Okay," and rose to walk Dunne to the door.

"Your new name is Andy Maguire. Don't do anything stupid, because this time it's on me. If you fuck up again, you will go back to prison, and people in the joint may discover that you were an FBI informer. Not nice. Hear me?"

"Understood. Thanks for trusting me. You won't be sorry."

Bogdanovich shook Dunne's hand and sent him off to Neverland.

# 38

Brooklyn, New York—June 2018

Jacob Rosenberg was at his computer, listening to the Comet Is Coming on his headphones, when his phone lit up with a text message from his friend and sometime mentor Jason Howe.

Rosenberg didn't look at the text from Howe right away, or any of the other messages that had backed up on his phone. He had a project to finish for Lorenzo Ricci, and it was already tomorrow in Italy. So he and his two apprentice geeks kept tending the graphics-processing units racked on the warehouse floor, trying to finish their almost-real video before midnight. The lights from the blade servers blinked in the darkened laboratory like distant stars.

Rosenberg had softened since his time in Urbino. He still had a goatee, but it was better trimmed now, and he'd stopped shaving his head, so that he had a neat cowl of black hair that he parted and combed every morning, like a normal person. He'd put on a little weight, too, eating and drinking in the restaurants and bars of Brooklyn. Life was about money now, not agitprop, and Rosenberg was settling down. He'd gotten a girl pregnant three months ago and, at first, he didn't tell her to abort the baby.

The laboratory was in a small warehouse in Williamsburg, on a street where every building was painted in fluorescent colors so that strolling outdoors was like walking through the pages of a comic book. Rosenberg's apartment was farther west in Brooklyn Heights, overlooking the bridge and the East River, near the building where Lorenzo had bought the penthouse flat. It was all too easy. Rosenberg was becoming just another computer criminal, as opposed to what he had imagined for himself several years earlier, when Jason had recruited him into the digital army.

Ricci had been specific about this new project: He wanted a piece of video that would cause a sudden, sharp fall in the share price of a company called Humford Holdings. He explained the basic story line to Rosenberg: The company was vulnerable. Short sellers believed it was overvalued because of the inflated reputation of Howard Schubert, its chief executive officer. Schubert had assembled a portfolio of companies that looked ordinary enough when you examined them individually, but as part of Humford Holdings they seemed to sparkle with fairy dust. If the market believed that Schubert was about to resign, reasoned Ricci, then the company's stock would be crushed.

"Make people believe that Schubert is quitting," Lorenzo said. "I don't care how you do that."

Rosenberg said he would make it so. At Stanford years before, he had told friends he wanted to be a screenwriter and only later became a software engineer. When he created a piece of video, he liked to tell a story that had the arc of a plot and conveyed a lesson beyond its impact on financial markets. That was why Ricci kept promoting him: He wasn't just a computer geek, he was an artist; he created false narratives that were believable.

Rosenberg toyed with various plotlines. Schubert was under investigation by the Securities and Exchange Commission. Schubert had been sued for sexual harassment by a former employee. Schubert's accounting firm had found irregularities and resigned from the account.

But as Rosenberg worked on the problem, the answer become obvious: Schubert was dying. He started tuning his network to create the evidence of this imagined fact so that it would appear to be a real fact. In his world, "real" was a term of art.

In the racks of servers arrayed beyond Rosenberg's desk lived the neural network he had been training so diligently these last weeks. He had started with a video template: a composite face of a middle-aged man with a facial structure and physical attributes similar to Schubert's. Then he added video of the actual Schubert, gathered by members of Lorenzo's team, and fed the clips into the neural net to create a believable face and voice for the fake CEO he was creating in the laboratory.

Rosenberg and his team shaped a first draft of their scripted drama. It was designed as a cell phone video, which would appear to have been shot secretly at a briefing given by the imaginary Schubert to several of his most senior managers. In the thirty seconds of video, a hoarse-voiced Schubert would explain to this intimate group that he would be having surgery in a week for stage four bladder cancer. The managers' faces wouldn't be visible as they heard this grim news, only Schubert's.

The cell phone camera would show him, full-face, pronouncing his own death sentence.

Then the computational work had started, and it continued to this moment. A first neural network created the imaginary death speech for Howard Schubert, simulating his face and voice. Then a second neural network detected small flaws in the simulation that made it less than perfectly believable: the shadow on Schubert's nose that didn't match the direction of the lighting; the slightly off-tone pitch of his voice when he began with the words "I have some bad news"; the momentary mismatch of his mouth with his voice.

Fixed. Fixed. Fixed. The first network corrected the flaws as soon as the second network detected them. It was like Darwin's natural selection; in the digital test bed, each dysfunctional error was erased; only the strongest, the most believable, survived. Rosenberg had a magisterial feeling as he watched the play of lights on the machines arrayed in the stack, their chips and processors forming a net that was so much like consciousness that it was consciousness. Fake; detect; fake; detect.

As Rosenberg watched the latest iteration of his generative adversarial network, he told his assistants: Our Howard Schubert is alive; he's real; he's dying of cancer. Then he sent it back for another round of create and re-create, to make it still more perfect.

The delivery system needed to be as believable as the image itself. The video would be loaded in a cell phone, and the phone would be shared, for a fee, with a hedge fund that had a big position in Humford Holdings stock. Obtained from a friend; can't say where; a word to the wise; time to push the button. And in the moment the sell order was executed, Rosenberg's performance—no, his art—would be complete. It wouldn't prompt a standing ovation, but something more powerful: a cascade of hundreds of millions of dollars, perhaps billions, as positions were unwound.

* * *

Rosenberg finished his last retake of the Schubert video just after midnight, a little later than he'd planned. The techs ordered cars from Uber and Lyft and said weary goodbyes, and finally Rosenberg was alone in his office at the far end of the warehouse and able to go through the messages that had been left on his phone.

He had a half dozen texts in three different encrypted apps. The one he read first was the long message from Jason Howe, the uber-geek, the man who liked to call himself "Eric" in homage to a radical historian nobody had ever heard of, and who had disappeared monk-like to distant Taiwan. Jason claimed he had decided to work on chip design in Taipei because it wasn't as boring as other things, but Rosenberg knew he had escaped to a safe harbor before one of the Italians convinced Ricci that he was a risk no longer worth taking.

"Take me with you," Rosenberg had said when Jason first told him of the Taiwan plan, and he had half meant it. But now the money was so sweet, and it turned out that what people always said about how crime doesn't pay wasn't true.

Rosenberg grasped his phone and clicked on the blue-and-white Signal icon. The message from Jason Howe was in a gray box, too long for one screen.

*J-Man. Core dump in Taiwan. Complete system crash. I'm in Palo Alto, living our origin story and over-caffeinating at ZombieRunner, but I need a serious favor. I want to come in from the cold, for real. I know Ricci and the fratelli probably think I'm a flake, especially after my hasty departure from Taipei. But I want to be part of the action when The Party goes down. Can I tuck myself in your suitcase? Seriously, I want to be there. Lots of stories to tell you, but they're all in Chinese.*

*You remember the Na'vi word for the neural connection when two crea-
tures connect their queues in Pandora? It's Tsaheylu. Your brother.*

Rosenberg thought about the request for a long minute, and then began
with a simple two-word answer.

*I'm here.*

He told Jason to send details about when he would be arriving in New
York, and he would take care of the rest.

Rosenberg skimmed through his other messages: Ricci wanted coding for
a new payload, using a zero-day exploit he had just acquired. Okay, tomorrow.
The director of security in Milan advised that Jason Howe had left Taiwan, and
to report any contact. Rosenberg just messaged: *Okay.* Let them do their own
spying on employees.

Finally, Rosenberg had three priority messages from Tom Goldman. The
first reported that he had begun final staging of the operation at the data-
recovery center in New Jersey; the second said he was awaiting word from
the techs about the precise time when the heat sensors would crash; the final
one reminded Rosenberg to have all necessary gear ready for Data-Save, at all
times, pending final notice by phone.

Rosenberg was tired. He found the flash drive that Goldman was so antsy
about and put it in his pocket. Sometimes he walked back to Brooklyn Heights,
but tonight after one a.m. it was sketchy in Williamsburg, with all the hookers
and drag queens and pimps outside the bars, and he ordered a black car. When
he got home, he had a shot of vodka, and then two more.

\*    \*    \*

Very early the next morning, Rosenberg was awakened in his Brooklyn loft by
a phone call from Goldman. The ring of his phone was insistent. Rosenberg let
it roll over to voice mail, but Goldman called again immediately.

"I need you now in New Jersey," he said. "Seriously. Now. It's going down
at Data-Save. How soon can you get here?"

"Shit," said Rosenberg. "What time is it?"

"Five o'clock. The system will crash at seven-fifty. You go in at eight. We have less than three hours. Hustle."

"Remind me where you are."

"Whippany. It's west of West Orange and north of Morristown, south of I-280. Tell me you remember."

"You drove last time. What's the address?"

"Put this in your phone. Nineteen-sixty Mt. Herman Avenue. It's a big, fat warehouse filled with computers. Meet me at the McDonald's across the street. I warn you: Lorenzo will not be happy if you're late."

"I'll be there. But, Tom, I don't respond well to threats. Especially this early in the morning. They make me anxious. I don't do my best work."

"Don't be a pussy. You sound like Howe. Just bring the flash drive, please. Otherwise this is a waste of time."

Rosenberg sighed. "I'm not an idiot. I have the flash drive." He pulled on his jeans and his black hoodie. He had promised Jason Howe back at Stanford that he would keep faith, no matter what.

* * *

Rosenberg arrived at the McDonald's across from the data center at 7:23. He had to take a yellow cab, which cost more than two hundred dollars, because no Uber driver answered his call. He was grumpy all the way out on the interstate. Dealing with Tom Goldman reminded him that this was a dirty business covered by smooth talk. The best thing about computer code was that it was simple, just a string of zeros and ones.

Goldman was sitting in a yellow plastic booth, looking at his watch, when Rosenberg arrived. His usually bland, genial features had a harder set.

"Glad you could make it," the lawyer said frostily. "We have less than thirty minutes until the system crashes. Twenty-seven, no, twenty-six minutes."

Rosenberg shrugged. "I'm here. What's the drill?"

"You remember the script?"

Rosenberg yawned. "Of course. Unless you changed it in the last two days."

"Play it back."

"The heat sensor glitches and says the floor is much colder than it actually is. The cooling eases up. The data-recovery servers get hot. One of the server racks on the third floor gets fried. Emergency service alarm. I'm on call. Poof! I go to the third floor where the trouble is, and while I am 'fixing' things, I stick the drive into a port in the server stack. Assuming I get in the door."

"I have credentials for you. You're Joseph Zelwig. You're on the four p.m. shift, normally, but this morning you're on call for emergencies."

"Okay. I guess. This feels more like burglary than computer science."

"Focus, Jake. This isn't the time to discover your conscience."

Goldman handed the goateed engineer a Data-Save identification card, and then gave him a black plastic device that was hot to the touch.

"Put this in your pocket when you go through the portal. It will neutralize the electronic security."

"So you say, but it's my ass."

Rosenberg was sweating. He wiped his brow with the sleeve of his sweatshirt.

"What about the data-port lock?" asked Rosenberg.

Goldman handed him a small key with four tiny teeth that fit the plastic caps that covered the USB ports in the server farm.

"Calm down, Jake. It's all cool."

"Show me the map of the servers."

Goldman removed a four-page document from his briefcase and handed it to Rosenberg.

"It's on page two. Just like we rehearsed: Take the stairs. Wear your ID around your neck. Don't ask directions. Your rack is on the third floor, aisle two-D. Floor three, two-Delta."

Rosenberg studied the floor plan. He closed his eyes and recited the location from memory and handed the sheets back to Goldman.

"How do I exit? Remind me."

"East door. Opposite side from where you entered. You forgot something in your car. You're coming right back."

"What about security cameras?"

"Forget about them. They will be wiped."

"Shit," said Rosenberg, shaking his head. Goldman looked at his watch.

"Move out, my friend. Now. Chop-chop."

* * *

The alarm was already buzzing when Rosenberg entered the data center through the west door. He flashed the badge, but in the chaos people barely looked. Junior managers were gathered outside a conference room trying to reach senior managers.

People were cursing as they tried to reach colleagues or summon extra help. "Backup power activated!" shouted one of the managers. A woman wearing a Data-Save T-shirt kept repeating, "Check the sensors, check the sensors," as if she didn't believe the readings.

"This has *never* happened before," said a man in a white shirt and tie, speaking loudly into a cell phone.

Rosenberg joined a queue of people heading upstairs. Others, in the confusion, were heading downstairs, away from the malfunction. When Rosenberg reached the third floor, he found people checking servers one by one. They knew the servers were failing, but they didn't know why yet. "The floor is hot," someone called out from a distant stack, but there was no response.

Rosenberg recalled the floor plan he had memorized a few minutes before, and headed to 3-G, then 2-F, then 2-E, and then he was at the designated stack, the lights still glowing and pulsing. The area nearby was empty. Most of the outages were a few dozen yards away, past the wall of black metal racks. He pulled up his hood and put on his plastic gloves.

Quickly, now. Quickly. Rosenberg found the control monitor for aisle 2-D. Using the key Goldman had provided, he unlocked the small plastic insert that blocked access to the computer's USB ports. He looked left, then right. He heard footsteps in the next aisle over, coming his way. The beeps of the alarm system were getting louder.

Do it now, Rosenberg told himself.

He took the flash drive from his pocket and inserted it in the open USB port. He heard voices in his corridor now, coming his way. He left the drive in for a count of five seconds and then removed it.

Someone was calling to him. Rosenberg pretended not to hear as he moved away from the control monitor, but the call was insistent.

"Is this row down, too?" a woman was asking. She looked frantic. She was more flustered than he was. Rosenberg relaxed.

"No. I just checked," he said. "They're okay. I'm going to make sure about 2-C."

"Okay, okay," the woman said, continuing down the dark corridor lined on both sides by needy machines. "I'll check 2-A."

Rosenberg made his way back to the stairwell. He went up to the fourth floor, where the alarm buzzers weren't ringing, and then walked deliberately around two sides of the building to the east wing, and descended the stairs to the east door.

"Wrong way, Charlie," called out a man entering the data center, just as he was leaving.

"Be right back," answered Rosenberg. "Forgot something in my car."

He walked several hundred yards down Mt. Herman Avenue to a Wendy's and called Goldman.

"Done," he said.

"Good boy. Any feedback?"

Rosenberg laughed, letting the fear and tension go.

"People are so stupid, Tom. I mean, that's the secret, right? It isn't the electronics. It's the fact that people are so goddamn stupid."

# 39

## Erie, Pennsylvania—June 2018

The wind raked the lakefront, bowing the trees on Presque Isle and rattling the empty, boarded-up storefronts downtown. A handsome new hotel and conference center capped the bayfront, and if you kept your eye on its towers and the fancy condos nearby, you might think nothing had changed from the days when Erie was one of the industrial diamonds of Lake Erie, along with Buffalo, Cleveland, and Toledo. But its manufacturing companies had mostly gone away. The big paper plant had closed, a planned steel mega-mill had never been built, and the electrical factory that once made locomotives and refrigerators had transferred production to Mexico. What was left was basically an insurance company, a university, and a lot of decent people who were too stubborn to move.

Dunne's FBI-furnished apartment was in an old brick ten-story building on State Street. His rooms were on the eighth floor, overlooking the lake. The apartment was cheaply furnished like a motel suite and had the commercial tidiness of a recent maid's visit. The room smelled of air freshener, not quite covering the musty odor left by a previous occupant. The refrigerator was empty, but a half-drunk bottle of vodka was nestled in the back of the freezer.

Dunne unpacked his suitcase and set up his computer. The FBI had given him his own portable Wi-Fi hotspot as part of its mobile phone package, but Dunne knew the Bureau would monitor it, so he had bought his own. He was tired, and he needed to relax. He put on a tweed jacket and a pair of jeans, and walked to a brewpub that he had noticed on the way in. Even though it was early summer, there was a chill in the air; Dunne turned up the collar of his coat and dug his hands into the pockets.

Inside, the bar was warm and noisy, filled mostly with students from the nearby university and by other drinkers who wanted craft beer instead of Budweiser. Dunne took a seat at the bar and ordered a pint of a local Belgian-style wheat beer called White Rascal.

"Cheers," said Dunne, tipping his glass to a big bearded man to his right, and then to the left, to two women, each with a sleeve of tattoos. It was the bearded man, who had finished off several pints of amber ale and was starting another, who wanted to talk.

"This country is fucked up," he said.

"I guess," said Dunne. He preferred to talk about sports or movies, or nothing at all, when he was in a bar with strangers. But apparently that wasn't to be.

"I'll be honest with you," said the bearded man in an unbidden, confidential voice, leaning unsteadily toward Dunne. "I voted for the president. Most people here did. 'Make Erie great again,' okay? This is the town that elected him, basically. You understand that, right? This is fucking ground zero."

"I don't think about politics much," said Dunne.

"Well, then, listen to the voice of Erie, Pennsylvania, my friend. Blue-collar town, heart of the Rust Belt. The Democrats thought they owned Erie. But they spent their time kissing the asses of rich Mexicans and Chinese and all that." He burped.

"Hey, friend, let's chill. I'm from Pittsburgh. I voted for the president. But my only politics right now is beer. Is that cool?"

"Listen, man. It's all cool. But you didn't let me get to the punch line." He took a massive swig of the amber ale, which dribbled down the black hairs of his beard.

"Okay, what's the punch line? Then I'm watching sports on TV."

"The punch line, my friend, is that the president hasn't done *shit* for Erie. It's worse now than before. And you know why that is?" He burped again.

"No, man, why is that?"

The bearded man leaned toward Dunne. He had a nasty twinkle in his eye, like a kid who was about to drop a firecracker on a frightened dog to impress his buddies.

"Because the blacks and Jews and Mexicans won't let him, that's why."

"Fuck you," muttered Dunne. He tensed for a moment, fists clenched under the bar, but the big inebriated man slumped back into his chair, cackling. Dunne didn't want to have to talk to the police. He picked up his beer and moved to the other end of the bar in front of a television set showing the Pirates game. The two tattooed women moved away, too.

"Racist prick," called out one of them.

The bearded man rocked in his chair, trying to get out of it to do something, he didn't seem sure what. Just then the manager came over and spoke quietly to him. He had a bushy beard, too, and seemed to know the loudmouth ale-drinker, addressing him as Al. The gist of the conversation was that Al needed to shut up or he would have to leave the bar.

Al ordered another beer, but the bartender said no, and he lurched out, cursing in every direction. The bar patrons ignored him.

Dunne listened to country music from the speakers near an empty dance floor, half watching the baseball game. The Bucs were losing. A Cleveland game was playing on another television down the bar, but for a Pittsburgh fan, watching the Pirates play badly was better than watching the Indians win.

\* \* \*

Dunne awoke the next morning, showered, and then shaved for the first time in more than a week. When he was dressed, he arranged his workspace in the living room of the FBI flat: His computer sat on the small desk; beside it was a legal pad and a felt-tip pen; three phones, all with their location services turned off, were lined up on a side table; a pillow softened the hard back of the desk chair; a cup of coffee purchased at a café down the street stood unopened.

The orderly workspace reminded him of his old desk on the third floor in Arlington, in the brief period before the walls fell in. He thought to himself: I want to go home.

Dunne took from his backpack a photograph of his daughter Luisa when she was three. He put it behind his computer. He had another photograph that he never displayed but always carried with him. It showed his ex-wife Alicia in Paris, just after they were married.

Dunne placed the photograph of his former wife on a windowsill above the desk. He put his head down on the desk and let himself think.

*   *   *

Dunne had been working at his desk for an hour when a cell phone began to ring. It was the one the FBI had given him as part of his informant identity. He didn't want to talk to anyone, and he was going to let the call roll over to voice mail, but that had problems, too. At the last minute, he answered.

"This is Bogdanovich," said a gruff voice. "Thought I should check in."

"What's up, Rick?" asked Dunne. It couldn't be good.

"I received a message from your old boss this morning. George Strafe. He said you were in trouble. The Chinese were coming after you. Some stunt you pulled in Taiwan, he said. He wanted to know where you were."

Dunne took a deep breath. He wondered how quickly he could get across the Canadian border if he needed to.

"What did you tell him?"

"I didn't tell him shit. I never trusted Strafe. He illustrates why FBI agents don't like CIA officers. The CIA lies for a living."

"Why did Strafe contact you, Rick?"

"He knows we're friends. From way back. He said he'd heard you'd moved to Pittsburgh, after you got out of prison. He wondered if we were in touch. I told him you'd stopped by to say hello, but that was it."

"Thank you. And you're right about Strafe. He's untrustworthy."

"You are in some serious shit, my friend. I don't know what's going on, but it scares me."

"I know," said Dunne. "I'm working on it."

*   *   *

The essence of Dunne's plan was simple: Even as he was running away from his adversaries, he would run toward them. "Active defense" was his new vocation, and it was the kernel of what he needed to do now. If he waited in hiding, hoping to escape detection, they would eventually find and destroy him. If he made himself visible, he became a target himself but also gained the initiative and the opportunity for surprise. The hunter might appear to have control, but not if the prey was armed and prepared.

As Dunne considered the vulnerabilities of the team arrayed against him, the personality that surprised him most was Adrian White. He had regarded White as someone like himself, a member of the CIA's blue-collar workforce, a man who like Dunne had a modest chip on his shoulder, but who focused on doing his job rather than taking credit for it.

How had White fallen into the orbit of a group of liars and manipulators whose primary mission seemed to be personal and collective enrichment? And how long had he been a knowing adversary? Had White been manipulating Dunne in Geneva, steering him toward the dance club and the seductress who tempted him? Had he laid a path of entrapment in Urbino, counting on Dunne's loyalty to his superiors?

White was clever and self-interested, but he wasn't a venal, calculating man. This vestige of decency might make him pliable.

Dunne scratched some ideas on his pad, barely legible even to him. His advantage was that his adversaries really wanted to find him. In their eagerness, they would make mistakes. He spent several hours assembling the elements of the operation in his mind and on paper.

He grew tired and restless, the plan not quite settled, so he took a run along the lakeside. His eyes caught the splash as the water broke against the sandy bank and scanned the spread of the thickening summer foliage, whose limbs and leafy branches began to cover the inlets and nooks.

Dunne's mind wandered to the spots where his dad took him fishing when he was a boy, trailering their little boat up to Lake Erie or renting a bigger craft lakeside, loitering in the coves and shallow bays waiting for smallmouth bass and the occasional rainbow trout. Once the fish were hooked, his father would reach out with his net, and they were soon gutted and on the grill, and his father would pop open the first of too many cans of beer.

\* \* \*

Dunne packed his phones and laptop in a backpack and retrieved his Ford Explorer from a pay-parking lot. He drove east for five minutes, then north toward the lake, to make sure that he was clean, and then headed west on I-90 for two hours to the Cleveland airport. He parked at the short-term lot, turned on the location services for his phones, and linked his laptop to the Wi-Fi connection.

Dunne had two old cell phone numbers for Adrian White and two email addresses, one a classified agency account and the other a Gmail in-box. Through all four channels, he sent the same imploring, uncertain, enticingly vulnerable message:

> Adrian: Bad things keep happening to me, and I don't know why. Have you been double-dealing me? I thought you were my friend. Maybe you could meet me and get me out of this jam. Can I trust you?

When the messages were gone, Dunne turned off the location trackers and the hotspot and put the phones in a Faraday bag that would block signals, in or out.

Dunne had an inventory of items he needed to gather quickly, on the fly. He drove back to Erie by a different route, moving east along I-80 and then turning north to Meadville. He visited the local college theater to ask if they had any old disguises for sale: wigs, prostheses, tummy pads. The manager sent him down the road to a community theater that had been in business for nearly a century. They were happy to part with some of their dusty props, especially to someone who paid cash.

Dunne stopped at a Costco just outside town and bought some supplies. The clerk looked at the unusual array in the basket.

"Big project?" asked the clerk.

"Repairing some damage," answered Dunne. Before he left Meadville, he took one of the phones from the Faraday bag and used it to search for cabins near Niagara Falls. He called a small, remote spot and booked a cabin for the following night.

*   *   *

Adrian White responded that evening: He texted just after ten p.m., to the burner phone Dunne had used.

*I can meet you tomorrow. Tell me where. I think I can help.*

Dunne hadn't hated Adrian White before, but he did now as he read those deceptive words. White and his friends thought they were setting a trap, but they were entering ground they didn't control.

Dunne answered carefully. He drove to Conneaut, just over the Ohio border, and, an hour later, sent his response using a second prepaid cellular phone, this one with a 415 area code, which he had purchased on his stopover in San Francisco.

Dunne's message was simple, with a date and time and an invitation.

*Tomorrow at 4:00 pm near Buffalo, in New York State. I'll send you the coordinates at 2:00. Come alone. If I see any surveillance, the meeting is off.*

Dunne had an S&T man's practiced intuition that White and his precious Consortium would take the bait, and he thought he had a reasonable chance of capturing White and taking him to a place where he could be persuaded to explain the conspiracy into which he had been recruited. But what would Dunne do with him then? Even in his rage, he wasn't a killer. He needed someone reliable who could keep White on ice after he had bled a little.

Dunne thought of the people to whom he could turn for help, but he realized that he couldn't trust most of the names. The friendships were transactional, or the people had complicating links with the federal government.

Eventually Dunne settled on a man he had known from his adolescence, who had proven faithful and discreet more than once. He placed the call to a number in Fox Chapel, in the suburbs of Pittsburgh, made his request, and, after an anguished conversation, got the answer he needed. As he drove back to Erie that night, he let himself think about his ex-wife.

# 40

Lake Erie Beach, New York—June 2018

The weather the next morning was hot and humid, with scattered thunderstorms along Lake Erie. Dunne rose early and rented a Chevrolet sedan at the local Enterprise agency when it opened at eight; he set off soon after, in disguise, to scout his location. Dunne had assumed many appearances over the years: long beards and short ones; different skin tones, noses, and facial structures. Today he wore a gray beard, a faded baseball cap, and lumpy pad around his stomach that made him look thirty pounds heavier.

The rendezvous point Dunne had selected was a small patch of sand grandly called Lake Erie Beach, across the state line into New York. It was a poor man's Riviera, with a tavern and a bar-and-grill framing the entrance to the beach. Working-class vacationers came here from Buffalo, a slight glimmer above the whitecaps, twenty-five miles northeast at the far end of the lake. Lake Erie had been a sinkhole these last decades as the mighty factories on its banks had slipped away, but at least now the lake was rimmed with green.

The sky darkened as the morning passed, and a sheet of rain advanced across the lake, a curtain of water that seemed at once to be falling up and down. A shard of lightning cut the distant sky, followed by a cymbal of thunder.

Dunne gazed at the bleak weather and smiled. The conditions would obstruct whatever surveillance his pursuers could put in the air.

Dunne left his rented car in the parking area. He pulled the hood of his jacket tight around his cap, beard, and false gut shielding his identity, and set off to reconnoiter the site. The "beach" was a sorry, scrubby bit of sand. A dog was chasing a Frisbee, and a few bathers were standing in the wet drizzle, determined to have their day at the shore.

Dunne walked slowly up the beach. A hundred yards north, the waterfront curved east at a crest called Point Breeze, overgrown with trees and shrubs that obscured the sandy ground beneath. Dunne circled the point and climbed down to the water's edge, testing the banks and eventually locating a spot that was obscured from view east or west.

He marked the location in his mind: A red oak stood twenty-five yards away in the firmer soil; closer to the water was a poplar tree, and by the bank itself was a thicket of dogwood shrubs, their spring blossoms gone but their green leaves festooned over the water, broad and deep enough to hide a small boat.

*    *    *

Dunne returned to his rented Chevy and drove a quarter mile northeast along Lake Shore Road to a little resort town where a sinuous estuary emptied into the lake. The water was just deep enough that a small boat could float free over the sandbar and into the long, protected finger of the river.

Here, too, Dunne walked the ground, looking for a place where a boat could hide. He found a little green patch by the river called Bennett Beach, with bushy trees overhanging the bank. Dunne returned to his rented car and steered it into a turnout fifty yards from the park and hidden from the road.

Dunne left the Chevy there. He walked back to Lake Shore and phoned for a local taxi to return him to Erie, where he had parked his green Ford Explorer.

Then Dunne made his next carefully considered move: He drove the big SUV up the shore road past Lake Erie Beach, a few miles farther on from Bennett Beach, until he reached a harbor known as Sturgeon Point. A lifetime before, he and his father had rented a boat there to cruise the lake all the way to Buffalo, whose skyscrapers nicked the horizon.

Dunne had called ahead that morning to reserve a one-day charter.

*   *   *

Dunne parked in a twenty-four-hour lot near the marina. Slouching low on the seat, he peeled off his beard and removed the tummy pad and the rest of his disguise. He needed, for a moment, to look like the picture on his Andy Maguire ID. He put the disguise in his pack with his other gear and set off for the boathouse.

The charter boats were in their slips, chafing against white-rubber bumpers. Dunne selected the smallest seaworthy vessel available, a seventeen-footer, equipped with a twenty-five-horsepower outboard motor. He gave the attendant a fake Maguire driver's license that matched his fake Maguire credit card and told the attendant he would return the boat the next morning.

The usual maximum rental was eight hours for $255, but Dunne offered to double that for overnight and made a quick deal. The man agreed to throw in an electric starter, so Dunne wouldn't have to pull the cord. On the way out, Dunne stopped by a nearby fishing store and made a purchase there, too.

Dunne set off in the little craft, heading southwest. The chop of the lake knocked against his metal hull with a regular thud as he crested each wave and hit the trough.

When the marina had faded to a speck in the distance, Dunne reapplied the false beard and the other elements of his disguise. The rain had slackened but the surface of the lake was still boiling. Dunne stuck close to shore all the way down to Lake Erie Beach. He found his little hideaway under the dogwoods, shipped the engine, and tied the boat to a nearby tree. He gathered shrubs and branches around the vessel so that it was invisible from land or water.

Then Dunne took his gear, stuffed it into his backpack, and retreated to the tavern nearest the beach to wait. At two, he texted the coordinates of Lake Erie Beach to Adrian White.

*   *   *

Just after two, Dunne slipped out the back entrance of the tavern and made his way to the grove of trees that sheltered Point Breeze. He squatted under the branches of a chokeberry bush and waited, binoculars to his eyes, focusing on the one access point to the beach. At three, a helicopter made a slow flight over the area; it lingered by the beach but made only a quick pass over the wooded area where Dunne was hiding. The chopper took one more run of the beach and the taverns and, finding nothing below, disappeared.

A few minutes later, a pair of burly bathers arrived, carrying beach bags big enough to hold semiautomatic weapons. They placed their towels on the sand and lay down awkwardly. One of them wore wraparound sunglasses on this cloudy day. The other began scanning the perimeter, 360 degrees, with electronic binoculars.

Dunne couldn't see any vehicles. There must be some, hidden somewhere, but they were far enough away that he would have a decent head start.

*   *   *

At four, precisely, Adrian White arrived. He walked down the access road and rounded the curve toward the sand. He looked far too cosmopolitan to be a Rust Belt beachcomber. He was wearing blue and green Hawaiian surf trunks, a black T-shirt with a picture of the rapper Drake, and a Dallas Cowboys cap that covered the top curls of his dreadlocks; the strands dangled to his shoulders.

White walked north of the two muscular bathers, ignoring them, to a point roughly halfway between them and the spot where Dunne was hiding.

White scanned the beach looking for his rendezvous. Dunne let him walk to the edge of the beach, the waves breaking on the sand just beyond his running shoes, before he texted a WhatsApp message. White heard the ding, took out his phone, and read the words:

*Walk along the bank to the wooded area to the north. If the two knuckle draggers on the beach follow, or I see any other watchers, no meeting.*

White turned and looked at the two security officers. Through his binoculars, Dunne could see the big man's lips move as he spoke into a hidden microphone. Reading the shape of the lips, the message was: "He's here," and then, "Don't follow." White walked slowly toward the spot that Dunne had commanded.

As White neared the top of the point and began passing out of view of the beach, Dunne texted him another message:

*Keep walking around the bend. Don't speak to your friends again.*

White kept walking, gingerly. Dunne retreated deeper into the grove, just before the lee bank, a few yards above where the boat was hidden. He had a gun in his back pocket, but that wasn't his instrument of choice.

Dunne held a fishnet in his left hand, the kind you might drag behind a trawler. In the other hand he held a big leather belt. But his chief weapon was surprise. He could hear White coming, from the crunch of the plants under his feet and the crackle of the shortwave radio in his ear.

*       *       *

Dunne waited until White was just past him, and then he pounced. In a first motion, he threw the entangling net over his prey, so that it caught his head and arms. He jerked hard on a cord attached to the net so that White stumbled. Then he jumped on White's back, strapping the belt quickly around his neck as the big man fumbled in the netting.

Dunne cinched the belt as tight as he could. White managed to shout, "Help," but that was all. Dunne reckoned he had about thirty seconds. White resisted, but he was choking for breath, gasping as he flailed inside the web.

As White feebly wheezed for air, Dunne pulled his hands behind him and cuffed them. He kneed his former colleague hard in the back of both thighs to weaken his legs, and then cuffed his feet. He dragged the immobile man toward his hidden boat, ten yards away in the brush. He tumbled him over the side and pushed the boat out in the water until he was knee-deep; he lowered the outboard motor and hopped in.

The engine started instantly, a loud whir of the prop in shallow water. Dunne cranked the power control all the way and the boat surged northeast, still hidden from view of the pursuers. White gave a last gasp before he passed out. Dunne kicked him.

"You bastard," he said over the roar of the outboard and the bump of the hull against the waves. "That's for my wife."

Dunne locked the motor so the boat surged straight ahead. He ripped the communications gear off White's body and threw it in the water. White was inert. Dunne needed him alive. He undid the belt and compressed White's chest several times.

White gurgled as he regained consciousness and then began to gasp for air. His eyes were bulging as he stared at Dunne, not just because he had been starved of oxygen, but because he was frightened. Dunne kicked him again.

"That's for my daughter," he said.

Dunne looked overhead for a chopper or a drone, but they hadn't scrambled one yet. If a boat was on the way, it was too distant to see or hear. The estuary was approaching. Dunne turned the boat to starboard and gunned the power. The little skiff shot through the narrow river opening and into the sheltering tree-lined creek.

He steered the boat toward the green shoulder of the park to the deserted spot he had chosen. White was moaning now. Dunne stuffed a handkerchief in his mouth and fixed it with duct tape.

Dunne beached the boat and trotted to the turnout, where he retrieved his rented Chevrolet. He drove it as close to the water as he could, left the engine running, and opened both back doors.

White was heavy. Dunne rocked the skiff until the body rolled out. The big man flailed on the grass, jerking to get free, so Dunne wrapped his arms and legs with more duct tape. Then he dragged White toward the Chevy a dozen yards away, heaved his shoulders up on the backseat, and then from the other side pulled his body inside the car. His legs didn't fit on the backseat, so Dunne punched his hand behind the knees to bend them and shoved the legs to the floor.

Dunne took his pistol out of his back pocket and put it in front of White's face.

"Do not fuck with me, Adrian. I used to like you, but I'm ready to kill you if you don't help me."

White nodded.

"Are you wearing a tracker?" asked Dunne.

White made a gasping noise through the gag that sounded like "No."

"I don't believe you," said Dunne. He fished in White's pockets, pulled down his shorts to look for something hidden up his ass, pulled off the running shoes and discarded them, and combed through the dreadlocks. He found nothing, but he was still suspicious.

Dunne examined White's lustrous black skin. Legs, torso, neck, all the places you might think to implant a tracker in someone's skin. But it was all smooth to the touch.

Dunne finally found it, on White's upper arm between his elbow and his shoulder, a small gash of scar tissue in the mahogany skin, from a recent incision.

"Sorry, brother," said Dunne. He took a pocketknife, cleansed it with disinfectant, and applied the blade gently to the skin. The GPS tracker popped out, with only a little gush of blood. Dunne wrapped the arm in gauze, and then swaddled the arms and legs in duct tape, to keep him still. Then he laid a gray blanket atop White.

Dunne took the GPS tracker and put it in the boat. He pushed the craft in the water again, turned on the engine, and powered it back toward the lake, the boat empty now except for the electronic ghost of its former passenger.

Dunne returned to the car and closed both doors. White was moaning from under the blanket.

"Just shut up," said Dunne.

Dunne drove back to the shore road. He heard distant sirens, and he could see the faint lights of a police car a half mile south, above Lake Erie Beach. They were still trying to figure out what had happened.

Dunne headed northeast and took his first turn onto a side road that crossed under the New York State Thruway and then ran parallel to it. Several miles on, he found an entrance ramp that joined the highway heading toward Buffalo. In the westbound lane, police cars were heading the other way.

Dunne stopped at the first gas station and bought some plastic sunshades for the back windows so that nobody could see inside.

# 41

## Niagara Falls, New York—June 2018

Dunne turned up the radio to cover the occasional muffled curses from the man under the gray blanket in the backseat. The Thruway was a well-groomed, old-fashioned motorway, the east-west lanes divided by a line of trees. Beyond the pavement stretched the flat terrain of upstate New York, rich and dotted with farms and forests. The landscape became more settled and suburban as they neared Buffalo. Dunne wanted to avoid passing through the heart of the business district, so he left the Thruway at an exit just past a suburban shopping mall. He found a smaller highway that ran along the banks of Lake Erie, past a steel plant in Lackawanna that was still operating somehow.

When he had settled into the drive, Dunne called the friend in Pittsburgh whom he had recruited as his accomplice. He told him that the plan he had described the night before was in motion, and that the friend should take the late afternoon flight to Buffalo and meet Dunne at a small motel near Niagara Falls, where he had reserved a cabin.

As Dunne drove, he wanted to talk to Adrian White. Partly it was to soften him up, and partly just to talk. He turned down the radio and spoke loudly so that the man under the blanket could hear him. At first White grunted back, but he soon fell silent.

"You did me wrong, Adrian," Dunne began. "I want to tell you about it, so you'll know why this is happening. My wife was named Alicia. She was the prettiest girl I ever met. After you and Strafe and your friends took me down, she divorced me. She took custody of my daughter Luisa, who I'll maybe never see again. But that's not the worst. Alicia lost our unborn son. Did Strafe and any of your other pals ever explain why that happened? Did they?"

There was only silence, so Dunne continued.

"It was because someone decided to squeeze me by publishing dirty pictures of my wife. Some I took and never deleted, some fake. Alicia was an innocent girl. She had only been with one man. Me. It destroyed her. Did you do that, Adrian?"

From the backseat there was a muffled sound of protest.

"Shut up, Adrian. You were part of it. It's on you. And I am telling you straight up that you are a dead man if you don't tell me what you know."

White gargled apologies against his gag. Dunne cut him off.

"No bullshit. I am going to kill you if you don't tell me what happened and what's coming down next. I mean it. I don't give a shit about the consequences. I have lost everything that matters to me. This is payback. Do you understand me?"

White grunted again, something breathier that sounded like assent, animated by fear.

The highway rolled north, elevated on concrete piers now, framed between the Buffalo River and the lake. Dunne quieted down. They crossed the river toward the Seneca Tower, a hulking refrigerator of a building that was Buffalo's closest claim to a skyscraper. Just to the west was a district called Canalside, where the Erie Canal met the lake.

Dunne looked at the area, gussied up now by developers, and remembered the way it had looked when he was a boy. He spoke again, in a reverie that was half meant for Adrian but mostly for himself.

"Here's another story for you, Adrian. You can't see it, but we're passing the part of town where all the bars and whorehouses used to be. They paved over all that shit, but I remember. My father would tell me about it when we came up to Buffalo. Ninety-three saloons, once upon a time, and God knows how many hookers. That's what he said."

Dunne paused. His mind filled with images from the past, a little boy in the passenger seat next to an abusive, alcoholic father, the kid wanting to be the lady-killer tough guy that his father pretended to be. Dunne cleared his throat and continued.

"My father told me what a stud he was, romancing all those women. Maybe that's why I'm fucked up, because I had to listen to that shit from my dad. But let's be honest, Adrian, this is on me, too. I was a weak man, and people like you knew how to use that, didn't you, you prick?"

Dunne paused again.

"You know what my father used to tell me? He'd say: Son, if you're not thinking about pussy, you're just not concentrating. He thought that was funny."

Through the gag, Adrian offered a sympathetic choke of laughter. Dunne's voice began again after another moment, low and bitter.

"Shut up. I am going to kill you, motherfucker, if you don't tell me everything I want to know. Just so you understand."

*   *   *

The afternoon was giving way to dusk as they headed north toward Niagara Falls. The sun had emerged from amid the clouds in the west, and the lake had a velvety sheen after the earlier turbulence. Canada was on the other side of the water, sunlight shimmering off the big lake and illuminating the ponds that dotted the way west.

Dunne drove just above the speed limit. Too careful looks suspicious, one of his mentors at the agency had told him years before.

Niagara Falls was twenty miles above Buffalo. They reached it just as the light was dying. Plumes of spray rose from the two cascading falls, and the particles of water seemed suspended in the vanishing light. And then it was dark, and you could barely see the water but could hear the roar as it rushed over the lip.

Dunne drove a few miles more and turned off the road to the rustic motel, back in the woods, where he had reserved a cabin. He parked in a secluded spot where nobody would hear the muffled sounds from his car. He put his pistol on the passenger seat and went to the main lodge, where he registered and got his key.

Dunne paid in advance, in cash, for three nights. He asked for a secluded cabin, telling the desk clerk that a friend would be dropping by later for some beers.

"Just don't break anything," said the clerk. "Any rowdy stuff, I'm calling the cops."

Dunne gave him a thumbs-up and returned to his car. He moved the Chevrolet to his cabin, parking it so that the back door opened just at the entrance.

It was pitch-dark now; Dunne waited until the area was deserted, and then dragged White into the room and slumped him onto the lumpy green chair just inside the door. He went back and parked his car in his assigned lane and returned with his pack.

He looked at his watch. With luck, his friend would arrive from Pittsburgh in an hour.

*   *   *

Dunne closed the shades tight. He turned on the faucet in the bathroom sink and the shower, too, so that the sound of the spurting water might fill the room. He pulled up a wooden desk chair next to White, who was still tightly bound and gagged. He laid the pistol on the floor nearby so he could reach it easily. From his pack he removed a long knife and withdrew it from its sheath. He put the tip of the blade against White's neck, just behind the carotid artery.

"Here's the deal: I'll take off the gag, if you don't call for help," said Dunne. "If you do, the knife goes in."

White nodded. With one hand, Dunne began unwrapping the gray tape, while the other held the blade. When the tape was unwrapped, he removed the handkerchief that gagged the mouth.

"Help me!" screamed White as soon as the cloth was gone. It was a piercingly loud sound.

Dunne pushed the knife till it broke the skin and drew blood. Not a gush of blood from the artery, but a sharp, painful stab.

White stopped his plea for help as the knife went in. Dunne relaxed his pressure on the blade.

"I will kill you if I have to, Adrian. I mean it. Don't fuck with me again."

"Yes, sir," said White.

Dunne got disinfectant and a gauze bandage from the kit. He stopped the bleeding and wrapped the bandage tight. Then he sat back in his chair, facing his prisoner.

"Talk to me, Adrian. If you tell me everything you know, I promise that you will survive. If you don't, this will have a bad ending. I promise that, too."

White nodded. "What do you want to know?"

"Tell me about George Strafe and the Italians."

"Shit," muttered White. He took a breath. "You know how it started. Ricci and his pals were doing things with technology. When Strafe sensed how good they were, he wanted in. That's why he sent you, to find out."

White's voice was hard to hear above the rush of water. Dunne went to the bathroom and turned off the shower; the basin faucet continued to run. He returned to White, who had stayed silent. Dunne patted him on the shoulder.

"I already know that, Adrian. Keep talking, or I'll bring back Mr. Knife. If you behave yourself, I'll take off some of the tape on your arms and legs."

"It hurts," protested White, but Dunne cut him off.

"Was Strafe playing me from the beginning?"

"Probably. He met me when I first joined your team, not on the seventh floor but somewhere in the basement where nobody would see, and he told me to keep an eye on you. He sent me messages through a separate channel when we were in Geneva."

"Why did he want me inside the Italian operation so badly?"

"You were the recon man. He needed to know what they were doing. What technology they had. Remember, we weren't supposed to spy on them until you agreed to do the job. It turned out they could do stuff we hadn't tried, even the Russians hadn't tried, nobody had. Once Strafe found out what they could do, he wanted a piece of it, quick. 'Il Consorzio,' they called it. The Consortium. You were in the way. You got caught in the churn."

"And you let him do it. You didn't stop him."

"Hey, Mike. I'm like you. I follow orders. I asked him why he was stiffing you, and he just said: 'Cost of doing business.'"

"Why did he take me down so hard? He destroyed my family. Why do that?"

"Because you were unreliable. He thought you were jerking him around after he brought you home. Not playing for the team anymore. Ratting him out.

That's what he told me, at least. It pissed him off. He wanted to make it look like the gearheads and Wiki-punks were trashing you, and you bought it."

Dunne nodded. He paused, but only for a moment.

"Was Veronika a setup? Did you know she was going to be at that bar?"

White nodded. "Yes. But you did the rest, brother."

"Yup." Dunne bit his lip. "Was Veronika part of this Consortium thing from the beginning?"

"No. But her mother was, I think."

Dunne thought of the face of the woman he'd seen entering the *Cosmos* in the harbor, who had been treated like royalty. Adele K. Hecht.

"The mother ran a bank, and a lot of other stuff, too," continued White. "Veronika went along. She didn't know what was going to happen to you. She was so upset she was going to tell the Geneva cops about her mother, Strafe said. They put her in a hospital to keep the lid on."

Dunne put his head in his hands and rocked slowly for a few seconds. Then he leaned over White's body and began unwrapping the duct tape from his torso a strand at a time. White's hands were still cuffed, and his legs were both cuffed and bound, but he could now stretch his upper body.

Dunne turned away from White for a moment. He took out his phone, out of sight of the other man. He clicked on the "Voice Notes" recorder app and laid the phone down.

"I'm running out of time," said Dunne. "These people are coming after me."

"Yes, sir. That's a fact."

"What are they planning? What's their big score? I hear the Italians were calling it 'La Festa.' The Party. What the hell is that?"

"It's a con job that's going to make everyone crazy rich. They're going to create fake information that will crash the markets. They're looking for a couple of partners who will do the trading for them."

"Like who?" Dunne looked at his watch. "Come on, time is running out."

"I don't know details. I'm just a foot soldier here, bro."

Dunne took his pistol off the floor and held it in his hand, uncocked but ready. He pointed it at White.

"Cut the 'bro' crap. You must know something."

"They only told me one name. There was a big hedge fund in Connecticut they wanted to use, but the fund said no. The CEO had his own disaster-prevention plan. I know about them because Strafe wanted me to visit them this week, before the Party went down, and remind them that if they said anything, they would end up dead. I was about to do that when you checked in."

"What's the name of the fund? And who's the guy you're supposed to intimidate?"

"Halcyon Capital Partners. They're in Darien, Connecticut. The head guy is named Lewis Spoon."

Dunne wrote down the names. He looked at his watch again. His helper should be here soon.

He looked Adrian White hard in the eyes, until he saw a flutter at the corner of the man's lips.

"I don't think you've told me everything, my friend." He raised the gun again and pointed it at Adrian's temple. This time he cocked the hammer.

"They'll kill me if I tell you."

"I will kill you if you don't. And I'm closer."

Dunne's finger tightened around the trigger and he began to squeeze. White gagged a moment in fear and then sputtered the words.

"Stop! I'll tell you. Put down the gun. Please, for god's sake."

Dunne uncocked the pistol, but kept it pointed at White's head.

"Talk," said Dunne.

"They're planning a trial run. A demo, to convince the investors they can pull this off. They had invited Spoon. They'll have a command post, a war room, so people can watch this shit go down."

"Where's the command post? And when is this supposed to happen? Come on, don't go stupid on me."

White was silent, and Dunne cocked the gun again.

"It's in Manhattan. Near the CIA base. I don't know the address."

"When is it? Come on, goddamn it."

"Next week sometime. Monday or Tuesday, I don't know."

"Oh, Jesus." Dunne put the gun down. It was Thursday. He had four days.

"Sit tight, Adrian. Your babysitter is coming."

Adrian looked at the gun, and the knife. "You are one crazy fucking white man, you know that?"

Dunne took that as a compliment. While they waited, he picked up his phone and played back the "Voice Notes" of what Adrian had said, just so they were clear.

# 42

## Niagara Falls, New York—June 2018

Just after eight, there was a knock on the door. Dunne opened it a crack and motioned the visitor inside. Into the cabin walked Richard Ellison, the African American from the Oakland neighborhood of Pittsburgh who had been Dunne's best friend in college. Ellison had gone on to become an assistant U.S. attorney and then general counsel for the biggest bank in Pittsburgh, but most important, he was the one man who had kept faith with Dunne, completely, while he was in prison, preserving for him the letter that contained the first threads of the string he had been following ever since.

Ellison stepped into the room and stood before the big Jamaican-born CIA man, his knotted dreadlocks against the green upholstery of the chair, cuffed and half wrapped in duct tape. White looked almost as surprised to see that Dunne's accomplice was a black man as Ellison was to see the mummified prisoner below him.

"What the fuck?" said Ellison. "What kind of crazy shit is this?"

"It's what I told you on the phone. This is Adrian White. He used to work with me. He was part of the group that ran me out of the agency. Now his friends are getting ready to do something seriously illegal. Isn't that right, Adrian? You tell my friend."

White stared at Dunne. "Your friend is a brother?"

"Obviously. He's also a former assistant U.S. attorney. Go on, tell him."

White turned to Ellison, who was still wearing a suit and tie from the office, where he had started the day.

"It's true," said White. "Mike was set up. I need to talk to a lawyer before I do any confessing, but what Mike says about a conspiracy is true."

Ellison studied the bizarre scene and tried to make sense of it: His friend, a former CIA officer who had served a year in prison, had evidently kidnapped a man who was a serving CIA officer, and was holding him hostage—and counting on Ellison to be his accomplice.

"Call the FBI," said Ellison. "They'll sort this out."

"Not now," said Dunne. "Not yet. These people are powerful. If we move now, they'll disappear. You saw what they did to me two years ago? They'll do it again. They don't care about the FBI. They have their own country."

"I could get disbarred. Lose my job."

"I know. It's a big ask. It's just, I'm on my own here. You're the only normal friend I have who I can trust."

Ellison lowered his head. He was a normal friend, it was true.

"I'm not agreeing. But what do you want me to do?"

"Watch Adrian. Feed him. Take him to the toilet. Keep the DO NOT DISTURB sign on the door. If you want to move him somewhere else, that's fine. Just make sure he doesn't communicate with anyone until Monday noon. That's all I need."

"But that's illegal."

"No, it's not. You're an officer of the court. You've become aware that a crime is about to be committed. I have the evidence recorded right here on my phone. You're protecting this witness from intimidation. Besides, he consents. Isn't that right, Adrian?"

Dunne picked up his pistol with one hand, and his phone with the other. He pointed the gun at White's head as he clicked the record button.

"Isn't that right, Adrian? You consent to remaining here under Mr. Ellison's protection voluntarily, don't you?"

"Yes," said White.

"Louder, and say the whole thing, please, so we can hear you."

"Yes, I voluntarily consent to remain here under Mr. Ellison's protection."

"Good. You two are going to be pals, I can tell. And the fact that you are cooperating with me and Mr. Ellison is going to help reduce the time you spend in jail later. Maybe you'll be so cooperative you won't spend any time in jail."

*    *    *

Dunne took Ellison into the bathroom for a private conversation. He turned on the shower again so that the man trussed in the green chair in the other room couldn't hear them. He explained more of what Adrian White had told him, and the seriousness of the financial chaos that could occur if they couldn't stop the plan to disrupt the markets with false information.

Dunne implored Ellison to give him enough time to reverse the flow of events, but he could see the doubt in his friend's eyes.

"This is wrong, Michael. I believe you, and I want to help you, but we need to do this legally."

Dunne thought a moment. He didn't want to hurt his friend Ellison, even to save himself. He reached for his wallet and took one of his Paladin LLC cards, and wrote on the back the cell phone number and personal email of Rick Bogdanovich at the FBI's Cyber-Forensics center in Pittsburgh.

"You know Bogdanovich, right?"

"Sure. He works for the Bureau. His office is in the tech park. He helped you get started."

"Call him tomorrow night. Tell him what's happening. Not too much, but enough to satisfy your conscience. He won't be able to scramble anyone until the weekend. Just give me twenty-four hours. Can you do that?"

Ellison thought about it, weighed his loyalty to Dunne against his own potential liability.

"Twenty-four hours. Yes, I can do that. Other than that, no promises."

"One last thing. Try to convince Adrian that no matter what, no matter who from the FBI or the CIA shows up, he shouldn't tell them that he gave me any information. Tell him you'll keep him out of jail, you'll be his lawyer, get him a great job, buy his mom a new house. Whatever it takes, just keep him quiet."

"Okay," said Ellison solemnly.

"Can I trust you, man? This is everything, right here."

Ellison put his arm around Dunne's shoulder. "Listen, brother: You can't find out whether someone is trustworthy except by trusting them. You helped teach me that, a long time ago."

"Amen," said Dunne.

He gave Ellison his kit of supplies, including the pistol, sheath knife, duct tape, and a water bag with a tube so that White could stay hydrated even if Ellison had to put the gag back in his mouth. At the bottom of Dunne's bag were two dozen power bars. He handed them to Ellison sheepishly.

"Maybe you can order a pizza," he said.

On his way toward the door, Dunne stopped and said a last word to Adrian White. "My friend Richard will take care of you. Don't do anything stupid."

White turned toward Dunne, pulling against his trusses. He cleared his throat. There was one more thing he had to say to Dunne, the one thing he had left out of his recitation, when the gun was pointed to his head. He offered it now not under compulsion, but out of remorse.

"They're going to come after your wife again," said White.

Dunne stopped suddenly and put down his pack. "What do you mean?" he asked. "How can they touch her? We're divorced. She lives in California. She's out of the picture."

"She's your weakness. They know you'll do anything to protect her. They talked about it. Before I went to meet you at that beach, they said if something went wrong, they would find her and squeeze her again, to get you off their back."

Dunne stood motionless for a moment, and then he bent down over Adrian White and gave him a kiss on his forehead, which was moist with sweat.

Dunne gathered his things. He put the DO NOT DISTURB sign in place on the outside knob. It was nearly nine p.m.

"See you on the other side," said Dunne. He closed the door, went to his car, and drove back to the main highway. He stopped at a gas station, filled the tank, and bought a six-pack of Red Bull.

# 43

## Darien, Connecticut—June 2018

The sun rose on the bubbles of wealth that glisten along the Connecticut shore-line, where many of the great hedge funds manage their trading thirty miles from the unpleasantness of Manhattan. Michael Dunne had driven through the night, traversing New York State on a buzz of caffeine. He arrived just before three a.m. and got a room at a simple hotel off the interstate. He slept five hours and awoke refreshed, with a sense that he was nearing the threshold of what he had been chasing for nearly two years—not simple revenge anymore, but something more powerful: knowledge.

Dunne called Halcyon Capital Partners and asked for the chief executive, Lewis Spoon. A skeptical assistant said her boss was busy. Dunne identified himself as a former officer of the Central Intelligence Agency who was calling on an urgent matter. She asked what this urgent business concerned, precisely, otherwise she couldn't disturb the chief executive.

Dunne rolled the dice and made a guess: He said he was following up a contact that had been made by a group of investors represented by a London lawyer named Tom Goldman. He wasn't acting with Goldman's group, Dunne said, but to investigate their activities. After a delay, the assistant put Dunne through. The CEO didn't bother with pleasantries.

"I hope you're calling to say that Tom Goldman has been arrested," Spoon said. "What he proposed is outrageous."

"Not yet," said Dunne. "I'm in the neighborhood, as it happens. Could I come see you this morning?"

"Wait a minute," said Spoon. He put Dunne on hold while he jiggered his schedule for that day. He came back on the line.

"I can see you now. Do you know where we are?"

"I have an address in Rowayton."

"Tell the guard your name. Michael Dunne, correct? He'll get you past the gate and the dogs. I'm in Building Number Three, up on the hill."

Dunne put on a blue suit he had carried all the way from Pittsburgh and his last clean shirt.

*   *   *

The gate swung open to the campus of Halcyon Capital. Three buildings with the austere, graceful lines of a Frank Lloyd Wright compound were set along a creek that sluiced down a gentle hillside to a pond lined with ferns and dwarf maples. The landscape was like a Japanese garden, groomed to appear raw and also perfectly ordered. Atop the hill stood Building No. 3, whose floor-to-ceiling windows overlooked the cove and the yacht club of the next dukedom east along the shore.

Spoon was standing at the door, in blue jeans and an open-neck shirt, rolled-up sleeves, a man rich enough to dress however he wanted. Halcyon Capital had more than $150 billion in assets under management as of that morning.

Spoon appraised Dunne: the swirl of red hair, ruddy complexion, lean body, deep circles under the eyes.

"You look the part," he said. "Come inside. Rosemary will get you some coffee."

Dunne took a seat on the couch, facing the big window. Several dozen sailboats were bobbing at their moorings in the anchorage across the bay. American flags flapped in the breeze at each dock and green lawn. It was easy to be patriotic if you were this rich.

Dunne had a fleeting thought: This is where all the money ended up, when they bled places like McKeesport dry.

Rosemary arrived with two steaming cups of coffee while Dunne was still settling.

"Let's have it, Mike," said Spoon.

"I need information about Tom Goldman and his group. They're dangerous. I need to know what he pitched you. Then maybe we can stop it."

Spoon laughed. He was used to getting information, not dispensing it.

"I thought you were going to explain all that to me, Mike. Officially, I don't know anything. Goldman made me sign a nondisclosure agreement before we talked."

"Did you report the conversation to the FBI?"

"Nope. My general counsel wanted me to, but I figured, why should I? Probably it was all bullshit, and if not, why make enemies? And there was that nondisclosure agreement. I could get sued."

"That agreement was dictated by a criminal, Mr. Spoon. Nobody will make you keep it."

"You obviously don't know much about business. But before I tell you anything, you need to answer me a question. Why did you get fired from the CIA and spend a year in jail? I checked, while you were on your way. That doesn't inspire confidence."

"I violated an agency rule, on the orders of my boss. I spied on an American. Illegally, they said. They went after me, and I signed a plea agreement and went to prison. But that's not why it happened. I got in their way, so they removed me."

"Who is 'they,' please."

"George Strafe, my former boss at the agency, is working with the man who came to see you, Tom Goldman. They run a network of the smartest hackers in the world. The chairman is a Swiss woman who owns a boat as big as a football field. I got in their way. Like I said, these are dangerous people. They create their own reality. They chew people up."

"You lost your family in all this, is that right?"

Dunne nodded.

"And you want to get them back?"

"That's probably impossible. I just want to stop more bad things from happening."

Spoon walked to his desk and buzzed his assistant. He asked her to summon two people to join the conversation. They arrived several minutes later, ascending the walk from Building No. 2. They took chairs, just back from where Dunne and Spoon were sitting.

"Michael Dunne, ex-CIA, meet Frederica Schwartz, my general counsel, and Anthony Spezos, my chief information officer. Mr. Dunne has come to see me about the unusual meeting I had last week with the lawyer from London who wanted us to help him invest money in a scheme to profit from market irregularities. We said no, emphatically, as you will recall."

The two assistants nodded.

"It turns out that Mr. Dunne here used to work with the people who organized that dubious effort. He is what you would call a whistleblower. He wants to go to the authorities, which I gather means the FBI. And I'm, what, curious about this whole thing. Freddy, is there any legal reason why I shouldn't talk to him?"

"Technically, yes," answered the general counsel. "But the nondisclosure would be very hard to enforce if the underlying proposal would violate the law. Let me amend that: It would be impossible to enforce."

"Thank you. I like lawyers who tell me it's okay to do what I want. Mike, I'm a soft touch, whatever people say. I feel sorry for you. Plus, I want to know more about this racket. So, I'm going to explain some of it to you, with help from Tony, who understands the AI part. And then you can do whatever you want with it."

"Thank you."

"I want one promise from you in return, which is that you will keep my name and my firm out of this, forever, period. That's the deliverable for me in this transaction: that Halcyon gets buried, if any bad shit happens. Do we agree?"

"Yes, sir." Dunne put his hand on his heart.

"Okay. Here's what your friend Goldman proposed to me. He said he had the ability to 'anticipate' certain market-moving events, meaning create them. The events would be very disruptive."

"Did he say what would happen?"

"Oh, yes. He said that records of trades in the market might disappear, electronically, so that firms like mine couldn't be sure what they were holding. The financial turmoil would be devastating, but the events wouldn't be real. People who bought assets at the bottom would get huge returns. He wanted to invest about a billion dollars with us, and have us leverage that, so the bet would be closer to a hundred billion."

"Holy shit," said Dunne.

"Precisely. So, I asked Goldman how he knew about all this scary stuff and he said he had contacts in the hacking world, Russians and Ukrainians and other people in the dark web who had gotten wind of the plan, and he was offering me a chance to benefit from it. Otherwise, he said, I'd get crushed like everyone else."

"What did you say? I mean, a hundred billion dollars is a lot, even for you, right?"

"I told him to fuck off. I said we didn't need his protection. We were already prepared for exactly what he was describing. We're not stupid. Anticipating risk is part of our business. Explain it to him, Tony. This is the part where my head hurts."

* * *

Anthony Spezos, the chief information officer, had a prominent nose and dark, thinning hair. He looked over the top of his black reading glasses toward Dunne as he spoke.

"People think of Halcyon as a financial company, but we're really an artificial intelligence company," he began. "I helped create the neural networks that beat the best Go players in the world, and then Lewis hired me to create something similar that could make money."

"I gave him his own fund within Halcyon," said Spoon. "It's up ten billion dollars since we closed the fund last year."

"My trading edge is that I understand how machines think," continued Spezos. "Computer brains are like humans'. They think slow and fast. The slow part is recognizing patterns. In the last facial recognition challenge, the winner took two hundred twenty-four seconds. Three years ago, it was twenty-nine hours, so 'slow' is getting faster, but still . . . Slow AI is machine learning, where the machine crunches every iteration, every trade, every crop and weather report, and everything else that's digitized—and tells you the probabilities based on past outcomes."

"Okay," said Dunne. "What's thinking fast?"

"The fast part is machine reasoning, intuition, let's say, based on the machine learning. That's more complicated. The models use smaller slices of data that still generate high-quality results. It's like unsupervised learning, compared to rote learning. This fellow Tom Goldman claimed his operation could combine the two."

"We weren't interested," broke in Spoon, "because we're already doing it. Tell him how we work analysts' calls, Tony."

The lawyer interjected. "Just to be clear: This is proprietary, Mr. Dunne. If you share it with anyone, we'll sue you."

"Got it," said Dunne.

Spezos, the computer scientist, leaned forward in his chair and continued.

"With the boss's permission: Every quarter, most big publicly traded companies have conference calls with financial analysts, where they try to set expectations for quarterly earnings, so the market doesn't freak out when the numbers are announced. What we did was to feed recordings of several thousand of those calls into computers, with algorithms that could correlate the words, pauses, inflections, and voice modulations of a CEO with what he said later in the call, good or bad, that would move the market."

"What use is that?" asked Dunne.

"When we listen to earnings forecasts now using this little system, we can predict what will be said at least ten seconds ahead. Ten seconds. That's all we need to make a killing on all the other traders."

"You can see into the future?" Dunne turned quizzically to Spoon.

"Yeah, basically," answered the chief executive. "It's less valuable now than it was a year ago, because other people have figured out how to do it. To make money, you need two things. Correct thoughts about what's ahead, and unique thoughts. What we have is correct, but it's not unique anymore, so Tony will figure out other ways."

Dunne was dazzled by the Halcyon money machine, but he was impatient, too. His clock was ticking.

"What was Tom Goldman's 'unique' thing? How's he planning to make money in a way that nobody else has?"

Spezos and the lawyer both turned to Spoon, who spoke quietly, with a combination of admiration for the Consortium's trading panache and horror at its consequences.

"They're going to create false events," said Spoon. "And they're going to wipe out the records of real events. They're going to create a panic, profit from it, and then restore order. It's brilliant, but incredibly irresponsible."

"What did they want from you?"

"Money to leverage their bets up to that hundred billion. Market presence. Insurance. They proposed a trial run, soon, to convince us that it would work. A proof of concept."

"How soon?" pressed Dunne.

"Next week. We said no."

"Why did you say no?"

"Because we already have the technology. Or, Tony does. We can reconstruct every single position we hold, even if there's a cyberattack or a dirty bomb on Wall Street or some other disaster that destroys all the electronic records. We can reengineer them, cross-referenced and time-stamped, so that everyone knows they're legit. That's part of what Halcyon sells its best clients. Their money will be safe, even after Armageddon."

"That's reassuring, I guess."

"It's business, Mike."

"When is the trial run scheduled?"

"This Monday, I think. Is that right, Freddy?"

"Yes, sir. Monday morning at ten. After the markets open."

"Where did they want you to go for the demonstration?"

"A trading room for one of the Swiss private banks. It's on Avenue of the Americas. What was the number, Freddy? Nineteen hundred block of the Avenue of the Americas, 1978, I think. Correct?"

The general counsel nodded.

"What's the name of the bank?" asked Dunne. But he knew. He'd known, really, for a long time, but he had been thinking slow.

"Maison Suisse," said Spoon. "It's a private bank based in Geneva, but it has big trading operations."

"I know it," said Dunne. "I used to have a friend who worked there. Who runs that bank, by the way?"

"It's odd, for a European bank. The CEO is a woman. Very beautiful and mysterious. People say she has more secrets than her clients, and that's why they trust her, but what would I know? I'm just a country boy here on the Connecticut shore. Her name is Adele Kruse, I think. Wait a minute. I think she had another husband. Adele Kruse Hecht. That ring any bells?"

"Possibly," said Dunne.

# 44

Darien, Connecticut—June 2018

Rosemary brought in more coffee, and some cookies and pastries. Dunne was too hungry to be polite. He ate a cranberry Danish, and then an oatmeal cookie. The breeze was stiffening on the water. Small boats were hoisting their sails, casting their moorings, and beating out toward Long Island Sound.

This was Dunne's one chance. Persistence and luck had brought him into this room, with a man who could help him accomplish what he had feared was impossible. Seize the moment or it would be gone.

"I think I can stop Goldman and Strafe before this goes down Monday morning," said Dunne. "But I need to ask a big favor."

"You're already overdrawn on that account," said Spoon. "What is it?"

"Do you have a private jet?"

"Of course. Three of them, to be exact."

"Can I use one of them to fly to California tonight? The Orange County airport first, and then San Jose. And then back here to New York."

"Westchester County, you mean. That's where the planes are kept. Why do you need to go to California?"

"To pick up one person who can help me. And to pick up two other people who are in danger. My wife and daughter. The family I lost, when things went bad."

Dunne opened his wallet and removed a picture of a radiant woman with a smile that, when the picture was taken, had only known joy.

"This is my wife, Alicia."

He took out a second picture, of a child whose delicate features matched those of her mother, but with the added exotic touch of red curls.

"This is my daughter, Luisa."

Spoon shook his head. "Beautiful. I'm sorry for you."

"It's going to happen again, if I can't protect them. Except this time it will be worse."

"What can I do?" Spoon opened his arms.

"I told you: Lend me your plane. If I try to fly commercial, I'll get stopped by someone. I'll never get to them."

Spoon didn't answer. Dunne looked at the floor. The chief information officer doodled a geometrical pattern on a piece of stationery. The general counsel leaned toward Spoon and whispered something in his ear.

"Would you excuse us for a moment? Freddy is telling me why I shouldn't do this, and I want to talk it over with her."

*　*　*

Dunne paced outside for ten minutes. Spezos excused himself and returned to his neural networks down in Building No. 2. Rosemary offered more sweets, but Dunne refused and asked for a Red Bull, and when told they had none, a Diet Coke. Eventually the door opened, and Spoon waved him back in the room. He was smiling, the look of a billionaire who had decided to make a risky bet, contrary to legal advice, because it would make him happy.

"I'm going to do it," said Spoon. "Freddy says I'm nuts—that I absolutely should say no—but that's her job. I'm going to hire you as a consultant, starting now, and give you identification for the pilot to put on the manifest. That will cover our ass, slightly."

"Thank you," said Dunne. "Most people would say no."

"Don't start with that," said Spoon gruffly. "You'll make me change my mind. I'm doing this because it's the right thing. And, also, because it will save my clients a lot of money if I don't have to reconstruct all their positions. You're taking all the risk, and I stand to profit. Why wouldn't I do that?"

*  *  *

Dunne was embarrassed by the luxury of the Gulfstream jet: the beige leather upholstery, the rosewood trays and inlays, the heavy crystal glass into which the flight attendant poured his sparkling water soon after he took his seat. The pilot introduced himself ceremoniously, as if it were Dunne's plane, and he asked for the names of the three passengers who would be added to the manifest for the return trip. The captain apologized that the plane's Wi-Fi system wasn't working, but maybe they could repair it in San Jose. He gave Dunne the locations of the general aviation terminals where they would land and take off.

Before the plane departed, Dunne asked for time to make two phone calls. He went aft, to the rest room in the back, where nobody would listen.

The first call was easy. Dunne contacted Jason Howe on Signal, as they had planned when they parted company at the San Francisco airport less than a week ago. He was in Palo Alto, hanging out with some of his geek friends from Stanford.

"I'm coming to see you tonight," said Dunne. "It's showtime. We're going to livestream La Festa, so that the Party ends before it starts."

"Nice," said Howe groggily. He had been up all night with his pals watching old Jean-Luc Godard movies on Netflix. "How should I get ready?"

"You need to find ways to penetrate a space in Manhattan. It's on Avenue of the Americas. It's the trading room of a private bank called Maison Suisse."

"That's Ricci's bank," said Howe.

"Correct. We need to get inside. We'll talk about the details tonight. Meet us tonight at Atlantic Aviation, where the private planes come into San Jose. Bring whatever gear you need to stream the big show. Then we'll fly back East."

"Wow!" said Howe. "You're really going to do it."

The second call was to Alicia. She was living in Irvine, in a little detached house off the Santa Ana Freeway. Dunne knew right where she lived, in a tidy Orange County bungalow near the school that Luisa attended. He used to look at it sometimes on Google Earth when he first got out of prison, and then stopped because he feared he would be accused of stalking his ex-wife.

Alicia hung up when Dunne called the first time. But he waited fifteen minutes and then tried again. When she answered, he repeated the same word four times.

"Please, please, please, please."

"What is it?" she answered. It was a voice beyond anger, hollowed out.

"I need to see you tonight. The people who hurt you before want to do it again."

"You hurt me," she said. "You promised you would stay away."

"Please, please, please, please," he repeated.

"What do you want?"

"I'm landing at John Wayne Airport at four p.m. your time this afternoon. I want you to get Luisa and go to the Hilton Hotel at the airport. At five, a driver will come bring you to the general aviation terminal at the airport. He'll have a sign with your name on it."

"Why are you doing this, Michael? We are healing. I have a new life."

Dunne choked back the emotion in his voice.

"I failed before. I fucked up. I'm trying to do it right this time, before something bad happens. We're both caught in the same thing now. The people who can create fake pictures are doing it again, on a much bigger scale."

"You did this. Nobody else." Her voice was bitter, but also resigned.

"I know. I've spent two years living with that. I wouldn't be calling you for the first time since we split if this wasn't real. You are in danger. I can't let it happen again. Please believe me."

Alicia didn't answer at first.

"You wouldn't lie about this," she said quietly.

"No. I wouldn't."

"How many days will we be away?"

"A few. I don't know. Pack enough for you and Luisa to get by until Monday."

"Where will we be?"

"Safe. That's all I can say."

* * *

The plane rolled down the runway, gaining speed until it was aloft. Dunne closed his eyes. He had an odd feeling that he was going home, after having wandered for a very long time.

# 45

## Irvine, California, and San Jose, California—June 2018

As the Gulfstream jet crested the Chino Hills and began a slow glide to touch-down at the Orange County airport, Michael Dunne's phone began buzzing with messages that had stacked up while he was in flight. They were texts from Alicia, his ex-wife, sent during the five hours they had been airborne. Dunne read the messages with a building sense of rage and futility, and when he was done, he let the phone fall into his lap.

*I got a call from your lawyer, Mark Walden, after we talked. He said you're in trouble again. He warned me that someone would be coming with a subpoena asking me to appear in court. He said I might be charged as an accomplice. What have you done?*

Then, thirty minutes later, another.

*A man from the U.S. Attorney's Office in San Diego just handed me a subpoena. What's happening? I don't feel safe. I'm bringing Luisa home from school. I had almost forgotten how angry I was at you, but now I remember.*

And then, forty-five minutes after that, another text.

*My mother is coming to get me and Luisa. I told her to call the Irvine Police Department. Don't try to stop me.*

An hour before the plane landed, she had sent a final message.

*Don't try to find me again, ever. You're a bad man. I feel sorry for you.*

Dunne tried to text her back. *Go to the airport. They're lying. I can protect you.* But the phone displayed only one checkmark, which meant that the message had been sent but not received.

Dunne thought for several minutes and then sent a second message: *I know I betrayed you once, but not this time. Watch television Monday morning. You'll see what I've been fighting against. I hope you'll be proud of me. If you trust me then, go to the same place we went for vacation the year after we married. Bring Luisa. Everything will be fine.*

Dunne remembered one of the samba songs she had sung to him on that beach at that hideaway in California. He spoke the English words tenderly into the phone and sent them as a voice message: *We'll make such sweet music / Until the night is done . . . / This is the time for that song, and this is the time for that dance.* The words brought tears to his eyes.

Those messages didn't go through, either. But maybe she would turn on her phone over the weekend, or in the days after, and hear what he had said.

As the plane taxied to a stop near the sky-blue marquee of the general aviation terminal, Dunne asked to speak to the pilot. He apologized that the passenger pick-up in Orange County wouldn't take place as planned. He asked the pilot to fly on to San Jose for the second pick-up.

"Why?" asked the pilot. "What happened?"

Dunne willed himself to speak quietly and calmly over the vortex of his emotions.

"Change of plans. The people we were going to pick up decided not to travel with us."

"That means we don't have to send anyone to the Hilton? I had already ordered the car. Should I cancel that?"

"Correct. Like I said, the passengers decided not come."

"Stuff happens," said the pilot. He went back to the cockpit.

*   *   *

Pilots live by schedules, and they don't like changes. The captain called Darien to get approval for the altered arrangements. Then he filed a new flight plan with air-traffic control, which took an hour for approval. He notified the backup crew in San Jose who would be flying the Gulfstream back to Westchester through the night.

Dunne sat in his plush cabin chair, trying to stay focused, making notes about what he would organize with Jason Howe's help. The flight attendant flirted with him. A handsome, red-haired man alone on a private jet, the guest of a multibillionaire, of course she did. Dunne said gently, and then more firmly, that he didn't need any help.

The Gulfstream took off again. The little plane climbed west over the ocean and steered north and toward the coast and up over the Central Valley; just over Palo Alto, it banked right sharply toward the runway at San Jose at the cusp of the bay.

The pilot was happier now. He and the copilot were overnighting in the city. The flight attendant gave Dunne a last pat on the shoulder, more like a squeeze, and then the new crew came aboard.

Dunne stayed in his seat, making notes. Thirty minutes later, a steward from Atlantic Aviation escorted a gangly man toward the plane, his pants low on his hips. Blond stubble had begun to grow on his shaved head, and he was wearing Ray-Bans, making him look considerably less like a monk than he had in Taiwan. He was towing a roller bag and had a pack slung over his shoulder. Behind him, a porter was rolling a cart that contained several boxes of computer gear.

Jason Howe climbed the carpeted steps of the Gulfstream and stuck his head in the door.

"Am I in the right place? This can't be your plane."

"Temporarily it is. Stow your gear so we can get out of here."

The porter put the boxes of computer gear in the rear storage, behind the toilet. Howe settled into the beige chair across the aisle from Dunne.

"*La Dolce Vita,*" he said.

"Not yet," said Dunne.

*    *    *

They were aloft thirty minutes later. Dunne asked the attendant to leave them alone for a few minutes so they could have a private conversation. Dunne looked into Howe's glassy eyes.

"Are you sober?"

"Yeah, man, of course. Except for being a little stoned. But it's just weed. Purely recreational."

"Does Rosenberg know you're coming?"

"Absolutely. I did just what you told me. We're going to meet up when I get to town. He's made so much money, I think he feels guilty."

"His motivation doesn't matter. The only important thing is that you two make a connection this weekend, after we land. You need to be inside his network."

"Cool," said Howe. He was fiddling with the controls for his big armchair seat, making it go up and back.

"Pay attention," said Dunne. "I need you to concentrate."

"Okay. What do you want me to do in New York? I'll take notes."

Howe reached for his computer, but Dunne blocked his hand.

"Just remember it," said Dunne. "No notes. No yellow Post-its. Here's what I need. Ricci and his friends are planning a demonstration for some Wall Street investors. It's supposed to happen Monday, at the place I told you about in Manhattan. Maison Suisse. You remember the address? 1978 Avenue of the Americas. You want to repeat that?"

"Yeah, sure. 1978 Park Avenue. Ha! Busted! 1978 Avenue of the Americas."

"Stop playing. This is serious. We need to be inside that place and wire it up. Did you bring all your stuff?"

"Absolutely. Cameras, mikes, routers. We could produce an episode of *The*

*Big Bang Theory* with all the gear I brought. Stream this freak show live, so the whole world can watch. That's what you want, right?"

"Correct. I think I can get inside the bank with one of our old S&T tricks. But I need a backup plan. That's Rosenberg. Does he know what you're doing, by the way?"

"Not really. I think he wants protection, so Ricci and Goldman can't burn him later if they want to get rid of him. He hates those guys. The more money they throw at him, the less loyal he is."

"My kind of guy," said Dunne. "Get some sleep. We have a long weekend. And no more weed."

"I'm high on life," said Howe. He pulled a blanket over his head and was soon asleep, snoring intermittently all the way back to the Westchester airport.

# 46

Manhattan—June 2018

A van from Halcyon Capital was waiting for Dunne and Howe when the plane landed in White Plains. It was a foggy dawn, vapor rising from the grass surrounding the runways. Frederica Schwartz, the general counsel, waited in the van as Dunne stowed the computer gear and other luggage in the rear of the vehicle. Howe chugged the remains of his second Red Bull of the morning, which he had procured from the flight attendant before the Gulfstream landed.

"I'm here as your compliance officer," said Schwartz, when Dunne had entered the van. "Mr. Spoon told me to help you do anything that's legal, and to stop you from doing anything illegal."

"That's easy, then," said Dunne. "You can go home now." But she didn't.

Dunne gave the driver an address in Tribeca, an empty loft that his friend and business mentor Vijay Prakash, the ex-FBI undercover man, had agreed to lend him when Dunne made an improvised plea for help a day before. The apartment was nestled in the ragbag of lower Manhattan.

The van rumbled past Foley Square and the forbidding fenced perimeter of the Metropolitan Corrections Center.

Dunne looked at the prison and shook his head.

"No way," he said. "Just so you know, Ms. Schwartz: Once is enough."

The van double-parked at the entrance to the tan-brick building where Prakash had his apartment.

"What are you going to do here?" asked Schwartz.

"Get some sleep," said Dunne. "Then we're going to think of legal ways to make trouble for people who want to corrupt our honest, efficient capital markets."

"Can I come up with you?" she asked.

"No. And you can't wait down here, either. But I'll call you when everything is ready. I promise. I don't want you and your boss to miss it. If we do this right, the whole world will be watching."

"What if you do it wrong?" she asked.

"That won't happen," said Dunne. "I only make mistakes once."

*  *  *

Dunne's advantage was that he had installed surveillance cameras in supposedly closed spaces many times before. That was what S&T officers did, and he was one of the best technicians the division had produced. He had two days, which was long enough for an adrenaline junkie, and he had the advantage that it was a weekend, when the trading floor of Maison Suisse would be deserted.

Dunne had already gathered most of the information he needed. He knew which weekend cleaning service the Swiss private bank used. It was based in Long Island City, and its servers were easy to hack; he had already downloaded credentials and schedules, and he knew the home address in Bushwick, near Bedford-Stuyvesant, of the Venezuelan man who was on duty as cleaning supervisor on Sunday morning.

Jason Howe had brought from Palo Alto six tiny cameras and microphones that could be hidden to capture every second of activity in the trading room on Monday morning. And he had the malware ready to take over Jason Rosenberg's phone, just in case he got skittish about cooperating.

Dunne had a floor plan of the trading room, hacked from the commercial real estate agent who had rented the space to Maison Suisse a decade before. He laid it out on the big oak table in the dining room of Prakash's empty flat, and, with Howe, he looked at every exit, stairwell, fire door, surveillance camera, and security post on the floor.

The hardest nut was the control station that operated Maison Suisse's power, lighting, and HVAC systems, which ran off a password-protected grid. The trading system used a separate network that was wired directly into the building's broadband fiber-optic system, with its own InfiniBand cable connectors. All Dunne cared about was the first; he wanted to be able to turn off the lights, if needed. Password crackers take a while, but they work eventually, and by midafternoon on Saturday Dunne was into the main power system.

Dunne did other housekeeping, too. He used old addresses and friends of friends to assemble the tools he'd need, including a dose of a potent anesthetic. Frederica Schwartz called him, twice, to make sure everything was all right, and Dunne gave her brief but reassuring responses.

*   *   *

Saturday evening, Jason Howe took the A train to Brooklyn. The station smelled of garbage and piss, the car was stuffy and sweltering, and he couldn't sit down because someone was sleeping on the blue plastic seat. Howe listened to music and watched two women, both dressed as Harley Quinn, comparing their cosplay costumes at the far end of the train.

Jacob Rosenberg was waiting in a bar on Atlantic Avenue that had its own indoor bocce court. He was wearing a black T-shirt that said CHANGE YOUR PASSWORD and a porkpie hat, way cooler than the last time Howe saw him.

Rosenberg gave a cool nod of his chin when he saw his old friend approaching. He tipped his glass of whiskey.

"You look the same," said Rosenberg. "Except worse."

"You, too. Except richer. And fatter."

Howe sat down and ordered a bourbon, and then a beer.

"How was Taiwan, man? We missed you."

"I was a pilgrim, Jake. What can I say? I sent you a picture of my favorite Buddha."

"I didn't open it. I don't open anything unless I know who it's from."

"It's from me, asshole. Check it out."

Rosenberg scrolled through his in-box, found the message from Howe, and clicked on the attachment. The phone displayed a picture of an enormous golden Buddha, 120 feet tall, flanked by eight pagodas.

"That's a big Buddha, man."

"The biggest. It's in Kaohsiung, in the south. It's like everything else in Taiwan. It says to Beijing: Hey, we're free Chinese! We're Buddhists, so get over it."

"I guess," said Rosenberg. He put down his phone. "To fallen empires," he said, clinking his glass against Howe's.

\*     \*     \*

It was that easy. Rosenberg's precious iPhone was infected. It was now a slave of Dunne's network. Dunne could see every file, every message, every video. Including the one that Rosenberg had just finished, which appeared to show the confidential declaration of a chief executive named Howard Schubert to his closest associates that he had been diagnosed with terminal bladder cancer.

Dunne would also be able to see and hear, through Rosenberg's phone, what happened in the trading room at Maison Suisse, if his other plans were derailed.

\*     \*     \*

The two men talked through three more rounds of whiskey and beer at the bar, and a double-vodka nightcap back at Rosenberg's loft. Rosenberg grew melancholy as the night wore on, asking his old friend if he still respected him.

"You seem to have a guilty conscience, buddy," said Howe.

"You think?" Rosenberg stroked his goatee and finished off his vodka.

"The root of suffering is attachment."

"What does that mean?"

"It's a Buddhist saying. It means I'm going to set you free. Do you really want to go to the Party Monday morning on the Avenue of the Americas?"

"How do you know about that? It's a big secret."

"I know *everything*, Jake. I would advise you not to go, my friend. Technology is fickle. You never know what might go wrong."

"Oh, bullshit," said Rosenberg. "You're drunk."

"I'm definitely drunk, but so what? That's why I'm offering to help an old pal. If you decide to take a powder on Monday, I'll be waiting from eight to eight-fifteen at the Starbucks a block from Avenue of the Americas."

"You're nuts. These people are killers. If I don't show up, my ass is grass."

Howe raised a finger, pointing heavenward.

"Ceasing to do evil, cultivating the good, purifying the heart: This is the teaching of the Buddhas."

"You're losing it, Jason. But I'll think about it."

# 47

## Manhattan—June 2018

Sunday morning at five a.m., Michael Dunne hailed a cab in Lower Manhattan and gave the driver an address in Brooklyn. He carried a backpack full of the electronic equipment he would need later in the day. Sitting in the backseat of the taxi, obscured from the driver's view by a bulletproof barrier, he put on a pair of surgical gloves. From the pack he took a new syringe and a plastic tube containing an anesthetic drug called Propofol. He drew a full dose into the syringe and capped the needle. He laid the syringe carefully in the pocket of his jacket and returned the other material to his pack.

The driver took the Brooklyn Bridge and the cab rolled across the top of Bedford-Stuyvesant into Bushwick. Hector Alarcon's place was in the eastern corner of the neighborhood, toward the cemetery. It was a semidetached house, with bars on the windows and new aluminum siding. His slice of the American pie.

Alarcon went on duty at Maison Suisse at seven-thirty on Sunday mornings. Dunne had figured that Alarcon would leave his home around six-thirty, and he had it right almost to the minute. Dunne waited in the alley closest to the house, and when Alarcon stepped out his front door and began walking to the Halsey Street subway station, he followed him.

The Venezuelan man was short, with a thin beard and dark features, neatly dressed in pressed chinos and a plaid cotton summer shirt. He was listening to music on a fat old pair of headphones.

The Sunday morning street was empty, and after a hundred yards Dunne made his move. He gently laid down his backpack and moved toward Alarcon at a faster pace. As they approached an alley mid-block, he doubled his steps. As he moved past the Venezuelan, he grabbed his left arm and injected the needle containing the Propofol. He pushed the plunger all the way. Alarcon waved his arms for a moment and then slumped, and in three seconds he was out cold.

Dunne dragged the inert body toward the alley and pulled it behind a parked car, so that it would be harder to see from the street. He retrieved his backpack and returned to Alarcon.

For Dunne, it was a kind of muscle memory. He'd done this before in training and, a few times, for real. The target, surprised from behind and listening to his music, never saw the attack coming and couldn't have identified his assailant.

Propofol is a wonderful drug. In addition to knocking people out, it makes them forget. Alarcon would sleep for several hours, with the dose Dunne had given him; when he woke up, he'd have only the dimmest memory of what had happened to him.

Dunne went through his pockets and found two identification badges, one issued by the company that maintained security for the whole building at 1978 Avenue of the Americas, the other for Maison Suisse's security system on the sixth floor. He pocketed both, along with Alarcon's driver's license. He took his credit cards, too, and $250 in cash, and left the wallet atop Alarcon's chest, as if it had been discarded there by a thief.

Alarcon was wearing a Houston Astros baseball cap with the name of Venezuelan baseball star Jose Altuve on the back. Dunne took the cap and put it on his own head.

*   *   *

Dunne walked a quarter mile west and then hailed a taxi that took him to midtown. He entered the private bank's building at the service entrance, a little early, and badged in, his cap pulled low over his head in the unlikely case that anyone was monitoring surveillance cameras early on a Sunday morning. He carried his backpack low, so that it would be shielded by his body from any camera.

He took the service elevator to the sixth floor and badged into the Maison Suisse employee entrance. Nobody else had arrived. He sat on a bench in the locker room that was used by the cleaning staff and carefully removed the contents of his pack: the pin cameras, needle microphones, and other surveillance tools that Howe had procured in Palo Alto. At the bottom of the pack were two processors: a small booster unit to capture, amplify, and relay the signals, and a modem router that would post the information to the Internet using a prepaid 3G phone card bought with cash. Anyone sniffing frequencies would see it as just another smartphone talking to a cell phone tower.

Dunne moved quickly into the main trading room, hiding each device in the spot he had selected, making sure that no traces were visible. He concealed the signal booster and router in cupboards used for office supplies.

Dunne had installed all the equipment by 7:25, and he was on the service elevator heading down and out the door just before the two junior workers assigned for that morning arrived at 7:30. He was back home in Tribeca by 8:30.

Dunne was hungry, and he found a restaurant open near the Hudson River docks. He bought a Sunday *New York Times*, but the news depressed him. The country was going down the toilet. He wondered how he could have been stupid enough to have voted for the president in 2016, but he knew the answer. He had been angry.

*   *   *

Sunday night, Dunne called Rick Bogdanovich at home in Pittsburgh. The Bureau could track his location eventually, but after Monday it wouldn't matter.

Bogdanovich's place was in Penn Hills, up the Allegheny, a cozy suburb that was a world away from the gritty, dispossessed industrial relics along the Monongahela. He was eating dinner with his family when Dunne's call came in, and it took the FBI man a moment to finish chewing what was in his mouth and say hello. When he realized it was Dunne on the other end, he exploded.

"Where the hell are you? I trusted you, goddamn it! You screwed me."

"Calm down, Rick. I'm sorry I took a runner after you'd given me a safe house and a cover. I had no choice."

"Bullshit. Everyone has a choice. Your friend Ellison turned over this CIA guy last night. He says you kidnapped him. Where are you? I'm bringing you in."

"It's not going to work that way," said Dunne firmly.

"What the hell is that supposed to mean? If you're threatening an FBI special agent, you are stupider than I thought. You keep this up and next time it won't be Petersburg but a supermax, and you'll never be released."

Dunne was undeterred. He could hear Bogdanovich's wife calling out, asking if everything was okay, and saying she would put his dinner in the oven to keep it warm.

"Here's how it's going to work," said Dunne. "I have identified a series of people who are committing major financial crimes against the United States. They have assistance from inside the U.S. government. You've already got one of them, Adrian White."

"Don't give me this crap. White says you jumped him and held him hostage. Your friend Ellison claims that isn't true, but I don't believe him."

"Forget about Adrian White. He's small fish. I am going to lead you to some very powerful people. You're going to watch them incriminate themselves, in the act of committing fraud, if you'll shut up and trust me, and then you can arrest them."

"I'm going to arrest you, Mike, as soon as I have the opportunity. Don't make this worse. Come in now. I'll try to get you a deal."

"No," said Dunne, louder. "That's not how it's going to happen. I'm going to tell you what to do, and you can either listen to me and be a hero, or ignore what I say and look like a complete fucking dumbbell. You choose."

Bogdanovich was silent for a moment, then responded.

"I'm listening."

"Tomorrow morning at ten a.m., a group of conspirators will meet in Manhattan at the office of a foreign-owned bank. The conspirators will demonstrate new technology they have developed for disrupting financial markets. They will attempt to gain the cooperation of one or more financial partners. I have the whole place wired for audio and video. If you go in early, you will fuck the whole thing up. Do you understand?"

"I hear the words."

"Hey, Rick, do you understand what I'm saying? If you try to bust this too early, you'll get nothing. You have to let this run. It's going to be streaming on every cable news channel on the planet, so just watch. When you've heard enough, break down the door and arrest them."

"What's the address in Manhattan where all this is going to happen?"

"Not yet, Rick. You have to promise me that you won't move too early and blow this up."

Bogdanovich made a noise that was a mixture of curse words and phlegm. "Listen, shithead, you don't get to ask for promises. You just committed a major felony."

"Then no address. I'll do this myself. Or let the NYPD make the collar."

Dunne's threat to give credit to another law enforcement agency got the FBI cyber expert's attention in a personal way.

"This is the Bureau's case. I'm not giving it up. Let's talk about it. What's the price?"

"If I give you the address of this bank, you won't go in early. And just to make sure, I'll be watching. If you break your word, I'll pull the plug and the deal's off."

"I don't make promises to potential criminal defendants, obviously. But it would be counter to FBI procedure if, when we are given the location of a prospective financial crime, we interrupt that criminal activity before we have sufficient evidence to make a prosecution. Statement of normal procedure. Okay? Is that good enough for you?"

"And you promise that you'll follow normal procedures in this case?"

"Yes. Of course. I promise to do my job."

"Okay. The bank is called Maison Suisse. It's located at 1978 Avenue of the Americas. The trading room where this will go down is on the sixth floor. The action will start at ten o'clock. It will be a demonstration. I'd give it ten, fifteen minutes."

"How will we know when it's going down?"

"I've wired the room for audio and video and will feed it to a site called Paladinvideo.net. The password is 'Petersburg2017!' You got that?"

"Web address is 'Paladinvideo.net.' Password is 'Petersburg2017!'"

"Correct. Unless I've screwed up, you'll have perfect audio and video. When you see the fraudulent trading technology, then move in with whatever task force you want."

"If you're messing with me, I swear to God—" Bogdanovich began, but Dunne cut him off.

"Save the threats, Rick. We're way past that. You've got a lot of work to do tonight to get a team ready. And remember, if you don't play by the rules we agreed on, this deal is off the table."

"I used to think you were a stupid hothead who had learned his lesson and wised up. Now I don't know what you are."

"I guess we'll find out," said Dunne. He ended the call.

# 48

Manhattan—June 2018

The building was an eight-story office block, faced with black glass, that stood amid a forest of taller buildings. The main entrance was on Avenue of the Americas, near Radio City Music Hall. New Yorkers called it Sixth Avenue, even though Mayor Fiorello La Guardia had officially changed the name in 1945 hoping to woo Latin American businesses and diplomatic missions. That had failed, but the avenue had managed to attract one Geneva-based Swiss private bank.

Dunne had taken a suite at the New York Sheraton, a block west. He moved in with Jason Howe on Sunday evening, after he made his call to Bogdanovich in Pittsburgh. The two began assembling their array of links and computer monitors to capture the audio and video feeds coming from Maison Suisse. They gathered the feeds on Paladinvideo.net, a password-protected site Dunne had created many weeks earlier. If all went well Monday morning, they would stream the best footage to Internet social media platforms and then push it out to YouTube and cable news channels.

Howe was deft at wiring this system. He had spent years creating social media sites to advance his causes, through Fallen Empire and his other crusades. Now he created a YouTube channel and repurposed several Facebook pages he had opened several years earlier in his social-banditry days. He was lost in his work, listening to music and intermittently singing passages of songs; he stopped, pulled the buds out of his ears, and turned to Dunne. The smile on his face was at once mischievous and angelic.

"This is the best." Howe beamed. "I mean, exposing evil actions by bad people, in a nice hotel."

Dunne ordered room service late in the evening, but the food was mostly left untouched. The two men were focused on their computers, setting each parameter, double-checking each connection, watching test footage, reframing it, checking audio levels. At midnight, Dunne told Howe they needed to get some sleep. They would be up again at five to fine-tune their systems. Howe agreed, but he stayed up for another hour playing with his new toys.

*   *   *

Maison Suisse employees began arriving at seven-thirty Monday morning. First came a wing of early birds, mostly traders, leaving the elevator and making their way to their desks. Howe monitored this video footage and framed and edited it, making sure he had the volume levels right and could see and hear what was being said in every part of the room.

The trading floor was brightly lit and crowded with desks. Most of them had four computer screens, so that traders could talk in chat rooms, monitor news, read the latest charts and graphs and other market intelligence, and do their buying and selling, all at once. Even as the desks began to fill up, the room was quiet. People didn't shout questions or command underlings. If they wanted something, they sent a chat message. On one side of the room, facing the street, was a row of offices for the senior managers, along with a small conference room. That area seemed to be the office gathering place; Dunne had covered it with several cameras and microphones.

At 7:50, Howe rose from his chair in their suite at the Sheraton. Dunne didn't pay attention at first. He thought his partner was stretching, or going to the bathroom, but when Howe headed toward the front door of the suite, Dunne called out.

"Where the hell are you going?"

"I'm meeting Rosenberg. I told him Saturday night that I would bring him in from the cold, if he wanted out."

Dunne, normally composed, was flustered. His cheeks reddened with surprise and anger.

"Are you crazy? He's not trustworthy. And we need his cell phone as a backup if the other systems go down."

"The other systems work fine. It's good karma to try to help Rosenberg. He's my friend. You save your people, I'll save mine."

Howe walked out the door and down the hall to the elevator bank. Dunne thought about trying to stop him, but he stayed where he was. Howe was right: They probably didn't need Rosenberg's phone, and it was good to keep faith with your friends, even when it carried risks.

Howe pulled up the hood of his jacket and walked to Starbucks. He stood in a dark corner for fifteen minutes, as he had promised. Nobody was watching the place, he was confident. But there was no sign of Rosenberg.

By eight-thirty, Howe was back upstairs in the suite at the Sheraton, at his screens again.

"Thanks," was all he said to Dunne. Then he put his buds back in his ears and began singing to himself again, as the last minutes ticked away.

\* \* \*

The members of the Consortium began arriving just before nine-thirty. The camera Dunne had placed at the entry to the trading room captured their arrival.

Lorenzo Ricci held the elevator door open for a woman who followed just behind him. She wore a classic navy-blue Chanel suit. Her hair was sculpted close to the head so what people saw wasn't the hairdo but the perfect lines of her face and the arctic-blue eyes. As she walked, she placed each heel as deliberately as a runway model.

Dunne knew the hidden weight her name carried: Adele Kruse Hecht.

"Start the feed to the Paladin channel," said Dunne. He had promised Bogdanovich that if the FBI stayed back, he would share everything he had.

The New York Stock Exchange rang its opening bell just as the two entered the crowded trading floor. Around the room, screens were lighting up and chat room messages were flashing, but most of the traders had their eyes fixed on the elegant woman who had just entered the room.

Adele Hecht had launched countless trades and made tens of billions of dollars for her clients, all of it, she always claimed, by what she called inspiration, which was really a calculation of the odds and weighing of risks, and then, instant decision.

\*    \*    \*

The traders were standing, applauding now, as Adele made her way across the room toward the conference room that overlooked the avenue. The men and women parted; a few of the women tried to reach out and shake her hand, or, failing that, just touch the perfect weave of her jacket.

Ricci followed behind, carrying a gray Louis Vuitton briefcase containing the computer that never left his side. His was a vulpine face, hard and predatory. But when he took off his glasses, you could see in his eyes the brilliance and ravenous curiosity that drove him.

Ricci followed Adele into the conference room, which was serving as a kind of green room before the performance that lay ahead.

Next to arrive at the elevator bank was Tom Goldman. He came alone, nodding to people on the way, on the assumption that others knew him.

Rage surged through Dunne as he watched this gathering convene. He had been manipulated at each turn of the events that surrounded his firing, prosecution, and imprisonment. Not now, he told himself. Anger will only produce more mistakes.

One more guest arrived in the elevator lobby. It was Jacob Rosenberg. He looked like a hipster: thick goatee, black leather jacket, tennis shoes, making no concession to conventional midtown standards of dress. He was carrying his iPhone in his hand, but nobody seemed to notice.

\*    \*    \*

"Check this out," called Howe from his command post.

One of the screens showed a bumpy point-of-view shot of the trading room as Rosenberg made his way past the desks toward the conference room. The malware that Howe had inserted in the phone worked. He owned that phone and everything in it.

Rosenberg joined the others in the conference room, his phone still in his hands. He stood back from the senior partners—Hecht, Ricci, and Goldman—a technician ready to display his work and assist where necessary.

* * *

As Dunne watched the parade, he had one thought, which he turned over for several minutes, as the elevator cars arrived and disgorged their passengers. He finally verbalized his concern aloud, though Howe couldn't hear through the earbuds.

"Where the hell is George Strafe?" said Dunne. "He should be here by now. They can't start without him. This is his show."

* * *

The cameras and microphones in the conference room captured a similar confusion among the principals.

Ricci spoke to the boss, Madame Hecht. *"Dov'è il signor Strafe. Dovrebbe essere qui ormai. Sono quasi le dieci. Non dovremmo iniziare senza lui."*

Hecht answered in English.

"Give him a few more minutes. He's a very busy man. Maybe he wants to wear a disguise."

She laughed at the thought of the CIA operations director donning a wig and a false beard, but Ricci nodded. Yes, maybe he was putting on a disguise.

* * *

At ten, there was a new commotion at the elevators, as the arrival bell rang. Dunne assumed it would be Strafe, finally, but it was instead two men dressed in very expensive suits. The Maison Suisse New York branch manager, an athletic man with a hearty voice, greeted them personally and walked them back to the conference room.

Tom Goldman made the introductions.

"Welcome to our party, gentlemen," he began. "You're the guests of honor."

There were handshakes around the room as Goldman continued.

"I would like to present Thierry Klein and Javad Qureishi," said Goldman. "They run private wealth funds in Cyprus and Kazakhstan. Between them they have more than three hundred billion in assets under management. Isn't that right?"

"Yes," answered Klein. He was a trim man, conservatively dressed, with hooded, pitch-black eyes.

"It's actually a little more than that," said Qureishi. He was hefty, well fed, with the look of an Ottoman courtier.

Goldman continued. "Our guests have signed nondisclosure agreements pledging silence about everything they will see and hear at our gathering today, witnessed by our general counsel. They report only to their principals back in Nicosia and Nursultan, respectively."

Heads nodded. Klein raised a finger.

"We understand the sensitivity of what will be presented this morning," offered Klein. "Our dual presence is, let me say, a mutual suicide pact. We will enforce each other's silence."

*   *   *

A block away, Dunne and Howe watched on their monitors.

"Are we ready to go live with the stream?" asked Howe. "We're getting to the good stuff now."

"Wait until George Strafe arrives," said Dunne. "If they decide to go ahead without him, then we roll."

*   *   *

Unseen by anyone on the sixth floor, or by Dunne and Howe at their monitors, a small group had gathered in the stairwell of the floor below, by confidential agreement with the chief of building security.

They had arrived an hour earlier, through a tunnel from the building next door. The building security director, a former FBI man himself, accompanied the group up the back stairs, scouting to make sure each flight was empty and secure. Behind him was Joe Sheehan, the special agent in charge of the FBI's

New York Field Office, accompanied by Rick Bogdanovich, the special agent in charge of the FBI's Cyber-Forensics lab in Pittsburgh.

A third senior official had joined the team that morning at Sheehan's request. He stood just behind the two SACs, collar up, brown hair stiff as if he hadn't showered in a week, dressed in an undertaker's suit, his face pitted by scars that had never quite healed.

Behind him stood a half dozen agents in their nylon FBI jackets, including two carrying the battering ram that would knock down the stairwell door when it was time to move.

Bogdanovich, at the head of the group, had opened a laptop computer, on which he and Sheehan were watching a video feed of the action from the floor above.

"It's past ten," said Sheehan. "They're late."

"Relax," said Bogdanovich. "They haven't done anything yet."

"This guy they're waiting for," said the man in the black suit. He spoke the words almost whimsically. "I don't think he's going to show up."

* * *

"We've waited long enough," said Adele Hecht magisterially. "It's time to show our guests what our engineers have created. Lorenzo, perhaps you could lead the demonstration."

Ricci stepped to the center of the group. He unbuttoned his blazer, and then buttoned it again. He spoke in a voice that combined the rhyme and rolling syntax of his native Italian with the round, ripe tones of Atlanta, Georgia, where he had done his studies.

"My name is Lorenzo Ricci," he said. "I am a computer scientist. With my team, I have done what we like to talk about often in the laboratory, but are able to do not so often, which is to change reality. Not forever, I am happy to say, but for long enough that people can profit from it. People like you, and us."

"I'm all ears," said Qureishi, who represented the massive, subterranean wealth of Kazakhstan.

"Myself, as well," said Klein, who spoke for Cyprus, the oligarchs' private banking hub.

"This is the real 'Alpha,' if I may say," continued Ricci. "Not just the skill to recognize unique value, the return that is above the mean, but the ability to *create* that value. To make the trading opportunities appear, and then act on them. As San Giovanni reminds us: *'All'inizio era la parola.'* In the beginning was the word."

\* \* \*

Dunne, watching the monitors a block away, shouted out to Howe.

"Take it live from here on. Push it to Facebook, YouTube, every platform you've got."

Howe moved deftly at several keyboards, sending the video stream, inset with a point-of-view feed from Rosenberg's iPhone camera. It was an arresting, startling video that conveyed immediately to viewers that they were watching something secret and stealthy happening in real time.

\* \* \*

Sheehan listened to Ricci's little speech about "Alpha" and nudged Bogdanovich.

"What do you think? Should we move in now?" The two agents carrying the ram hefted it to their shoulders. The other members of the team unholstered their pistols, preparing to go through the open door, up the stairs, and into the trading room above.

"Not yet," said the man with the pitted face. "It gets better."

# 49

Manhattan—June 2018

Lorenzo Ricci powered on a large video monitor in the conference room. He removed his computer from the briefcase and placed it with a flourish on the conference table. He removed his cashmere jacket and folded it neatly over a chair, revealing his crisp shirt of fine Egyptian cotton. It took only a few moments for his computer to boot up. He turned to the group. Ricci made a flourish with his hand, like a magician about to begin a trick.

"Listen carefully, my friends and fellow investors: In about sixty seconds, when I activate a program instruction, certain servers of the data center in New Jersey that backs up records of all trades on the New York Stock Exchange will be corrupted. The backup data will no longer match the trading records that have been generated by the main system. There will be a . . . discontinuity."

"You can do that?" asked Qureishi, wide-eyed.

"Yes. I can do that. When algorithms detect these anomalies, the system will halt trading. For a time, no financial firm that holds shares of firms listed on the NYSE will be certain what the prices are, or the value of its positions. It will take many hours, perhaps days, to reconstruct reliable price and trade data."

"Oh, my god!" said Klein. "That is the scariest thing I ever heard."

"Perhaps the most profitable," said Ricci. "Now, before I push the button, would anyone like to call his trading desk and short Dow or S&P 500 futures?"

"No," said Klein.

"Yes," said Qureishi, almost at the same time.

"Yes," said Klein, correcting his answer.

The two fund managers moved to separate corners of the room and called the people who ran their trading desks. Each took a relatively conservative bet, one shorting the equivalent of $5 billion in futures, the other about $2.5 billion, cut into multiple orders to prevent detection. In terms of their overall portfolios, these were modest amounts, but this was a test, after all. A proof of concept.

*　*　*

Out on the trading floor, a few of the portfolio managers had tuned to CNBC, which was cutting intermittently to what it described as a "bizarre, unconfirmed event" at a bank in Manhattan. The Maison Suisse employees recognized their conference room, but most thought it was a joke or a prank of some sort.

The phones and message boards began to light up, too, as friends from other banks and funds on the Street began to call, wondering: What the hell? But people are always slow to recognize the drama that doesn't sneak up on them, that's happening right in their midst.

*　*　*

The New York branch manager thought his bosses should know they were on television, at least. He was knocking on the door, interrupting Ricci's presentation. Adele Hecht opened the door a crack and said icily, "Not now."

Ricci saluted her. "Have you placed your bets?" he asked the two fund managers.

The two men said yes, and the Italian typed a command into his computer.

"The disaggregation process will take between fifteen minutes and a half hour. Then you should begin to see the first signs of market disorientation, as new prices fail to match old recorded prices."

Klein looked at his watch. "Can I increase my short position?"

Ricci nodded, and the two men called their trading desks.

"I'd like each of you also to make a leveraged bet for me, please. As much as your desks can handle."

The two bankers scrambled to comply.

"I want you to remember," Ricci said when the bankers had given their orders, "that this technology is proprietary. We can create these effects whenever we want in the future. We—the partners in this venture—will essentially hold the power to disorder the financial markets as we choose, or refrain from doing so, at a price."

"Sweet," said Goldman, unable to suppress any longer his appreciation for what Ricci and his engineers had accomplished.

"I have one more piece of technology that I would like to show you, please," said Ricci, "with the assistance of my colleague Mr. Jacob Rosenberg."

Rosenberg stepped forward, iPhone in hand. By now several million people were watching, including many of the Maison Suisse traders out on the floor. There was a pounding at the conference room door again, more insistent. Hecht sharply warned those on the other side not to bother them again and turned the lock.

\* \* \*

"Now, for Christ's sakes!" said Sheehan down on the fifth floor.

The man with the pitted face and upturned collar nodded. "Yes, now."

The FBI team rushed up the stairs to the sixth floor, where the lead agents wielded their battering ram to splinter the door. The squad burst into the trading room, guns drawn, shouting: "Arms in the air! This is the FBI."

\* \* \*

Ricci, oblivious to the commotion, asked Rosenberg to cue the video, which appeared on the conference room monitor.

"Do either of you have positions in the shares of Humford Holdings?" asked Ricci.

Both Klein and Qureishi said they did; one was long on the stock, the other short.

"You will find this of interest," said Ricci. He clicked the arrow to start the video and there on the screen was the face of one of the most familiar men in the investment world, Howard Schubert.

"I have some bad news that I need to share with my team," Schubert said on the vertical cube of the iPhone video, his voice recognizable, but gruff and raspy from stress.

"I visited with my doctor a week ago to see what was causing blood in my urine and other discomforts. The doctor did exploratory surgery, to see what might be wrong. I'm sorry to say . . ."

There was pounding on the door again, this time not the branch manager of Maison Suisse, but a voice shouting: "Open up, FBI!" The sorrowful voice continued on the iPhone video that was being displayed on the monitor.

". . . I am sorry to say that I received the results of the biopsy yesterday. The doctor told me that I have stage four bladder cancer. The operation will take place next week."

"Poor Howard," said Klein sorrowfully.

"Where did you get this?" asked Qureishi.

"It's fake," said Ricci, proudly. "It's money in your pocket if you trade on it now."

Just then the door burst down, and into the room walked the two FBI chiefs, followed by George Strafe.

*  *  *

"You bastard!" Michael Dunne screamed at the monitor. It was prolonged wail of rage, like the agony of a grieving spouse or the convulsive sob of a parent who has lost a child. Then he stopped and was utterly silent for a moment.

Dunne walked over to Howe, who was transfixed by what he was watching on the screen.

"That's George Strafe. That's my boss, the man who destroyed my life. The prick found a way to change sides."

Dunne looked around the room, uncertain what to do, and then grabbed a jacket that was lying on a couch. He went into the bedroom and found the pistol he had locked in the safe; he stuck it in the back of his pants and then, after a moment's reflection, put it back in the safe. But he withdrew something else: the slim, long-bladed knife he had used to threaten Adrian White.

"I have to go," said Dunne. "Keep the video feed running until someone tells you to turn it off."

# 50

Manhattan—June 2018

Dunne ran through the Sheraton lobby and pushed his way up the street to the side entrance of the black cube that housed Maison Suisse. A crowd of people had gathered outside, office workers who been watching on cable television or YouTube feeds and had rushed out of neighboring buildings to watch the bizarre drama unfold. They were pointing up to the sixth floor where the events were happening live. Some people in the crowd were shouting, "Fake News." A left-wing group began chanting, "Hey-hey, ho-ho. Maison Suisse has got to go."

Dunne still had Hector Alarcon's badge, which got him through the first perimeter of employee security. He took the stairs to the fifth floor and, seeing that access to the floor above was blocked by an FBI agent, he crossed thirty yards along a service corridor at the back of the building to a small stairway he'd seen on the floor plans. He opened the fifth-floor door, setting off a security alarm, ran up the stairs, and kicked open the door on the sixth floor, setting off another set of bells.

No one noticed: The trading room was pandemonium already.

Stunned traders crowded the floor, each craning for a view of the conference room, which was now surrounded by FBI officers. Ricci, Goldman, and

Hecht had been put in handcuffs, along with Klein and Qureishi, the two fund managers.

Dunne pushed his way across the room, shouldering aside gawkers, so that he intercepted the law enforcement group and its prisoners just as they were turning the corner toward the elevator. Sheehan was in front, followed by Bogdanovich and Strafe, and behind them the agents who were marching each of the arrestees forward.

Dunne pressed toward them. An FBI man at the perimeter tried to stop him, but Dunne shouted, "Hey, Rick, it's me." His agitation caught Bogdanovich's eye.

"Let him through," said Bogdanovich. He pulled Dunne's arm as he approached and grasped him in a bear hug.

"This is the guy who made it happen," he said to Sheehan, his colleague. "This is the man, right here."

Sheehan extended a hand. Like Dunne, he had red hair and ruddy complexion. But Dunne's eyes were on someone else.

"I need to talk to that man for a moment," Dunne said, pointing to George Strafe. "Is that okay with everybody?"

Sheehan protested that they had to move now, transport vans were waiting and the crowd on the street was getting unruly.

"Okay by me," said Bogdanovich. "If our colleague doesn't mind."

"It's fine," said Strafe. "Mike and I will go back to the conference room and talk for a minute. I'll meet you guys at Federal Plaza."

*　　*　　*

Michael Dunne didn't say anything for a moment when they were locked in the room overlooking the avenue. Some of the furniture had been overturned in the chaos, and the cameras and microphones had been removed. The video monitor displayed dull gray snowflakes after the connections had been broken.

Strafe was wearing his black suit, not quite pressed, one of a half dozen he bought every other year at a discount men's store in Washington. His short hair spiked in different tufts and swirls; people charitably might have imagined it had been gelled, but it was just a bad haircut, sloppily combed. Some of the deep scars on his face had a reddish tint under the shine of the fluorescent light.

"You fucked me," said Dunne when they were alone.

Strafe shrugged. "It's more complicated than that."

"You switched sides."

Strafe shrugged again. "I was playing both sides. I needed a way into Ricci's operation. You were my ticket. Then he got greedy and I needed to get out. You helped me again. You were my mule, both ways. You just didn't realize it."

"You are a lying piece of shit."

Strafe laughed. "You really don't understand our business, do you? We're paid to lie. Most people have to bet on red or black. We don't. We get to bet on both. Even if we lose, nobody sees it, and there's always another pot of money."

Dunne was trying to stay calm. He breathed as slowly and deeply as he could. But this recitation of amoral tradecraft sickened him.

"You destroyed me. You ruined my marriage. You let me go to prison. What kind of a person are you?"

"I don't know. A bad person, I guess. What kind of person are you, Mike? You did a lot of this shit yourself. You can be pissed off at me, if it makes you feel better. But you were a big boy. You knew what you were doing."

Dunne looked at Strafe more carefully now. What he was saying was true, in part. Dunne had been the architect of much of his own undoing. But Dunne had built his life back, moment by moment, brick by brick, to where he was whole again. If there were any strings still connecting him to Strafe and his world, he wanted to cut them.

"Let me ask the spymaster: Were you playing me from the beginning?"

Strafe gave a last shrug.

"Pretty much. I knew we needed to penetrate the Italian group. I wanted someone really good, who wouldn't ask questions, because the operation I was planning was illegal. But I didn't completely trust you, either. So I needed a little, what, control."

"And then?"

"I had Adrian watch you and give you a nudge. You always had a bad-boy side, it was in your file, and I knew you'd eventually get yourself in trouble. When you did, click-click. But it only motivated you more. Good job, too, getting into Ricci's shop and finding what I needed to know. Good tradecraft."

"Fuck you."

"Too bad about that chick. I heard her mother put her in a mental hospital. 'Delusional.' She wasn't diming you, by the way, but her mother was."

"Veronika didn't send me to prison. Neither did her mother. You did."

"Yeah, I guess. When you made trouble on the legal case, it pissed me off, frankly. So, yes, I set you up. So what?"

"I lost a child."

"Not my problem. Guilt trips don't work on me, my friend. My guilt reservoir is overflowing. There isn't room for any more. So, tough shit."

Dunne took a step toward his tormentor. He removed the long knife from his back pocket. As he raised it above Strafe, Dunne saw the sudden fear in the older man's eyes. This was the one thing Strafe hadn't imagined. Arrogance makes people stupid that way. They think they can write their own ending.

Dunne slowly extended his right arm until the knife was pointed directly at Strafe's chest. He held it there, for a long five seconds, watching the other man tremble.

"No," said Strafe. "My God. Please." It was a whimper, not an order.

Dunne nodded. In one, quick, graceful motion, he lowered the right arm holding the knife and swung hard with his left. It was a roundhouse punch that knocked Strafe to the floor. Blood trickled from Strafe's nose. Dunne returned the knife to his pocket.

Strafe screamed as he fell, and an FBI special agent who had been standing outside the door rushed into the room. He saw Strafe sprawled on the floor, his hand at his nose, dripping blood.

"What happened, sir?" asked the young FBI agent, extending a hand to the CIA deputy director.

Strafe took a long, wary look at Dunne, his eyes blinking back tears of pain and shock. Blood was still flowing from his nose. He turned back to the FBI man.

"I slipped," he said. "I'll be okay."

As Strafe walked unsteadily from the room, Dunne spoke quietly, just behind the black-suited man who had once been his boss.

"Watch your step," whispered Dunne.

"You're a loser," sneered Strafe, holding his white handkerchief with the *GS* monogram to his face. "People like you are what keeps people like me in business."

"Don't bet on it," said Dunne. "When you're falling asleep at night, just remember: That crazy bastard you tried to fuck over is still standing. And one day you're going down for the count."

# 51

## Carmel-by-the-Sea, California, and Washington, D.C.—July 2018

Michael Dunne took the first flight the next morning from JFK to San Jose. The plane was cramped and uncomfortable, but Dunne barely noticed. A middle seat was all that was left, but he didn't mind that, either. He dozed and day-dreamed. An English teacher at Pitt had once told Dunne, while he was having a late-adolescent crisis, to imagine that he was adrift at sea. He couldn't see it, in his confusion, but land was in every direction; he just had to begin swimming and think how it would feel when his toes first touched the sand and he climbed ashore.

Dunne had only realized later, when he described the image to a classmate, that his professor had been paraphrasing a passage from the *Odyssey*.

And that was what Dunne could feel now: the sand between his toes as he began to walk toward solid ground.

Dunne rented a car at the airport and drove through the fertile valley toward the seaside resort of Carmel, where he had brought his bride the year after they married. He went first to the little inn where they had stayed, think-ing she might have gone there, but the desk clerk looked genuinely mystified when he asked about a golden-skinned mother and child. Dunne tried another hotel where they'd had dinner on that long-ago trip, thinking she might have booked there, but that was a bust, too.

Dunne began to worry, for the first time since he had left New York. Maybe she never got the message he sent. Perhaps she hadn't been watching television Monday morning. Possibly Mark Walden or one of Strafe's other hidden cut-outs had stolen her away. Perhaps she hadn't been able to catch a flight north from Los Angeles. Or maybe, the worst but most likely possibility, maybe she hadn't forgiven him.

The sun was falling toward the horizon. Dusk was another few hours away. Dunne had an image in his mind from years ago: a beach, a braided strand of brown hair, a skipping motion along the shore as a young woman danced at the edge of the waves.

Dunne drove down Ocean Avenue and parked near the beach. It looked just the way it had nearly a decade before; the lengthening summer sun gave a rosy tint to the sand, the rays catching pods of kelp that had washed in from the sea and making them glow a shiny green. Which way had they gone that time? South along the curve of white sand was Carmel Point, and far beyond, the rocky promontory of Point Lobos. No, they'd walked north, toward the cypress trees that guarded Pebble Beach.

Dunne started walking, and then he ran. In the far distance, skittering at the edge of a wave, was a young girl, and next to her a tall woman, who scooped the girl in her arms, lifted her from the waves, and spun her in a circle.

The woman looked startled at first as Dunne approached. She held her daughter close. Dunne slowed. He walked the last few yards toward her, feeling the sand firm under his feet.

* * *

George Strafe must have assumed that he had wiped his own crime scene clean of any prints. He was a hero, to read the newspaper accounts describing the successful bust of the Italian conspiracy to hack the financial system. People even talked about promoting him to director. But Strafe hadn't reckoned on Roger Magee.

Magee had spent a lifetime keeping his mouth shut. And he would have done so this time, if people hadn't overreached. But he was proprietary when it came to the Directorate of Science and Technology. He had talked to Dunne; he knew the truth.

When the grandees on the seventh floor began a housecleaning at S&T, removing the people who had been aware, in ways large and small, of the manipulation that surrounded the case of Michael Dunne, the cord of silence that Magee had spliced and retied for thirty years finally snapped.

He phoned George Strafe at home, on a private line that nobody had, and said: "You piss me off." That was it. He hung up, and Strafe probably assumed he was just a grumpy old tech who'd had too much to drink.

*   *   *

Magee called a reporter at the *Washington Post* who covered the intelligence beat and invited him to a small restaurant out in Vienna, Virginia, so far in the suburbs it wasn't really Washington anymore. Magee arrived an hour early, and sat in his favorite booth in the back, drinking beer and watching the door.

The long wisps of Magee's beard had gone white, like the fringe of hair around his bald spot. He looked like a mean, semi-alcoholic version of Santa Claus. The reporter arrived ten minutes late. He was tall and thin and looked way too healthy to have seen life's darker side. Magee beckoned for him to take a seat.

"I don't like reporters, personally," said Magee. "I never have. But I want you to listen to me carefully. Because I'm going to give you one hell of a story."

# Acknowledgments

I am grateful to many people who helped me explore the world of fact so that I could begin to imagine this piece of fiction.

My thanks, first, to two Central Intelligence Agency veterans: Glenn Gaffney, former director of the CIA's Directorate of Science and Technology and now head of security at In-Q-Tel, the CIA's in-house venture-capital firm; and Sean Roche, former associate deputy director of the CIA for Digital Innovation; and to the agency's public affairs office, which arranged the meetings.

The FBI public affairs office kindly organized visits with Keith Mularski, head of the FBI's National Cyber-Forensics & Training Alliance in Pittsburgh, and Mike McKeown, a supervisory special agent for cybercrime at the FBI's Pittsburgh Field Office.

Several tutors tried to help me understand the startling new technologies of artificial intelligence and deepfakes, including Jack Clark, policy director for OpenAI; Jared Cohen and Dan Keyserling at Alphabet's (aka Google's) Jigsaw unit; and Amir Husain, chief executive of SparkCognition. Special thanks to Justin Kosslyn, formerly at Google and now at TED, who read the manuscript and suggested technical changes. I am also grateful to my friend David McCormick, chief executive of Bridgewater Associates, and his colleague

David Ferrucci, who led the design team for IBM's "Watson" project and is now a senior technology officer at Bridgewater.

For help on cybersecurity, my thanks to Milan Patel, the former supervisory special agent in the FBI's cyber operations and now chief client officer of BlueVoyant, a cyber consulting firm; to Laura Rosenberger of the German Marshall Fund's Alliance for Securing Democracy; and to Thomas Rid, a professor at the Johns Hopkins School for Advanced International Studies.

Many years ago, Giovanni Lanni and Gabriele Cavalera hosted me in Urbino, Italy. I told them that someday I'd write about their exquisite hometown, but they probably didn't believe me. Thanks also to the German Marshall Fund, which sponsored my trip to Taiwan, and to the many friends I met there. In Erie, Pennsylvania, I'm grateful to my hosts Ferki Ferati and Ben Speggen of the Jefferson Educational Society. Pittsburgh, the emotional center of this novel, is where I got my start as a journalist in 1976, covering the United Steelworkers of America for the *Wall Street Journal*, and where I met my beloved wife Eve, who was the first reader of this book, as of every previous one.

Garrett Epps gave this book a wise reading, as he has all my other novels. I owe special thanks for this book to Lincoln Caplan, who helped me imagine the plot and characters, read the book when it was in raw, fragmentary form, and gave me insightful comments on many succeeding drafts. To him and his wife Susan Carney I gratefully dedicate this novel. I'm thankful for the support of my publisher, W. W. Norton, and especially to Starling Lawrence, one of the great editors in the book business. As always, thanks to my literary agent, Raphael Sagalyn, at ICM/Sagalyn, and to Bruce Vinokour at Creative Artists Agency for his perceptive notes. Thanks, finally, to my colleagues at the *Washington Post* who allow me to live in two worlds at once, especially to editorial editor Fred Hiatt and publisher Fred Ryan.